THE HEIRESS BRIDE

ALSO BY CATHERINE COULTER

The Hellion Bride
The Sherbrooke Bride
Season in the Sun
Beyond Eden
Impulse
False Pretenses
Secret Song
Earth Song
Fire Song

ALSO BY CATHERINE COULTER

The Hellion Bride
The Sherbrooke Bride
Season in the Sun
Beyond Eden
Impulse
False Pretenses
Secret Song
Earth Song
Fire Song

THE HEIRESS BRIDE

Catherine Coulter

G. P. PUTNAM'S SONS
NEW YORK

G. P. Putnam's Sons
Publishers Since 1838
200 Madison Avenue
New York, NY 10016

Published simultaneously in Canada

ISBN 0-399-13778-5 (acid-free paper)

Printed in the United States of America

To Stacy Creamer—

A woman who loves her crazed career, does it very well, and never loses her enthusiasm. A woman who's honorable, bright, and a jock. And she likes my writing.

All my thanks, Stacy. I hope you and I are together until either you lose your passion for pounding the pavement or I expire over my computer keyboard. I'm happy. I'm happy.

THE HEIRESS BRIDE

Prologue

Vere Castle, 1807
Near Loch Leven, Fife Peninsula, Scotland

HE STOOD STARING out the narrow window down into the courtyard of his castle. It was April, but spring wasn't much in evidence yet save for the wildly blooming heather that poked through the patches of fog to dazzle the eye with a rainbow of vivid purples. Scottish heather, like his people, would burst through rock itself to bloom. This morning, fog hung thick over the stone ramparts; thick and gray and wet. He could hear his people clearly through his window two stories up in the north circular tower—old Marthe clucking to the chickens as she tossed them grain, Burnie yelling at the top of his lungs at young Ostle, a new stable lad who was also his nephew. He heard bowlegged Crocker yelling at his dog, George II, threatening that he'd kick the shiftless bugger, but everyone knew that Crocker would kill anyone who even said a cross word to George. The morning sounded no different from any he'd heard since he was a child. Everything was normal.

Only it wasn't.

He turned away from the window and walked to the small stone fireplace, splaying his hands to the flames. This was his private study. Even his brother, Malcolm, when alive, had kept away from this particular room. It was warm in the room despite the sluggish fire, for thick wool tapestries woven by his great-grandmother were hung on every wall to keep away the damp and chill. There was also a beautiful old

Aubusson carpet that covered most of the worn stones on the floor, and he wondered how his wastrel father or his damned brother had overlooked the carpet; it was worth a good deal of money, he imagined, and could have provided at least a week's worth of gaming or wenching or a bit of both. So the carpet was left, and the tapestries, but little else of value. Over the fireplace on a nearly rotted tapestry was the coat of arms of the Kinrosses: *Wounded But Unconquered.*

He was nearly mortally wounded. He was in very deep trouble and the only way out of it was to marry an heiress, and quickly. He didn't want to. He would rather swallow one of Aunt Arleth's tonics than marry.

But he had no choice. The debts incurred by both his father and his now-dead elder brother had left him bowed to his knees and nearly beyond desperate. He was the only one to be responsible, no one else. He was the new earl of Ashburnham, the seventh bloody earl, and he was up to his peer's neck in financial woes.

All would be lost if he didn't act quickly. His people would starve or be forced to emigrate. His home would continue to decay and his family would know nothing but genteel poverty. He knew he couldn't allow that. He stared down at his hands, still stretched toward the fire. Strong hands he had, but were they strong enough to save the Kinross clan from the gut-wrenching poverty that had been his grandfather's plight after 1746? Ah, but his grandfather had been a wily man, quickly adjusting to a new reality, quickly ingratiating himself with the few powerful earls left in Scotland. He'd also been smart, not disdaining the smell of the factories; and he'd invested the few groats he could get his gnarly hands on in iron and cloth factories springing up in the north of England. He'd been successful beyond his wildest dreams. But he'd died like all men must. Luckily for him he died old and quite pleased with himself, not realizing that his son was a rotter and would bring Vere Castle back to its knees.

Hell, what was a wife anyway, he mused, particularly an English wife? He could, if he wished, simply lock her in one of the musty rooms and toss away the key. He could beat her if he found her proud and unbending. In short, he could do anything he pleased to a damned wife. Perhaps he would be lucky and she'd be as malleable as a sheep, as witless as a cow, as bland as the castle goats who were at their happiest chewing on old boots. Whatever she would be, he would deal with it. He had no choice.

Colin Kinross, seventh earl of Ashburnham, strode from the study room at the top of the north tower. The next morning he was on his way to London to find a bride with a dowry as great as Aladdin's treasure.

1

London, 1807

SINJUN SAW HIM the first time on a Wednesday night in the middle of May at a rout given by the Duke and Duchess of Portmaine. He was a good thirty feet from her across the massive ballroom, partially obscured by a lush palm tree, but it didn't matter. She saw him quite clearly enough and she couldn't look away. She craned her neck around two dowagers when he walked gracefully to a knot of ladies, bowed over a young one's hand, and led her in a cotillion. He was tall; she could see that because the lady came only to his shoulder. Unless, of course, the young lady was a dwarf, and Sinjun doubted that. No, he was tall, much taller than was she, the saints be praised.

She continued to stare at him, not knowing why she was doing it and not caring in the least, until she felt a hand on her forearm. She didn't want to look away from him, not now. She shook the hand away and walked off, her eyes still on him. She heard a woman's voice from behind her but didn't turn around. He was smiling down at his partner now, and she felt something deep and strong move within her. She walked closer, circling the dance floor, drawing nearer. He was no more than ten feet away now and she saw that he was magnificent, as tall as her brother Douglas, and as massively built, his hair blacker than Douglas's, ink-black and thick, and his eyes—good Lord, a man shouldn't have eyes like that. They were a rich dark blue, a blue deeper than the sapphire necklace Douglas had given Alex for her birthday. If only she were close enough to touch him, to set her fingers lightly upon the cleft in his chin, to sift through that shining hair of his. She knew in that moment that she would be perfectly content to look at him for the rest of her life. Surely that was a mad thought, but it was nonetheless true. He was well built; she wasn't ignorant about things like that, not with two outrageous older brothers. Yes, he had an athlete's body, strong and hard and tough, and he was young, probably younger than Ryder, who had just turned twenty-nine. A small, insistent voice told her that she was being a silly twit, to open her eyes, to stop this infatuated nonsense, for after all, he was just a man, a man like any other man, and in all good likelihood he was cursed with a troll's character to go along with his magnificent looks. That, or worse: He was a complete bore, or no brain worth speaking of, or he had rotted teeth. But no, that wasn't true, for he just threw his head back and laughed deeply, showing beautiful, even, white teeth, and indeed, that laugh bespoke great intelligence to her discerning brain, a rich, deep laugh, just like his eyes, and weren't they intelligent? Ah, but he could be a drunkard or a gamester, or a rake or any number of other exceptionable things.

She didn't care. She just kept staring. A great hunger welled up in her, a hunger that spread into a great coalition of hungers she didn't understand, but she knew that he had put them there, deep inside her. Finally the cotillion ended and he bowed over the young lady's hand, delivered her back into the bosom of her chaperon, and went to join a small group of gentlemen. They greeted him with loud and merry voices. So he was a man popular with other men, just like Douglas and Ryder, her brothers. The group went off toward the card room, much to Sinjun's disappointment.

Someone patted her bare arm again.

"Sinjun?"

She sighed even as she turned to her sister-in-law Alex. "Yes?"

"Are you all right? You've been standing there as still as one of the Northcliffe Greek statues for the longest time. Before, I called to you, but you didn't seem to even see me."

"Oh yes, I'm quite all right," she said, and looked back to where she'd last seen him. Then she heard a man laugh and knew it was his laugh, pure and resonant. It filled her with warmth and excitement, and made that something deep inside her move again, move powerfully. She felt it to her toes.

No man could be the ideal of perfection that she'd bestowed upon him at first sight. No, it was quite impossible. She wasn't stupid or naive or a silly little debutante, not with two brothers so flagrantly brazen in their behavior and speech. He was probably a troll, at least on the inside.

"Sinjun, what the devil is wrong with you? Are you sickening with something?"

She drew a deep breath and decided to keep her mouth shut, which was quite unlike her. But this was too new, too uncertain. She grinned hugely. "Alex, I quite like her grace, the Duchess of Portmaine. Brandy is her nickname and she begged me not to call her that horrid name Brandella. Isn't that exceedingly clever to shorten Brandella in such a manner?" Sinjun leaned down close to her sister-in-law's ear. "And would you just look at her grace's bosom—is it possible that she is more impressive than you? Of course, she is a bit older than you, I expect."

Douglas Sherbrooke, not stifling his laugh, said, "Good Lord, do you think that age is a factor, Sinjun? A lady's years adding to her endowments? My God, by the time Alex is sixty, she wouldn't be able to walk upright. But this calls for a closer study of the duchess. On the other hand, I must point out, Sinjun, as your eldest brother, that it is most inappropriate for you to remark upon her grace's assets and Alex's lack thereof."

Sinjun laughed at her brother's words and the look on his wife's face as he continued to Alex in a mournful voice, "I had thought you the most nobly endowed lady in all of England. Perhaps it is only in southern England that you hold that distinction. Perhaps it is only within the immediate vicinity of Northcliffe Hall that you lord it over other less worthy bosoms. Perhaps I have been taken in, perhaps I have been duped."

His fond wife punched his arm. "I suggest that you keep your eyes and thoughts at home, where they belong, my lord, and leave the duchess and her endowments to the duke."

"Just so," the earl said, then turned to his sister, who looked suddenly different to his critical and fond eye. She hadn't looked at all different earlier in the evening, but she did now. She looked abstracted, yes, that was it, which was odd, very odd indeed. Sinjun was usually as clear as a summer pond, her thoughts and feelings clearly writ on her expressive face; but now he didn't have the slightest idea what was in her mind. It bothered him. It was like a hard kick from a horse he'd just turned his back on. He suddenly felt as if he didn't know this tall, quite lovely young lady, not at all. He tried for neutrality. "So, brat, are you having a good time? This last cotillion is the only dance you haven't danced the entire evening."

"She is nineteen, Douglas," Alex said. "Surely you must soon stop calling her brat."

"Even when she continues to play the Virgin Bride to torment my sleep?"

Whilst the two of them argued over the luckless sixteenth-century ghost of Northcliffe Hall, Sinjun had time to think and decide what to say. When they finished, she sidestepped her brother neatly, saying only, "No ghosting about for me, at least in London, Douglas. Oh dear, there is Lord Castlebaum with his fond mama. I had forgotten that he has the next country dance. He sweats dreadfully, Douglas, and his hands are wet—"

"I know. He's also a very nice young man. But Sinjun," he continued quickly, raising his hand to still her, "it doesn't matter if he were a very dry saint. You don't have to marry him. Accept his sweat and his niceness and simply try to enjoy yourself. Remember, you are here in London to have fun, nothing more, just to enjoy yourself. Don't listen to Mother."

Sinjun couldn't hide her sigh. "Mother," she repeated. "It's difficult, Douglas. She says I must hie myself to the altar or I shall be on the wretched shelf. This shelf is the dreaded Spinster Shelf, and she always says it in capital letters. She continues to list out all the shelf's incumbent horrors, including becoming Alex's drudge once Mother has cast off her mortal coil. She even remarked that I was getting long in the tooth. When I looked at my teeth in the mirror, I swear one of my molars had lengthened just a bit."

"Don't listen to her. I am the head of the Sherbrooke family. You will enjoy yourself; you will laugh and flirt to your heart's content. If you don't find a gentleman to please you, it doesn't matter."

His voice was austere and very lordly, and Sinjun was forced to smile. "I'm also nineteen, and that, apparently, is nearing a disastrous age for a girl to be yet unwed, and completely unacceptable for a girl not to have even one beau. She even points to Alex being eighteen when she wed you. Then she says that Sophie was lucky to have coerced Ryder into marriage, because she was nearly twenty and likely to be a lifetime spinster. Taking in Ryder, she claims, was the smartest thing Sophie ever managed. It is also my second Season. Mother says I must keep my mouth shut because gentlemen don't like ladies who know more than they do. She says it drives them to the brandy bottle and to gaming hells."

Douglas said something crude and quite inelegant.

Sinjun laughed, but it was a sham laugh. "Well, one never knows, does one?"

"All I know is that Mother says a lot, too much."

But even as Douglas spoke, clearly harassed, she saw the man in her mind's eye and she smiled, this one real, filling her eyes with warmth and dreams. She realized that her sister-in-law Alex was looking at her closely, and that her expression was puzzled. But she said only, "Feel free to speak to me anytime you wish to, Sinjun."

"Perhaps soon. Ah, here's Lord Castlebaum, wet hands and all. But he does dance very well. Perhaps I shall discuss shelves with him. I will see both of you later."

She stepped on Lord Castlebaum's toes three times in an attempt to find the man again. Later she began to think that her eyes must have lied, that no man could be so immensely glorious to behold. But she dreamed of him that night. They were together, and he was laughing and standing close to her, touching his fingertips to her cheek, and she knew she wanted him and she was leaning toward him, wanting to touch him, and it was there in her gaze, all the wanting she had for him, and he saw it and knew it as well. The scenes softened and slowed, melding together into vague colors and intertwining bodies, and she awoke near to dawn, her heart pounding, perspiration lying heavy on her skin, and a moan in her throat. Her body felt languid and slow. There was a strange ache deep in her belly. She knew she'd dreamed the mystery of lovemaking, but only in blurred images. She had yet to solve the mystery, yet to know him, yet to be intertwined with him. She wished she'd discovered his name, for to be that intimate with a nameless man wasn't something she could accept.

She saw him the second time at a musicale at the Ranleagh town house on Carlysle Square three nights later. A very large soprano from Milan thumped the piano with her fist as her Viennese accompanist tried to keep his fingers on the trembling keys and mark a strong beat at the same time. Sinjun was soon bored and twitching with restlessness. Then, quite suddenly, she felt something strange sweep over her and knew, simply knew, that he had come into the room. She turned slightly in her chair and there he was. She sucked in her breath at the sight of him. He had just divested himself of a black cloak and was speaking quietly to another gentleman. He looked even more splendid to her than he had at the Portmaine ball. He was dressed all in black with a very white batiste shirt. His thick hair was brushed back, a bit long for current fashion, perhaps, but to her, perfection itself. He was seated at a diagonal from her, and if she kept her profile toward the bellowing soprano, she could look at him as much as she wanted. The moment he was seated, he grew instantly still. She watched him remain perfectly still, even as the soprano pumped up her lungs and gained a ringing high C. A man with courage and fortitude as well, she thought, nodding to herself. A man with manners and good breeding.

Her fingers itched to touch that cleft in his chin. She saw that his jaw was strong and well defined, that his nose was elegant and thin and that his mouth made her want to . . . no, she had to get hold of herself. The dream images mixed in her mind for a moment and she knew herself well lost. Goodness, it was quite likely that he was already wed, or betrothed. She managed a show of outward calm until there was, at last, an adjournment to the supper room.

She said in an offhand manner to Lord Clinton, a friend of Douglas's from the Four Horse Club, who had escorted her to dinner, "Who is that man over there, Thomas? The tall one with the very black hair? You see him, he's with those three other men who aren't nearly as tall as he is or nearly as impressive."

Thomas Mannerly, Lord Clinton, squinted in the direction she was pointing. He was myopic, but the man in question did stand out, no question about that. The man was very tall and too well built for his own good, the bastard. "Ah, that's Colin Kinross. He's new to London. He's the earl of Ashburnham, and a Scot." The last was said with a hint of disdain.

"Why is he here, in London?"

Thomas stared at the lovely girl at his side, nearly as tall as he was, and that was surely a bit off-putting, but he didn't have to marry her, just keep an experienced eye on her. He said now, carefully, as he brushed some invisible lint from the sleeve of his black coat, "Why do you care, Sinjun?" At her silence, he stiffened. "My God, he hasn't offended you in any way, has he? Those damned Scots, they're barbarians, even when they're educated in England, as he was."

"Oh no, no. I just asked out of curiosity. The lobster patties are quite good, don't you think?"

He agreed, and Sinjun thought: *At last I know his name*. At last. She wanted to shout her victory. At last. Thomas Mannerly happened to look at her just then and he sucked in his breath at the most beautiful smile he'd ever seen in his life. He forgot the lobster patty on his plate. He said something to her, something polished and just a bit intimate, and was chagrined when she didn't appear to have even heard him. She was, if he wasn't mistaken, staring at that damned Scot.

Sinjun was fretting within five minutes. She had to know more than just his name and the fact that he was a Scottish nobleman and why Thomas Mannerly had sounded a bit stiff about that. She didn't have much opportunity to find out more about Colin Kinross that night, but she didn't despair. It would soon be time to act.

Douglas Sherbrooke, earl of Northcliffe, was happily ensconced in his favorite leather chair in the library, reading the *London Gazette*, when he chanced to look up to see his sister standing in the doorway. Why the devil was she just standing there? She would normally come caroling in, speaking and laughing even before she had his attention, and her laughter would make him smile, it was so carefree and lovely and innocent. And she would lean down and kiss him on the cheek and hug him hard. But she wasn't laughing now. Why the hell was she looking so damned diffident? As if she'd done something unbelievably awful? Sinjun didn't have a shy bone in her body, not from the moment he'd first picked her up out of her cradle and she'd grabbed his ear and twisted it until he'd yowled. He folded the paper on his lap. He frowned. "What do you want, brat? No, you're too advanced in age for brat anymore. My dear, then. Come in, come in. What is the matter with you? Alex said there was something on your mind. Out with it. I don't like the way you're acting. It isn't like you at all. It makes me nervous."

Sinjun came slowly into the library. It was very late, nearly midnight. Douglas waved her to the seat opposite his. It was odd, she thought, as she approached. She had always believed Douglas and Ryder were the two most handsome men in the entire world. But she'd been wrong. Neither of them came close to Colin Kinross.

"Sinjun, you are behaving quite strangely, not at all like yourself. Are you ill? Has Mother been tormenting you again?"

She shook her head and said, "Yes, but she always does, saying it's for my own good."

"I will speak to her again."

"Douglas."

She stopped, and he blinked to see that she was staring down at her toes and she was actually plucking at her muslin skirt.

"My God," he said slowly, the light dawning finally, "you've met a man."

"No, I haven't."

"Sinjun, I know you haven't overspent your allowance. You're so tight with your purse strings that you'll be richer than I am in a matter of years. Mother picks at you, but most of it bounces off. You pay her no mind, truth be told. Alex and I love you within the bounds of common sense, and we've tried to make you as comfortable as we can. Ryder and Sophie will be arriving in a week or so—"

"I do know his name, but I haven't met him!"

"Ah," said Douglas. He sat back, grinning up at her, steepling his fingers. "And his name is?"

"Colin Kinross, and he's the earl of Ashburnham. He's a Scot."

Douglas frowned. For a moment he'd hoped it just might be Thomas Mannerly she liked. No such luck.

"Do you know him? Is he married? Betrothed? Is he a gamester? Has he killed men in duels? Is he a womanizer?"

"You would have to be different, wouldn't you, Sinjun? A Scot! No, I don't know him. If you haven't even met the man, then why are you so damned interested?"

"I don't know." She paused, and looked extraordinarily vulnerable. She shrugged, trying for a glimmer of her old self, and gave him a crooked smile. "It's just there."

"All right," Douglas said, eyeing her closely. "I'll find out all about this Colin Kinross."

"You won't say anything to anyone, will you?"

"I will to Alex but no one else."

"You don't mind that he's a Scot, do you?"

"No, why should I?"

"Thomas Mannerly had a touch of scorn in his voice, called him a barbarian, that kind of thing."

"Thomas had a father who believed to the soles of his viscount's feet that a true gentleman must be born breathing the fine, just air of England. It appears that Thomas has adopted his departed sire's absurdities."

"Thank you, Douglas." Sinjun leaned down and kissed his cheek.

As he watched her leave the library, a thoughtful frown settled on his forehead. He tapped his fingers slowly together. The only thing he had against a Scot was that if she married one, she would live very far away from her family.

He followed his sister upstairs not long thereafter. He walked into the bedchamber to see Alex brushing her hair, seated at her dressing table. He met her eyes in the mirror, smiled, and began to take off his clothes.

Her brush stilled. She put it down and turned to face him.

"You will watch me all the way to my bare hide?"

She just smiled and nodded.

"You are staring, Alex. Are you concerned that I have gained flesh? You wish to see that everything is still lean and all my parts are in good working order?"

She just smiled more widely, and this time she just shook her head and said, "Oh no. I suspect you are quite perfect. You were last night and this morning and—" She giggled.

When he was quite naked, he walked over to her, picked her up in his arms, and carried her to their bed.

When he was able to speak coherently again, he stretched out beside his wife and said, "Our Sinjun is in love."

"So that's why she's been behaving so oddly," Alex said on a huge yawn and came up on her elbow beside her husband.

"His name is Colin Kinross."

"Oh dear."

"What is it?"

"Someone pointed him out to me the other evening at the musicale. He looks very forceful, Douglas, and stubborn."

"All this from just a viewing of the man?"

"He's quite tall, perhaps even taller than you. That's good, because Sinjun is very tall for a woman. Ruthless, that's what I meant to say. He looks quite capable of doing anything at all to get what he wants."

"Alex, you can't tell all that about a man just by looking at him. Now, I will take away your clothes for two days if you don't stop speaking nonsense."

"I don't know anything about him, Douglas."

"He's tall and he's tough-looking. He's ruthless. A fine place for me to start."

"Yes, and you'll see I'm right." She laughed, her breath warm and soft against his shoulder. "My father despises the Scots. I hope you don't feel that way."

"No, I don't. Sinjun hasn't yet met him, she told me."

"She will, very soon, I doubt not. She's very resourceful, you know."

"In the meantime I'll endeavor to find out all I can about our Scottish gentleman. Ruthless, hmm?"

. . .

The next evening Sinjun felt like dancing in her bedchamber. Douglas was taking her and Alexandra to the Drury Lane Theatre to see *Macbeth* performed. Surely as a Scot and a Kinross, with scores of cousins named Mac Something, he would also be there. It was opening night. Surely, oh surely he would be there. But what if he accompanied another lady? What if he . . . She stopped herself. She had spent an hour on her appearance, and her maid, Doris, had merely nodded, smiling slyly. "You look beautiful, my lady," she had said as she lovingly threaded a light blue velvet ribbon through Sinjun's hair. "Just the same color as your eyes."

She did look well enough, Sinjun supposed, as she studied herself one last time in the mirror. Her gown was a dark blue silk with a lighter blue overskirt. The sleeves were short and puffed out, and there was a matching pale blue velvet sash bound beneath her breasts. She looked tall and slender and fashionably pale. There was just a hint of cleavage, no more, because Douglas felt strongly about things like that. Yes, she looked just fine.

Sinjun didn't see him until the intermission. The lobby of the Drury Lane Theatre was crowded with the glittering *ton*, who gossiped and laughed and whose jewels were worth enough to feed a dozen English villages for a year. The lobby was also very hot. Some unfortunate patrons were splattered with dripping wax from the hundreds of lit candles in the chandeliers overhead. Douglas took himself off to fetch champagne for Alex and Sinjun. A friend of Alex's came up, and thus Sinjun was free to search in every corner of the vast room for her Scot, as she now thought of him. To her delight and speechless excitement and horror, she saw him standing not eight feet behind her, speaking to Lord Brassley, a friend of Ryder's. Brass, as he was called, was a rake and kindhearted, a man who commendably kept his wife in more luxury than his mistresses.

Her heart speeded up. She turned completely to face him and began to walk forward. She bumped into a portly gentleman and automatically apologized. She simply kept walking toward him. She wasn't more than three feet away when she heard him laugh, then say quite clearly to Lord Brassley, "Good Lord, Brass, what the devil am I to do? It's damned painful—I've never in my life seen such a gaggle of disasters, all of them in little knots or herds, giggling and simpering and flapping and staring. It isn't fair, no it isn't. I must needs wed myself to an heiress or lose everything I own, thanks to my scoundrel of a father and brother, and all those females I've met who fit the groat requirements scare me to my toes."

"Ah, my dear fellow, but there are other females who aren't disasters," said Lord Brassley, laughing. "Females you don't have to marry, just enjoy. You simply amuse yourself with them. They will relax you, Colin, and you certainly could use some relaxation." He slapped Colin Kinross on his shoulder. "As for the heiress, be patient, my boy, be patient!"

"Ha, patience! Every day that goes by brings me closer to the brink. As for those other females, hell, they would also want to spend all the groats I don't have, and expect that in my undying gratitude I would shower them with endless baubles. No, I have no time for distractions, Brass. No, I must find myself an heiress and one that is reasonably toothsome."

His voice was deep and soft and filled with humor and a goodly dose of sarcasm. Lord Brassley laughed, hailed a friend, and took himself off. Without further hesitation, Sinjun walked to him, stood there right in front of him until his beautiful dark blue eyes finally came to rest on her face and a black brow rose in question. She thrust out her hand and said quite clearly, "I'm an heiress."

2

COLIN KINROSS, seventh earl of Ashburnham, stared at the young woman standing in front of him, her hand outstretched toward him, staring at him with utter sincerity and, if he wasn't mistaken, a goodly dollop of excitement. He felt knocked off his pins, as Philip would say, and stalled for time to get his brain back in working order. "Forgive me. What did you say?"

Without hesitation, Sinjun said again, her voice strong and clear, "I'm an heiress. You said you needed to marry an heiress."

He said slowly, his voice light and insincere, still stalling for mental reinforcements, "And you are reasonably toothsome."

"I'm pleased you think so."

He stared at her outstretched hand, still there, and automatically shook it. He should have raised her hand to his lips, but there that hand was, stuck out there like a man's, and so he shook it. A strong hand, he thought, slender fingers, very white, competent. He released her hand.

"Congratulations," he said, "on being an heiress. And on being toothsome. Ah, do forgive me, ma'am. I'm Ashburnham, you know."

She simply smiled at him, her heart in her eyes. His voice was wonderful, deep and smiling, much more beguiling than either of her brothers'. They didn't come close to this marvelous man. "Yes, I know. I'm Sinjun Sherbrooke."

"An odd name you have, a man's nickname."

"I suppose. My brother Ryder christened me that when he tried to burn me at the stake when I was nine years old. My real name is Joan, and he wanted me to be Saint Joan but it became Sinjun for Saint John, and so . . . there it is."

"I like Joan. I prefer it. It is feminine." Colin ran his fingers through his hair, realizing that what he'd said was ridiculous and not at all to the point, whatever that was. "This has taken me aback, truly. I don't know who you are, and you don't know who I am. I really don't understand why you've done this."

Those light blue eyes shone up at him as guileless as a summer day as she said clearly, "I saw you at the Portmaine ball and then at the Ranleagh musicale. I'm an heiress. You need to marry an heiress. If you are not a troll—your character, of course—why then, perhaps you could see your way clear to marrying me."

Colin Kinross, Ashburnham or simply Ash to his friends, could only stare at the girl who couldn't seem to look away from his face. "This is quite the oddest thing that has ever happened to me," he said, a baffling understatement. "Except for that time at Oxford when the don's wife wanted me to make love to her with her husband teaching Latin in the other room to one of my friends. She even wanted the door cracked open so she could see her husband whilst she was making love to me."

"Did you?"

"Did I what? Oh, make love to her?" He coughed, recalling himself. "I don't remember," he said, suddenly frowning, his voice austere. "Besides, it is an incident better forgotten."

Sinjun sighed. "My brothers would have confided in me, but you don't know me, so I can't expect you to be more forthcoming yet. I know I'm not beautiful, but I am passable. I'm in my second Season without even a betrothed, or even a remotely attached gentleman to my name, but I am rich, and I'm a kind person."

"I can't accept all of your assessment."

"Perhaps you have already found a lady to meet your groat requirements."

He grinned at that. "Plain speaking, huh? No, I haven't, as I suspect you already know, having overheard my whining plaints to Brass. Actually, you are quite the loveliest young lady I have met. You're tall. I don't have to get a painful crick in my neck speaking to you."

"Yes, and I can't help it. As to my loveliness, certainly my brothers think so, but you, my lord? This is my second Season, as I said, and I didn't wish to have it, for there is so much sheer boredom about, but then I saw you."

She stopped talking but didn't stop staring at him. He was startled at the hunger in those quite lovely light blue eyes of hers. This was really beyond anything in his experience. He felt bowled over, off kilter, and really quite stupid. The vaunted control he was known for was gone. It was disconcerting.

"Come over here, out of the crush. Yes, that's better. Listen, this is difficult. It is also a highly unusual situation. Perhaps I could call on you tomorrow? I see a young lady walking toward us, and she looks quite purposeful."

She gave him a dazzling smile. "Oh yes, I should quite like that." She gave him the Sherbrooke town house address on Putnam Place. "That is Alex, my sister-in-law."

"What is your complete name?"

"Everyone calls me Sinjun."

"Yes, but I don't like it. I prefer Joan."

"All right. It's Lady Joan, actually, for my father was an earl. Lady Joan Elaine Winthrop Sherbrooke."

"I will call on you in the morning. Would you like to ride with me?"

She nodded, looking at his white teeth and his beautiful mouth. Unconsciously, she leaned toward him. Colin sucked in his breath and quickly backed away. Good Lord, the chit was as brazen as a Turkish gong. So she'd fallen for him the first time she'd seen him. Ha! He would take her riding tomorrow, discover why she was playing this insane jest, and perhaps kiss her and fondle her just a bit to teach her a lesson. Damned impertinent chit—and she was a Sassenach to boot, which made sense since he was in London. Still, he believed Sassenach young ladies to be more reticent, more modest. But not this young lady.

"Until tomorrow, then," he said, and was gone before Alex could bear down on them.

Colin searched out Brass and unceremoniously plucked him out of the theater. "No, don't complain. I'm taking you outside, away from all these female distractions, and you're going to tell me what the devil is going on here. I think you're probably behind this absurd jest, and I want to know why you set that girl on me. The gall of her still has my head spinning."

Alex watched the man, Colin Kinross, pull Brass from the huge lobby. She looked back at Sinjun to see that she was also staring after him. She correctly assumed that Sinjun's thoughts about the man weren't nearly as prosaic as her own.

"He is an interesting-looking gentleman," Alex said, getting the ball rolling.

"Interesting? Don't be ridiculous, Alex. That's utterly inadequate. He's beautiful, perfectly beautiful. Didn't you see his eyes? And the way he smiles and speaks, it—"

"Yes, my dear. Come along now. The intermission is over and Douglas is getting testy."

Alex bided her time, but it was difficult. The moment they arrived back at the Sherbrooke town house, she kissed Sinjun good night and grabbed her husband's hand, dragging him into their bedchamber.

"You want me that badly?" Douglas asked, staring at her with some amusement.

"Sinjun met Colin Kinross. I saw her speaking to him. I fear she's been rather forward, Douglas."

Douglas looked down at his hands. He then lifted a branch of candles and carried it to the table beside their bed. He studied it for a while, in meditative silence, then shrugged. "We will leave it be until tomorrow. Sinjun isn't stupid, nor is she a silly twit. Ryder and I raised her properly. She would never ever jump her fences too quickly."

At ten o'clock the following morning, Sinjun was ready to jump. She was waiting on the front steps of the Sherbrooke town house, dressed in a dark blue riding habit, looking as fine as a pence, so Doris had told her firmly, and she was lightly slapping her riding crop against her boot.

Where was he? Hadn't he believed her? Had he just realized that she wasn't to his taste and didn't intend to come?

Just before she was on the edge of incoherence, she saw him cantering up, astride a magnificent black barb. He pulled up when he saw her, leaned down just a bit, and gave her a lazy smile.

"Aren't I to be allowed in your house?"

"I don't think so. It's too soon."

All right, he thought, he would accept that for the moment. "Where is your horse?"

"Follow me." She walked around the back of the house to the stables. Her mare, Fanny, was standing placidly, calmly accepting the caresses bestowed on her neck by a doting Henry, one of the stable lads. She waved him away and mounted by herself. She arranged her skirts, knew in her heart that she wasn't physically capable of presenting a finer picture, and prayed. She gave him a tentative smile. "It's early. Shall we go to the park?"

He nodded and pulled alongside her. She didn't say a word. He frowned as he neatly guided his stallion around a dray filled with kegs of beer and three clerks dressed in funereal black. The streets were crowded with hawkers, shopkeepers, wagons of all sorts, ragged children from the back streets. He stayed close, saying nothing, keeping a look out for any danger. There was danger everywhere, naturally, but he realized that she could deal with most anything that could happen. If she couldn't, why then, he was a man, and he could. Whatever else she was, she was an excellent rider.

When they reached the park, he said as they turned into the north gate, "Let's gallop for a bit. I know a lady shouldn't so indulge herself, but it is early, as you said."

They raced to the end of the long outward trail and his stallion, strong as Douglas's horse, beat Fanny soundly. She was laughing when she pulled her mare.

"You ride well," Colin said.

"As do you."

Colin patted his stallion's neck. "I asked Lord Brassley who you were. Unfortunately he didn't see you speaking to me. I described you, but to be frank, ma'am, he couldn't imagine any lady, particularly Lady Joan Sherbrooke, speaking to me as you did."

She rubbed the soft leather of her York riding gloves. "How did you describe me?"

She'd gotten to him again, but he refused to let her see it. He shrugged and said, "Well, I said you were reasonably toothsome in a blond sort of way, that you were tall and had quite lovely blue eyes, and your teeth were white and very straight. I had to tell him that you were brazen to your toenails."

She was silent for a moment, looking over his left shoulder. "I suppose that's fair enough. But he didn't recognize me? How very odd. He's a friend of my brother's. He is also a rake but good-hearted, so Ryder says. I fear he still tends to see me as a ten-year-old who was always begging a present off him. He had to escort me once to Almack's last Season, and Douglas told me in no uncertain terms that Brass wasn't blessed with an adaptable intellect. I was to remain quiet and soft-spoken and on no account to speak of anything that lay between the covers of books to him. Douglas said it would make him bolt."

Colin chewed this over. He simply didn't know what to think. She looked like a lady, and Brass had said that Lady Joan Sherbrooke was a cute little chit, adored by her brothers, perhaps a bit out of the ordinary from some stories he'd heard, but he'd never noticed anything pert about her himself. He'd then lowered his voice, whispering that she knew too much about things in *books,* at least he'd heard that from some matrons who were gossiping about her, their tones utterly disapproving, and she was indeed tall. But then again, she'd been waiting on the front steps of the town house for him to arrive, certainly not what the young lady of the house would do, would she? Wouldn't an English young lady be waiting in the drawing room, a cup of tea in her hand? Brass had also insisted that Joan Sherbrooke's hair was a plain regular brown, nothing out of the ordinary, but it wasn't. In the early sunlight it was at least a dozen colors, from the palest blond to a dark ash.

Oh, to hell with it. He didn't understand, and he wasn't at all certain he believed her. More likely, she was looking for a protector. Perhaps she was the lady's maid to this Lady Joan Sherbrooke, or a cousin. He should just tell her that he had no money and all she could expect from him would be a fun roll in the hay, no more, no less.

"I have taken you by surprise," Sinjun said, watching the myriad expressions flit over his face. On the heels of her calmly reasoned understatement, she said in a rush, "You're the most beautiful man I have ever seen in my life, but it's not that, not really. I wanted you to know that it wasn't only your face that drew me to you, it was . . . well, just . . . oh goodness, I don't know."

"Me, beautiful?" Colin could only stare at her. "A man isn't beautiful, that is nonsense. Please, just tell me what you want and I shall do my best to see that you get it. I can't be your protector, I'm sorry. Even if I were the randiest goat in all of London, it would do me no good. I have no money."

"I don't want a protector, if by that you mean you would take me on as a mistress."

"Yes," he said slowly, fascinated now. "That is what I meant."

"I can't be a mistress. Even if I wanted to be, it wouldn't help you. Surely my brother wouldn't release my dowry if you didn't wed me. I suspect he wouldn't be pleased if I did become your mistress. He is very old-fashioned about some things."

"Then why are you doing this? Pray, tell me. Did one of my benighted friends put you up to this? Are you the mistress of Lord Brassley? Or Henry Tompkins? Or Lord Clinton?"

"Oh no, no one put me up to anything."

"Not everyone likes the fact that I'm a Scot. Even though I went to school with a good many of the men here in London, they think it just fine to drink with me and sport with me, but not for me to wed their sisters."

"I think you could be a Moroccan and I would still feel as I do."

He could but stare at her. The soft blue feather of her riding hat—a ridiculously small confection of nonsense—curled about her face, framing it charmingly. Her riding habit, a darker blue, darker than her eyes, he saw, fit her to perfection, and it wasn't flirtatious, that habit, no, it was stylish and showed off her high breasts and narrow waist and . . . . He cursed, fluently and low.

"You sound just like my brothers, but usually they're laughing before they get to the end of their curses."

He started to say something but realized that she was staring at his mouth. No, she couldn't be a lady. She was a damned jest, paid for by one of his friends. "Enough!" he bellowed. "This is all an act, it has to be. You can't want to marry me, just like that, and proceed to announce it in the most brazen way imaginable!" He turned suddenly in his saddle and jerked her against him. He pulled her out of her sidesaddle and over his thighs. He held her still until both horses quieted, not that he had to do anything, because she didn't fight him, not at all. She immediately pressed her breasts against him. No, she couldn't be a lady, no way in hell.

He forced her against his left arm and lifted her chin with his gloved fingertips. He kissed her hard, his tongue probing against her closed lips. He raised his head, anger in his voice. "Damn you, open your mouth like you're supposed to."

"All right," she said, and opened her mouth.

At the sight of her open mouth, Colin couldn't help himself. He laughed. "Bloody hell, you look like you're about to sing an opera like that vile soprano from Milan. Oh, damnation!" He set her again onto Fanny's back. Fanny, displeased, pranced to the side, but Sinjun, even a Sinjun who was nearly incoherent with pleasure and excitement and amusement, managed to bring her easily under control.

"All right. I will accept that you are a lady. I will . . . no, I cannot accept that you saw me at the Portmaines' ball and decided you wanted to marry me."

"Well, I wasn't precisely certain I wanted to marry you then, at that moment, just that I thought I could look at you for the rest of my life."

He was disarmed immediately. "Before I see you again—if I see you again—I would that you cloak yourself in a bit of guile. Not a tremendous amount, mind you, but enough so that you don't leave me slack-jawed, with nothing to say when you announce something utterly outrageous."

"I'll try," Sinjun said. She looked away from him for a moment, across the wide expanse of thick green grass, to the riding trails that intersected the park. "Do you think perhaps I could be maybe pretty enough for you? Oh, I know all the other about toothsomeness was just a jest. I wouldn't want you to be ashamed of me, to be embarrassed if I did become your wife."

She met his eyes as she spoke. He just shook his head. "Stop it, do you hear me? For God's sake, you're quite lovely, as you must certainly know."

"People will tell any number of lies, offer more Spanish coin than would fill a cask if they believed one an heiress. I'm not stupid."

He dismounted his stallion, hooked the reins about his hand, and strode to beneath a full-leafed oak tree. "Come here. We must talk before I willingly incarcerate myself in Bedlam."

Ah, to stand close to him, Sinjun thought, as she obeyed him with alacrity.

She looked up at that cleft in his chin, and without thought, she raised her hand, stripped off the glove, and her fingertip traced the cleft. He stood completely motionless.

"I will make you an excellent wife. Do you promise you don't have a troll's character?"

"I like animals and I don't shoot them for sport. I have five cats, excellent ratters, all of them, and at night they have the hearth all to themselves. If ever it is really cold in the dead of winter, they sleep with me, but not often, because I tend to thrash about and crush them. If you mean, would I beat you, the answer is no."

"You're obviously very strong. I'm pleased you don't hurt those who are weaker. Do you also care about people? Are you kind? Do you feel responsible for those people who are your dependents?"

He couldn't look away from her. It was very distressing, but he said, "Yes, I suppose so."

He thought of his huge castle, only half of it really a castle, and that one not medieval by any means but built by a Kinross earl in the late seventeenth century. He loved the castle with its towers and its crenellated battlements and its parapets and deep embrasures. Ah, but it was so drafty in some parts, so dilapidated, that one could catch an inflammation of the lung just standing in one spot for ten minutes. So much had to be done to bring the entire castle back up to snuff. And all the outbuildings and the stables, the crofts and the drainage system. And the depleted herds of sheep and cattle, and his crofters, so many of them, poor and dispirited because they had nothing, not even enough seeds to plant for crops to feed themselves, and the bloody future was so grim and hopeless if he didn't do something. . . .

He looked away from her, toward the line of immense town houses that lined the far side of Hyde Park. "My inheritance was sorely depleted by my father and polished off by my brother, the sixth earl, before he died. I need a lot of money or my family will be reduced to genteel poverty, and many of my dependents will be forced to emigrate, that or starve. I live in a huge old castle set at the eastern side of Loch Leven, beautiful really, not far to the northwest of Edinburgh, on the Fife Peninsula. But still, you would see it as a savage land, despite all its arable land and gentle rolling hills. You're English and you'd see only the barren heights and crevices, and savage, rocky crags and hidden glens with torrents of rushing water bursting through them, water so cold your lips turn blue just to drink it. It's usually not all that cold in the winter months, but the days are short and the winds occasionally heavy. In the spring the heather covers the hills with purple, and the rhododendron spreads over every crofter's hut and even climbs the walls of my drafty castle, in all shades of pink and red and magenta."

He shook himself. He was prosing on like an idiot poet about Scotland and his part of it, as if he were parading his credentials for her inspection, and she was looking up at him, her expression rapt, taking in every word and watching his mouth. It was absurd. He wouldn't, couldn't, accept it. He said abruptly, "Listen, it's true. My lands have the possibility of wealth because of all the arable acres, and I have ideas how to help my crofters improve their lot and thus improve my own in the process. No, we're not like the Highlands that must even now import sheep to survive. It's called enclosing, and it's a pernicious practice, for all the men and women who have lived on their plots of land for generations are being systematically disinherited. They're leaving Scotland or coming to England to work in the new factories. So I must have money, Joan, and there is no other way for me to save my inheritance except by marrying it."

"I understand. Come home with me and speak to my brother Douglas. He's the earl of Northcliffe, you know. We will ask him exactly what my dowry is. It's bound to be very generous. I heard him saying to my mother once that she should stop her picking at me for being on the shelf. Since I was an heiress, he said, I could marry anyone I wanted, even if I was fifty years old and had no teeth."

He looked at her helplessly. "Why me?"

"I haven't the foggiest notion, but there it is."

"I could stab you in your bed."

Her eyes darkened and he felt a surge of lust so great it rocked him on his heels.

"I said stab, not tup."

"What does tup mean?"

"It means . . . oh, damnation, where is that wretched guile I asked you to fetch up? Tup is a crude word, forgive me for saying it."

"Oh, you mean lovemaking, then."

"Yes, that is what I mean, only I was referring to it in a more basic way, what it usually is between men and women, not the high-blown romantic nonsense that females must call lovemaking."

"You are cynical, then. I suppose I can't expect you to be perfect in every way. My two brothers make love, they don't tup. Perhaps I can teach you all about it. But first, of course, you will have to show me the way of such things. It wouldn't do for you to continue to shout with laughter when I open my mouth for you to kiss me."

Colin turned away from her. He felt marooned on a very insubstantial island, one that kept shifting beneath his boots. He hated losing control. He'd lost control over his inheritance, and that was enough to try any man. He didn't want to lose control with a woman to boot, but she kept thrusting and parrying, being utterly outrageous and taking it for granted that it was just fine, that it was normal, almost that it was expected. No Scottish girl would ever behave like this supposedly refined English lady. It was absurd. He felt like a damned fool. "I won't promise you love. I cannot. It will never be. I don't believe in love, and I have very good reasons. I have years of reasons."

"That's what my brother Douglas said about his bride, Alexandra. But he changed, you know. She kept after him until he converted himself, and now I do believe that he would gladly lie down in the middle of a mud puddle and let her tread across him."

"He's a bloody fool."

"Perhaps. But he's a very happy bloody fool."

"I won't speak of this further. You are driving me into the bloody boughs and down again. No, be quiet. I'm taking you home. I must think. And so must you. I'm just a man, do you understand me? Just a man, no more, no less. If I married you, it would be for your groats, not for your lovely eyes or your probably very nice body."

Sinjun just nodded and asked very quietly, "Do you really think I have a nice body?"

He cursed, gave her a boot up, and climbed back into his own saddle. "No," he said, feeling more harassed than he'd ever felt in his life. "No, just be quiet."

Sinjun was in no hurry to return to the Sherbrooke town house, but Colin was. She paid him no heed when they arrived, merely guided Fanny to the stables at the back of the mansion. He was forced to follow.

"Henry, do see to the horses, please. This is his lordship, Lord Ashburnham."

Henry tugged on the bright red curl that dipped onto his forehead. He looked very interested in him, Colin saw, and wondered at it. Surely this outrageous girl had dozens of men panting around her, if for nothing more than to see what she would say next. Lord, her brother must have to warn every man who came through the front door about her excessive candor.

Sinjun skipped up the front steps and opened the door. She stood aside to wave him into the entrance hall. It wasn't the size of the Italian black-and-white marble entrance hall at Northcliffe, but it was of noble proportions nonetheless. White marble with pale blue veins stretched to the pale blue walls, most of them covered with paintings of past Sherbrookes.

Sinjun closed the door and looked around to see if Drinnen, the butler, or any of his minions were anywhere to be seen. There was no one. She turned back to Colin and gave him a brilliant smile and a very conspiratorial one, truth be told. He frowned. She took two steps and stopped, toe to toe with him.

"I'm glad you came in. Now you believe I'm who I said I am. That's good, though the thought of being your mistress does interest me. The concept, you understand. Should you like to speak to my brother now?"

"I shouldn't have come in. I've thought about it all the way back from the park, and it can't be happening, not like this. I'm not used to having a girl chase me down like a fox in the hunt, it isn't natural, it isn't—"

Sinjun merely smiled up at him, put her arms around his neck, and brought him down to her mouth. "I'll open my mouth but not so much this time. Is this right?"

It was more than right. Colin stared for a very brief instant at that soft, open mouth and pulled her tightly against him. He forgot that he was in the entrance hall of the Sherbrooke town house. He forgot that there must be servants about, abounding in hidden places. He forgot all about the Sherbrooke ancestors staring down on them.

He kissed her, his tongue lightly tracing over her lips, then slowly going into her mouth. It was wonderful, and he felt her lurch against him and knew that she felt wonder as well. He kissed her more deeply and she responded freely, fully, and he forgot everything. He hadn't bedded a woman for a month, but he knew even so that this effect she had on him wasn't usual. His hands swept down her back, touching her, learning the feel of her, and he cupped her buttocks, lifting her tightly against his belly.

She moaned softly into his mouth.

"*My God! What the hell is going on here!*"

Those words pierced through the fog in Colin's brain at the same time he was literally dragged away from her, spun around, and struck with blinding ferocity in the jaw. He went down like a stone on the white marble. He grabbed his jaw, shook his head, and stared up at the man who looked ready to kill him.

"Douglas! Don't you dare. This is Colin Kinross, and we're going to be married!"

"Like hell you are! Did you see— No, dear God, a man who hasn't even had the breeding to speak to me, and here he is making love to you in the entrance hall! His hands were on your damned butt. My God, Sinjun, how could you allow a man to do that? Go upstairs, young lady. Obey me. I will see to this bastard, and then I will see to you."

Sinjun had never seen her brother so angry, but she really didn't care if he swung from the chandelier in his rage. She calmly stepped in front of him even as he was ready to advance on Colin again. "Oh, no you don't, Douglas. Just stop it. Colin can't hit you back because he's in your house, and it's at my invitation. I won't allow you to hit him again. It wouldn't be honorable."

"Like hell!" Douglas shouted.

Sinjun wasn't aware that Colin was now standing behind her until he said, "He's right, Joan. I shouldn't have gotten so carried away, here, in his house. Forgive me. However, my lord, I can't allow you to hit me again."

Douglas was beside himself. "You have won yourself a beating for that, you damned bastard."

He flung Sinjun aside and hurled himself at Colin. The two men grappled, pushing and pulling and grunting, fairly evenly matched.

Sinjun heard one groan from a fist to someone's stomach. It was enough. She heard a cry from Alex, who was now dashing down the stairs. The servants were gathering, wide-eyed, huddled beneath the stairs and in the doorway to the dining room.

"Stop it!"

Sinjun's voice didn't result in a truce. If anything, they went at it all the harder. She was furious, at her brother and at Colin. Men! Couldn't they just talk things out? Why did they have to revert to being little boys? She yelled at Alex, "Just stay there, I'll handle this. Oh my, yes, and with great pleasure."

She pulled a long, stout walking stick from the rosewood stand in the corner next to the front door, lifted it, and struck Douglas hard on his shoulder. Then she brought it down equally hard on Colin's right arm.

"That's enough, you bloody fools!"

The two men fell apart from each other, panting. Douglas was holding his shoulder, Colin his right arm.

"How dare you, Sinjun!"

But Douglas didn't wait for an answer, just growled and turned back to the man who'd had the damned gall to caress his little sister's buttocks in the middle of the entrance hall. And to stick his tongue in her mouth, the damned bastard. In her mouth!

Sinjun just started swinging. Not hard, just enough to get their attention. She heard Alex yelling, "Just stop it, Douglas!" Then Alex struck her husband with her own walking stick hard against his back.

Just as suddenly, Douglas realized what he was doing. He stopped cold. There was his small wife and his flushed sister whirling walking sticks about like mad dervishes.

He drew a deep breath, looked over at the damned Scottish ravisher, and said, "They'll kill us. We have to either go to a boxing saloon or put our fists in our pockets."

Colin was looking at the tall young lady who had proposed marriage to him. She'd struck her brother to protect him. It was amazing. Now she had moved toward him so that she was standing between them, that walking stick held firmly in her strong hands. It was more than amazing. It was also humiliating.

"Fists in pockets, if you please, my lord," Colin said.

"Good," Sinjun said. "Alex, what do you think? Shall we put the sticks away or keep them just in case the gentlemen here lose their breeding and tempers again?"

Alex, frowning ferociously, didn't answer. She dropped the stick and sent her fist into her husband's belly. Douglas, too surprised to do anything but grunt, looked at his wife, then over at Sinjun, and sighed. "All right, fists in pockets."

"Civilization is not a bad thing," Sinjun said. "To cement the truce, we'll have some tea. But first, Colin, you must come with me for a moment. There is blood on your lip. I will clean it off for you."

Alex said, "And you're a mess, Douglas. Your knuckles are raw and you've ripped your shirt, the one I made especially for you on your birthday. But you didn't think of that, did you, when you dove headfirst into these absurd fisticuffs? Oh goodness, there's some of Colin's blood on the collar. I doubt even Mrs. Jarvis's best potions will get that out. Sinjun, we will all meet in ten minutes in the drawing room." She looked around, saw Drinnen standing there looking drawn and white, and said calmly, "If you please, disperse the staff, Drinnen. And bring tea and scones to the drawing room. His lordship here is Scottish and doubtless will be very critical. Be certain the scones are up to snuff."

And it was done. By two women. Colin followed Joan Sherbrooke without a word. From the corner of his eye, he saw the earl likewise trailing in the wake of his very small wife, that lady's shoulders back, her chin high as a general's.

Colin Kinross, seventh earl of Ashburnham, felt as if he'd been trapped in a bizarre dream. It wasn't a nightmare, but it was beyond passing strange. He looked at the mass of loose brownish-blond hair that streamed down her back, pulled loose of pins during their skirmish. He didn't know what had happened to her riding hat. Thick hair, quite lovely really. She was toothsome, no doubt about that, and kissing her had been more enjoyable than anything he could remember.

But this interference, he couldn't tolerate it. The fight was between two men. Ladies had no say. No, he couldn't, wouldn't, tolerate such interference from her again.

3

"ENOUGH OF THIS, Joan. I will not be led around like a damned goat."

Sinjun turned at the irritated voice of the man she had decided irrevocably she would marry and smiled. She patted his arm. "I myself don't like to be led around, either, particularly in a strange house. I don't mean that the house is strange, just that it is unknown to you. Walk beside me, then we'll both be leading."

"It has nothing to do with the strangeness of the damned house. Or my strangeness or anyone else's strangeness." But nonetheless, he fell into step beside her, feeling like an idiot.

She led him into the nether regions of the large house, down a passageway and through a door into a huge kitchen that was cozy and warm and smelled of cinnamon and nutmeg and sweet bread baking in old stone ovens. He sniffed scones and his mouth watered. He'd been too long from home. "Sit down here at the table, my lord."

He gave her a very irritated look. "For God's sake, with all that's happened in less than twenty-four hours, I think you can call me Colin."

She gave him a dazzling smile. If he hadn't felt so irritated he might have grabbed her and kissed her again. As it was, he just sat in that damned wooden chair like a docile dog and let her dab a damp cloth against his mouth. It burned like the devil but he kept still.

"I would have preferred to take you to my bedchamber," Sinjun said, pausing a moment to view her handiwork, "but Douglas would probably have immediately canceled the truce. He is, at times, unaccountable."

He grunted.

"As it is, you get to meet Cook, Mrs. Potter by name, and she makes the best scones you will ever eat in England. Dear Mrs. Potter, this is Lord Ashburnham."

Colin nodded to the immense woman all garbed in white, including her apron, holding a long-handled bread paddle. She gave him a suspicious stare. He stared at the paddle and the meaty hand holding it.

"Who was that small woman?"

"Douglas's wife, Alexandra. She loves him dearly and would give her life for him."

Colin grew very still. An odd concept that, and he wasn't certain he could even begin to believe it. He reached up his hand and grabbed her wrist, drawing it down. He pulled slightly and soon she was leaning down to him, not three inches from his face. "Do you believe in such loyalty?"

"Yes."

"You struck your brother, true, but then you turned and struck me harder."

"I did try to be fair, but in the heat of battle, so to speak, it's difficult to mete out an exact equality of blows."

He had to smile, which he did.

"If you don't release me, I think Mrs. Potter is going to hit you with the bread paddle."

He let her go. She finished patting the cut on his lip. "Hot tea will burn a bit, but it will taste good, too. Now, onward to the drawing room. You must deal with Douglas, since he is the head of the Sherbrooke family."

I don't believe this is happening to me, Colin thought as he strode beside the tall girl with her coltish walk and her tumbled hair. She began to whistle, just like a boy. He started, then just shook his head. He said aloud, "This really isn't what I expected. I didn't know you existed until last night, and now here I am in your house and your brother attacked me and I've even been in your kitchen."

"Douglas firmly believed you deserved it. He didn't know you then. All he saw was this very handsome man holding me up with his hands."

"That's not all I was doing with my hands."

Instead of blushing like an English heiress maiden should, she stared at his mouth and said in a very wistful voice, "I know. It was very nice, although it was startling. No one has ever done that to me before. I quite liked it."

"You must keep your mouth shut, Joan. The guile I spoke of, it's a useful thing. You must protect yourself."

"I can and I do, though there is seldom the need. How old are you, Colin?"

He sighed and let it go. "I'm twenty-seven. My birthday is in August."

"I thought you were about Ryder's age. He's one of my brothers. You will meet him soon. He's quite outrageous and funny and charming and quite the philanthropist. He used to hate anyone knowing how kind and good he was because he liked his wicked rake's image. As to my youngest brother, Tysen the Holiness we call him, I will protect you from his vicaring, which is what Douglas calls his prosing on and on about good deeds and the many paths to hell and such. But he is my brother and I love him despite his narrow vision of things; and then there is his wife, Melinda Beatrice. Ryder said two names were too many, and besides she has no bosom."

Colin could only stare at this outpouring. "I've never met a family like yours before."

"No," Sinjun said comfortably, "I expect not. My brothers and sisters-in-law are wonderful. All except Melinda Beatrice, and she's really a bore, to peel the bark off the tree. Do you know they've been married four years and have three children? My brothers are forever twitting Tysen about unvicarlike potency and lack of control and overloading Noah's ark with all his offspring."

They had reached the drawing room. Colin turned to her and smiled. "I won't attack your brother, I promise. Hands in pockets."

"Thank you. I also hope that my mother keeps herself absent until after you've left. I must deal with her gently but firmly, and that will require having Douglas on my side first."

When he remained quiet, Sinjun turned and asked, "Do you want to marry me, Colin?"

He looked thoughtful. "I want to meet your mother first. It is said that daughters become the very image of their mothers."

Sinjun, aghast, poked him in the arm. "Oh dear," she said. "Oh dear." When he laughed, she poked him again and dragged him into the drawing room.

She said to her grim-faced brother and a smiling Alex, "Now we shall do things properly. This is Colin Kinross, the earl of Ashburnham. He is twenty-seven years old and he is considering marrying me, Douglas, so you see it was all right for him to take, er, liberties with my person."

"He was caressing your bottom, dammit! A man only does that to his wife."

"Douglas!"

"Well, he was caressing her, Alex. Was I to stand there watching the bounder seduce my little sister?"

"No, of course not. I apologize for not quite understanding the situation. Drubbing him was exactly the proper thing to do. Ah, here's Drinnen with tea. Do come in. Sinjun, you and Colin please sit over here on the sofa."

Colin Kinross looked at the earl of Northcliffe. He saw a man some five or so years older than he was, an athlete, no dandied-up fop like many of their contemporaries. "I apologize for taking liberties with Joan. I suppose that since I have, it would only be honorable for me to marry her."

"I don't believe any of this," Douglas said. "And you call her Joan! Only Mother calls her that. It's repellent."

"I don't care for the mannish nickname."

Douglas just stared at him.

"I assure you I don't care," Sinjun said, then smiled grandly. "He can call me anything he wishes to. Now, I thought if one put one's mind to it, this courtship and marriage business wouldn't be all that difficult. You see, I was right. It's grand to get things moving properly. What would you like in your tea, Colin?"

"Just a moment," Douglas said. "There is nothing simple about any of this, Sinjun. I want you to listen to me." But he turned to Colin. "I have found out, sir, that you are on the hunt for an heiress. You haven't been at all discreet about it. You doubtless know very well that Sinjun here will be quite rich upon her marriage."

"So she tells me. She came up to me and announced she was an heiress. She wanted me to speak to you to find out exactly what she's worth."

"She *what?*"

Sinjun only smiled at her brother. "It's true, Douglas. I knew he needed a wife with money, and so I told him I was perfect for him. Groats and toothsomeness all in one female person. To make it even grander, he catches all the other Sherbrookes in the family net as well as me."

Alex laughed, she couldn't help it. "I hope, Colin, that you can control this minx. She tackled me once in the immense entranceway of Northcliffe Hall, in front of everyone, and held me down until Douglas could be released from the room I'd locked him in. You must be careful, for she's really quite very determined once she sets her course."

She went into peals of laughter, and Sinjun grinned. Douglas looked wooden as a church pew, and Colin looked as if he were indeed in Bedlam and the inmates were ganging up on him.

"I'll tell you all about it later," Sinjun said, and lightly patted his biscuit-colored coat sleeve. She made the mistake of looking at his face and felt her own color rise at her very interesting thoughts.

"Stop it, Joan," he said low, through his teeth. "You're a danger to yourself. Just stop it. Do you want your brother to attack me again?"

"Listen, all of you just cease and desist for a minute." Douglas rose and began pacing the drawing room. He was also carrying his teacup and sloshed tea onto his hand. He grimaced, set the cup down, and resumed his pacing. "You saw him for the first time five days ago, Sinjun. *Five days!* You can't possibly know that you'd be content with this man—he's a bloody stranger."

"He said he wouldn't beat me. He said he was kind and felt responsible for his dependents. When it's really cold he lets his cats sleep with him. What else should I know, Douglas?"

"You might want to know if he cares for anything other than your money, my girl!"

"If he doesn't now, he will come to care for me. I'm not a bad person, Douglas. You like me."

Colin rose to stand his full height. "Joan, you will cease to answer for me as if I were a half-wit and not even here."

"Very well," Sinjun said, and primly folded her hands in her lap.

"Damnation, my lord, I don't have a bloody word to say to you! This isn't . . ." Words failed Douglas. He stomped to the door and turned to say over his shoulder, "I will speak to you again, Colin Kinross, this time next week. *Seven days!* Seven additional days, do you understand me? You're to keep away from my sister. One week, mind, no sooner. And keep your damned hands off my sister before you leave her in ten minutes!"

He slammed the door shut behind him. Alex rose then and grinned at them. "I fancy I will anoint his troubled brow with rosewater. It will soothe him." She giggled and followed her husband from the salon. She said at the door, not turning, "Keep your hands off him, Sinjun, do you hear me? Men have no tolerance in matters of affection. You mustn't drive him over the brink. Even in only ten minutes, gentlemen can forget every proper behavior they ever learned."

Were all the Sherbrookes—even those not born Sherbrookes—quite mad?

"I am pleased to have accorded your sister-in-law so much amusement," Colin said, and there was more irritation in his voice than there was tea in his cup. "If you want me to keep my hands off you, then stop staring at my mouth."

"I can't help it. You're so very beautiful. Oh dear, all we have are ten minutes."

Colin jumped to his feet, and he took up Douglas's pacing. "This is all immensely unlikely, Joan," he said, pivoting to walk toward the marble fireplace. "And in the future I will speak for myself." And just what would he say? Damnation. He paused, looking down into the empty grate. It was pale pink Italian marble, expensive and fashioned by masters. Then he pictured in his mind the huge blackened fireplace in the great hall of Vere Castle that could hold an entire cow. Old and filthy, the bricks cracking, the mortar falling out in chunks. Jesus, even the magnificent painting of a pastoral scene over the Italian marble mantel was old and reeked of solid wealth and an acceptance of great privilege. Wealth and privilege of many generations. He thought of the winding narrow stairs that climbed to the second-floor north tower, so dangerous now because of wood rot from the cold wind seeping through the gaps in the outer stone. He drew a deep breath. He could save Vere Castle. He could save his people. He could replenish the sheep. He could even plant crops, since he'd learned all about crop rotation. He could buy grain. He turned to his future wife and said, "I will accept your belief that I'm beautiful. A man, I suppose, wants to be thought reasonably acceptable to the woman he marries."

"More than acceptable," Sinjun said, and felt her heart thump wildly in her breast. He'd accepted her. Finally. She wanted to kick her heels in the air.

He sighed then and plowed his fingers through his hair, making it stand on end. He stopped cold when she said in a marveling voice, "I didn't ever think I would fall in love. No gentleman has ever made me think there was anything to this love business. I found some of them amusing, but nothing more than that. Others were stupid and rude and had no chins. Some thought me a bluestocking, and all because I'm not ignorant. I couldn't imagine having any of them kissing me. Goodness, if any of them had even touched my bottom, I should have shrieked and killed them. But with you . . . it's different. I understand that you don't love me. Please believe me that it doesn't matter. I will do my best to make you care for me. Now, there is nothing more I can say other than I will try to make you a good wife. Would you like to eat one of Mrs. Potter's scones, or would you like to leave and go somewhere private to brood?"

"Brood," he said. "There is so much you don't know about me. You might very well change your mind."

She gave him a long, thoughtful look. She said quite calmly and with great finality, "You will care for me, will you not, if we marry?"

"I will protect you with my life. It would be my responsibility."

"You would give me respect?"

"If you deserve it."

"Very well, then. You can tell me anything you wish to after the ceremony. Not before. And know now that nothing you say to me will change how I feel about you. It's just that I don't want anything untoward and unimportant coming to Douglas's ears before we're married."

He would wed her. He desperately needed the money, and he liked her, despite her outlandishness. It was frightening, this openness of hers, this truth that knew no tempering. Well, he could teach her to moderate her tongue. He knew he wouldn't find it at all difficult to bed her. Yes, he would wed her. But he would wait the week her brother had demanded. But it had to be soon after that. The situation back home was growing worse by the day. She would do just fine. And she'd presented herself to him on a wondrous silver plate. Only a fool would look such a gift-heiress in the mouth. Colin Kinross wasn't a fool.

He strode over to her, pulled her to her feet, and just looked down at her silently. Then he kissed her lightly on her closed mouth. He wanted more but forced himself not to take any more from her, even though he imagined he could ease her down to the floor this very minute and take her without much fuss. But he didn't. He would keep himself within safe bounds. He said, "I would like to see you again, despite your brother's edict. Would you like to go riding tomorrow? We'll be discreet."

"I would love to. Douglas will never know. Oh, Colin?"

He turned.

"Will you teach me how to speak Scottish?"

"Aye, and 'twill be my pleasure, lassie." His voice was lilting and smooth as honey. "Ye'll be my sweetheart, dinna ye ken?"

"I've never been a sweetheart before. It sounds grand."

All he could do was shake his head at her.

Douglas said to his wife, "I've discovered nothing ill about Ashburnham. He is liked and respected. He attended Eton and Oxford. He has many men friends in society. The only thing any of them can say is that he must marry an heiress." Douglas, in a habit that was becoming more pronounced, plowed his fingers through his hair again. He continued his pacing as his wife watched him from her dressing table. It was still early in the evening, three nights from the week Douglas had demanded. Both of them knew that Sinjun had met Colin the day after the historic brawl, but neither wanted to make an issue of it. As far as Douglas knew, Sinjun hadn't seen him since. But who could know with Sinjun? She was damnably resourceful.

"How long has he been the earl of Ashburnham?"

"Just six months. His brother was a wastrel, as was his father. Together they ran the estate into the ground. He has a huge barn of an old castle that will require vast sums to bring it back to what it was. Then there are the crops, the sheep, the poverty of his people—crofters, they're called in Scotland."

"So," Alex said slowly, "when he became the earl and discovered the true state of his affairs, he made a decision, the only one he could make. You don't dislike him for that, do you, Douglas?"

"No. It's just that—"

"That what, my dear?"

"Sinjun doesn't know him. She's infatuated, that's all. She'll end up in Scotland, with no one to protect her, and what if—"

"Do you believe that Colin Kinross is an honorable man?"

"I have no idea. On the surface, I'd say yes. What goes on in his mind? In his heart?"

"Sinjun will wed him, Douglas. I only hope she doesn't seduce him before they're wed."

He sighed. "I hope so, too. Now I must go to speak with Mother. She is squawking again, driving her maid insane, demanding that the young man be brought to her. She is threatening to send Sinjun to Italy until she has forgotten this foreign bounder. The strange thing is that she doesn't at all mind that he is marrying her daughter for money. What she minds is that he is a Scot. She says all Scots are hard and mean-fisted and *Presbyterian.*"

"Perhaps you should quote some Robert Burns poetry to her. It's really quite lovely."

"Ha! It's a foreign language and she'd have even more fits than she's having now. Damnation, I wish Sinjun weren't lying in her bed with a headache. She is never about when I need her."

"Shall I come with you?"

"If you were to do that, Mother would rage until we were both deaf. You still haven't won her over, my dear. I doubt not she will soon come around to blaming you for this debacle." Douglas sighed and left the room, mumbling about his damned sister and her equally damned headache.

Sinjun didn't have a headache. She had a plan and she was well into its execution. She had carefully molded a bolster into a reasonable human shape and covered it. Excellent. If there were no close inspection, the bolster would pass muster as a likely female. She patted her own pants leg, straightened her jacket, and pulled her felt hat more fully down over her forehead. She looked like a boy, no doubt about it. She turned and looked at her back in the long mirror. Just like a boy, even to her black boots. She whistled softly. Now all she had to do was climb down the elm tree into the garden. Then she was off.

Colin's lodgings were on the second floor of an old Georgian town house on Carlyon Street, only three streets away. It wasn't yet dark and she kept whistling to keep away any fears that might try to nibble at her, and to make anyone who saw her see only a boy, out for the evening. She saw two gentlemen in their swirling cloaks, laughing and smoking cheroots, but they paid her no heed. There was a ragged boy sweeping the path for anyone who passed, and she thanked him and gave him a pence. Sinjun found his lodging without problem and strolled to the front door as if she hadn't a care in the world. She pounded the huge eagle's-head knocker.

There wasn't a sound from within. She knocked again. She heard a giggle and a girl's high voice scolding, "Now, sir, don't you do that! No, no, not there, you mustn't. Now, we've a visitor. No, sir—" There were more giggles and when the door opened, Sinjun was face-to-face with one of the prettiest females she'd ever seen. The girl's neckline was low over very white, full breasts, and her pale hair was mussed and her eyes were bright with excitement and fun. She was grinning wickedly.

"And just who'd you be, my fine lad?" she said, striking a pose, one hand on her hip and her chest poked out.

The fine lad answered with a wide smile, "Who do you want me to be?

Your father, perhaps? No, that isn't possible, is it? I would have to scold the gentleman who was making you laugh, and you wouldn't want that, would you?"

"Oh, you're a fine one, you are! All jests and games and a well-oiled tongue. You want to see someone here?"

Sinjun nodded. She saw a gentleman from the corner of her eye as he slipped into a door off the main corridor. "I'm here to see Lord Ashburnham. Is he in?"

The girl struck another pose, this one even more provocative, and giggled once again. "Aye, a pretty one, his lordship is. But he's poor, you know. Can't afford a nice girl, he can't, or a gentleman's man to help him. Talk is he's marrying an heiress, but he won't say boo about it. Probably the heiress is a stoat all dressed in fancy silk, poor man."

"Some heiresses can even whistle, I've heard," Sinjun said. "Now, his lordship's apartment is on the second floor, isn't it?"

"Yes," the girl said. "Hey, wait! I don't know if he's here or not. Haven't seen him for two days now. Tilly, one of the girls, went up to see if he wanted some fun—all willing to give it to him on the house, she was—but he wasn't there. Leastwise he didn't answer. And what man wouldn't answer when he heard Tilly calling out to him?"

Sinjun took the stairs two at a time, saying over her shoulder, "If he isn't there, perhaps I shall return and you and I can, er, have a cup of tea and a chat."

The girl giggled. "Ah, go along with you, my cute lad! Ah, 'tis you, sir, back again. Now, where were we? Ah, what naughtiness you are!"

Sinjun was still smiling when she reached the landing. It was a solid house with a wide hallway. Well maintained, the paint fresh, a gentleman's establishment. Were the pretty girls here all the time? She found Colin's door and knocked. There was nothing. She knocked again. Please, she thought, please let him be here. It had been too long. Four whole days without him. It was too much. They'd fooled Douglas that first morning, but Colin hadn't called on her since. She had to see him, to touch him, to smile at him.

Finally she heard a deep voice call out, "Whoever you are, go to hell."

It was Colin, but he sounded strange, his voice low and raw. Was he with someone? A girl like the one downstairs?

No, she wouldn't believe that. She knocked again.

"Damnation, go away!" The curse was followed by a hacking cough.

Sinjun felt a spurt of fear. She gripped the door handle, and to her immense relief it wasn't locked. She pushed the door open and walked into a small entrance hall. She looked to her right into a long, narrow drawing room that was well enough furnished, she supposed, but impersonal, without any individual character. It called up nothing of Colin. Nothing of anyone except perhaps a musty gentleman from the past century. She called out, "Colin? Where are you?"

She heard some cursing coming from beyond the drawing room. She hurried now, pushed the door open, and came face-to-face with her betrothed. He was sitting up in the middle of a rumpled bed, quite naked, the sheets drawn only to his waist. Sinjun stood there a moment, just gawking. Goodness, he was big, and there was black hair all over his chest, and he looked strong and muscular and lean and she couldn't stop staring at his chest and his arms and his shoulders, yes, even his throat. There were black whiskers on his face, his eyes were bloodshot, and his hair was standing on end. He looked quite wonderful.

"Joan! What the hell are you doing here? Are you out of your damned mind? Are you—"

His voice was a croak. Sinjun was across the room to him in a moment to stand by the side of the bed. "What's wrong?" Even as she asked him, she realized he was shaking. And she'd been standing there staring at him like a half-witted fool. "Oh goodness." She pushed him back down and pulled the covers up to his chin. "No, no, just hold still and tell me what's wrong."

Colin lay flat on his back, looking up at Joan, who was trying to look like a boy, which was ridiculous. But perhaps it was the fever; perhaps she wasn't really here, perhaps he'd just conjured her up.

He said tentatively, frowning, "Joan?"

"Yes, love, I'm here. What's wrong?" She sat beside him and laid her palm on his forehead. He was hot to the touch.

"I can't be your love," he said. "It's much too soon. Damnation, I'm tired or something, and weak as a day-old pup. Why are you pretending to be a boy? It's silly. You have a woman's hips and long legs that aren't at all remotely like a boy's."

It was an interesting avenue of conversation, but Sinjun was too scared to be sidetracked. "You have a fever. Have you been vomiting?"

He shook his head, then closed his eyes. "Have you no damned sensibilities?"

"Your head hurts?"

"Yes."

"How long have you felt bad?"

"Two days now. I don't feel bad, I'm just tired."

"Why didn't you send for a doctor? For me?"

"I don't need anyone. It's just a passing fever, nothing more. I was out in the rain, at a boxing match on Tyburn Hill. I'm just tired."

"We'll see," she said. Men, she thought, as she leaned down and pressed her cheek to his. They couldn't bring themselves to admit to any weakness. She drew back. The heat was incredible. His eyes flew open, but she said as she gently laid her fingertip on his lips, "No, don't move. I will see to everything now. When did you last eat?"

He looked as irritated as his voice sounded. "I don't remember. It isn't important. I'm not hungry. Just go away, Joan. It's vastly improper for you to be here."

"Would you leave me if you found me sick and alone?"

"It's altogether different, and you know it. For God's sake, I'm bare-assed."

"Bare-assed," she repeated, smiling at him. "My brothers have never said that before. No, no, don't frown at me or curse at me anymore. Just lie down and I will see to things."

"No, dammit, just go away!"

"I will, and I will soon be back with help. Lie down and keep warm, Colin. Now, would you like some water?"

His eyes lit up and he nodded.

Once he'd drunk his fill, she said matter-of-factly, "Do you need to relieve yourself?"

He looked ready to spit. "Go away."

"All right." She leaned down and kissed his mouth and was gone in the next moment.

Colin pulled the covers to his nose. His thoughts were vague. The room blurred. When he opened his eyes again, he was alone. Had she really been here? He wasn't so thirsty anymore, so someone must have come in. Lord, he was cold and he couldn't seem to stop shivering. His head pounded and his thoughts grew vaguer. He was ill, more wretched than he'd been when he'd cracked two ribs in a satisfying fight just two months before his brother had gotten himself killed and Colin had inherited a title he'd wanted only because he hated the destruction of his home.

He closed his eyes and saw Joan dressed like a boy and she was smiling down at him. Unaccountable girl. She would be back, of that he had no doubts—that is, if she'd ever been here in the first place.

An hour later he received a shock when not only Joan returned, but her brother Douglas with her. He saw that she was still wearing boys' clothes. Didn't her brother discipline her? Wasn't she given any guidance on how a young lady of quality was to behave?

Colin stared at the earl, who was staring back at him. He was unable to find a single word to say. Douglas said calmly, "You're coming back to Sherbrooke House. You're ill, I can see that, and my sister doesn't want to marry a man who's nearly dead."

"So you were really here," he said to Sinjun.

"Yes, and now all will be well. I'll take excellent care of you."

"Dammit, I'm only tired, not ill. You're making too much of this, and I just want to be left alone and—"

"Do be quiet," Douglas said.

And Colin, because he felt worse than a half-starved mongrel, shut his mouth.

And that, he thought, too ill to care, was that.

"Sinjun, get out of here. The man's naked and you aren't to stay about and embarrass him. Send in Henry and Boggs to help me get him into clothing."

"I can dress myself," Colin said, and Douglas, seeing the fever burning bright and hot in his eyes, agreed.

He didn't do it well, but he managed to dress himself quickly. However, the ride to the Sherbrooke town house was a nightmare Colin would just as soon not have lived through. He passed out when Henry and Boggs were helping him up the wide stairway.

It wasn't until they were in the guest bedchamber that Douglas discovered the jagged four-inch-long knife wound at the top of Colin's right thigh.

4

"YOU MUST GET SOME REST, Sinjun. It's nearly one o'clock in the morning."

Sinjun didn't wish to look away from his still face, but she forced herself to glance up at her sister-in-law. "I'm resting, Alex. It's just that I must be here if he wakes up. He's always so thirsty, you know."

Alex said calmly, "He's a strong man. He won't die. I'm not worried about him now. I don't want you to lose your health."

"Do you promise, Alex?"

"Yes, I promise. His breathing is a bit easier, I can hear it. The doctor said he would survive this. He will."

"I still don't want to leave him. He's had horrible nightmares."

Alex handed Sinjun a cup of tea and sat beside her.

"What sort of nightmares?"

"I'm not sure. He's frightened and he's confused. Whether it's real or just the fever, I don't know."

Colin heard her voice. It was pitched low and it was calm, but the underlying worry was there, thick and deep. He wanted to open his eyes and look at her, but he couldn't. It was that simple. He was deep within himself, and he was afraid; she'd been right about that. He'd seen Fiona again, and she was lying there at the base of the cliff, quite dead, her body sprawled on the jagged rocks. He was standing there looking down at her. Fear welled up in him and he wanted to get away from it, but it pursued him, overwhelmed him, and he was dying of the fear and the terror of what he couldn't or wouldn't remember, and the god-awful uncertainty. Had he killed her? No, dammit, he hadn't killed his wife, he hadn't. Even this nightmare couldn't make him believe that he had. Someone had brought him here, perhaps Fiona herself, and she'd fallen, but he hadn't killed her. He knew it deep down. He'd backed away from the cliff edge very slowly, one step, then another. He felt dizzy and strangely detached from himself. He'd led men back there, to where he'd found her, and no one had asked him what had happened, how it was that Fiona was lying there thirty feet below, her neck broken.

Ah, but there was talk, endless talk, and that talk was more devastating than an outright accusation, for it swirled around him, always out of his reach, those damned whispers and innuendos; and it ate at him because he knew he could shout his innocence, but how could he explain how he'd come to be there on the cliff edge himself? That he didn't know, didn't remember. He'd just come to himself and he'd been there. There was no reasoning he could grasp, nothing. The only person he'd told everything he remembered had been Fiona's father, the laird of the MacPherson clan, and he'd believed him. But it wasn't enough, never enough, for he couldn't remember and it preyed on him, brought him down when he slept, when he was at his weakest, this guilt that wasn't really guilt. But he still felt the nightmares to be a penance he was obligated to pay.

He was thrashing now, moaning deep in his throat. The knife wound in his thigh burned and gnawed at him. Sinjun was on her feet in an instant, gently holding him still, her hands on his shoulders. "Hush, Colin. It's all right. They're just nightmares, nothing more than nightmares. Just phantoms to plague you. Nothing more. That's right, listen to me. I won't lie to you. Come closer, yes, here's some water, it will make you feel better."

She tipped the water glass slightly and he swallowed. She held the glass until he turned his head away. She dabbed the water from his chin, saying quietly to her sister-in-law, "I put some laudanum in the water. It should help him into a deeper sleep, away from the nightmares."

Alex said nothing. She knew no one could pull her away from Douglas were he ill. Thus, she just patted Sinjun's arm and left the bedchamber.

Douglas was awake. He pulled Alex against him and held her close. "How is he?"

"Very ill. He's having nightmares. It's awful, Douglas."

"Couldn't you get Sinjun to leave him to Finkle for the rest of the night?"

"No. Finkle would fall asleep and probably wake poor Colin up with his snoring. You told me about the times when you were campaigning that Finkle would wake you up with his noises even after you'd been in battle for twelve hours and exhausted. No, let Finkle see to Colin during the day. Sinjun is young and strong. She needs to be with him. Let her."

Douglas sighed. "Life is bloody unexpected. I forbade him to enter the house, knowing deep in my brain that the two of them would naturally see each other. Damnation, he could have died if Sinjun hadn't taken matters into her own hands and gone to his lodgings. It's my bloody fault. She doesn't know about the knifing, does she?"

"No. Now, if you continue to blame yourself, Douglas, for something that could never be remotely your fault, I shall write to Ryder and urge him to come here immediately and bash you into the ground."

"Ha! Ryder wouldn't do that. Besides, I'm bigger than he is. I'd thrash him into a lump."

"Ah, but then you'd have to deal with Sophie."

"A terrifying thought."

"I hope you don't mind that she and Ryder can't come to London just now. With two of the children hurt in that fall from the hayloft, they wouldn't much enjoy it; they'd be too worried. Also, the twins are quite happy there with their cousin and all the other children."

"I miss the little heathens," Douglas said fondly.

"All twelve of the children plus our two and Ryder and Sophie's one?"

"Two at a time is preferable. I like the notion of trading children around. They never quite have time enough to roll you up so you'll do whatever they want."

"You're right about that. Ah, but my dear, with Colin so ill and the wedding to be seen to, it is better, I suppose, that we leave the boys with their aunt and uncle."

"I think Sinjun will want to marry Colin just as soon as possible. If that's so, then Ryder and Sophie won't be here."

"I'm too tired to think more on the situation. Let's get some sleep."

Douglas felt a soft hand stroke down his chest and smiled into the darkness. "Ah, I thought you were tired. You have regained your vigor? Am I to be rewarded?"

"If you promise not to shout too loudly and awaken your mother again." Alex shuddered, remembering the one night she and Douglas had enjoyed themselves immoderately, and his mother had burst into the room, thinking Alex had killed her beloved son. The memory still made her stiff with mortification.

"I'll stuff a handkerchief in my mouth."

He was whole-witted at last, but so weak he couldn't seem to raise himself so he could use the chamber pot. It was damnable. At least the fever was gone and the pain in his leg was tolerable. He'd been a fool not to see a doctor when it had happened, but he simply wasn't used to having some quack dose him, for God's sake, for whatever reason. Never had he seen Dr. Childress, the Kinross physician for over thirty years, for anything more than childhood illnesses. He was young and strong and healthy as a stoat. A simple little knife cut and here he was flat on his back, sick with fever and out of his head.

He watched with half-closed eyes as Joan came into the room. He was testy and hungry. He didn't want her there. He needed a man to help him.

"Ah, good, you're awake," Sinjun said, giving him a smile that lit up the bedchamber. "How do you feel?"

He grunted.

"Should you like me to shave you? I shaved Tysen's head once while Ryder held him down. Not more than ten years ago. I could try, and I would be very careful."

"No."

"The strangest thing, Colin, there's a man downstairs who claims he's your cousin."

That brought him bolt upright in the bed. The covers fell to his belly and he could but stare at her. Which cousin? None of his cousins knew he was here, did they? Ah, MacDuff did.

"That's not possible," he said, and fell back to the pillows. Sinjun was looking at the line the covers made below his waist. She swallowed. He was so beautiful, all hard and long, black hair covering his chest, ah, but it narrowed to a soft black trail and disappeared beneath the covers. He was too thin, she could see his ribs, but that would change.

"You must stay warm," she said, and pulled the covers up to his shoulders, even though she wanted to pull them to his feet and look at him for six hours at least.

"Joan, you're not jesting? MacDuff is here?"

She blinked. "MacDuff? He didn't give me his name, just said he was your favorite cousin. MacDuff, as in Shakespeare's MacDuff?"

"Yes. As boys, we all called him MacCud—"

"As in a Scottish cow?"

He grinned. "That's it. His real name is Francis Little, absurd for someone of his height, breadth, and width, so we chose MacDuff for him when we were boys. As I recall, he threatened to smash us in the dirt if we didn't stop calling him MacCud and change it to MacDuff."

"It fits him better than Francis Little, which isn't at all right for a man with a chest the width of a tree trunk. MacDuff! That's very clever, Colin. I imagine you devised that name. You know, he's got the reddest hair and no freckles. His eyes are as blue as a summer sky—"

"His eyes are just the same shade as yours. Stop your rhapsodizing about my bloody giant of a cousin. Bring him up."

"No," Sinjun said. "Not until you've eaten your breakfast. Ah, here's Finkle right now. He'll assist you with other matters as well. I will be back in a few minutes and help you eat."

"I don't need your help."

"Certainly not, but you will enjoy my company, won't you?"

He just looked at her. She smiled at him, kissed his closed mouth lightly, and nearly danced from the room.

She turned at the doorway. "Should you like to marry me tomorrow?"

He gave her a look that held irritation rather than shock, and said, "You would have a memorable wedding night. I would be lying dead to the world at your side and that would be it."

"I shouldn't mind. We have the rest of our lives together."

"I refuse to wed you until I can bed you properly." It was a stupid thing for him to say, he realized. He needed to wed her in the next hour, if it were possible. Time was growing short. He desperately needed her money.

Sinjun sat back, watching the two cousins talk. They were speaking quietly, so she couldn't understand them, nor did she really want to eavesdrop, something at which she was really quite accomplished. With three older brothers, she'd learned at a very young age that most information kept from her, wicked or otherwise, was best discovered through a keyhole. She looked out the window down into the enclosed garden. It was a cool day, but the sky was clear and blue and the flowers and plants in the garden were in full bloom. She heard Colin laugh and looked up, smiling. MacDuff—surely that nickname was stranger than her own nickname, Sinjun—seemed a pleasant man, and more important, very fond of Colin. Even sitting by the bed he looked huge, not fat, no, not at all, just huge like a giant. His laugh was huge, too, shaking his entire body. She liked him. She had no qualms about MacDuff because she'd told him that if he tired Colin, she would personally boot him out.

He'd looked down at her from his vast elevation and grinned. "You're no coward, I see, just a bit stupid to take this mongrel into your home. Nay, I'll close my trap when the time comes so as not to tire out the poor lad."

In perfect accord, she'd taken him in to see Colin.

Even now he was rising and saying to Colin, "It's time you rested, old man. No, no arguments. I have promised Sinjun and I have a mighty fear of her."

"Her name is Joan. She isn't a man."

MacDuff raised a violent red eyebrow. "A bit irritable, are we? A bit of a green color about the gills? I will see you in the morning, Ash. Do what Sinjun tells you to do. She's invited me to the wedding, you know."

And MacDuff the tree trunk was gone.

"He has no Scottish accent, just as you don't."

"MacDuff, despite his nickname, prefers the English side of his family. My father and his mother were brother and sister. His mother married an Englishman from York, a very wealthy ironmonger. Both of us were educated in England, but he went more deeply into it than I did. I used to think he would cut all ties with Scotland if he weren't tied to it so closely, at least that's what he always said. But now I believe he's changed his mind, because during the past few years he's lived most of the time in Edinburgh."

"You're tired, Colin. I want to hear all about this, but later, my dear."

"You're a nag."

He sounded sour, which pleased her. He was mending.

"No, not a nag. One rides a nag," she said, patting the covers at his shoulders.

He stared at her. "Your sexual innuendos aren't at all the thing for a virgin."

He realized she had no idea what he was talking about and snorted at her. "Just go away, Joan."

"All right. Forgive me, Colin. You're tired and must rest."

She turned at the door. "Would you like to marry me the day after tomorrow?"

"Perhaps if I can walk tomorrow I shall be able to ride the day after tomorrow."

She cocked her head to one side in question, and when he just continued to look sour, she smiled and left him.

Colin lay back and closed his eyes. He was worried, very worried, and so angry he wanted to spit. MacDuff had come to tell him that the MacPhersons were moving on Kinross lands. They'd heard about his financial ruin, knew he was out of Scotland, and had thus taken advantage. They were, according to MacDuff, freely raiding Kinross land and sheep. They were vultures, normally incompetent and content to whine about all their misfortunes—all brought on by themselves. They'd even killed several crofters who'd tried to save their homes from pillage. His people were doing what they could, but there was no leader there for them. Colin had never felt more helpless in his entire life. Here he was, lying in this lovely damned bed in this beautiful house, weak as a day-old foal, and useless to himself and to his family and his people.

Marrying Joan Sherbrooke was the most important thing he could accomplish. It wouldn't have mattered if she'd had rabbit teeth, so long as her guineas were shining and numerous. Nothing mattered except smashing the cowardly MacPhersons and saving Vere Castle and all the other Kinross properties. He had to move quickly. He tried to rise, gritted his teeth at the wash of pain through his thigh, and fell back again. Colin's head began to pound. The next time Joan asked him to wed her, he'd ask that the preacher be brought in the next five minutes.

Douglas Sherbrooke very carefully folded the letter and slid it back into its envelope.

He began to pace the length of the library, then stopped, pulled the letter from the envelope, and read it through again. The big block letters were in black ink and carefully printed. He read:

Lord Northcliffe,

Colin Kinross murdered his wife. He will wed your sister and then do away with her. Doubt it not. He is ruthless and would do anything to get what he wants. The only thing he wants now is money.

It was the sort of thing that Douglas hated. An anonymous accusation that left one furious and disbelieving because it was anonymous, but still planted a seed of doubt despite what one felt about the one being accused. The letter had been delivered just an hour before by a small urchin, who simply told Drinnen that a cove bid 'im to deliver this letter to the lordship o' this fancy 'ouse.

Drinnen didn't ask the lad to describe the cove. A pity. He assumed it had been a man. He paced again, now crumpling the letter in his hand.

Colin was mending rapidly. Sinjun was already dancing about, wanting to marry him by the end of the week. Jesus, it was already Tuesday. What to do?

He knew deep in his gut that Sinjun wouldn't care if the wretched letter accused Colin of murdering an entire regiment. She wouldn't believe it. She would never believe it. She'd go to war with her entire family before she'd believe it.

Damnation. He knew he couldn't ignore it, and thus, when Alex and Sinjun left the house to fetch Sinjun's wedding gown from Madame Jordan's, he didn't put it off. He strode up to Colin's bedchamber.

Colin was wearing one of his own dressing gowns, thanks to Finkle and several footmen, who had returned to his lodgings and packed all his clothing and brought his two trunks here. He was standing beside the bed, looking toward the door.

"Do you need some assistance?" Douglas asked as he stepped into the room.

"No, thank you. I'm endeavoring to prove that I can walk across this room and back three times without falling on my nose."

Douglas laughed. "How many times have you done it?"

"Twice, at five-minute intervals. This third time looks to be the death of me though."

"Sit down, Colin. I must speak to you."

Colin sat gingerly in a wing chair near the fireplace. He stretched his leg out in front of him, wincing as he did so. He began to gently message the leg. "You didn't tell Joan, did you?"

"No, only my wife, although I don't know why you care if Sinjun knows or not."

"It would infuriate her and worry her and she wouldn't stand for it. She would probably hire a Bow Street Runner and the two of them would go haring off to track down the man who did it. She would probably place an advertisement in the *Gazette* for information leading to his capture. She could hurt herself. She obviously needs to be protected, more from herself than anything else."

Douglas could but stare at him. "You've known her such a short time and yet . . ." He shook his head. "That's exactly what she'd do. I sometimes feel the good Lord doesn't know what she plans to do until she does it. She's very creative, you know."

"No, but I suspect I'll learn."

"You have yet to tell me how you got knifed in the thigh."

Colin didn't meet Douglas's eyes. "It was a little bully who wanted to rob me. I knocked the man down and he pulled a knife from his boot. My thigh was as high as he could reach."

"Did you kill him?"

"No, but I probably should have, the damned blighter. He wouldn't have gotten much from me had he succeeded in picking my pocket. I had no more than two guineas with me at the most."

"I got a letter just a while ago, accusing you of murdering your wife."

Colin became very still. It was as if, Douglas thought, he had pulled inside himself, away from pain or perhaps guilt? He didn't know. Colin looked beyond Douglas's left shoulder toward the fireplace.

"It wasn't signed. The person who wrote it sent a boy around with it. I don't like letters like this. They're poisonous and they leave one feeling foul."

Colin said nothing.

"No one knew you'd already been married."

"No. I didn't think it was anyone's affair."

"When did she die?"

"Shortly before my brother died, some six and a half months ago."

"How?"

Colin felt his guts twist and knot. "She fell off a cliff and broke her neck."

"Did you push her?"

Colin was silent, a hard silence both deep and angry.

"Were you arguing with her? Did she fall accidentally?"

"I didn't murder my wife. I won't murder your sister. I gather the writer of the letter warned you about that."

"Oh yes."

"Will you tell Joan?"

Douglas blinked. He still couldn't accustom himself to Colin's calling Sinjun Joan. "I must. It would be preferable, naturally, if you told her, perhaps gave her explanations that you've not given to me."

Colin said nothing. He was stiff, wary.

Douglas rose. "I'm sorry," he said. "She is my sister and I love her dearly. I must protect her. It is only fair that she know about this. I do feel, however, that before the two of you marry, this must be resolved. That is something I must demand."

Colin remained silent. He didn't look up until Douglas had quietly closed the door behind him. He leaned his head back and closed his eyes. He rubbed his thigh; the stitches itched and the flesh was pink. He was healing nicely.

But was he healing quickly enough?

Who, for God's sake? Who could have done this? The MacPhersons were the only ones who came to mind, and it was a powerful motive they had, if they were indeed responsible. His first wife, Fiona Dahling MacPherson, had been the laird's eldest daughter. But old Latham had supposedly absolved him, at least he had at the time of Fiona's death. Of course her brother hadn't, but the laird had kept Robert in line. During the past several months Colin had heard that the laird wasn't right in the head, that his health was failing rapidly, which was only to be expected, since the man was as old as the Gaelic rocks at Limner. Ah, yes, the letter had to be from the MacPhersons, the wretched cowards, there was no one else.

The damned letter paled into insignificance. He had to marry Joan, and quickly, or all would be lost. He closed his eyes.

He forced himself to rest. Several hours later Colin rose from the chair and walked the length of the bedchamber, two times, then three. He was gaining strength, thank God. He just prayed it was quickly enough.

It was during dinner that evening, Joan eating her own dinner beside him, that he made up his mind. He looked up from the fork bite of ham to realize that she was speaking.

". . . Please don't misunderstand me, the wedding gown is lovely, truly, but it's all such a fuss, Colin. My mother would probably display you like some sort of trophy, she's so pleased that I'm finally to be yanked off the Spinster Shelf. Oh, I do hate the trappings of it all. How I should simply like to whisk you away from here so we can begin our lives together. All this other nonsense is just that, nonsense."

His jaw dropped. Relief flooded him. Manna from heaven, all of it flowing from her mouth. He'd floundered and thought and thought some more, rejecting one idea after another, and here she was, giving herself to him, without reservation.

"I'm not yet very strong," he said, concentrating on chewing the ham.

"You will be strong enough by Friday. Perhaps even sooner. Ah, if only you could be well right this minute."

Colin drew a deep breath. "I must tell you something, Joan. No, please, listen to me. It's very important. Your brother will forbid the marriage. He has told me he will, that he must, to protect you."

Sinjun just looked at him, the peas on her fork, hovering above her plate. She waited, slowly ate the peas, then drank some of her wine. She continued to wait, saying nothing.

"Oh, the hell with it! Your brother believes that I killed someone. He will tell you about it if I don't. He must protect you, as I said. He wants everything resolved before we marry. Unfortunately, there is no way to resolve any of it, ever. I didn't tell him that, but it's true. We won't marry, Joan, I'm sorry. Your brother won't allow it and I must go along with his wishes."

"Who did you supposedly kill?"

"My first wife."

Without hesitation, Sinjun said, "How utterly absurd. Not that you are so young and already once wed, but that you would hurt her or anyone for that matter, and certainly not your wife. Nonsense. How did he hear such a ridiculous thing?"

"An anonymous letter."

"There, you see. Someone is jealous of you; that, or someone simply has taken you into dislike because you are so handsome and have cut such a dash in London. I will speak to Douglas and set him straight on this."

"No."

She heard the determination in that one word. She said nothing. She waited. Patience was difficult, but for once she managed it.

She was rewarded after an interminable wait when he said slowly, looking right into her eyes, "If you want to marry me, we will have to leave, tonight. We will go to Scotland and marry over the anvil, but not in Gretna Green, for that would be the first place your brother would go. It will be done, and your brother will not be able to do a thing about it. We will stop at the Kinross house in Edinburgh and have a proper wedding." There, he'd done it. Dishonor filled him. But what else could he do? There was no damned choice, and she had offered herself to him on the proverbial platter.

Sinjun was silent for a very long time. When she spoke finally, he nearly fell back against the pillow with relief. "I wasn't weighing your suggestion, Colin, I was planning. We can do it. My only concern is that you aren't at your full strength just yet, but no matter. I will take care of everything. We will leave at midnight." She rose and shook out her skirts. She looked every bit as determined as her brother had. "This will hurt my brother, but it is my life and I must choose to do what I believe is best for me. Oh goodness, there is much to be done! Don't worry. You must rest and regain your strength." She leaned down and kissed him. He had no chance to respond, for she was already striding toward the door, her steps so long that the material of her gown pulled across her buttocks and thighs. She turned, her hand on the doorknob. "Douglas isn't stupid. He will know immediately what we've done. I will plan an alternate route. We must throw him off. It's a good thing that I'm tightfisted. I have a good two hundred pounds of my own. After we're wed, Douglas will have no choice but to give you my dowry, and you won't have to worry about losing everything anymore. He must do it quickly—we will make him understand that—I know that you must have the money very soon. I'm truly sorry about that letter, Colin. Some people are the very devil." With that, she was gone. He could swear he heard her whistling.

It was all right. He'd won; against all odds, he'd won, and he was doing only what she wanted, after all. She'd been the one to push it, not he. Ah, but the guilt was there, deep and roiling inside him. Even having known Joan only a short time, Colin had no doubt that she would have them off exactly at the time she'd determined, in a very comfortable carriage that her brother would have a devil of a time tracing. He wouldn't be surprised if she even had matching grays pulling the carriage. He closed his eyes, then opened them. He had to eat everything on his plate. He had to become strong again, and very soon.

My brothers will kill me, she thought as the closed carriage bowled through the dark night toward the Reading road. Colin was sleeping beside her, exhausted. She leaned over and lightly kissed his cheek. He didn't stir. She tucked the blankets more closely around him. He was quiet, his breathing deep and even. Excellent, no nightmares. It still surprised her that the illness had so weakened him. But it didn't matter now. He would be well again, very soon, particularly since she would be the one to see to him.

She loved him so much she hurt with it. No one would ever come between them. No one would ever harm him again. It is my life, she thought, not Douglas's or Ryder's or anyone else's. Yes, it's my life, and I love him and trust him and he is already my husband, my mate in my heart.

She thought of her mother and how she'd managed to grind poor Finkle under just that afternoon, and sailed into Colin's bedchamber like the Queen's flagship. Colin had grinned as he'd told her that her mother had stood there, eyeing him for the longest time, and then she'd said, "Well, young man, I understand you want to marry my daughter for her dowry."

Colin smiled at Joan's mother and said, "Your daughter resembles you greatly. She's lucky, as am I. I must marry for money, ma'am, I have no choice in the matter. However, your daughter is beyond anything I could have expected. I will take good care of her."

"You speak with a honeyed tongue, sir, and it is entirely acceptable to me that you continue doing so. Now, pay attention to me. Joan is a hoyden. You will have to find some way to control her pranks, for she is quite good at them; indeed, she is known far and wide for them. Her brothers have always applauded her escapades, for they are imbeciles when it comes to proper feminine propriety. It is thus your responsibility now. She also reads. Yes, I am being truthful to you, I feel I must. She *reads*"—the dowager drew a deep, steadying breath—"even treatises and tomes that should rightfully be covered with dust. I am not responsible for this failing. It is again her brothers who haven't shown her the correct way to comport herself."

"She truly reads, my lady? Tomes and such?"

"That is correct. She has never bothered even to hide her books beneath her chair when a gentleman visits. It is provoking and I try to scold her, but she only laughs. What could I do? There, I have told you the truth. Joan may suffer for it if you decide her character is too malformed for you to wed her."

"It will be my problem, my lady, as you said. I will ensure that she reads only those things I deem appropriate for a young wife."

The dowager countess beamed at him. "This is excellent. I am further pleased that you don't speak like a Scottish heathen."

"No, ma'am. I was educated in England. My father believed that all Scottish nobility should speak the King's English."

"Ah, your father was a wise man. You're an earl, I understand. A seventh earl, which means that your title goes back a goodly way. I don't approve of newcomers to the peerage. They're upstarts and believe themselves to be equal to the rest of us, which, of course, they're not."

He nodded, his serious expression never faltering. The interrogation had continued until Sinjun had flown into the room, gasped, then said firmly, "Is he not handsome and terribly clever, Mother?"

"I suspect he'll do, Joan," the dowager countess said as she turned to face her daughter. "He has come to rescue you from a spinster's fate, thank the good Lord. Were he ugly or deformed or obnoxious of character, I should have to refuse him—though it would be a close thing, since you grow older by the day, and thus fewer gentlemen want you for their wife—but our consequence would demand it. Yes, this is a good thing. He is handsome, although too dark. He resembles Douglas. Odd that neither you nor Alexandra seems to mind. Now, Joan, you will not allow him or yourself to fall into slovenly Scottish ways once you return to that *place*. I am glad you brought him here to the house. I shall visit him every day and teach him about the Sherbrookes and his duty to you and to our family."

"I should be charmed, ma'am," Colin said.

That had gone off splendidly, Sinjun thought, calming her breath. She'd been scared to death when Finkle had told her that her mother had descended upon Colin. She saw that Colin was grinning at his own cleverness, and she leaned down and kissed him. "You did well with her. Thank you."

"I outlasted her, that's all. And I heaped her coffers with Spanish coin. She likes Spanish coin."

"It's true. Neither Douglas nor Ryder is much in the habit of flattering her. She misses it. You did well, Colin."

She wanted to kiss him now, but she feared to awaken him. There would be time, all the time in the world. By the time they reached Scotland, by way of the Lake District, she would not be a virgin any longer, she was planning on that. A girl couldn't elope with a gentleman and emerge unscathed. She would ensure that she was very well scathed indeed. Their marriage, once in Scotland, would be a mere formality.

Sinjun slipped her hand beneath the blanket and closed her fingers around his hand, a strong hand, lean and powerful. She thought of his wife, a woman now dead. She'd asked him nothing more about it, and she wouldn't. If he wished to tell her more about his first wife and how she had died, he would. Sinjun wondered what her name was.

She also wondered if she would ever tell him that her brother had spoken to her of the letter long before she'd gone to his room. She'd even read it, twice. She'd argued only briefly with Douglas, knowing well he was worried about her, and knowing as well that she must argue with him, else he would be suspicious. Oh yes, she'd agreed with him, yielding to his demand that the marriage be postponed until the charge of murder could be resolved. All the while she was determined to elope with Colin that very night. Perhaps Colin would find out that it had been she who had maneuvered him into making his elopement suggestion, perhaps sometime in the misty future.

It was a pity that she must hold her tongue when it itched to be nothing more than truthful, but she knew men abhorred the notion that they could be manipulated. The thought of a woman managing them sent them into a rage. She would spare his male pride, at least until he was completely well again. And perhaps until he came to care for her. For a moment, the thought of telling him the truth made the misty future look on the dark and gloomy side.

5

"WE ARE ONLY GOING as far as Chipping Norton, to the White Hart," Sinjun told Colin when he stirred. "We will be there in another hour. How do you feel?"

"Bloody tired, dammit."

She patted his arm. "You didn't say that with much heat, Colin, which means you're probably a good deal more than tired; you're exhausted, what with all our hurrying and sneaking about. But you'll get your strength back more and more each day. Don't worry. We won't be to Scotland for another six days as best as I can figure it. You will have plenty of time to mend."

Because it was dark inside the carriage Sinjun couldn't see the irritation in his eyes, and it was there, for he felt helpless, unmanned, like a small child in the care of a nanny, only this nanny was just nineteen years old. He grunted.

"Why in God's name did you pick the White Hart?"

She giggled. An unexpected sound from a nanny, Colin thought with surprise. "It was because of the stories I heard Ryder and Douglas telling Tysen, and he was appalled, naturally, since he was studying to be a man of the cloth. Of course Ryder and Douglas were laughing their heads off."

"And none of them had any idea that you—the infant daughter of the house—were eavesdropping."

"Oh no," she said, waving her hand airily as she smiled. "No idea at all. I got quite good at it by the time I was seven years old. I have this feeling you know all about the White Hart and how the young gentlemen at Oxford spent many evenings there with their light-o'-loves."

Colin was silent.

"Are you remembering your own assignations?"

"Yes, as a matter of fact. The wife of one of my dons used to meet me there. Her name was Matilda, and she was so blond her hair was nearly white. Then there was the barmaid at the Flaming Dolphin in Oxford. She was a wild one, insatiable I remember, loved the feather ticks at the White Hart. Then there was Cerisse—a made-up name, but who cared? Ah, all that red hair."

"Perhaps we shall have the same bedchamber or bedchambers. Perhaps we should simply hire the entire inn, to cover all the possibilities, so to speak. A symbolic gesture of your sown wild oats."

"You're a very inappropriate virgin, Joan."

She looked at him closely. The moon had finally come from behind thick dark clouds, and she could at last see his face. He was pale, she could see that, and looked dreadfully pulled. The fever must have been more devastating than she'd thought to have left him so very weak. "You don't have to worry about merely sleeping next to me tonight, Colin. You can even snore if it pleases you to do so. I don't mind being a virgin until you have all your strength back."

"Good, because that's what you're going to remain." He felt the rawness in his thigh and wondered why he yet cared that she shouldn't know about it. It didn't really matter, not now.

"Unless, of course," she said, leaning closer to him, her voice dropping to what she hoped was a seductive whisper, and wasn't at all, "you would like to tell me how to go about accomplishing what it is that should be done. My brothers always accused me of being a dreadfully fast learner. Would you like that?"

He wanted to laugh, but ended by groaning.

Sinjun was forced to assume that was a no, and sighed.

The White Hart stood in the middle of the small marketing town of Chipping Norton, comfortably set in the Cotswolds. It was a fine, very picturesque Tudor inn, so old and rustic Sinjun felt charmed at the same time she was praying for it not to fall down around their ears. So this was where many of the young men came for their trysts. It did look rather romantic, she thought, and sighed again.

There wasn't a soul to be seen, for it was three o'clock in the morning. Still, Sinjun was far too excited to be tired. She'd managed to escape her brother, and that was no mean feat. Sinjun was out of the carriage in a trice, giving orders to the driver, a man of few words, bless him, and big pockets to hold more guineas than she'd planned to pay him. But she wasn't at all worried. If she ran out of money, she'd simply sell her pearl necklace. Nothing was more important than Colin and getting herself safely wedded to him. She turned to help him down from the carriage.

"You'll be in bed in a trice. I'll go in if you'd like to wait here, Colin, and—"

"Hush," he said. "I will deal with our ostler. He's a dirty old lecher, and I don't want him getting the wrong idea. Damn, I wish you had a wedding ring. Keep your gloves on. You are my wife and I will see to things."

"All right." She beamed at him, then frowned. "Oh dear, do you need money?"

"I have money."

Nevertheless, Sinjun dug into her reticule and pulled out a sheaf of pound notes. "Here. I would feel better if you keep it." She gave him a sunny smile.

"Let's get this over with before I fall on my face. Oh yes, keep your mouth shut."

It was as they walked across the quiet, dark courtyard that Sinjun noticed how badly he was limping. She opened her mouth and then closed it again.

Ten minutes later Sinjun opened the door to a small bedchamber set under the dark eaves and stepped back for Colin to enter first. "I think the ostler believes we lied," she said, not at all concerned. "But you did very well with him. I think he's afraid of you. You're a nobleman, and thus quite unpredictable."

"Aye, he probably did think I lied, the fat old carp." Colin looked toward the bed and nearly moaned with the pleasure that awaited him. He felt her hands on his cloak and stilled. "I doubt he'd recognize a husband and wife if he attended their wedding."

"Let me help you." She did, efficient as a nanny, and it irritated him, but he held still, just looking at that bed. He wanted to sleep for a week.

"If you will sit down I'll pull off your boots."

That was soon done. She'd had enough practice with her brothers. Sinjun stepped back. "Shall I do more?"

"No," he said. "Just turn your back."

She obligingly did as he bade, removing her own shoes and stockings, hanging up her cloak and his in the small armoire provided. She turned back when she heard the bed creak. He was lying on his back, his eyes closed, the covers drawn up to his bare chest. His arms were at his sides, on top of the blanket.

"This is all very odd," she said, chagrined that her voice sounded so much like a maiden's, all skinny and scared.

He didn't answer her and she was emboldened to continue. "You see," she said slowly, "it's true that I am rather outspoken, I guess you'd say, but my brothers have always encouraged me to speak my mind. So it was the same with you. But now, well, it feels strange, being in this room with you, and I know you don't have your clothes on and I'm supposed to climb in on the other side of that bed and—"

Her monologue was interrupted by a low rumbling snore.

Sinjun had to laugh at herself. All her soulful meanderings, only for her and the armoire and a sleeping man. She walked quietly to the bedside and looked down at him. He was hers, she thought, all hers, and no one would take him away from her, not even Douglas, no one. Murdered his wife! What arrant nonsense. Lightly, she stroked her fingertips over his brow. He was cool to the touch. The fever was long gone but he was still so very weak. She frowned, then leaned over and kissed his cheek.

Sinjun had never slept with anyone before in her nineteen years, particularly a man who was large and snoring, a man who was so perfect to her that she wanted to spend the rest of the night looking at him and kissing him and touching him. Still, it was strange. Well, she would get used to it. Douglas and Alex always slept in the same bed, as did Ryder and Sophie. It was the way married people did things. Well, except perhaps for her parents; and truth be told, she wouldn't have wanted to sleep in the same bed with her mother, either. She crawled in next to him, and even from nearly a foot away, she could feel the heat from his body.

She lay on her back and stretched out her hand to find his. Instead her hand found his side. He was naked, his flesh smooth and warm. She didn't want to leave that part of him, but she did. It wouldn't be fair to take advantage of him when he was asleep. She laced her fingers through his. Surprisingly, she was asleep very shortly.

Sinjun awoke with a start. Sunlight was pouring through the narrow diamond-paned window. It certainly wasn't the crack of dawn. On the other hand, to get strong again, Colin had to sleep, and a bed was preferable to the jostling he got in the carriage. She lay there a moment, aware that he was beside her, still sleeping soundly. He hadn't moved, but then neither had she. She realized then that the covers weren't tucked up about his neck, where they were supposed to be. Slowly, knowing she shouldn't but unable not to, she turned and looked at him. He'd kicked the covers off and they were tangled around his feet. As for the rest of him, he was there in the bright sunlight for her to see. She'd never before seen a naked man, and she found him as beautiful as she thought she would. But too thin. She stared at his belly and his groin, and at his sex nestled in the thick hair. His legs were long and thick and covered with black hair. He was beyond beautiful; he was magnificent, even his feet. When she finally forced her eyes away from his groin—a difficult task, for she was frankly fascinated—she blinked at the white bandage around his right thigh.

Of course the fever alone hadn't been responsible for his continued illness. She remembered that damned limp of his the previous night. He'd been hurt somehow.

Anger and worry flooded her. She'd been a fool not to suspect that some other injury was at work here. Why the devil hadn't he told her?

Damnation. She scrambled off the bed and pulled on her dressing gown.

"You wretched man," she said under her breath, but it wasn't under enough. "I'm your wife and you should trust me."

"You're not my wife yet and why are you bleating at me?"

His jaw was a stubble of black whiskers, his hair was mussed, but his eyes were alert, such a deep blue that she forgot to speak for a moment, content just to stare at him.

Colin realized that he was naked and said calmly, "Please pull the covers over me, Joan."

"Not until you tell me what happened to you. What is this bandage for?"

"The reason I was so ill was because I was knifed, and like a fool, I didn't see a physician. I didn't want you to know because I could just see you tearing London apart with your bare hands to find the villain and bring me his head on a platter. Now we're out of London so it doesn't matter. You're safe from yourself."

Sinjun simply looked at him. He had a point. She would have been greatly incensed, no doubt about that. She smiled down at him. "Does the bandage need to be changed?"

"Yes, I suppose so. The stitches need to come out tomorrow or the next day."

"All right," she said. "I'll do it. The good Lord knows I've had enough practice with all of Ryder's children."

"Your brother? How many children does he have?"

"I call them his Beloved Ones. Ryder saves children from dreadful situations and brings them to live in Brandon House. There are about a dozen children there right now, but one never knows when another will arrive, or when one will leave to go to a family Ryder has carefully selected. Sometimes it makes you cry, Colin, to see a little one battered by a cruel drunken father or just left in an alley by a gin-soaked mother."

"I see. Get yourself dressed, but first cover me up."

She did, reluctantly, and he found he was chuckling. Never in his life had he met any female like her. Her interest in his body was embarrassing it was so blatant.

Sinjun solved the privacy problem with a blanket hung over an open armoire door. She didn't stop talking to Colin while she dressed. While she was eating her breakfast, she watched him shave. She volunteered to help him bathe, but that treat was denied her. Again, she was ordered to pack their things, her back turned to him. He did, however, allow her to look at his thigh. The wound was healing nicely. Sinjun lightly pressed the flesh around the stitches. "Thank God," she said, "I was so afraid."

"I'm fine now. It's just a matter of building back my strength."

"This is all very strange."

He eyed her, the flamboyant girl who didn't seem to have a fear of anything or anyone, who looked at the world as if it were hers to rearrange and reshape just as she wished. Life, in his brief experience, had a way of knocking that out of one. He found himself rather hoping it wouldn't be knocked out of her for a good long time. She was strong, no fluttering miss, and for that he was grateful. A fluttering English miss would never survive Vere Castle and all its denizens, of that he was sure. Just then he saw a hint of panic in her eyes, and it was that small sign of vulnerability that kept him quiet. She would find out quickly enough.

Then she was laughing and smiling again, even at Mr. Mole, the ostler of the White Hart. When he made a leering comment to her as they were leaving, she merely turned to him and frowned. "It is a pity, sir," she said, "that you must needs be so disagreeable and show so little breeding. My husband and I stopped here only because he is ill. I assure you that we will never come here again, unless he is ill again, which is unlikely because—"

Colin laughed and took her hand.

He soon became markedly silent, and Sinjun left him to his thoughts. He continued silent through the day and the evening and into the next day. He was preoccupied, frankly absent from her, and she decided to allow him the peace to work out whatever was bothering him. What bothered her most was that he had ordered two bedchambers for them, without explanation. She'd left it alone.

It was late the following afternoon, as the carriage bowled toward Grantham, that he turned to face her in the carriage and dropped the boot. "I have given this a lot of thought, Joan. This is difficult for me, but I must do it, to absolve myself of a veritable little bit of my guilt. I abused your brother's hospitality by slipping out like a thief in the night with his sister. No, no, keep quiet. Let me finish. In short, I cannot justify what I've done, no matter how hard I try to rationalize it. However, there is one thing I can do that will hold some honor, that will help me live with myself. I won't take your virginity until our wedding night."

"*What?* You mean I've left you to yourself, been silent as a punch bowl, and over the past day and a half all you've come up with is that bit of arrant nonsense? Colin, listen, you don't know my brothers! We must, that is, you must make me your wife and this very night, else—"

"Enough! You make it seem like I'm going to torture you, for God's sake, rather than preserve your damned innocence. It isn't nonsense, arrant or otherwise. I won't dishonor you in that way; I won't dishonor your family in that way. I was raised to hold honor dear. It's in my blood, in my heritage, generation upon generation of it, even through all the killings, the savage battles, there was honor somewhere lurking about. I must marry quickly to save my family and my holdings, you know that well enough, and to protect them from the damned raiding and lying MacPhersons, but one thing I don't have to do is be a rutting stoat on an innocent girl who isn't yet my wife."

"Who are the MacPhersons?"

"Damnation, I didn't mean to mention them. Forget them."

"But what if Douglas catches us?"

"I will handle it when and if it happens."

"I understand about honor, I truly do, Colin, but somehow it's more than that, isn't it? Do you dislike me so much? I know I'm too tall and perhaps too skinny for your tastes, but—"

"No, you're not too tall or too skinny. Just leave it be, Joan. My mind is made up. I won't take your virginity until we're wed, and that's that."

"I see, my lord. Well, my lord, my mind is also made up. I fully intend for my virginity to be but a memory by the time we reach Scotland. I don't think it reasonable to think that you can simply *handle* Douglas if he catches us. You don't know my brother. I might think I'm clever, all my machinations to evade him, trying alternate routes and all that, but he's as cunning as a snake. No, my virginity is more than just a marital thing, Colin. It's necessary that you rid me of it quickly. I feel very strongly about this, so it's not just that's that. Now, just whose mind is it that will carry the day?"

She wished he'd yell as Douglas and Ryder did, but he didn't, saying only, very calmly, very coldly, "Mine, naturally. I'm the man. I will be your husband and you will obey me. You can begin obeying me now. It will doubtless be good for your character."

"No one has ever spoken to me like that except my mother, and she I could always ignore."

"You won't ignore me. Don't be childish about this. Trust me."

"You're as autocratic as Douglas, damn you, even though you haven't yelled."

"Then you should realize your only choice is to shut your mouth."

"Take out your own stitches," she said, utterly infuriated with him, and turned to look out the window.

"A spoiled English twit. I might have known. I'm disappointed but not surprised. You can back out of this, my dear, you surely can, with all your English virtue still intact. You're not only outspoken, you're a termagant if you don't get your way, a hoyden, and perhaps even bordering on an overbearing shrew. I begin to think your groats aren't worth all the suffering."

"What suffering, you beetle-brained clod? Just because I disagree with you, it doesn't make me a termagant or a shrew or anything else horrible you just called me."

"You want to back out of this? Fine, have the man turn the carriage around."

"No, damn you, that would be too easy. I will marry you and teach you what it is to trust someone and confide in someone, to compromise with someone."

"I'm not used to trusting a woman. I already told you that I liked you, but anything else was out of the question. Believe it. Now, I'm so tired my eyes are crossing. You will be my wife. Act like a lady, if you please."

"As in fold my hands in my lap and twiddle my thumbs?"

"Yes, a good start. And keep your mouth closed."

She could only stare at him. It was as if he were trying to drive her away, but she knew he couldn't want her to back out of the marriage. It was male perversity. Besides, she also had no choice but to marry him. She wanted to yell that it was too late for her, far too late. She'd given him her heart. But she wasn't about to let him become a tyrant, and groveling at his feet with such a confession would surely make him into a veritable Genghis Khan, given his present attitude. Oh yes, she knew all about tyrants, even though Douglas assumed the tyrant mantle now very rarely. Ah, but she remembered those early days when he'd first wed Alexandra. She gave Colin a sideways look but held her peace. She became silent as a stone. Colin slept until they arrived at the Golden Fleece Inn in Grantham late that evening.

Sinjun assumed that Colin did take out his own stitches, for he again procured two bedchambers, bade her a dutiful good night before her door, and left her. The next morning he hired a horse, merely telling her shortly at breakfast that he was bored with riding inside the damned carriage. Ha! He was bored with riding with her. He rode outside the carriage for the entire day. If his leg bothered him, he gave no sign of it. In York, Sinjun hired a horse, with a look daring him to object, but he only shrugged, as if to say, it's your money. If you insist upon wasting it, it doesn't surprise me. She was glad now that he'd decided not to go to the Lake District, though she'd argued vehemently with him at the time. He wanted to get home more quickly, and even her warnings of Douglas with three guns and a sword hadn't dissuaded him. She thought, as the wind whipped through her hair, that Lake Windermere was too romantic a spot to share with him. This endless gallop north with the silent man riding just ahead of her wasn't at all the way she'd imagined her elopement to Scotland to be.

The morning they rode ahead of the carriage across the border into Scotland, Colin reined in and called out, "Stop a moment, Joan. I would speak to you."

They were in the Cheviot Hills, low, rangy mounds that were mostly bare, stretching as far as she could see. It was beautiful and lonely as the devil and not a soul was to be seen, not a single dwelling. The air was warm and soft, the smell of heather strong. She said to him, "I'm pleased you remember how to speak, given how long it's been."

"Hold your tongue. It defies belief that you are angry with me just because I wouldn't bed you, and here you are a young lady of quality."

"That isn't the point—"

"Then you're still holding your sulk that we didn't go to the Lake District, a ridiculous ploy that wouldn't fool an idiot."

"No, I'm not angry about that. All right, what do you want, Colin?"

"First of all, do you still want to marry me?"

"If I refuse, will you force me because you must marry me because you need my money?"

"Probably. I would think about it, perhaps."

"Excellent. I won't marry you. I refuse. I will see you in hell first. Now force me."

He smiled at her, the first time in four days. He actually smiled. "You aren't boring, I'll give you that. Your outrageousness even occasionally pleases me. Very well, we'll marry tomorrow afternoon when we reach Edinburgh. I have a house on Abbotsford Crescent, old and creaky as the devil and needs money poured into it, but not as badly as Vere Castle. We will stop there and I will try to have a preacher wed us. Then we will ride to Vere Castle the following day."

"All right," she said, "but I will tell you again, Colin, and you really should believe me. Douglas is dangerous and smart; he could be anywhere waiting for you. He conducted all sorts of dangerous missions against the French. I tell you, we should wed immediately and—"

"That is, we will ride to Vere Castle unless you're too sore to ride. Then I will prop you up in the carriage."

"I don't know what you're talking about."

"I'm talking about taking you—our wedding night—until you're raw with it."

"You're being purposefully crude, Colin, purposefully nasty and unkind."

"Perhaps, but you're in Scotland now, and you will soon be my wife, and you will learn that you owe me your loyalty and your obedience."

"You were one way when we first met. Then, when you were ill, you were really quite nice, albeit irritable because you hate weakness. Now you're just being a fool. I will marry you and every time you're a fool in the future, I'll do something to you to make you regret it." There, she thought, that was setting things straight. She loved him to distraction—a fact she knew well that he knew, and thus his outlandish behavior toward her—but she wouldn't allow his character flaws or his outmoded notions of husbands and wives to interfere with what she insisted that he be.

He laughed. It was a strong, deep laugh, a laugh of a man who knew his own worth and knew it to be above that of the girl who rode beside him. He was well again and strong of body and ready to take on the world—with her groats. "I look forward to your attempts. But be warned, Joan, Scottish men are masters in their own homes, and they beat their wives, just as your honorable and kind Englishmen occasionally do."

"That is absurd! No man I know would ever raise a finger against his wife."

"You have been protected. You will learn." He started to tell her that he could easily lock her in a musty room in his castle, but he kept quiet. They weren't yet married. He gave her a look, then a salute, and kicked his horse in his sides to gallop ahead of her.

They arrived at the Kinross house on Abbotsford Crescent at three o'clock the following afternoon. It had been drizzling lightly for the past hour, but Sinjun was too excited to be bothered about the trickles of water down her neck. They'd ridden the Royal Mile, as fine as Bond Street, Sinjun gawking all the way at the fine gentlemen and ladies who looked just as they did in London, and all the equally fine shops. Then they turned off to the left onto Abbotsford Crescent. Kinross House was in the middle of the crescent, a tall, skinny house of red aged brick, quite lovely really, with its three chimney stacks and its gray slate roof. There were small windows, each leaded, and she guessed the house to be at least two hundred years old. "It's beautiful, Colin," she said as she slipped off her mare's back. "Is there a stable for our horses?"

They cared for their own mounts, then paid the driver and removed their trunks and valises. Sinjun couldn't stop talking she was so excited. She kept tossing her head toward the castle that stood atop its hill, exclaiming that she'd seen paintings of it, but to actually see it all shrouded in gray mist, the power of it, how substantial and lasting it was, left her nearly speechless. And Colin only smiled at her, amused at her enthusiasm, for he was tired, the rain was dismal, something he'd grown up with, and the castle, indeed, was a fortress to be reckoned with, but it was just there, brooding over the city, and who really thought about it?

The door was opened by Angus, an old retainer who had been a servant to the Kinross family his entire life. "My lord," he said. "Dear me and dear all of us. Oh Gawd. Aye, the young lassie is wi' ye, I see. More's the pity, aye, sech a pity."

Colin grew very still. He was afraid to know, but he asked nonetheless, "How do you know about my young lassie, Angus?"

"Och, dear and begorra," said Angus, pulling on the long straight strands of white hair that fell on each side of his round face.

"I hope you don't mind that I invited myself in. Your man here didn't want to let me over the threshold, but I insisted," Douglas said as he came up behind Angus. He was smiling through his teeth. "You damned bastard, do come in. As for you, Sinjun, you will feel the flat of my hand soon enough."

Sinjun looked at her furious brother and smiled. It was difficult, but she managed it, for she wasn't at all surprised to see him. Ah, but Colin was, she saw. She'd warned him, damn his stubborn hide. She stepped forward. "Hello, Douglas, do forgive me for giving you such a worry but I was afraid you would be intractable. You have that tendency, you know. Welcome to our home. Yes, Douglas, I'm a married lady, married in *all* ways, I might add, so you can forget any notions about annulment. I would appreciate your not trying to kill him, for I'm too young to be a widow."

"Blessed hell! The damned devil you say!" And there was her brother Ryder, standing at Douglas's elbow, and he looked fit to kill, flushed to his eyebrows, unlike Douglas, who never stirred when his anger was deep and burning, just remained cold-stone still and yelled. "Is this the fortune-hunting bastard who stole you from Douglas?"

"Yes, that's him," Douglas said through still-gritted teeth. "Blessed hell, your *husband!* Damn you, Sinjun, there's been no time. Ryder and I have ridden like the very devil. You're lying, Sinjun, tell me you're lying, and we will leave right now, right this instant, and return to London."

Colin stepped into his own house and raised his hands. "Be quiet, all of you! Joan, step aside. If your brothers want to kill me, they will, regardless of your trying to protect me by flapping your petticoats at them. Angus, go see to some refreshment. My wife is thirsty, as am I. Gentlemen, either kill me now or come into the drawing room."

This all seemed very familiar, and Sinjun was forced to smile. "There are no umbrella stands about," she said, but Douglas wasn't to be drawn. He was stiff and cold and looked severe as an executioner.

"Ryder, this is my husband, Colin Kinross. As you can see, he shouts as loudly as you and Douglas do, and he looks a bit like Douglas, only he's more handsome, much wittier, and of a more reasonable nature."

"Bosh!"

"How do you know, Ryder? This is the first time you've ever met him. Colin, this is my brother Ryder."

"It's certainly going to be interesting," Colin said.

Ryder studied him closely, all the while yelling, "I can tell by the look of him that he's none of those things. He's about as reasonable as Douglas here, no more, certainly. Damnation, Sinjun, you've been a perfect idiot, my girl. Let me tell you—"

"Go into the drawing room, Ryder. You can tell me all you wish to there." Sinjun turned to Colin and raised a brow.

"This way," he said, and led them across the narrow entrance hall that smelled musty and clogged the nostrils with dust, through a single door into a room that could kindly be called elegantly shabby.

"Oh dear," Sinjun said, eyeing the room. "It's proportions are quite nice, Colin, but we must get a new carpet, new draperies—goodness, those must be eighty years old! And just look at those chairs—the fabric is rotting right off them."

"Be quiet!"

"Oh, Douglas, I'm sorry. You aren't interested in all my housewifely plans, are you? Please sit down. As I said, welcome to my new home. Colin tells me the house is all of two hundred years old."

Douglas looked at Colin. "Are you well yet?"

"Yes."

"You swear you're fully and completely healed and back to your strength?"

"Yes."

"Good, damn you!" Douglas leaped on him, his hands going for his throat. Colin, no fool, was ready for him. They went down to the floor, dust billowing up from the faded carpet, and rolled, Douglas on top, then Colin, each kicking the other with his legs, each rolling the other over.

Sinjun looked at Ryder, whose lovely blue eyes were narrowed and filled with fury. "We must stop this. It happened before. It would be a very bad melodrama were it not so dangerous. Will you help me? It is absurd. You're all supposed to be civilized gentlemen."

"Forget civilization. If by any wild chance your *husband* just happens to knock Douglas out, it's my turn."

Sinjun shouted, "Blessed hell! Stop it!"

There was no discernible effect.

She looked wildly around for a weapon. No blessed umbrella stand or any other piece of dilapidated furniture she could use to bash Douglas's head.

Then she saw just the thing. She calmly picked up a small hassock nearly hidden behind a sofa and swung it with all her might, striking Douglas's back. He roared, jerking about and staring at his sister, who now had the hassock raised over her head.

"Get off him, Douglas, or I swear I'll break your stubborn head."

"Ryder, take care of our idiot sister whilst I kill this mangy bastard."

But it wasn't to be. The panting, the cursing, the grunts were all abruptly stopped by the obscenely loud report of a gun. In the closed room it sounded like a cannon.

Angus stood in the open doorway, an old blunderbuss smoking in his hands. There was a huge hole in the ceiling of the drawing room.

Sinjun dropped the hassock with a loud thud. She looked at that hole, smoking and blackening the ceiling all around it, and said to Douglas, "Is my dowry large enough to repair even that?"

6

ANGUS STOOD QUIETLY in the corner of the drawing room, holding the blunderbuss close, eyes still watchful, even after he'd announced, "Forgive me, my lords, but her ladyship here bain't much of a Kinross yet, and thus if someone must have his neck shot through, it will be one of ye even though yer her brothers. Ye also be Sassenach toffs, an' that makes me finger itch like th' divil."

And that was that, Ryder thought, after he'd figured out the essence, which wasn't at all good as far as he and Douglas were concerned.

Now Colin and Sinjun sat side by side on the worn pale blue brocade sofa, Ryder and Douglas on equally worn chairs facing them. There was no rug between them. Silence was the news of the day.

"We were married in Gretna Green," Sinjun announced.

"The devil you were," Douglas said. "Even you, Sinjun, wouldn't be that stupid. You would think that I would go there immediately, and thus you would go elsewhere."

"No, you're wrong. After I thought that, I realized that you wouldn't go there, that you would come to Edinburgh instead and quickly find Colin's house. You see, I know you very well, Douglas."

"This has nothing to do with anything," Ryder said. "You're coming home with us, brat."

Colin raised a black eyebrow. "Brat? You're calling her brat and she's Lady Ashburnham, my wife?"

Sinjun said to him as she patted his hand in what she hoped was a wifely gesture, "It takes my brothers time to change and adapt to things. Ryder will come about, just give him a year or so."

"I am not amused, Sinjun!"

"No, neither am I. I am married. Colin is my husband. It was doubtless the damned MacPhersons who wrote the anonymous letter to Douglas claiming Colin killed his wife. They're cowards and liars and they're out to destroy him, and what better way to go about it than to begin by ruining his nuptials with me?"

Colin stared at her. She was frightening. He'd mentioned the MacPhersons but one time, yet she'd put it all together. Of course, he hadn't really spoken to her for nearly three days. She'd had a lot of hours to think and sort through things. Thank God she didn't know the full extent of it—yet.

A very fat woman came into the room. She was wearing a huge red apron that went from right beneath the massive bosom of her black gown to her knees. She was smiling widely. "Och, ye're here, me lord. It's home ye be at last. And this sweet little lassie be yer wife?" She curtsied, using her apron.

"Hello. What is your name?"

"Agnes, me lady. I'm here wi' Angus. I do what he doesn't, which be most of everything. Look at the hole in the ceiling! My Angus always was excellent at his work. Be any of ye hungry?"

There was a chorus of yeas and Agnes took herself off. Angus hadn't moved from his spot in the corner, blunderbuss still held firmly against his chest.

It was at that moment Colin realized that he'd been silent as the grave. He cleared his throat. It was his home, after all. "Gentlemen, would you care for a brandy?"

Ryder nodded and Douglas clenched his fists again and said, "Yes. Good smuggled French brandy?"

"Naturally."

Well, that was something, Sinjun thought, relaxing just a bit. Men who drank together couldn't smash each other, not with brandy snifters in their hands. Of course, they could throw the snifters, but she'd never seen either Ryder or Douglas do that.

"How are Sophie and all my nephews, and the children?"

"They're all well except for Amy and Teddy, who were fighting in the hayloft and a bale of hay rolled off its stack and knocked both of them out and down to the ground. No broken bones, thank God."

"I expect Jane lambasted them but good." Jane was the directress of Brandon House, or Bedlam House, as Sinjun called the lovely large three-story house that lay but one hundred yards from Chadwyck House, the residence of Ryder, Sophie, and their young son, Grayson.

"Oh yes, Jane had a rare fit, threatened to pull ears and dish out bread and water after they recovered from all their bruises. I think that's what she did do, adding just a dollop of jam to their bread. Then Sophie kissed them both and yelled at them as well."

"And then what did you do, Ryder?"

"I just hugged them and said if they were ever so stupid again, I would be very upset with them."

"A dire threat," Sinjun said, and laughed. She rose and walked to Ryder, leaned down, and hugged him close. "I've missed you so very much."

"Blessed hell, brat, I'm exhausted. Douglas dragged me out of bed—and Sophie was so warm, it was damned difficult to leave her—and he forced me to ride like the devil himself were snapping at our heels. He said he would outfox you, bragged, he did, but you won, didn't you?"

"Here is your brandy, my lord."

"I'm not a lord, Kinross. I'm a second son. I'm only an honorable, and that strikes me as a mite ridiculous. Just call me Ryder. You are my brother-in-law, at least until Douglas decides whether or not he will kill you. Take heart, though. Not many years ago Douglas gave a good deal of thought to killing our cousin Tony Parrish—called him a rotten sod—but in the end he gave it up."

Angus relaxed a bit.

"That situation is nothing like this one, Ryder."

Angus snapped back to attention.

"True, but Sinjun is married to the fellow, Douglas, no way around that. You know she's never one to do things half-measure."

Douglas cursed foully.

Angus relaxed a mite, for curses were a wise man's way to relieve his spleen.

Colin strolled to Douglas and handed him a brandy. "How long do the two of you plan to stay? Don't get me wrong. You're welcome as my brothers-in-law to remain as long as you wish, but there are few furnishings here and thus it wouldn't be very comfortable for you."

"Who are the MacPhersons?" Douglas asked.

Colin said calmly enough, "They are a clan who have feuded with my clan for several generations. Indeed it all started around 1748, after the Battle of Culloden. There was bad blood there because the laird of the MacPhersons stole my grandfather's favorite stallion. The feuding finally stopped when I married the current laird's daughter, Fiona Dahling MacPherson. When she died so mysteriously some six months ago, her father seemed not to blame me. However, the eldest brother, Robert, is vicious, unreasonable, greedy, and utterly unscrupulous. When my cousin visited me in London, he told me the MacPhersons, led by that bastard Robert MacPherson, had already raided my lands and killed two of my people. Joan is correct. It is very likely one of them penned that letter. The only thing is, I can't imagine how they knew where I was or how any of the sniveling cowards had the cunning to come up with such a plot."

"Why the hell do you call her Joan?" Ryder said.

Colin blinked. "It's her name."

"Hasn't been for years. Her name is Sinjun."

"It's a man's nickname. I don't like it. She is Joan."

"Dear God, Douglas, he sounds just like Mother."

"True," Douglas said. "Sinjun will bring him around. Back to the MacPhersons. I don't want my sister in any danger. I won't allow it."

"She may be your sister," Colin said very quietly, "but she is my wife. She will go where I go and she will do as I bid her. I will keep her from harm, you needn't worry." He turned to Sinjun. His eyes glinted in the soft afternoon light but his expression remained utterly impassive, as did his voice. "Isn't that right, my dear?"

"Yes," she said without hesitation. "Shortly, we will travel northward to Vere Castle. I will take very good care of Colin, neither of you need worry."

"It isn't that poaching bastard I'm worried about," Douglas yelled at her. "I'm worried about you, dammit."

"That's very nice of you, Douglas, and understandable, since you're fond of me."

"I'd like to take a strap to your bottom."

"Only I will take straps to her in the future," Colin said firmly. "She doesn't believe that now, but she will learn."

"Sounds to me," Ryder said very slowly, looking back and forth between the two of them, "yes, it does seem that you just might have met your match, Sinjun."

"Oh yes," she said, purposefully misunderstanding her brother. "He is my match, my mate for life. I was waiting for him and at last he found me." She walked over to her soon-to-be-husband, who was standing by the mantel holding a brandy snifter. She put her arms around his chest, leaned up, and kissed his mouth. Douglas growled and Ryder, dear blessed Ryder, laughed.

"All right, you're no longer a brat," Ryder said. "I would like another brandy, Colin, if you please. Sinjun, do remove your arms from him, it might save him from further pummeling by Douglas."

"This isn't settled yet," Douglas said. "I'm very upset with you, Sinjun. You could have trusted me, you could have spoken to me. Instead you just stole out of the house like a damned thief."

"But Douglas, I understood your position, truly, and I respected it. But the fact was and is that Colin is innocent of any wrongdoing, and what's more, he had instant need of my money and simply couldn't wait for some sort of resolution that probably would never come. I was rather concerned about that, since both you and my money would still be in London. But that's not the case now, thank God. I am glad you came—albeit you weren't happy when you arrived—so that you and Colin can work it all out."

"Joan," Colin said very quietly, "one doesn't speak about settlements in such a way. Certainly not in front of ladies, and not in the drawing room, under such oddly unconventional conditions."

"You mean because there's a hole in the ceiling?"

"You know very well what I mean."

"But why ever not? It's my dowry, and you're my husband. Let's get on with it."

Douglas laughed, he couldn't help himself.

"I think," Ryder said, "that this means your hide just might remain on your body, Colin. Sinjun, take yourself off and the gentlemen will deal with all the money matters."

"Good. Don't forget Great-Aunt Margaret's inheritance to me, Douglas. You told me once it was an impressive number of groats and all invested on the 'Change."

"We're as good as married, Colin."

He turned to face her in the dark-cornered earl's suite at the end of an equally dark and quite dismal corridor on the second floor of Kinross House. There was but one branch of candles lit and he was holding it. He set it down on a battered surface that had once held all his father's shaving objects.

He just shook his head. "I know we must pretend that we are, and I intend to do so until your brothers leave. I will sleep with you in that bed, and as you can see, it's large enough for a regiment. You will keep your hands to yourself, Joan, else I'll be displeased with you."

"I simply don't believe this, Colin. I do hope you aren't the sort of person who makes a decision, then sticks to it whether it's good or miserably bad."

"I'm right in this decision."

"You're ridiculous."

"A wife shouldn't be so disrespectful to her husband."

"You're not my husband yet, damn you! What you are is the most stubborn, the most obstinate—"

"There's a screen in the corner. You may change behind it."

When they were lying side by side in the mammoth bed, Sinjun staring up at the dark bed hangings, which smelled moldy, he said to her, "I like your brothers. They're honorable and quite fit as friends. As relatives, they're superlative."

"So nice of you to say so."

"Don't sulk, Joan."

"I'm not sulking, I'm cold. It's damp in this dreadful room."

He wasn't cold, but then again he was rarely cold. But he knew that if he pulled her into his arms, he would make love to her, and he wouldn't break his vow, particularly with her brothers here under his roof, flesh-and-blood reminders of his perfidy.

He leaned up and grabbed his bedrobe that he'd tossed at the foot of the bed. "Here, put this on. It will wrap around you twice and keep you very warm."

"I am overcome with your generosity and reasonableness."

"Go to sleep."

"Certainly, my lord. Whatever you wish, whatever you demand, whatever you—"

He began snoring.

"I wonder why Douglas didn't demand to see our marriage lines. That isn't like him not to be thorough."

"He just might, mightn't he? Shall we wed tomorrow, whilst your brothers are visiting the Castle? It turns out Douglas has a friend who's a major there, and he wants Ryder to meet him."

"That would be just excellent," Sinjun said. "Colin?"

"What now?"

"Would you just hold my hand?"

He did, and felt very warm fingers. So she was on the verge of freezing to death, was she? He imagined that his soon-to-be-wife would do just about anything to gain what she wanted. He would have to watch her carefully. "I hope you enjoy my dressing gown."

"Oh yes, it's soft and smells like you."

He said nothing to that.

"Wearing it, I can fancy you're touching me everywhere."

At ten o'clock in the morning the following day, Colin and Sinjun were wed by a Presbyterian preacher who had been friends with Colin's uncle Teddy—not his father, Colin explained to her, because his father had been all that was sinful and a rotter. Reverend MacCauley, an ancient relic, was blessed with more hair than any old man should have, but best of all, he was fast with his lines and pronouncements and dictums, the latter being the most important consideration. When they emerged as Lord and Lady Ashburnham, Sinjun gave a skipping little step. "'Tis done, at last. Now, shall I volunteer to show my brothers our marriage lines?"

"No. Stop, I want to kiss you."

She became still as a stone. "Ah," he said, gently taking her chin in the palm of his hand and raising her face. "You're no longer hell-bent on being bedded, are you? It was all an act. But why?" He stiffened then, his fingers tightening a bit on her chin. "I see now. Even last night you were worried that Douglas and Ryder just might discover that we weren't yet wed. You wanted to protect me, didn't you? You wanted to get your dowry into my hands."

"No," she said. "Not entirely. I could look at you naked until I die. Even your feet are lovely."

"You're always taking me off-stride, Joan. I like it sometimes. Also, just being naked isn't the same thing. What will you do when you're lying on your back in bed naked and I'm standing over you, ready to come to you?"

"I don't know. Close my eyes, I suppose. It sounds rather alarming, though, but not repellent, at least not with you."

He grinned. "I should like to do something about this right this minute. At least within the next hour, at the most. But your brothers are here and I don't think Douglas would take it kindly were I to throw you over my shoulder and haul you upstairs. Tonight then, Joan. Tonight."

"Yes," she said, and stood on her tiptoes, her lips slightly parted. He kissed her lightly, as he would an aunt, and released her.

Abbotsford Crescent was only a fifteen-minute walk from Reverend MacCauley's residence. Colin had stopped Sinjun and was pointing out an old monument from James IV's reign when suddenly, without warning, there was a pinging sound and a shard of rock shot up to strike Sinjun, slicing her cheek. She'd moved in front of Colin and bent over to look at those age-blurred words just a moment before. She jumped now with the shock of it, and slapped her hand to her face. "What was that?"

"Oh hell," Colin shouted, and pushed her to the ground, covering her with his body. Passersby stared at them, hurrying their step, but one man ran over to them.

"A man shot at ye," he said, spitting in the next instant in disgust. "I saw him, standing over there by the milliner's shop, he was. Are ye all right, missis?"

Colin helped Sinjun to her feet. Her hand was pressed to her cheek and blood oozed between her fingers. He cursed.

"Ah, the lassie's hurt. Come along to my house, 'tis just over there, on Clackbourn Street."

"No, sir, thank you very much. We live just in Abbotsford Crescent."

Sinjun stood there numb as a frozen toe, listening to them exchange names and addresses. Colin would come by and speak to the man later. *Someone had shot at her.* It was incredible. It was unbelievable. She still felt no pain in her face, but she felt the wet, sticky blood. She didn't want to see it, so she just kept her palm and fingers pressed tightly to her cheek.

Colin turned back to her, frowning. Without a word, he picked her up in his arms. "Just relax and rest your head against my shoulder."

She did.

Unfortunately for both of them, Ryder and Douglas had just returned when Colin walked in with her. There was no way to hide the blood still seeping from between her fingers, and thus there was pandemonium and flying accusations and questions and yelling, until Sinjun calmly said, "That's quite enough, Douglas, Ryder. I fell, that's all, I just fell like a clumsy clod and cut my face. Stupid, I know, but at least Colin was there with me and carried me home. Now, if you will both just be quiet, I should like to see how much damage there is."

Of course the brothers weren't at all quiet. Sinjun was carried to the kitchen, just as she had once taken Colin to see to his cut lip in the London Sherbrooke kitchen, a fact that wasn't lost on him, she saw. She was set down on a chair and told to hold still.

Douglas automatically demanded warm water and some soap, but it was Colin who firmly removed the soft cloth from his hand and said, "Take your hand away, Joan, and let me see how bad it is."

She closed her eyes and didn't make a sound when he touched the damp cloth to her flesh, wiping away all the blood. The shard of rock had grazed her, and not deeply, thank the good Lord. It looked like a simple scratch, and for that he was grateful, what with her two brothers hovering over him, watching his every move, ready, he supposed, to fling him aside if he didn't do things as they would have done them.

"It's not bad at all," Colin said.

Ryder moved him aside. "An odd cut, Sinjun, but I don't think you'll be scarred. What do you think, Douglas?"

"It doesn't look like a simple scratch; rather, it looks like something sliced across your cheek with great force. How did you do it, did you say, Sinjun? You really didn't expect me to believe this is from a fall?"

Sinjun, without hesitation, collapsed against Colin and moaned. "It hurts so much. I'm sorry, Douglas, but it does hurt."

"It's all right," her husband said quickly, "I'll see to it."

While Colin was dabbing some alcohol on the cut, Douglas was frowning.

Sinjun didn't like that frown at all. "I don't feel well. I daresay I'll be ill very soon. My stomach is turning over."

"It's only a small cut," Douglas said, his frown deepening. "Something that wouldn't even slow you down."

"True," Colin said, "but sometimes a sudden injury knocks the body off its bearings. I do hope she won't retch." It sounded like a threat, and Sinjun said, "My stomach is settling even as you spoke, Colin."

"Good. Look, Douglas, she's very tired, as I imagine you can understand."

There was dead and utter silence. Both brothers stared from their new brother-in-law to their little sister—their little *virgin* sister, their former little virgin sister. It was a huge pill to swallow. It was difficult. Finally Douglas said on a loud sigh, "Yes, I suppose so. Go to bed, Sinjun. We will see you later."

"I won't bandage the cut, Joan. It will heal faster."

She gave her husband a brave smile, yet a smile so pathetic and wretched that Ryder began to frown.

"I don't like this at all," he said to the kitchen at large. "You have no more guile than a pot of daisies, Sinjun, and you're a wretched actress and—" It was then that Agnes walked in and Sinjun closed her eyes in relief. The three men were given to know in short order that they were all next to useless and they'd gotten blood on the kitchen table. And here was the poor little missis, all hurt and them carrying on like three roosters with only one hen.

Ten minutes later Sinjun was lying on the bed in the earl's suite, two blankets pulled over her.

Colin sat down beside her. He looked thoughtful. "Your brothers suspect your retching and moaning was an act. Was that an act?"

"Yes, I had to do something quickly. I wanted to faint, but neither of them would have believed that. I'm sorry, Colin, but I did as best I could. We can't have them know the truth. They'd never leave here, else they'd cosh you on the head and steal me. I couldn't allow that."

He laughed even though he was amazed. "You're apologizing because you got shot and tried to pull the wool over your brothers' eyes. Don't worry, I'll maintain the charade. Rest whilst I speak to them, all right?"

"If you kiss me."

He did, another light, disgustingly brotherlike kiss.

Sinjun wasn't sleeping when Colin came into their bedchamber. She was scared, excited, and at the moment she was holding her breath. He strode to the bed and stood there, staring down at her, the branch of candles raised high in his hand.

"You're turning blue. Breathe."

Her breath came out in a whoosh. "I forgot to for the longest time."

"How does your cheek feel?"

"It's fine, just throbs a bit. I thought dinner went off smoothly, don't you?"

"As well as can be expected with each of your brothers taking turns studying your cheek. At least Agnes sets an excellent table."

"Is all my money in your hands now?"

He thought it a rather odd way of putting it, but merely nodded. "Douglas has written me a letter of credit. In addition, we will visit the manager of the Bank of Scotland tomorrow. He will have his man of business send me all the information I will need for any future financial transactions and the status of all your investments. All is done. Thank you, Joan."

"Was I as much an heiress as you hoped I'd be?"

"I'd say you were more than an adequate heiress. What with your inheritance from Great-Aunt Margaret, you are one of the plumpest-in-the-pocket young ladies in England."

"What are you going to do now, Colin?"

He set the branch of candles down and sat beside her. "Are you cold?"

She shook her head and said, "Yes."

He lightly touched his fingertips close to the now-red slash across her smooth flesh. "I'm very sorry about this. We must talk about it, you know. I hope the bullet was meant for me and you were in the way at the last moment."

"Well, I certainly don't hope that! I don't want anyone trying to shoot you. On the other hand, I don't particularly want to be shot, either." She fell silent, from one instant to the next, silence, and she was still as a stone, frowning.

"What is it?"

"The knife wound in your thigh. What if it wasn't just a robber? What if it was another attempt on your life?"

He merely shook his head. "No, don't go so far afield for blame. London is a nasty place, truth be told, and I wasn't in a very prime location at the time it happened. No, it was just a little bully trying to line his pockets and I was his mark, nothing more. Now, would you like to be made love to? This is your wedding night, after all."

That certainly gave her thoughts a new direction, Colin thought, looking down at his bride of one day. She was wearing a virginal white lawn nightgown that very nearly touched her chin it was so high. Her long, tousled hair was loose to the middle of her back, with several tresses over her shoulder. He lifted a handful of hair and brought it to his face. Soft and thick and the scent of jasmine, if he wasn't mistaken. "So many different shades," he said, quite aware that she was leery about the entire business now, since there was no more need for bravado and self-sacrifice in order to save him. He knew if he'd allowed it, she would have very likely stripped off her clothes, stretched him out on his back, and done the deed herself. And all to protect him and give him her money. She was sweet and guileless and determined and smarter than she should be. He would have to deal strictly with her, this wife of his, else she would take him over, and he would never allow that. Somehow, though, he couldn't quite see himself locking her in a musty tower room.

He was lucky to have found her, no doubt about that. Then he thought about that bullet hitting the rock and the shard slicing her cheek. What if the bullet had hit her? What if the rock shard had struck her eye? He drew back from those thoughts. It hadn't happened. He intended to take measures to protect her, beginning the moment her brothers left on the morrow. They would leave shortly thereafter for Vere Castle. That was the one place in Scotland he could be sure she was safe.

He leaned down and kissed her mouth. She started, then opened her lips, just slightly, but he didn't take her invitation. He continued to kiss her lightly, his tongue stroking her bottom lip but not entering. He continued to kiss her until he felt her begin to relax. He wasn't about to touch her yet. He just held that thick tress of hair in his hand and rubbed it against his face.

He raised his head a bit and said, "You're quite pretty, Joan, quite pretty indeed. I would like to see the rest of you now."

"Isn't my face enough for the moment?"

"I should like to see more of the picture." He should have lit a fire in the blackened fireplace, he realized. He would have liked to stretch her out on her back and look his fill at her, but she'd freeze, and that would never do. Instead, he helped her lift the nightgown over her head, then he gently pressed her again onto her back and drew the covers to just beneath her breasts. He wanted to see and touch and kiss her breasts.

"Now, let me look at you."

Sinjun didn't like this. She covered her breasts with her hands, realized how ridiculous her action was and dropped her arms to her sides. He was completely dressed and here she was like a white lump just lying here. She wasn't in control, he was. She didn't like it one bit.

He straightened and looked at her breasts, not touching them, just looking. "Very nice," he said, a vast understatement. He was surprised that they were so full. She walked like a boy, a coltish walk that was free of the coquette, free of any feminine swaying and teasing. Ah, but her breasts were very nice indeed, high and full and the nipples a soft deep pink.

"Colin?"

"Is that little thin voice actually coming from the woman who wanted to rip my breeches off and have her way with me the instant we left London?"

"Yes, but I don't like this. This is different. The motives are no longer there for getting it done. What's more, you're looking at me—"

"As I recall, you did the same to me, only the covers were down around my ankles. You looked your fill, did you not, and you were fully dressed?"

"Not at first. I was in my nightgown at first."

"But you wouldn't cover me until you'd looked your fill."

"It wasn't enough, Colin. I could have looked for a good deal many more hours."

He had no smart reply to that. He leaned down, not touching her with his hands, and gently took her nipple in his mouth.

He thought she'd try to fling him off her, but she only quivered a bit, then became still as a stone.

"What are you doing, Colin? Surely that—"

He blew warm breath over her and she gasped.

"This is my prelude," he said, and lowered his head again to his pleasant task. Her scent filled his nostrils and he strengthened his pressure on her soft flesh.

"Oh dear, Colin, that feels quite strange."

"Yes, I trust it is also enjoyable."

"I don't know. Perhaps. No, not really . . . oh goodness."

He very gently lifted her breast in the palm of his hand, pushing her firmly against his mouth. When he raised his head to look at her face, he also saw the darkness of his flesh against the white of hers. So different they were.

Perhaps having a wife wasn't going to be such a disaster after all. He wanted to come inside her now, this instant, but he knew he would have to wait. He knew that women needed encouragement, particularly stroking between their thighs, and he knew also that he wanted to taste her, to learn the textures of her soft flesh against his mouth and his tongue.

Enough was enough. It was time to expand upon his prelude. He rose quickly to stand beside the bed. He was quiet a moment, just staring down at this new bride of his, the bride he hadn't wanted, the bride who had saved him and his family for generations to come. He took off his clothes, calm and controlled, just smiling down at her, seeing the anticipation, the banked excitement in her incredible blue eyes—Sherbrooke blue eyes he'd heard them called in London. But he also saw the wariness there; her eyes were following his every move. He shrugged out of his shirt, then sat down to pull off his boots. He didn't turn around when he stripped down his britches; indeed, he never looked away from her. He straightened when he was naked and smiled at her, his arms at his sides. "Look your fill, my dear."

Sinjun looked and she kept looking. Then she shook her head as she said, clearly appalled, "This will never work, Colin. It can't."

"What can't work?" He followed her eyes and looked down at himself. He was fully aroused, something of a surprise since he hadn't really gotten things started yet; he was also a large man, and although in his experience women usually grew quite excited at the sight of him, he imagined that a virgin wouldn't be quite so enthusiastic, at least not at first.

"That," Sinjun said, pointing unnecessarily at him.

"It will be all right, you will see. Could you try to trust me?"

Her throat worked. She couldn't seem to get the words out. She just kept staring at him. "All right," she whispered, pulled the covers to her chin, and slid over to the far side of the bed. "But I don't think trust has much to do with it."

He waited a moment, then said, "Do you have any idea of how all this will work?"

"Oh yes, certainly. I'm not stupid or ignorant, but what I thought can't be right. You're too big and even though I trust you it can't be the way I thought it would be. It's utterly impossible. Surely you can see that."

"Well, no, I can't," he said, and, still smiling at her, he walked to the bed.

7

SHE'D BEEN SUCH A TEASE, so certain of herself, utterly outrageous in her speech, trying to get him to bed her, yet in truth she was terrified. It amused him, this virginal fear of hers, given all the invitations she'd forced down his throat. He looked down at her, aware that she was trying to shift away from him.

He lifted the covers and climbed in beside her. He came down over her, and her breasts pressed against his chest. She sucked in her breath at the same moment he sucked in his. "This is very nice, Joan," he said, and kissed her even as he rubbed himself against her breasts.

"You feel furry, and it sort of tickles. It's very strange, Colin."

"And you feel soft and warm, like silk slowly rubbing against one's flesh."

His tongue entered her mouth at the same time his hand moved flat and smooth over her belly to curve around her.

His fingers rested there, not moving, just touching her to feel the heat of her and for her to feel the heat of him. Then he merely pressed down, giving her the weight of his hand against her flesh. She quivered, he felt it, and it pleased him. He was also harder than a stone; it was unnerving, nearly painful, and it was also driving him witless.

Sinjun was looking at him when he kissed her. His eyes were closed and his thick black lashes were against his lean cheeks. He was utterly beautiful, and this was what she wanted, what she'd wanted since she'd decided to have him, but goodness, there was so much of him, surely too much of him, much too much, and it couldn't be pleasant, not remotely pleasant. Ah, but his hand and his fingers, resting there, just lightly pressing against her, and it was such a private place, this part of her, yet it felt right for him to have this intimacy with her, perhaps. Perhaps not. This wasn't unpleasant, certainly not, and perhaps he would content himself with this. She rather prayed that he would. Then he opened his eyes.

"Any closer and your eyes will cross," Colin said, and laughed, a rather painful sound because he'd grown even harder than a stone in the past minute, nearly gone beyond anything he could remember except when he'd been a boy and so randy he'd been in constant need; and he wanted to come inside her this moment, this very instant, deep and deeper still, and . . .

"Please," she said, and wrapped her arms around his neck. "Please teach me how to kiss, Colin. I do like kissing. I could kiss you forever."

"There's much more than kissing, but we'll begin there and always come back to it. Just open your mouth to me and give me your tongue."

She did, and when her tongue searched his out, she felt his fingers sliding down, rubbing lightly against her flesh, and she squirmed at the strange sensations it brought to her, so deep inside her, so very low, and she moaned into his mouth, startling both of them.

He lifted his hand and looked at her face at the same time. Her disappointment was clear for him to see. He smiled, albeit painfully. "You like that. Shall I continue?"

"Perhaps it would be all right."

He laughed as he kissed her again, but her moan when he eased his finger inside her made him forget everything but the pounding need he felt, a need that was growing beyond him, beyond his control.

She was very small, this bride of his, and he knew he had to keep control of himself. He wanted to give her pleasure, but he doubted it would be possible this first time. Perhaps it was better just to get this first time over with, and quickly. She was easing around his finger, her warm flesh accommodating him now, and he moved deeper. Yes, she was softening for him and the moistness of her made him picture his sex deep inside her and he nearly went over the edge with lust.

He moaned and shuddered and moaned again, and Sinjun, momentarily loosening herself from the feelings he was building in her belly, snapped her eyes open. "Colin? What's wrong? Did I hurt you?"

"Yes, and it's wonderful. Joan, I must come into you now. You're eased for me, truly, but it will be tight. Trust me. I'll go very slowly, but come into you I must. This first time must be done or there couldn't be a second time, which will be wonderful for you, you'll see, just trust me."

Every pleasant feeling evaporated in the flash of an instant. Sinjun stared at him, now between her legs, raising her knees, positioning her for himself. He was too big, far too big, it was unimaginable. "No," she said, panicked now, as she pressed her fists against his hairy chest. "Please, Colin, I have changed my mind. I should like to wait, perhaps Christmas might be a nice—"

He came into her and she yelled, pressing her hips into the feather mattress, but he only grasped her hips in his hands and pushed deeper and deeper still. She tried to hold herself still, to keep her cries deep in her throat, but it was difficult. She closed her eyes against him and against the pain, but it became only more rending. Then she felt him stop inside her and he was breathing hard, his voice trembling when he said, "Your maidenhead, I've got to get through it. Don't scream. Sweet Jesus, I'm sorry, sweetheart." He pushed forward even before he stopped speaking, and she yelled, loud and hoarse, and he brought his hand down quickly over her mouth, muffling her cries, and he was touching her womb and she hated it, hated the pain and the rawness of it, the alien invasion of her body, but he wasn't hurt, oh no, he was a wild man, driving into her then pulling out, again and again until suddenly he was rigid over her, his back arched, stiff as a board, and she opened her eyes and stared up at him to see that his eyes were closed, his head thrown back, his throat working against what seemed to her to be a raging cataclysm.

He moaned, then yelled, muted because of her brothers, she assumed, then he fell forward on her. She felt him then inside her, the wetness of him, his man's seed, and she felt . . . she didn't know what she felt. The pain he'd inflicted in her body, yes that, certainly, but more than the throbbing pain, the rawness. He'd lied, telling her to trust him, and like a twit she had, at least a little bit, until he'd forced himself into her.

She felt betrayed.

He was breathing hard, his face beside hers on the pillow. His body was heavy on hers. She felt the sheen of sweat on him and on her.

It was difficult for her to speak calmly, because she wanted to strike him and scream at him, but she managed it. "I didn't like that, Colin. It was awful."

His heart was drumming in his ears. He was breathing so hard he thought he would burst with it. He felt as if he'd been flattened, and every minute of his flattening had been wondrous, beyond anything he could have imagined. . . . And she didn't like it? It was awful? No, it couldn't be true. He shook his head. He must have misunderstood her.

He calmed his breathing. It took him a good deal of time. She remained quiet, not moving beneath him, and he imagined that he was heavy on her, but he didn't move. He was still inside her, not so deep now, but the feel of her flesh made him shudder with pleasure and need. Finally he managed to raise himself on his elbows. He stared down at his wife.

Unconsciously, he pushed forward and high into her, breaching her deeply, and she winced, gritting her teeth. He stopped immediately.

"I'm sorry," he said, but he wasn't, not for what had happened, because he had enjoyed it more than he ever had in his life. "Your virginity, it's past now, and there won't be any more pain."

Her calm was cracking. "You lied to me, Colin. You said it would work. You told me to trust you."

"Naturally, I'm your husband. It did work, can't you feel me? I'm supposed to be inside you. I'm supposed to spill my seed in your womb. It will be easier next time. Perhaps you will even enjoy it. You did somewhat this time, didn't you?"

"I don't remember."

She didn't damn remember? Ah, but he wanted her again. It surprised him and dismayed him. Surely he wasn't a rutting savage to maul his innocent bride yet again. No, he wasn't. He groaned, feeling her tight and hot around him. It was too much, it was more than a man with few wits left could handle. He stiffened above her and drove deep into her once more.

She yelled at the shock and pain of it. She hit him with her fists, shoving against him, trying to throw him off her, but it only sent him deeper and he just kept driving, feeling her flesh convulse around him, driving him and pushing him, and he couldn't stop himself. He heard her cries but he didn't slow, he couldn't, and again he climaxed, raw groans ripping from his throat.

He was flat on top of her again, breathing hard, wondering what the devil had come over him.

"How many times will you do that?"

"I think I've stopped for a while. Joan, you're not crying, are you? No, tell me you're not crying. I'll hold very still now, I promise."

Her voice came steadier, which relieved him, until he heard her say, "I do care for you a lot, Colin, but it will be difficult to bear this often. It wasn't pleasant. I know we had to do it so that Douglas couldn't take me back to London with him and annul the marriage. But now that you've done it, will you have to do it often?"

He wanted to tell her that he could easily take her again, a third time, perhaps a fourth, but he held his tongue. He'd hurt her, and she had no idea of what pleasure could be. "I'm sorry," he said, and slowly forced himself to pull out of her. He felt the pulling of her flesh, heard her whimper.

"I'm sorry," he said again, and disliked himself for apologizing like a damned parrot.

"I don't understand though."

"What don't you understand?"

"I always thought that Douglas and Alex—that's his wife, you know. Well, I always believed that she much enjoyed staying with him in the same bed. And Ryder and Sophie, too, but now . . . perhaps it's just kissing they enjoy, and the other, they must bear it, they choose to bear it because they love their husbands. But it's difficult, Colin. I didn't realize what it would be like."

"I told you that when I take you again you will enjoy it. I promise you that."

She clearly didn't believe him, not that he could blame her, for hadn't he just lost himself again, slamming into her when he knew it would hurt her? "I'm sorry," he said for yet a third time. "I will make it up to you."

She lay there, sprawled on her back when he rose to stand beside the bed. There was his seed and her virgin's blood on her thighs and on the white sheets. He leaned over her, and Sinjun, fearing the worst, yelled at the top of her lungs.

Then, in the next instant, there was a hammering on the bedchamber door and Douglas was yelling, "What's happening in there? Sinjun, what's wrong?"

"Move out of the way, Douglas, he's killing her!"

It was Ryder who flung open the door and burst into the bedchamber, Douglas on his heels.

There was appalled silence. They stood there, their dressing gowns flapping around their bare legs, staring at their new brother-in-law, who was standing naked by Sinjun, who was sprawled on her back on the bed, but that was just for a flash of an instant, for in the next, she grabbed the covers and pulled them to her neck. "Get out!" she screamed at her brothers, so filled with humiliation she thought she'd die of it. "How dare you! Damn you both, get out!"

"But Sinjun, we heard you yelling, screaming in pain—"

She got ahold of herself. She didn't think it was possible, but she did it. She even managed to smile at them, but it was wobbly and mean and utterly mortified. "Now, Douglas, I've heard Alex yelling her head off—many times, in fact. Can't I yell as well?"

"Yours wasn't pleasure yelling," Ryder said, his voice so cold she shivered at the sound of it. "Yours was pain yelling. What did this bastard do to you?"

"Dammit!" Colin roared. He grabbed his own discarded dressing gown and shrugged into it. "This is bloody ridiculous! Cannot I have privacy in my own house? Yes, she yelled, damn you both to the devil. What the hell do you expect? She was a bloody virgin and I had to get through her bloody maidenhead!"

Douglas looked at Ryder, then back at Colin. He roared in rage and yelled at the top of his lungs, "You cunning bastard, you despicable savage, I'll bloody well kill you this time, you lying sod!"

"Not again," Sinjun said.

"Yes, again, dammit!" Ryder now, and his jaw was working he was so angry. "You were a *virgin,* Sinjun? You, who have been married to this damned heathen for how long now? *Completely* married, you told us? In *all* ways, you said. Well then, just how the hell could you still be a virgin? This rutting stoat doesn't look like he'd wait for anything or anyone."

Sinjun pulled the covers around her and brought her legs over the side of the bed. Colin was looking like a dog ready for a good fight, bent forward, hands fisted, his eyes mean as a snake's. Her brothers were coming closer and closer, just as ready to spill blood.

"Stop it, all of you!" she yelled. Where was Angus with his damned blunderbuss? She jumped in front of her brothers. "No more, do you hear me? No more!" They were ignoring her, intent on bashing Colin. She spoke calmly now, colder than they'd ever heard her voice. "You will leave my bedchamber now, both of you, or I swear it, Douglas, Ryder, I will never speak to either of you again. I swear it."

"No, you can't mean that," Douglas said, paling.

"You can't know what you're saying," Ryder said, taking a step back. "We're your brothers, we love you, we—"

"I do mean it. Get out, both of you. We will speak of this in the morning. You have embarrassed me to my toes, both of you, and if—" Her voice broke off and she burst into tears.

It was so utterly unexpected that both Douglas and Ryder rushed forward to her. Colin raised his hand and said quite calmly, "No, gentlemen. I will see to her. We will speak in the morning. Go away."

"But she's crying," Ryder said, clearly aghast. "Sinjun never cries."

"If you've made her cry, you bastard—"

"Douglas, leave us alone." Colin tightened his arms around his wife's back.

Ryder and Douglas backed off. They didn't want to, but they had no choice. Both left the bedchamber cursing.

Colin said nothing. He simply held her tightly against him, watching the door close finally.

"I should have locked the damned door," he said, filled with disgust for himself. "That will teach me to be more careful when my wife has two brothers who love her so much they'd kill anyone who broke her fingernail."

"They would have broken the door down. It would have made no difference. And you broke more than a fingernail."

"Why, she speaks," he said. "How grand. A bride who bursts into tears one minute and speaks calm as a clam the next." He shoved her away from him. Her eyes were wet with tears, but none had spilled over. It didn't slow him though. He grabbed her shoulders, squeezing tight, and shook her. "I will tell you this once, Joan, and I don't expect to have to repeat myself. This is my house. You are my wife. Damn you, I am a man, not some sort of sniveling hound for you to protect by shoving me behind your damned skirts. Do you understand me, madam?"

She tried to pull free of him, but he held on tightly. She wanted to strike him herself, hard. She snarled like an animal at him, "Blessed hell, they would have killed you! They would have bashed you to the floor. And if you would open your eyes, you would notice that a skirt isn't what I'm wearing."

"Don't you dare try to distract me. You will never again jump in front of me. Do you understand me, madam? For God's sake, there could be real danger, possibly, and you could be hurt. This is Scotland, a land vastly different from that gentleman's paradise to the south. There is always the chance of violence here. I won't tolerate your foolish behavior, ever again. Do you understand me?"

"You're not a sniveling hound, you're a bloody stupid fool! You're raging about like a bull, Colin, and it's absurd! I merely pretended to cry, just to stop them, and it did. Whatever was wrong with that?"

"Enough!" He slammed his palm against his forehead. "It is too much, dammit! Get into bed, Joan, you're shivering."

"No, I shan't. You'll do those horrible things to me again. I don't like it, Colin. I don't want you to do that again. I don't trust you."

He could only stand there, in the middle of the dim bedchamber, with its too-dark walls, shabby furnishings, frayed draperies. And here was his bride telling him he wasn't to bed her again. It was enough. It was too much. And she'd had the gall to interfere again between him and her brothers. He was enraged. He was quite beyond logical and calm thought. He was on her in an instant, ripping the covers off her. He picked her up and threw her on the bed.

"Stay there!"

He untwisted the covers and tossed them over her. "Get yourself warm."

"You won't stick yourself in me again, Colin, I shan't allow it. It was horrible and you won't do it. Damn you, get away from me!"

It sent him right over the edge. First her brothers and now her, giving him orders, and she was his wife, and it was time to begin as he meant to go along. He felt himself hardening, and it was enough. He slammed down on top of her. He immediately clapped his hand over her mouth, then shoved her legs apart. She fought him in earnest this time, but it didn't help. He was between her legs, spreading them wider until he was satisfied, and then he came into her, slower this time, and since she was slick with his seed and with herself, he moved quickly to seal himself deep inside her. When he moved, it didn't hurt quite so much, but enough, because her flesh was raw. This time she didn't cry out. The last thing she wanted was for her brothers to burst into their bedchamber again, for he still hadn't locked the door. She suffered him, closing her eyes, her hands at her sides now, fisted. She turned her face away, pressing it against the mattress, and lay still. He wasn't violent with her, nor was he at all rough. He moved deep then eased out, once, twice, three times, and yet again. It didn't last long. He tried to kiss her, but she kept her head turned to the side. She heard his breathing quicken, felt his body pulse and shudder with his exertions. When he released his seed, he groaned deep in his throat. When it was over, he didn't fall on her as he'd done before. He pulled out of her immediately. She nearly cried out. She felt raw, so bruised by him she wondered if she would be able to walk. She knew he was standing beside the bed, looking at her, but she didn't care. What did it matter that her legs were sprawled? That she was naked and lying there? It didn't matter now, nothing did. If he wished, he could take her again, and there was naught she could do about it. Let him look. She didn't care. He said nothing; she could still hear his breathing, harsh and fast.

"I'm all sticky and I want to bathe."

He stilled himself. Jesus, he could just imagine how wet and sticky she was. He'd spilled his seed in her three times. He sighed, drawing on his control, dampening his guilt, willing his anger at the absurd situation to quiescence. "Just lie still. I'll get you some water and a cloth."

Sinjun didn't move. She closed her eyes. This was her wedding night and it was a shambles, painful and embarrassing, and then Douglas's and Ryder's bursting in. She turned her back to Colin and pulled her legs to her chest. She wished she were the Sinjun she'd been just a month before. Everything had been simple and straightforward to that Sinjun; that Sinjun knew about fun and humor and had dreamed about love. She had looked upon Colin and seen her dream come true. Ah, and what a dream it was to this Sinjun: a mess, a girl who didn't know a blessed thing. Everything had gone awry.

She cried, for the first time in three years.

Colin stood by the bed. He felt like the damned rutting bastard Douglas had accused him of being. He felt helpless. Her sobs weren't delicate and feminine, they were hoarse and ugly and immensely real.

"Well, hell," he said, climbed into the bed, and cupped his body around hers. Her tears lessened. She began to hiccup. He kissed the back of her neck. She stiffened. "Please, Colin, don't hurt me again. Surely I don't deserve any more of your punishment."

He closed his eyes against her words, words she meant, no doubt about that. And it was his fault, because he'd been too rough with her, had moved too quickly, good Lord, he'd taken her three times, and that third time hadn't been well done of him. The second time was not all that well done, either, but at least that second time was perfectly understandable. But he had punished her with the third, pure and simple. No, he'd not behaved as he should have. "I won't come inside you again," he said. "Besides I can't. I have no more seed to spill in you. Go to sleep."

Surprisingly, Sinjun closed her eyes and did just that. She slept long and deep. It was Colin who woke her up the next morning as he turned her on her back. She shivered at the sudden cool air on her skin and opened her eyes. He was standing over her, holding a damp cloth.

"Hold still and let me bathe you."

"Oh no." She jerked away from him, rolling over until she was on the far side of the mammoth bed. "No, Colin, I will see to myself. Please, go away now."

He stood there, frowning at her, holding the cloth in his outstretched hand, feeling like a fool. "Very well," he said at last. He tossed the cloth to her, hearing it slap against her wrist. "Angus is bringing up buckets of hot water for your bath. Get it done quickly, for I, too, wish to bathe, and you don't seem at all interested in sharing the tub with me, more's the pity, though I am now your husband, something you wanted more than anything, if you would be honest with yourself, marriage and my man's body, but not in that order, not at first."

"You're angry," she said as she pulled the covers to her nose. She was utterly confused. "This is very odd, Colin, since it is you who hurt me. How can you dare be angry?"

"I'm angry at this damnable situation." There was a knock on the door. "Don't move," he said over his shoulder. "Keep yourself wrapped in the covers."

It was Angus, not her brothers brandishing swords, and he was carrying two steaming buckets of water.

Once they were poured into the porcelain tub, he looked up and said, "Do you fancy walking naked over here and climbing in?"

She didn't fancy it at all. She shook her head. "You may go first."

He stripped off his dressing gown, climbed into the tub, leaned back, and let his knees stick up. Sinjun would have laughed if she hadn't felt so miserable. She didn't want to get out of the bed. She didn't want to face her brothers.

They said not a word. Both Douglas and Ryder seemed determined that there be no more fights, no more arguments with Colin. They actually seemed to understand that they'd embarrassed her to her very toes. It embarrassed her even more to know that they must have discussed the situation and had decided upon a course of behavior. To be talked about, even by her brothers, was almost more than she could bear.

After a second cup of coffee, Ryder said, "Douglas and I are leaving this morning, Sinjun. We're both sorry that we've intruded and made you uncomfortable. However, should you ever need us, you need but write or send a messenger to Douglas or to me. We will come to you immediately. We will do anything you wish us to do."

"Thank you," she said. Suddenly she wished they wouldn't leave her, wouldn't promise not to interfere again. They always had. They loved her. Even last night—it was because they loved her.

When they took their leave an hour later, she felt hollow inside. She felt utterly alone and, for the first time, truly afraid of what she'd done. She threw herself into Douglas's arms, hugging him tight. "Please take care. Give my love to Alex."

"I will."

"And to the twins. They are destroying Ryder's home with their exuberance, he told me. It must be wonderful. I miss all the children so much."

"Yes, I know, love. I miss them, too. It's fortunate both Ryder and Sophie adore children, even those who are destructive little heathens. I've closed up the London house. Alex and the boys will be at Northcliffe Hall when I return. Don't worry about Mother. I will see to it that when she writes you, it will be pleasant, and not endless carping."

When Ryder gathered her against him, he said, "Yes, I shall kiss Sophie for you and hug and pet all the little heathens. And I'll miss you like the very devil, Sinjun."

"Don't forget Grayson, Ryder. He's so beautiful, and I miss him dreadfully."

"He's the picture of Sophie, only with Sherbrooke blue eyes and the Sherbrooke stubborn-as-hell chin."

"Yes, and I love him dearly."

"Shush. Don't cry, love. I understand a bit how you must feel, for Sophie had to leave her home in Jamaica to come to England, and I know she was sometimes heartsick. At the very least she was cold here. But Colin is your husband and he will take care of you."

"Yes, I know."

But she didn't sound like she knew it, Ryder thought. Oh hell, what were they to do? She was married to the man. Ah, but to leave her here alone . . . he didn't like it. But Douglas had insisted that they'd interfered enough. "Sometimes at the beginning of a marriage, things aren't quite as straightforward as one would wish them to be." She just looked at him, her expression remote, and he floundered on. "That is, occasionally there are slight problems. But any problems are resolved with time, Sinjun. You must be patient, that's all."

He had no idea if what he'd said made any sense to her situation, but the pain in her eyes smote him. He didn't want to leave her in this damned foreign land with this damned husband she'd only just met.

Colin stood apart from the three of them, watching and frowning. He felt jealous, oddly enough, and he recognized it for what it was. The three of them were so very close. He and his older brother, Malcolm, had always been at each other's throats. And their father had just laughed and sided with his brother, because he'd been the future laird, the future earl, and it was his opinion that counted, his words that were believed, his wishes that were important, his never-ending gambling debts and wenching expenses that must be paid. Then Colin had refused to join with Napoléon, knowing that his father was skirting disaster with his damnable beliefs, beliefs that weren't really all that strongly held, no, they were beliefs that it amused his father to hold, nothing more. And his brother shared the beliefs as well, to taunt him, to try to make him leave Scotland, but he wouldn't go. He wanted a commission in the English army, but naturally his father refused to buy it for him. No, his father had other plans for him. He'd been used to end the feud with the MacPhersons. He'd wedded Fiona Dahling MacPherson when he was twenty years old. It had ended the feud—until a month ago. Until something had happened that had set Robert MacPherson off.

"Is something wrong, Colin?"

It was Douglas speaking, and Colin quickly brought himself away from his miserable memories. "No, certainly not. I will take care of your sister. Don't worry."

"You will also bring her to visit her family early next fall. Is it possible, do you think?"

Colin thought for a moment, then nodded. "You have now given me the means to recover myself, my home, and my lands. There is much for me to do. However, all should be in good order by the fall."

"All the money was rightfully Sinjun's, not mine. I'm glad it will be put to good use. I personally hate to see an estate fall into ruin."

"Perhaps," Colin said slowly, looking toward the two magnificent Arabian stallions who were blowing and snorting, one held by Angus and the other by a clearly frightened stable lad, "you would wish to come and visit us sometime in the future. After, of course, Vere Castle has been refurbished a bit. The drive to the castle is very beautiful, all tree-lined, and now, in the early summer, the leaves form a canopy overhead."

"No doubt we would be pleased to," Douglas said. "Ryder can bring all the children."

"I like children," Colin said. "Vere Castle is a large place, surely there are enough rooms to house all of you."

Then Douglas and Ryder were gone, with one last wave, riding down the cobblestoned street, their great coats billowing out behind them.

Sinjun stood there on the street, watching them, feeling more miserable than she could remember. She wouldn't allow that misery to remain clogged in her heart and in her mind; no matter this sex business, she was married to Colin. Ryder was right. She must be patient. After all, she adored her husband, despite what he'd done to her. She would deal with it. There was much to be done. She wasn't one to lie down and moan her distress. Of course, in the past there never had been much distress to consider moaning about.

She turned then and smiled at her husband, not really much of a smile, but an honest effort at one. "I should like another cup of tea. Would you?"

"Yes, Joan, I believe I would." He fell into step beside her. "I like your brothers."

She was silent a moment, then said with desperate cheerfulness, "Yes, I rather do, too."

"I know you will miss them. We'll see them soon, I promise you."

"Yes, you promise."

He gave her a quick look but said nothing.

8

THE DOCK ON THE FIRTH OF FORTH was a nasty place, smelling of fish in all stages of rot, unwashed bodies of yelling stevedores, and other odors she couldn't, thankfully, identify. It was filled with so many carts and drays and boats of every size in the water that it was difficult to see why they hadn't all crashed into each other. In that moment, two drays did collide, tipping an oak barrel off the end of one of the drays. It bounced hard on the cobblestones and then rolled, picking up more speed, until it slammed into an iron railing, cracking wide open. Rich dark ale spilled out, filling the air with its pungent smell. Sinjun smiled and sniffed. She supposed the London docks were much the same, but she'd never been to see them. Colin took her elbow, saying nothing, and directed her to a ferry that looked to be on its last legs, had it been a horse. It was a long, narrow barge with unpainted wooden railings, and its name was *Forth Star,* surely an ambitious title for such a scrawny boat. The horses were already on board, standing very close to the people, and not happy about it. The ferry was owned by an old man who had the foulest mouth Sinjun had ever heard. He cursed at the people, at the animals, at all the valises and trunks. He even yelled at the opposite bank of the Forth. Sinjun regretted that she could only understand just a bit of what he said. She did see Colin wince several times when the old man got bitten in the shoulder by a horse and yelled his displeasure to all within three miles.

When the ferry got under way, Sinjun watched with horrified eyes, knowing it had to run into other boats. One ship from Holland came within scraping distance. Another from Spain was so close the sailors were leaning over the sides with long poles to push any boat away that came too close. Nothing seemed to bother Colin—natural, she supposed, because he was, after all, a Scot, and none of this was new to him. Even the horses started blowing loudly in the salty clean air. Thank God it was a beautiful day, warm and balmy, the sun high in a cloud-strewn sky. As they neared the other side of the Forth, she saw that the Fife Peninsula seemed from here to look every bit as English as Sussex. The green was soft and pure and deep, and the hills were rolling and gentle. It was lovely, and Sinjun felt a stirring of enthusiasm. At that moment, the *Forth Star* hit another small barge. The two captains howled at each other, the horses whinnied, and the people shook their fists. Sinjun tried not to laugh as she yelled at the other captain herself.

The ferry crossed at the narrowest point, called the Queensferry Narrows, not a beautiful spot, for the water looked thick and dirty and swirled about the barge. Ah, but looking toward the east, to the North Sea, was beautiful.

Colin said unexpectedly, "At this point the Forth is a long tidal estuary. The river itself begins nearly all the way to the western sea. It's a mighty river there, deep and so blue it makes you want to cry. Then it narrows and meanders over a flat peaty wilderness to Stirling."

Sinjun breathed in deeply. She nodded at his offering, then turned back to lean her elbows on the railing. She was afraid of missing something. She also didn't particularly wish to speak to her husband.

"If you turn about you can see the Castle. It is clear today and the view is rather spectacular."

Sinjun obligingly turned and looked. "I thought it more mysterious, more ethereal perhaps, last evening, when it was shrouded halfway up in fog. Every once in a while you could hear the soldiers yelling and it seemed like ghost voices coming out of the gray mist. Wonderfully gothic."

Colin grunted at that and turned back to look down at the swirling waters. "You will have to accustom yourself to the mists. Even in summer we can go weeks at a time without the sun. But it is warm and it stays light enough to read even at midnight."

Sinjun brightened at that. "You have a well-stocked library, Colin, at Vere Castle?"

"The library is a mess, as is most everything else. My brother didn't particularly care, and since his death I haven't had time to see to things. You will have to go through it and see if there is anything that interests you. I also have a library of sorts in my tower room."

"Perhaps you have some novels?" Her hopeful voice made him smile.

"Very few, I'm afraid," he said. "Remember, you're deep in Presbyterian country. Hellfire would surely await anyone so ill-advised as to read a novel. Try to imagine John Knox enjoying a Mrs. Radcliffe novel. It boggles the mind."

"Well, hopefully Alex will send me all my books when she sends us our trunks."

"If your brother didn't order all our things burned first."

"A possibility," Sinjun said. "When Douglas is angry, he can do the most awesome things."

Sinjun hoped the trunks would arrive soon. She was perilously close to having very little to wear. Even her blue riding habit, of which she was inordinately fond, was looking sadly distressed. She swiped the dust off her sleeve as she looked at her fellow passengers. Most were country people, dressed in rough homespun woolens of dull colors, and clogs and open leather vests. There was one aristocratic fellow with very high shirt points who looked a bit green from the swaying of the barge. There was another man who looked to be a prosperous merchant, who kept spitting over the side of the barge, his teeth as brown as his spittle. And the speech, it wasn't English, even though Sinjun could understand most of it. It was filled with slurring and lilting sounds that were melodic and coarse all at the same time.

Sinjun didn't say anything else to her husband. At least he was trying to be pleasant, as was she. But she didn't want to be pleasant. She wanted to hit him. She looked at his profile, drawn to look at him really because he was so beautiful. His black hair was blowing in the gentle breeze. His chin was up and his eyes were closed in that moment, as if he were reaffirming that he was a Scot and he was home. A sea gull flew perilously close, squawking in his face. He threw back his head and laughed deeply.

She wasn't home. She stuck her chin up as high as his was. She breathed in the sea air, the nearly overpowering smell of fish and people and horses. She looked at the terns and the gulls and the oystercatchers.

They were all putting on a grand show, hoping for scraps from the passengers.

"We will ride to Vere Castle today," Colin said. "It will take us about three hours, no more. The sun is shining and thus it will be pleasant. Ah, do you think you will be able to do it?"

"Certainly. It's strange you would ask. You know I'm an excellent rider."

"Yes, but that was before. I mean, you're not too sore, are you?"

She turned slowly to face him. "You sound very pleased with yourself. How odd."

"I'm not at all pleased. I'm concerned. You're obviously hearing what you want to hear, not what's there."

"There is a wealth of conceit in your tone. All right, Colin, what if I said I was too sore? What would you do? Hire a litter, perhaps? Put a sign around my neck reading that I was unable to ride because I'd been plowed too much—like an overused barley field?"

"An analogy that is perhaps amusing but nothing more. No, if you were too sore, I would carry you before me. You would rest on my thighs and ease the pain you perhaps might be feeling."

"I would prefer to ride by myself, thank you, Colin."

"As you wish, Joan."

"I would also prefer that we had not yet left Edinburgh."

"You have already expressed yourself at some length on that subject. I've told you why we left so quickly. There is danger and I don't want you exposed to it. I am taking you to Vere Castle. I will return to Edinburgh. There is much that both of us need to do."

"I don't really want to be left alone in a castle with people I don't know, Colin."

"Since you are the mistress, what should it matter? If something displeases you, you may discuss changing it with me when I return. You may even make lists, and I will certainly review them."

"I sound like your child, not your wife. If a servant displeases me, do I dismiss the servant or just add it to the list so that the master—"

"I'm the laird."

". . . so that the laird may review it like a judge and issue forth a decision?"

"You are the countess of Ashburnham."

"Ah, and what does that entail, other than making lists and learning how to plead my cases before you?"

"You are being purposefully annoying, Joan. Look at that bird, it's a dunlin. On your English coast you call them sandpipers."

"How knowledgeable you are. Did you know they get a black stripe on their bellies when they wish to mate? No? Well, they certainly didn't do all that well with your education at Oxford, did they? But perhaps some of it was your fault. You spent far too much time tupping all your ladies at the inn in Chipping Norton."

"Your memory is lamentable. Tupping is crude. You won't use it again. Your tongue also runs too smoothly, Joan, so smoothly that you are in danger of being tossed overboard."

She continued, not hesitating, "Now, let me present my only item to you—the judging laird. I wish to remain with you. I'm your wife, despite everything."

"What do you mean, despite everything? Are you referring to your less than wonderful experience in our marriage bed? All right, so you weren't that pleased with the result of our union. You are small and I was too enthusiastic. I shouldn't have forced it that third time. I have apologized to you several times. I have told you it will get better. Can you not trust me?"

"No. You will remain as you are, and that is too rough and too big."

"A bit salty of tongue now, aren't you?"

"Oh, go to the devil, Colin!"

"Have you looked at your face, Joan? 'Tis still red from the stone that slashed across it. That was a bullet. You could have been hurt, killed even. You will stay at Vere Castle until I have seen that it will stop and that you will be in no more danger."

"But I didn't even get to visit Edinburgh Castle!"

"Since you will live in Scotland for the rest of your life, I daresay that you will see the Castle as often as you wish."

"The MacPhersons live in Edinburgh?"

"No, they are some fifteen miles from my lands, but the old laird is there, I was told. They've a comfortable house near the Parliament Building. I must see him. There are also, as I've already told you several times, many things for me to see to. Bankers and builders to speak to. New furnishings to consider. Sheep to buy and have transported to Vere and—"

He fell silent when she simply turned away from him. Damn him, as if she didn't care about new furnishings, new stock for the land, new plans for building. But no, he was excluding her. She'd already given him all her arguments. None seemed to matter.

She sat down on a valise. It collapsed under her weight and she remained seated on a smashed-down valise, and tucked her legs under her. She said nothing more to her husband. At least he hadn't attacked her again before they'd left Kinross House. She was sore, very sore, but she would never admit it to him. She would ride and she wouldn't say a word, not if it killed her, which she hoped it wouldn't.

An hour later they had debarked from the *Forth Star* and were on their way to Kinross land and Vere Castle, their valises strapped on the backs of their saddles.

"Perhaps later in the summer we can travel into the Highlands. The scenery is dramatic. It is like going from a calm lake into a stormy sea, everything is churned about, its civilized trappings stripped away. You will like it."

"Yes," Sinjun said, her voice abrupt. She hurt from the horse's gait. She was an excellent rider but the pain was something out of her experience, and no matter how she shifted her position, the saddle seemed to grind into her.

Colin looked over at her. She was staring straight between her horse's ears, her chin high, as it had been now for the past two days. She was wearing the same dark blue riding habit she'd worn since she'd begun riding beside him during their elopement, a beautiful, starkly fashioned outfit that suited her, for she was tall and elegant, this wife of his, and pale-skinned, her hair tucked neatly beneath the matching blue velvet riding hat, the ostrich feather curling gently around her right cheek. It was dusty and looked a bit worse for wear, but still, he liked it. Now that he had money, he would be able to buy her lovely things. He thought of her long white legs, the sleek muscles of her thighs, and his guts knotted.

"We will stop for lunch at an inn near Lanark. You can have your first real taste of our local dishes. Agnes at Kinross House has always fancied herself above all our native dishes. Her mother was Yorkshire-bred, you know, and thus it is English beef and boiled potatoes for her, quite good but not Scottish. Perhaps you can try some broonies."

He was trying, she'd give him that, but she didn't care at the moment. She simply hurt too much. "How far is the inn?"

"Two miles or so."

Two miles! She didn't think she would make another two feet. The road was well worn, wide, surrounded by rolling hills and more larch and pine trees than she could begin to count. There were farms and carefully tilled lands, reminding her of England, and grazing cattle.

They were riding northward through the Fife Peninsula that lay between the Firth of Forth and the Firth of Tay, Colin had told her earlier, a region protected from the Highlanders from the north and the English invaders from the south, which had thus been the historical cradle for religion and authority. Again, she recognized that the land was beautiful, and again, she simply didn't care.

"Over there are some strange-looking hills—they're basalt thrown up by old volcanoes. They become quite thick soon and they cover a lot of land and go quite high. There are even lochs scattered in amongst them. There is some good fishing to be had in many of them. We haven't time today, but soon we'll ride to the coast. It's rugged, strewn with rocks, and the North Sea batters against the land with the fury of an enraged giant. There's a string of tiny fishing villages, many of which are very picturesque. I'll take you climbing up West Lomond, the highest point. It's shaped like a bell, and the view from the top is spectacular."

"Your lectures are very edifying, Colin. However, I should prefer hearing about Vere Castle—this dumping ground you're taking me to."

"West Lomond is just southwest of Auchtermuchty."

Sinjun yawned.

His jaw tightened. "I am rather trying to entertain you, Joan, to teach you something of your new country. Your continued sarcasm doesn't sit well with me. Don't make me regret our alliance."

She twisted about in her sidesaddle to stare at him. "Why not? You have certainly made me regret it." She saw the anger build in his eyes, and she felt her own anger building apace. She urged her horse forward into a gallop, away from him. She regretted it instantly, for she slammed up and down on the saddle. The pain rocketed through her. She bit her lip. She felt tears sting her eyes, but she didn't slow down.

The Plucked Goose—surely an odd name for an inn—lay in a small village at the base of some of those damned steep basalt hills. The large, freshly painted sign that swung from its chains was of a large goose with a small head and a long neck and utterly bare of feathers. The inn was quite new, which surprised Sinjun, who thought every inn in England and Scotland must go back at least to Elizabeth I, and the yard was clean. She heard Scottish coming from every window and door in the inn, but this was a different accent, and despite her misery she smiled.

She pulled her horse to a halt and just sat there for a moment, trying to calm her body from its assault. She looked over to see Colin standing beside her, his hands outstretched to lift her down. Normally she would have simply laughed and jumped from her horse. Not today. She allowed the courtesy. He eased her down the length of his body as he lowered her. And when she was finally on her feet, he said, "I've missed you," and he leaned down to kiss her.

He felt her stiffen and released her. They were, after all, in the public yard of a very public inn. The innkeeper's wife, Girtha by name, who welcomed Colin as if he were her long-lost nephew, exclaimed how thin he was and how pretty Sinjun was, how sleek their horses looked even though they were obviously rented hacks, commented on how the blue of Sinjun's riding habit matched her eyes, all without taking a breath.

The taproom in the inn was dark and cool and smelled of ale and beer, very pleasant really. There were only a half dozen locals drinking there, and they were quietly talking, paying the earl and countess no heed.

Colin ordered broonies for himself and for Sinjun. When they came, he watched as she bit into the oatmeal gingerbread. They were wonderful, and she nodded her enthusiasm to the hovering innkeeper's wife.

"Now," he said, "let's have some haggis."

"I know what's in it. I asked Agnes. It doesn't sound very appetizing, Colin."

"You will accustom yourself. Everyone around you will eat it and enjoy it. Our children will be weaned on it. Thus, I suggest you try it now."

Their *children!* She stared at him, her mouth open. Children! Good God, they'd been married less than a week.

He grinned at her, understanding her reaction. "I worked you too hard, very true, but I did spill my seed in you three times, Joan. It's possible you are already carrying my child."

"No," she said very firmly. "No, I am too young. Besides, I'm not at all certain I want to do it yet. When poor Alex was pregnant she vomited all the time, at least at first. She would suddenly turn white and simply be sick. Hollis, our butler, had a sick pan placed discreetly in every room at Northcliffe Hall." She looked pained at the memories and shook her head again. "No, I won't do it, Colin. No, not yet."

"I fear you have no choice in the matter. It is many times the result of lovemaking and—"

That got her attention. She dropped her fork and stared at him. "Lovemaking. What an odd way to refer to what you did to me. Surely there is something else more appropriate to call it. Like your infamous tupping."

"There are many words that are used to refer to the sex act," he said in a pedantic voice, ignoring her sarcasm. "However, in my experience, ladies prefer poetry and euphemisms, so lovemaking is the more accepted form of reference. Now, you will lower your voice, madam. If you haven't noticed, there are people around us and they may be savages in your aristocratic English eyes, but they are my people and not at all deaf."

"I didn't ever say that. You're being—"

"I'm being realistic. You could be pregnant and you'd best face up to it."

Sinjun swallowed. "No," she said. "I won't allow it."

"Here, have some haggis."

It was a bagged mess of livers and heart and beef suet and oatmeal all served up with potatoes and rutabagas. Sinjun took one look at the bloated sheep stomach it was served in and wanted to run.

"You didn't order it from the innkeeper's wife," she said slowly, just staring at that foreign-looking stretched hot bag filled with things she'd just as soon never see in her life. "There hasn't been time."

"I didn't have to. It's the main dish served here and has been since the inn opened five years ago. Eat." So saying, he cut into the skin and forked down a goodly bite.

"No, I can't. Give me time, Colin."

He smiled at her. "Very well. Would you like to try some clapshot? It's a dish from the Orkneys, supposedly coming to us from the Vikings. All vegetables. It's usually served with haggis, but eat it by itself and see if it settles nicely in your belly."

She was grateful. The rutabagas were nasty things, but she could shove them to the sides of the plate. The potatoes were good, and the hint of nutmeg and cream made it quite tasty. There was no more conversation between her and Colin.

Sinjun spent the next hour and a half in a daze of pain. She didn't notice the damned countryside, even though Colin kept up a stream of travel commentary. She was nearly to the point of telling him she couldn't ride another yard, another foot even, when he said, "Pull up, Joan. Yon is Vere Castle."

There was a wealth of pride and affection in his voice. She craned up in her saddle. Before her, sprawled out over an entire low hillock, was an edifice that was the size of Northcliffe Hall. There all similarities ended. The west end was a true fairy-tale castle, with crenellated walls, round towers, and cone-topped roofs that rose three stories. It was a castle from a children's storybook. It needed but flags flying from all the towers, a drawbridge, a moat, and a knight in silver armor. It wasn't massive, like Northcliffe Hall, but it was magical. It was connected to a Tudor home by a two-story stone building that resembled a long arm with a fist at each end. A fairy castle at one end and a Tudor manor at the other—in this modern day two such disparate styles should have been a jest, but in reality the whole was magnificent. It was now her home.

"The family lives primarily in the Tudor section, although the castle part is the newest, built back at the turn of the seventeenth century. That earl, though, didn't have quite enough money to do it right, thus it is rotting at a faster pace than the Tudor section, which is nearly one hundred and fifty years older. Still, I love it. I spend much of my time there, in the north tower. When we entertain, it's always in the castle."

Sinjun stared. "I hadn't expected this," she said slowly. "It's massive and all its parts, well, they're so different from each other."

"Of course there are different parts. The original Tudor hall dates back to the beginning of the sixteenth century. It has a fireplace large enough to roast a large cow. In the Tudor wing there's a minstrel's gallery that would rival the one at your Castle Braith in Yorkshire. Oh, I understand. You expected something of a hovel, something low and squalid and probably smelly, since Scots, of course, have their animals living with them. Something not nearly as impressive as your wondrous Northcliffe Hall. It isn't stately, but it's real and it's large, and it's mine." He fidgeted a moment. "The crofters many times have their animals in their houses with them during the winter. That is true, but we don't at Vere Castle."

"You know, Colin," she said mildly, looking at him squarely, "if I indeed were expecting a ratty hovel, why, then, wouldn't that prove how much I wanted to marry you?"

He looked nonplussed at that. He opened his mouth, then closed it. She turned away from him but not before he saw, for the first time, the utter weariness and pain in her eyes that she'd kept hidden from him. At least this was something tangible, something he could get his teeth into. "Sweet Lord," he bellowed, "why the devil didn't you say anything to me?" He sounded utterly furious, which he was. "You're in pain, aren't you? Yes, you are, and you didn't say a damned word to me. Your stubbornness passes all bounds, Joan, and I won't have it, do you understand me?"

"Oh, be quiet. I'm fine. I wish to—"

"Just shut up, Joan. Not too sore, are you? You look ready to fall down and expire. Are you bleeding? Have you managed to rub yourself raw?"

She knew she wasn't going to stay on her horse's back for another moment. She simply couldn't. She pulled her leg free and slid off her horse's back. She leaned against the horse until she could get control of herself. When she had control, she said, "I will walk to your castle, Colin. It's a beautiful day. I wish to smell the daisies."

"There aren't any damned daisies."

"I will smell the crocuses, then."

"You will just stop it, Joan." He looked enraged. He cursed, then he dismounted.

"Stay away from me!"

He drew up three feet from her. "Is this the girl who wanted me to kiss her in the entrance hall of her brother's home in London? Is this the girl who walked up to me at the theater, thrust out her hand, and informed me she was an heiress? Is this the girl who kept insisting that I bed her immediately? Even in the carriage? Where is she, I ask you?"

Sinjun didn't answer. She didn't care. She turned away from him and took a step. She felt pain grind through her. She stumbled.

"Oh damnation, just hold still and be quiet."

He grabbed her arm and turned her to face him. He saw that damned pain again in her eyes and it struck him silent. Gently now, he drew her against him, supporting her with his arms around her waist. "Just rest a moment," he said against her hair. "Just rest and then allow me to hold you. I'm sorry, Joan." He pressed her face against his shoulder. She breathed in the scent of him.

She didn't say a word.

She arrived at her new home in the arms of her husband atop his horse, just like a fairy princess being brought to her prince's castle. However, unlike that fairy princess, Sinjun was wrinkled and dusty and painfully aware that she looked a wreck.

"Shush, don't stiffen up on me," he said in a low voice, his breath warm on her cheek. "I don't believe that you're frightened, not you, a Sherbrooke of Northcliffe Hall. My family and my people will all welcome you. You will be their mistress."

She was quiet. They rode beneath the incredible canopy of green formed by the tree branches meeting across the drive. As they drew nearer, there were men and women and children and all sorts of animals appearing along the road to welcome Colin home. There was great cheering. Some of the men threw their caps into the air, women waved their aprons. Several mangy dogs yapped and jumped about Colin's horse, who took it all in stride. There was a goat chewing on a length of rope, not appearing to care that the master was once again gracing them with his presence.

"Everyone knows you're my bride, my heiress bride, here to save my hide and my castle and keep my people from starvation or emigration. They are probably cheering God's beneficence rather than us. Though you did find me. I should perhaps let that be known. Then you would be soundly cheered. MacDuff should still be here. I wanted you to have a warm welcome."

"Thank you, Colin. That's kind of you."

"Will you be able to walk?"

"Certainly."

He smiled over her head at the utter arrogance in her voice. She had guts. She would need them.

Sinjun awoke with a start to pale evening light. For a moment she was confused, then memory righted and she closed her eyes against it. It seemed impossible, but it wasn't. Colin hadn't told her. He'd conveniently remained silent on what she considered to be a very important part of her life here at Vere Castle, as his wife. She shook her head, blanking out incredulity and anger at him for his damnable silence, and stared about the huge bedchamber, the laird's bedchamber, with a gigantic bed set up upon a dais, a bed that would hold six men lying side by side. The room was wainscoted with dark oak, beautiful really, but the dull, very dusty burgundy draperies that were all pulled nearly closed made the room as somber as a monk's cell. The furniture was old, and she recognized the Tudor style of the huge armoire that dominated one entire corner of the room.

She still didn't move, just looked about her. She thought of the list of things to be done that was already forming in her mind. So much to be done. Ah, but where to begin? She didn't want to think about her reception as the countess of Ashburnham, but she had to.

Colin had kept his arm about her waist as he led her through the gigantic oak front door into the large square first floor. He kept his arm around her even when all the servants appeared, all of them staring at her, all of them doubtless seeing it as a very romantic gesture. The minstrel's gallery rose on three sides on the second floor, the railing old and ornate. A quite large chandelier hung down from the third story. There were high-backed Tudor chairs against the walls, and little else. She saw all of this in a haze, listening to Colin as he introduced one person after another. She hurt, but she wasn't a coward or a weak-kneed miss. She smiled and repeated names. But she couldn't remember a one after the repetition came out of her mouth.

"This is my aunt Arleth, my mother's younger sister. Arleth, my wife, Joan."

An older, sharp-chinned face came into view and Sinjun smiled and took the woman's hand, bidding her hello.

"And this is—was—my sister-in-law, Serena."

Ah, a very pretty young woman, not many years older than Sinjun, and she smiled nicely.

"And these are my children. Philip, Dahling, come here and say hello to your new mama."

It was at that point that Sinjun simply stopped cold in her tracks. She stared at her husband, but he said nothing more. She thought she couldn't have understood him properly. But there, walking slowly toward her, their faces sullen, their eyes narrowed with suspicion, were two children. A boy, about six years old, and a little girl, four, perhaps five.

"Say hello to Joan. She's my new wife and your new stepmother." Colin's voice was deep and commanding. She would have answered if he'd spoken to her in that tone. He'd made no move toward his own children.

"Hello, Joan," the boy said, then added, "My name's Philip."

"I'm Dahling," said the little girl.

Sinjun tried to smile, tried to be pleasant. She loved children, she truly did, but to be a stepmother without any warning? She looked again at Colin, but he was smiling down at the little girl. Then he picked her up and she wound her arms around his neck and said, "Welcome home, Papa."

Papa! It couldn't be true, but it was. Sinjun managed to get out, "Are you really darling? All the time?"

"Of course, what else could I be?"

Colin said, "Her name's actually Fiona, like her mother. There was confusion, so everyone started calling her Dahling, her second name." He then spelled it for her.

"Hello, Dahling, Philip. I'm pleased to meet both of you."

"You're very tall," Philip said, the image of his father, except for cool gray eyes that were staring at her hard.

"You're all rumpled," Dahling said. "There's an ugly scar on your face."

Sinjun laughed. You could always count on children for unadorned candor. "That's true. Your father and I rode all the way from Edinburgh— indeed, nearly all the way from York. We're both in need of a good bath."

"Cousin MacDuff said you were nice and we were to be polite to you."

"It sounds like a good idea to me," Sinjun said.

"Enough, children," Aunt Arleth said, coming up to them. "Excuse them, er—"

"Oh, please call me Sinjun."

"No, call her Joan."

Serena looked from one to the other. It was at that moment that Sinjun wished with all her heart that she were standing on the cliffs next to Northcliffe Hall, looking out over the English channel, the sea wind ruffling her hair. She hurt between her legs, hurt very badly. She looked at Colin and said calmly, "I'm afraid I don't feel very well."

He was quick, she'd give him that. He picked her up and, without another word to anyone, carried her up a wide staircase, down a wide, very long corridor that was dark and smelled musty. It seemed to Sinjun that he'd marched a mile with her in his arms before he entered a huge bedchamber and put her down on the bed. He then started to pull up her riding skirts.

She batted at his hands, yelling, "No!"

"Joan, let me see the damage. For heaven's sake, I'm your husband. I've already seen everything you have to offer."

"Go away. I'm not very fond of you at the moment, Colin. Please, just go away."

"As you will. Shall I have some hot water sent up?"

"Yes, thank you. Go away."

He did. Not ten minutes later a young girl peeked in the room. "My name's Emma," she announced. "I've brung yer water, m'lady."

"Thank you, Emma." She excused the maid as quickly as she could.

She was indeed a mess, her flesh raw and very sore from all the riding she'd done today. She cleaned herself up, then crawled into the bed, staying close to the edge. She felt out of place, she felt fury at Colin for his excruciatingly important omission. She was a stepmother to two children who, it appeared, couldn't bear the sight of her. To her relief, she'd fallen asleep quickly and deeply.

But now she was awake. She would have to get up. She would have to face Colin, his aunt, his sister-in-law who wasn't anymore, and the two children, his children. She didn't want to. She wondered what Colin had said to everyone. Certainly not the truth. Now they would believe her a weakling, an English weakling. She was on the point of getting out of the bed when the door opened and a small face appeared.

It was Dahling.

9

"YOU'RE AWAKE."

"Yes, I am," Sinjun said, turning to see Dahling peering into the room. "I was about to get up and get dressed."

"Why did you get undressed? Papa wouldn't tell us what was wrong with you."

"I was just tired. It was a long trip from London. Your papa wanted to get home quickly to you and Philip. Is there something you wanted?"

Dahling sidled into the room. Sinjun saw that she was wearing a heavy woolen gown that was too short for her, and stout boots that looked too small and very scuffed. Surely the child must be uncomfortable in such clothing.

"I wanted to see if you were as ugly as I thought."

Precocious little devil, Sinjun thought, reminded of Amy, one of Ryder's children, a little girl who was an imp and brazen as a brass gong, hiding, Ryder knew, a fear that was deep, very deep. "Well then, come closer. You must be fair, you know. Yes, climb up here on the bed and sit really close to me. Fairness is very important in life."

When the little girl reached the dais, Sinjun reached down and lifted her beneath her arms and up onto the bed. "There, now make a study of me."

"You talk all funny, like Aunt Arleth. She's always yelling at Philip and me not to speak like everyone else does, except Papa."

"You speak very well," Sinjun said, holding very still, for the little girl was now running her hands over her face. Her fingers lightly touched the red mark on her cheek. "What is this?"

"I was hurt when your father and I were in Edinburgh. A flying rock. It's nothing, and the mark should go away soon."

"You're not too ugly, but just a little bit ugly."

"Thank you for relieving me of such a major curse and leaving me with just a minor one. You're not ugly, either."

"Me? *Ugly?* I'm a Great Beauty, just like my mama. Everyone says so."

"Oh? Let me see." Sinjun then did exactly what Dahling had done to her. She ran her fingers over the little girl's face, pausing here and there, saying nothing.

Dahling began to fidget. "I *am* a Great Beauty. If I'm not now, I will be when I'm grown up."

"You also have the look of your father. He's very handsome, so that's all right. You have his eyes. Beautiful dark blue eyes he has, and so do you. Mine are also beautiful, don't you think so? They're called Sherbrooke blue. That's my family name."

Dahling chewed on her bottom lip. "I suppose so," she said at last. "But that doesn't mean you're not still a little bit ugly."

"You have your father's dark hair. That's also nice. Don't you like my hair? It's called Sherbrooke chestnut."

"Maybe it's all right. It's very curly. Mine isn't. Aunt Arleth just shakes her head and says I must bear with it."

"But you're still a Great Beauty?"

"Oh yes, Papa told me so," Dahling said with complete conviction.

"You believe everything your papa tells you?"

The little girl cocked her head to one side. "He's my pa. He loves me, but sometimes he doesn't see me or Philip, now that he's the laird of the Kinross clan. It's a very important job. He's very important and everybody needs him. He doesn't have much time for *bairns*—children."

"You don't have your father's nose. Yours is turned up on the end. Is that like your mother's?"

"I don't know. I'll ask Aunt Serena. She's Mama's younger sister. She takes care of me when the governesses all leave, but she doesn't like to. She'd rather be out picking flowers and wearing flowing gowns like a girl waiting for a prince to come."

Sinjun felt a sinking at that artless news. "Governesses? You and Philip have had more than one?"

"Oh yes, we never like them, you see. They're all English—like you—and ugly, and we make them leave. That, or they didn't like Mama, and she'd make them leave. Mama didn't like other ladies around."

"I see," Sinjun said, but didn't. "How many governesses have you had since your mama went to heaven?"

The little girl said very proudly, "Two. But mind you, it's only been seven months. We can make you leave, too, if we want."

"You think so, do you? No, don't answer that. Now, my dear, I must attire myself for dinner. Should you like to help me, or would you like me to help you?"

Dahling frowned. "What's wrong with me?"

"Do you dine in the nursery or with the family?"

"Papa decides. He decides everything now that he's laird. Aunt Arleth doesn't like it. I've seen her eyes turn red sometimes she's so angry at him. Papa says that sometimes we're the very devil and he doesn't want us around when he's eating his soup."

"Well, why don't you dine with us this evening, to celebrate my being here. Do you have another gown?"

"I don't like you and I don't want to celebrate. You're not my mama. I'll tell Philip that we'll make you leave."

"Do you have another gown?"

"Aye, but not new. It's short, just like this one. Papa says we don't have any groats for fripteries—"

"Fripperies."

"Yes, that's it. Aunt Arleth says I grow too fast and Papa mustn't waste his groats on me. She says she's not surprised that we're poor, since he should never have been the laird in the first place."

"Hmmm. Your papa now has sufficient groats for new dresses. We'll ask him."

"They're your groats. I heard Cousin MacDuff talking to Aunt Arleth about how you were a great heiress and that's why Papa married you. She sniffed and said it was proper that he had sacrificed himself. She said it was the first decent thing he'd done in his life."

Good grief, Sinjun thought, momentarily stunned. Aunt Arleth sounded like a thoroughly nasty old bird. She said, calmly enough, even with a smile hovering, "That's right. The poor boy is very noble and pragmatic. So you shouldn't want to send me away, because I'm here for a higher purpose than your governesses."

"Aunt Serena said that Papa had your money now and that maybe you'd go to heaven, like my mama."

"Dahling! Shut your mouth!"

Colin strode into the bedchamber, his eyes on the little girl, who was gazing at him with adoration and now some perturbation, because he hadn't sounded pleased with her. Sinjun stared at him. He looked stern and forbidding, striding into the room, the laird, the master, the earl, and he looked harassed.

"She was just giving me the family news, Colin," Sinjun said mildly. "Surely you want me to know what Aunt Arleth and Auntie Serena think of me. I have also decided that you're right and Dahling just might be a Great Beauty. Lord knows she's precocious. But she does need some new gowns. More than enough reason, don't you think, that I accompany you back to Edinburgh?"

"No. Dahling, go to your aunt Serena. You'll be dining with us at the big table tonight. Go now."

Dahling scooted off the bed, looked back at Sinjun, shook her head, and skipped from the room.

"What was she telling you?"

"Just children talk, Colin, about everything and about nothing. As I told you, I quite like children and I'm with them a lot, what with my three nephews and all of Ryder's Beloved Ones. Why the devil didn't you tell me about them?"

She saw then that Colin could be just like Douglas and Ryder and Tysen. She supposed that it was a trait all men shared. When they were clearly in the wrong, or when a topic wasn't to their liking or made them uncomfortable, why then, they simply ignored it. He said now, "What did she say?"

However, living with three brothers had taught her perseverance. "Why didn't you tell me?"

He raked his fingers through his black hair, making it stand on end. "Damnation, Joan, it doesn't matter now."

Sinjun leaned back against the pillows, pulling the covers over her more securely. "I can see your point of view, Colin. Actually, I can see it quite clearly. You were afraid I wouldn't want you for a husband if you'd told me I'd be the proud stepmother of two children who chase away every governess that you or your wife ever hired. Isn't that right?"

"Yes. No. Maybe. I don't know, dammit."

"Are there any more little surprises you've got waiting for me? Perhaps a mistress in one of those castle towers, who has long golden hair and unrolls it out of the window to pull you up? How about a couple of illegitimate children wandering about? Or perhaps a mad uncle locked away in the Tudor section in a priest hole?"

"Do you have a gown to wear this evening?"

"Yes, but I'll need Emma to press it for me. I do have only one, Colin. Are there any more surprises?"

"I'll get Emma, and no, there aren't, except . . . how did you know about Great-Uncle Maximilian? He is mad, true, and he does howl at the full moon every month, but who could have told you? Normally he's content to quote Rabbie Burns and drink gin."

"I will assume you're jesting."

"Yes, damn you, I am. But the children, that's different. They're just children, Joan, and they're smart little beasts, and they're mine. I hope you won't take them into dislike and abuse them just because you're angry at me for not telling you about them."

"As in throw rocks at them?"

"I'm serious."

"Perhaps, then, I can throw rocks at you?"

"If you're well enough to throw rocks, why then, you're well enough for me to take you again tonight." He felt instant guilt, because she actually paled at his words. "Oh, stop it! I'm not a damned savage."

"I'm relieved. How many governesses have Philip and Dahling enjoyed, say, in the past two years?"

"I don't know. Not more than three, maybe four. Fiona didn't like one of them, so the children weren't responsible. The last one was a fainting ninny and she had no guts."

"No guts, huh? All right, please tell Emma to press my gown for me. I will have it for her when I have unpacked my valise."

"She will do that for you."

"No, I prefer to."

"How do you feel?"

"Fine. There's no dressing screen in this room. I trust you will fetch one."

"Why? You're my wife and I'm your husband."

"It isn't proper for me to dress and undress in front of you. Besides, I will need assistance. Where is the countess's bedchamber?"

"Through that door," he said, and pointed to a door that she could barely see because it was built into the wainscoting.

"Is that where your former wife slept?"

"Joan, what's wrong with you? It doesn't matter, none of it. She's dead. You're my wife and—"

"Since you have my groats, you can send me to heaven with Dahling's mama. You say that bullet in Edinburgh was intended for you. Perhaps it wasn't, Colin."

He picked up a pillow and threw it at her. It hit her smack in the face.

"Don't you ever speak like that again, do you hear me? Damn you, you're my bloody countess!"

"All right. I was just angry with you and that's why I was nasty. Forgive me."

"I will, this time. Kindly moderate your insults in the future, and stop carping at me. Now, you must hurry. Dinner is served in forty-five minutes. I'll get Emma."

He left her without another word.

Well, Sinjun thought, smoothing her hand over the pillow he'd thrown at her, his reaction was interesting. Perhaps he did care for her a bit.

Cousin MacDuff was the first family member she encountered when she came downstairs. He was standing at the foot of the staircase, a brandy snifter in his hand, looking very pensive. He looked even more massive than she remembered. His violent red hair was pomaded down, and his clothes were quite natty, black britches, white linen, white silk stockings.

She was nearly upon him before he noticed her presence. "Joan! Hello and welcome to Vere Castle. Forgive me for not being here when you arrived."

"Hello, MacDuff. Please call me Sinjun. Only Colin persists in this Joan business."

"You'll bring him about, I daresay."

"You think so, do you?"

"Yes. He told me about your reception in Edinburgh—your brothers being there and all." He paused and looked upward at the minstrel's gallery, all in gloom now, frowning a bit. "I should like to have seen it. It sounds like you had quite a bit of fun. Did Angus really shoot a hole in the drawing room ceiling?"

"A very big hole. It made everything quite black and smelly."

"I'm always on the short end of adventures. It doesn't seem fair, since

I'm so big, does it? I could champion any number of lovely young ladies just by frowning at the opponents. They would scatter to the winds, I daresay, were I to wave one of my gigantic fists at them. Colin also told me about the shot." He paused and studied her face, touching the mark with his blunt, large fingers. "There won't be a scar, thank the good Lord. Don't worry, Colin will bring the culprit to justice. What do you think of your new home?"

Sinjun looked at the dusty oak wainscoting, the dull and dirty stair railings that were so beautifully carved. "I think it's magic. I also think a lot of dirty hands have touched the railings and a lot of other hands have been idle."

"No one has done much of anything since Fiona and Colin's brother died."

"Including simple housekeeping?"

"So it would appear." MacDuff looked around the large first floor. "You're right. I hadn't noticed. But you know, things have been like this since Colin's mother died some five years ago. It's good you're here, Sinjun. You can see that all is brought back up to snuff."

"Her name is Joan."

"Your one refrain, Colin?" His voice was amiable. He shook his cousin's hand, making Colin wince.

"Joan is her name."

"Well, I prefer Sinjun. Now, let's go into the drawing room, shall we? Doubtless your bride would like a sherry."

"Yes, I would," Sinjun said, and looked at her husband and swallowed. He was beautiful in black evening garb and pristine white linen. He was immaculate and so handsome she wanted to hurl herself into his arms. She wanted to kiss his mouth, his earlobe, the pulse in his neck.

"Good evening, Joan."

"Hello, Colin."

He arched a black brow at the interested tone of her voice, but said nothing, merely bowed.

Aunt Arleth was the only one in the dark and dour drawing room, sitting near a sluggishly burning peat fire. She was dressed in unrelieved black, a beautiful cameo at her throat. She was very thin, her hair black and luxuriant, pulled up in an elegant twist, white wings sweeping back at her temples. She had once been quite pretty. Now she looked annoyed, her mouth thin, her pointed chin up. Aunt Arleth rose and said without preamble, "The children are eating with Dulcie in the nursery. My nerves are overset, nephew, what with the arrival of this Young

Person, whom you had to carry upstairs, with everyone looking. I don't want the children at my table tonight."

Colin merely smiled. "I, on the other hand, have missed my children." He motioned to a footman, who was wearing a very ragged livery of dark blue and faded white. "Fetch the children, please, Rory."

There was a hiss of anger, and Sinjun turned to Aunt Arleth and said, "Please, ma'am, it is I who wish to have them at the dinner table. They're now my responsibility and I should like to get to know them."

"I have never believed children should be allowed to eat with the adults."

"Yes, Aunt, we know your feelings. Indulge me for this evening. Joan, some sherry? Aunt, what would you like?"

Aunt Arleth accepted her sherry, sat down, and became markedly silent. Serena came into the drawing room at that moment, looking like a princess in a very formal gown of pale pink silk, her lovely dark brown hair threaded through with matching pink ribbon. She was smiling, her eyes bright and very gray and staring directly at Colin. Oh dear, Sinjun thought, and accepted her sherry from MacDuff. What, she wondered, was it going to be like when Colin left? Serena then nodded to Sinjun and gave her a smile that said quite clearly that she knew she was beautiful and Sinjun must know it as well.

Sinjun smiled at her, willing to try, and to her surprise Serena smiled back. It seemed a genuine smile, and Sinjun prayed it was, but she wasn't stupid. There were deep waters in Vere Castle, very deep. Then the children were ushered in by Dulcie, the nursery maid, a young girl with merry dark eyes and a lovely smile and a very big bosom.

Both children were beautiful. Philip, the image of his father, stood tall and proud and scared. His eyes darted from his father to Sinjun and back again. He made no move toward anyone, nor did he say anything. Dahling, on the other hand, walked over to her father in her too-short gown and a pair of slippers that had certainly seen better days, and said, "Dulcie said if we weren't good at the dinner table and made you yell at us, the ghost of Pearlin' Jane would get us."

"Och, what a bairn!" Dulcie exclaimed, throwing up her hands and laughing. "Yer a wee nit, ye are, my lass!"

"Thank you, Dulcie," Aunt Arleth said, clearly dismissing the girl. "You may return to fetch them in an hour, no longer, mind."

"Aye, ma'am," Dulcie said in a squashed voice as she curtsied.

"I don't like you filling the child's mind with those absurd ghost stories."

"No, ma'am."

"There are many who have seen Pearlin' Jane," MacDuff said mildly. He turned to Sinjun. "She's our most famous ghost, a young lady who was supposedly betrayed and heartlessly murdered by our great-grandfather."

"Nonsense," said Aunt Arleth. "I've never seen her. Your great-grandfather wouldn't have hurt a gnat."

"Fiona saw her many times," Serena said quietly to Sinjun. "She told me that the first time she saw her in her white pearl-sewn gown, she nearly fainted with fright, but the ghost didn't try to harm her or scare her. She just sat there, atop the castle gate, her face as white as death itself, and stared at her."

"I fancy that was just about the time Fiona discovered Colin had a mistress."

Sinjun gasped. She stared at Aunt Arleth, not believing what the woman had said. It was outrageous; it was unbelievable. Now she said to Sinjun, her voice full of spite, "Don't be a ninny, girl! Men are men no matter where you are, and they all have mistresses, aye, and Fiona found out about that little slut he'd taken to his bed."

Sinjun looked swiftly at Colin, but there was only a sardonic look on his face. It was as if he were quite used to this sort of attack and didn't regard it. But Sinjun had no intention of ignoring it. She was infuriated. She said in a very loud and clear voice, "You will not speak of Colin again in that discreditable way. He would never break his vows, never. If you think he would, why then, you are either blind or stupid, or just plain mean. I won't tolerate it, ma'am. You live in my husband's house. You will treat him with the respect he deserves."

How to make an enemy in just a few short seconds, Sinjun thought. Aunt Arleth sucked in her breath but said nothing. Sinjun looked down at her clasped hands. There was utter silence.

Then Colin laughed, a deep, full, rich laugh that reverberated off the water-spotted wallpaper of the large drawing room. He said with very real humor, "Aunt Arleth, beware. Joan here must needs protect me. She won't allow any insult against me. She needs but a horse and some armor and she would go into a tourney to defend my honor. I suggest, ma'am, that you moderate your speech when around her. I have found that even when she is angry with me, she is still ferocious in her defense of me. Only she is allowed to cosh my head, no one else. It's odd, but it's true. Now, shall we all adjourn to the dining room? Philip, take Dahling's hand. Joan, allow me to show you the way."

"She needs to be taught manners," Aunt Arleth said under her breath, but of course not under enough.

"My groats are on you," MacDuff said in her ear as Colin seated her in the countess's chair down the long expanse of mahogany dining table. It was Aunt Arleth's chair, Sinjun knew that. She held her breath, but Aunt Arleth merely paused a moment, then shrugged. She seated herself in a chair held by Colin, on his left hand. No upset, no uproar, for which Sinjun was grateful. The children were placed in the middle, MacDuff on one side, Serena on the other.

"I wish to propose a toast," Colin said, and rose to his feet. He lifted his wineglass. "To the new countess of Ashburnham."

"Hear! Hear!" MacDuff shouted.

"Yes, indeed," said Serena warmly.

The children looked from their father to their new stepmother. Philip said very clearly, "You're not our mother even though Father has had to make you the countess to save us from ruin."

Aunt Arleth smiled maliciously at Sinjun.

"No, I'm not your mother. If you hadn't noticed, Philip, I'm far too young to be your mother. Goodness, I'm only nineteen. It was a strange thing for you to say, you know."

"Even when you're old you won't be our mother."

Sinjun only smiled at the boy. "Perhaps not. Soon my mare, Fanny, should arrive. She's a great goer, Philip. Do you ride?"

"Of course," he said in a scornful voice. "I'm a Kinross and someday I will be the laird. Even Dahling rides, and she's just a little nit."

"Excellent. Perhaps both of you will show me some of the countryside on the morrow."

"They have their lessons," said Aunt Arleth. "I must teach them, since the governesses won't stay. It's Serena's duty, but she shirks it."

Colin said mildly, "Joan is a treat, Aunt. Let the children attend her. No matter their snits, she is their stepmother and is here to stay. They must get to know her." He then bent a very stern eye on his son. "You won't torment her, do you understand me, Philip?"

"Yes," Sinjun agreed in high good humor, "no snakes in my bed, no slimy moss dredged up from a swamp for me to sit on or clutch in my hand in the dark."

"We have better things than that," Dahling said.

"The slime is an interesting thought," Philip said, and Sinjun recognized that intense contemplative look. She'd seen it a number of times on every child's face she'd ever known.

"Eat your potatoes," Colin said. "Forget slime."

There was haggis for dinner, and Sinjun wondered if she would fade away and become another resident ghost through lack of food. At least there were several removes, so she managed to eat enough to satisfy her. She listened to Colin and MacDuff discuss several business ventures and problems with local people. She drifted a bit, for there was still pain between her thighs, dull and throbbing now, but still there. She jerked her head up when she heard Colin say, "I'll be leaving in the morning to return to Edinburgh. There is much to be done."

"Now that you have her money?" Aunt Arleth said.

"Yes," Colin said. "Now that I have her money I can begin to solve all the miserable problems left by my father and brother."

"Your father was a great man," said Arleth. "None of it was his fault."

Colin opened his mouth, then merely smiled and shook his head. He continued his conversation with MacDuff. Sinjun would have liked to throw her plate at his head. He truly was going to dump her here in this strange place, and without a by-your-leave. Wonderful, just wonderful. Two children who would do their best to make her life miserable, and two women who would probably just as soon see her jump from one of the crenellated towers as speak to her.

Serena said, "We must have a party for your wife, Colin. It will be expected. All our neighbors will be aghast to learn that you've married again so quickly—after all, it's only been seven months—but since you only did it for her money, it's best that they understand it as quickly as possible. Don't you agree, MacDuff?"

Cousin MacDuff said nothing, merely turned to Colin when he said, "When I return we will discuss it."

Sinjun forked down a bit of potatoes and gave her attention to her new home. It was far more pleasant than her dinner companions. The Tudor dining room was, somewhat to her surprise, utterly charming. It was long and narrow, with portraits covering nearly every inch of wall. The huge table and ornately carved chairs were heavy and dark and surprisingly comfortable. The draperies that ran the entire brace of long windows at the front of the room were old and shiny, but the quality was there and the color was superb. She fancied that she would match the same soft gold brocade.

"Vere Castle is the finest house in all the county."

She smiled toward Serena. "It's magical."

"It's also falling down about our ears," Aunt Arleth said. "I don't imagine that Colin has got you with child yet."

That was straight talking, Sinjun thought. She heard a fork clatter to a plate and looked up to see Colin staring at his aunt. It was a bit of impertinence, but since Colin had already spoken of it, Sinjun wasn't shocked as she had been at first.

"No," she said mildly.

"You will remember the children are here, Aunt."

"We don't want any of her children around," Philip said. "You won't allow it, will you, Papa? You have me and Dahling. You don't need more children."

"We wouldn't like them at all," Dahling said. "They'd be ugly, like her."

"Now, now," Sinjun said, laughing. "They could be quite beautiful, like your father. And, Dahling, you did admit that my Sherbrooke blue eyes were nice as well as my Sherbrooke chestnut hair."

"You made me," said Dahling, her lower lip jutting out.

"True. I twisted your arm and stuck pins in your nose. Already I'm such a wicked stepmother."

"Pearlin' Jane will get you," Dahling said as a last resort.

"I look forward to seeing her," Sinjun said. "I will see if she is as impressive as our own Virgin Bride."

"Virgin Bride?" MacDuff cocked his head to one side, his bushy red eyebrows hiked up a good inch.

"She's our resident ghost at Northcliffe Hall, a young lady of the sixteenth century who was just wedded when her groom was murdered before he could come to her."

Dahling's eyes were fixed on Sinjun's face. "She's real? You've seen her?"

"Oh yes. She appears to the ladies of the family, but I know for a fact that my brother the earl has seen her as well, though he refuses to admit it. She's quite beautiful, really, with very long pale hair and a flowing gown. She speaks to you but never out loud, it's in your mind you can hear her, I guess you'd say. She seems to want to keep the ladies of the house safe."

"Utter nonsense," said Colin.

"That's what Douglas says. But he has seen her, Alex told me so. He just can't bring himself to admit it out loud, because he fears people will think him hysterical and he will think himself hysterical as well. All the Northcliffe earls have written about her, but Douglas refuses to. A pity, really."

"I don't believe you," Philip said. "Virgin Bride, what a silly name!"

"Well, I don't believe you either. Pearlin' Jane is a pretty silly name, too. No, I shan't believe you until I've seen Pearlin' Jane for myself." As a challenge, it was excellent, Sinjun thought, looking at Philip from beneath her lashes. She wouldn't be at all surprised to have a rendition of Pearlin' Jane haunting her room once Colin had left.

"Children, you will leave now. Here's Dulcie."

Sinjun didn't want the children to leave. At least she'd gotten their interest. Philip gave his father a pathetic look, but Colin only shook his head and said, "I will be up later to tuck you up. Be good now and go with Dulcie. Joan, when you are finished, you may take Aunt Arleth and Serena into the drawing room. MacDuff and I have some more plans to discuss. We'll join you shortly."

"What a pity that you interest him so little that he must leave you."

Ah, Auntie, Sinjun thought, you'd best mind your tongue. She smiled lovingly at the woman and said, "I agree. If his marvelously great father hadn't been such a wastrel bastard, perhaps he wouldn't have to leave."

She heard Colin laugh from behind her. She had played her cards all wrong, she decided later. He would leave with no concern that she would have any problems with his relatives. If she had only had the foresight to burst into helpless tears, just maybe he would have remained—that, or taken her with him back to Edinburgh.

"I think Colin is quite the handsomest man in all of Scotland," Serena said.

"You're stupid and silly," Aunt Arleth said. "Just like your sister was."

Sinjun drew a deep breath and kept a smile pinned to her mouth.

It was after midnight when Colin came quietly into the laird's bedchamber. Joan was sleeping very close to the far edge of the bed, the covers pulled to her nose. He smiled, then stripped off his clothes. Naked, he walked to the bed and stepped onto the dais. Slowly, he eased the covers down. She stirred, batting at the covers with her hands, but she didn't awaken. Slowly, he eased up her long cotton nightgown. Easy and slow, he told himself. He'd gotten it up to her thighs when he was content to stop for a moment and look at her long white legs. Very nice legs, very nice indeed. He felt himself swell, but knew she couldn't accommodate him tonight. No, he wanted to see if he could accommodate her. He gently lifted her hips and pulled the nightgown to her waist. He moved the candle closer. Ah, but she was lovely. He stared at the chestnut hair that covered her woman's mound, her flat white belly that could even now have his child growing there. It was a heady thought. She tried to twist away from him, moaning a bit in her sleep. He eased her legs open, and she obligingly parted them more widely. Now, he thought. He bent her knees up and parted her flesh. He winced at the sight of that soft flesh roughened from the hard riding they'd done. He parted her with his fingers, wincing again at the redness. "I'm sorry," he said quietly, and wondered if he should try to give her pleasure. Why not? She needed to learn that it was possible to enjoy him. He leaned down and lightly touched his mouth to her white belly. She quivered; he felt the smooth muscles tighten at the touch of his mouth. He continued kissing her, light, nipping kisses, until he eased down between her legs and found her and blew his warm breath over her flesh. She squirmed. He smiled, pleased.

He parted her soft flesh and lightly touched her with his tongue. In the next instant, she screamed, jerking away from him, flinging her hands out to ward him off, pulling her nightgown down.

"Hello," he said, grinning up at her. "I love your taste, but I must have more of you to be certain. What do you think, Joan?"

10

SINJUN OPENED HER MOUTH to yell again, then closed it. He was lying between her legs, his arms hooked around her thighs, his chin lightly resting on her belly. He was grinning at her.

"Well? Would you like me to do more?"

She got hold of herself, by a meager thread. It was difficult because she'd never imagined such . . .

She said aloud, "What you were doing—it was startling. It is very embarrassing. Are you certain such things are done?"

He leaned down and lightly kissed her again, then raised his head, pushed her legs more widely apart, and gave her a beautiful smile. "You do taste good, Joan. Yes, my dear, a man much enjoys kissing a woman between her legs."

"I feel very odd, Colin. Would you please let me go? I am not used to having my nightgown around my waist and anyone positioned precisely where you are. It is disconcerting. And you are a man, after all."

"If I continue to kiss and caress you here, you will enjoy it immensely."

"Oh no, how could that be true? Really, Colin, let me go now. Goodness, you're naked!"

"Yes. Don't be frightened. I have no intention of taking you again.

Actually I wanted to see how badly you'd hurt yourself by riding today."

"I hurt *myself!* What gall! 'Twas *you* who hurt me."

He drew himself up between her legs and she saw that he was staring down at her and now his fingers were lightly stroking over her and she was so embarrassed she couldn't think of a word to say. "You're raw, I'm afraid. But you will heal. Just stay off a horse for a while." Then he kissed her belly, lowered himself over her, and settled himself comfortably. She felt his sex hard and pressed against her and tried to bring her legs together, foolish, of course because he was lying between them.

"Your breasts feel nice against my chest. What do you think?"

"I don't like this. I don't think you can control yourself. I don't want you to hurt me again."

"I'm a man, Joan, not a randy boy. I won't take you, I promise. Now, kiss me and I'll leave you alone."

She pursed her lips, but he just laughed and ran his tongue along her bottom lip. "Open your mouth. Don't you remember begging me to teach you to kiss? How could you have forgotten so quickly?"

"I haven't forgotten. I just don't want to do it right and have you become a ravening barbarian again."

"A good point." He kissed her again, lightly, then rolled off her. He watched her quickly jerk her nightgown down to her toes, then pull the covers over both of them and lie down on her back, all the world like a supine statue.

"If you like, you can give me pleasure, then."

He was balanced on his elbow, facing her. His eyes were dark, his cheeks flushed, and she knew it for what it was. A man's desire. "How is that possible? You promised, Colin, not to hurt me again."

"Oh, it's very possible. I was touching you and fondling you between your legs. You can do the same to me."

She looked at him as if he were mad, completely and utterly mad.

"It's done all the time between people who care about each other."

"I'm not quite certain I understand, Colin."

"My sex, Joan. You can kiss and caress my sex."

"Oh."

"On the other hand, perhaps it's better that I go to sleep now. I must leave early tomorrow morning."

"Really? You would like that? It would give you pleasure, Colin?"

He wasn't deaf to the utter bewilderment and disbelief in her voice, and said quickly, "It's all right. I do have to get some sleep."

"I'll try it, if you wish."

"What?"

"I'll kiss you there, if you wish."

He saw then that she wasn't at all repelled by the thought of him. On the contrary, she was quite intrigued by the notion, and he felt himself begin to shake. He wondered if he'd spill his seed if he allowed her mouth on him. His sex throbbed. No, best not to disgust her, because he couldn't be certain that he could control himself. He shook his head vehemently and said, "All right."

He lay on his back but did nothing more. Sinjun raised the covers and stared at him. He felt her staring at him and throbbed all the more. "Touch me."

Very slowly, she lowered the covers to his feet, then she simply stared at him for a very long time. She finally flattened her palm on his hard belly just at the instant before he believed he would yell with the need for her to touch him. "You're beautiful, Colin."

He couldn't help it. He moaned, even as he pressed upward. When her fingers lightly touched him, he quivered like a raw young boy.

He held himself rigid, his hands fisted at his sides. "Touch me, Joan. With your mouth."

She stared at him again, then lightly closed her hand around him. She eased down on her knees beside him, her hair cascading over his belly, but he didn't notice the beauty of it, the warmth of it, because he was focused on his sex and on her mouth. He felt her hot breath and nearly died from the intense pleasure. When she lightly nipped at him, he very nearly yelled.

"You're very different from me," she said, and caressed him; oh, it was tentative, but that made it all the more seductive. "I could never be as beautiful as you." He wanted to tell her that was nonsense, but he was silent, straining, wanting so much for her to take him into her mouth, but she didn't, not understanding, really, but she would learn, and he wanted her to do things at her own pace. She experimented and he squirmed and wanted to groan, but held his mouth shut, not wanting to frighten her.

When she finally took him into her mouth, he knew he couldn't control himself. The nearly painful sensations that rocketed through him shook him deeply. He had to stop this. He had no intention of shocking her or repelling her, and thus, even though he felt more frenzied, more urgent than he ever had in his life, he pulled her away.

She twisted about to look at him and her hair tumbled over his belly and chest. "Didn't I do it right?"

He looked into her beautiful Sherbrooke blue eyes and tried to smile—not much of a success that smile, but he tried. "I'm a man, Joan, and it's difficult for me. Now, no more questions. Settle here, against me, and let's go to sleep."

She nestled against him, her palm over his racing heart. She said nothing. Finally, his heart began to slow. She kissed his chest, then said, "I'll try to do things properly, Colin, and touching you with my hands and my mouth is quite nice, really, for you are so splendid. But this other business of your body—you are much too large, surely you must realize that. It won't work, you have already seen that it won't. I'm sorry, but there it is."

"You're a ninny who doesn't know anything." He kissed her nose, then squeezed her more tightly against him. "I should prefer it if you removed that ridiculous nightgown."

"No," she said after several thoughtful moments. "I don't think that's a good idea."

He sighed. "You're probably right."

"Colin?"

"Hmmm?"

"Will you bed other women when you return to Edinburgh?"

He was utterly silent. "Do you believe I took a mistress while my first wife was alive?"

"Certainly not!"

"Well then, why would you believe I would sleep with another woman whilst wedded to you?"

"Men do, I know, except for my brothers. They're faithful to their wives because they love them very much. I hope you are more like them than all those other men who have no honor. On the other hand, you don't love me. So it is a question."

"Will you seduce any men while I'm gone?"

She hit him in the belly, and he obligingly grunted. Then her hand smoothed over where she'd hit him, her fingers splaying downward to touch him, and then he did moan. "No," he said, his breath hard and deep. "Don't, please."

She drew her hand away, and he was both relieved and hated it.

"Why did your aunt Arleth say you'd taken a mistress while your wife was still alive?"

He didn't answer her but said instead, "She doesn't much care for me, as you will discover, since you're my wife and you now live here. I don't know why."

"One could believe her, you know," she said, "except it's obvious she doesn't know how you're made. I know how large you are, I know how a woman would look at you and want to run. That is, you're beautiful, Colin, but as I told you, that part of you that—"

"It's called my sex, Joan."

"Very well, your sex, Colin. What woman could possibly want to do that willingly? It would have to be your wife and thus she'd have to do it."

He laughed, he couldn't help it. "You will see. Yes, you will see."

"Are other men even larger than you?"

"How do I even attempt to answer that question? I'll sound like a conceited sod if I say no, certainly not, and I'd bludgeon my own male pride if I said yes. I haven't seen all that many naked men, actually, particularly when they're aroused. Nonetheless, you don't know anything about it. You will learn, however. Now, go to sleep."

She fell asleep before he did. His mind was filled with visions of Robert MacPherson, and the bastard was plotting his demise. He also thought about his very innocent wife, who had no qualms at all about asking him questions about his male parts with the utmost candor. It was amusing, really. He'd never met a girl like her in his life. Ah, and the feel of her mouth on him—it was enough to make a stoic man cry.

He really didn't want to leave her just yet, but there was no choice. He had so much to do, and he simply refused to put her at risk. She would be safe here. MacDuff had told him MacPherson was in Edinburgh, far from Vere Castle. Yes, she'd be safe here, and he would be able to track Robbie MacPherson down and make the ass see reason, that or kill him. At least he wouldn't have to worry that his wife would try to protect him and attack MacPherson herself.

When Sinjun went downstairs the following morning, Colin was already gone. She stared at Philpot, the Kinross butler, and said blankly, "He left already?"

"Aye, my lady, with the sun."

"Well, blessed hell," Sinjun said, and walked to the dining room.

Sinjun was staring up at the Kinross coat of arms above the huge fireplace in the medieval central section of the house. Three silver lions were painted on a shield of gold. Two larger lions were holding the shield upright, and a griffin flew atop. It said beneath the shield: *Wounded But Unconquered.*

She laughed. It was a wonderful motto and at the moment, with the soreness still in evidence between her thighs, it was even somewhat apt for her.

"Fiona always liked the Kinross coat of arms, but she never laughed that I remember."

Sinjun turned to face Serena. She smiled. "The motto just reminds me of something. I had thought to fetch Philip and Dahling after lunch. Do you know their schedule?"

"Aunt Arleth has the headache. Philip and Dahling are probably riding roughshod over Dulcie."

"Goodness, I wish I'd known. If you will excuse me, Serena, I'll go see to them."

"He won't ever love you, you know."

That was plain speaking, Sinjun thought, staring at the woman. "Why not? I'm not a bad person nor am I ugly, even though it pleases Dahling to think so."

"He loves another," Serena said, her voice verging on the dramatic. Sinjun nearly laughed. She pressed her hand against her breast and breathed, "Another?"

"He loves another," Serena said again, and walked like a graceful princess from the huge Tudor entrance hall.

Sinjun could only shake her head. She was waylaid on her way to the nursery by the housekeeper, Mrs. Seton, a lady with very dark eyes and thick dark eyebrows that very nearly met over her eyes. She was the wife of Mr. Seton, a very important man in the local kirk, Colin had mentioned to her, and also the Kinross steward. Sinjun gave her a bright smile.

"My lady, I understand—indeed, all understand—that we are no longer in Dire Straits."

"This is true. His lordship is in Edinburgh right now to pull us all out of the River Styx."

Mrs. Seton drew a deep breath. "Good. Vere Castle has been my home all my life. It's disgraceful, all this neglect."

Sinjun thought of Philip and Dahling and decided they could happily torment Dulcie for a little while longer. "Why don't I come to your rooms, Mrs. Seton, for a nice spot of tea? We can make a list of what we need."

A list. Then it had to be approved by Colin. What an absurdity. What did Colin know of bed linens or draperies or rents in chair fabrics or dishes and pans?

"Then you must tell me where we can go to replace all that we need."

She thought Mrs. Seton would burst into tears. Her thin cheeks filled out and turned quite pink with pleasure. "Oh aye, my lady, oh aye, indeed!"

"I also notice that the servants aren't garbed all that well. Is there a good seamstress in Kinross? The children need new clothes, as well."

"Oh aye, my lady! We'll go to Kinross—a small village just at the other end of the loch. Everything we'll need will be there right and tight. No need to go to Edinburgh or Dundee, good enough goods up here, ye'll see."

"Colin won't like you interfering like this. You have just arrived, you don't really belong here, and yet you're trying to take over. I won't have it."

Sinjun winked at Mrs. Seton before turning to Aunt Arleth. "I had thought you prostrate with the headache, ma'am."

Aunt Arleth's lips thinned. "I roused myself because I was afraid of what you might do."

"Do begin the list, Mrs. Seton. I shall join you in your sitting room shortly. Oh yes, I should like to inspect all the servants' rooms as well."

"Yes, my lady," Mrs. Seton said, and her departing walk was brisk with energy.

"Now, Aunt Arleth, what would you like to do?"

"Do? Whatever do you mean?"

"I mean, do you intend to keep sniping at me? Do you intend to continue in your unpleasant vein so that all are made miserable by your behavior?"

"You're a young girl! How dare you speak to me like that?"

"I am Colin's wife. I am the countess of Ashburnham. If I wish to tell you to go to the devil, Aunt Arleth, I am within my rights to tell you to."

Aunt Arleth looked so flushed Sinjun was momentarily concerned that she'd overdone her dose of honesty and the good lady would swoon at her feet with palpitations. But then the lady got herself well in hand. Aunt Arleth was made of sterner stuff, and Sinjun realized it fully when the lady said, "You are from a privileged, wealthy family. You are English. You don't understand what it's like to see everything rot around you. You haven't the least idea what it's like to see the crofters' children crying with hunger. And yet you come here and flaunt your money and expect all of us to fall at your feet."

"I don't believe I expected that at all," Sinjun said slowly. "What I expected was to be given a fair chance. You don't know me, ma'am. You are spouting generalities that rarely have anything to do with anyone. Please, can't we try to live in peace? Can you not just give me a chance?"

"You are very young."

"Yes, but I daresay that I will add to my age as the years progress."

"You are also too smart, young lady!"

"My brothers taught me well, ma'am."

"Colin doesn't belong here as the earl of Ashburnham. He is a younger son, and he refused to obey his father, refused to join with the Emperor."

"I'm very relieved that he didn't have anything to do with Napoléon. However, Colin did oblige his father. He stopped the feud with the MacPhersons by marrying Fiona. Isn't that true?"

"Aye, but then look what happened—he killed the bitch. Tossed her over the edge of that cliff, then pretended he didn't know what had happened, pretended he didn't remember. Oh aye, and now he's the laird and the MacPhersons are out for blood again."

"Colin didn't kill Fiona and you know it. Why do you so dislike him?"

"He did. There was no one else to have done it. She'd played him false, aye, with his own brother. That's a nice shock for you, isn't it, you ignorant little English twit. Well, it's true. Colin found out and killed her, and I wouldn't doubt it if he didn't also kill his brother, the beautiful boy, *my* beautiful clever boy, but that wretched Fiona flaunted herself to him and seduced him all unawares, and he couldn't help himself, and look what happened."

"Aunt Arleth, you are saying a good many things and all of them are quite confused."

"You stupid girl! Taken with Colin's good looks, weren't you? You couldn't wait to bed him, couldn't wait to have him make you a countess! All the girls want him, no sense at all, none of them, no more sense than you likely have and—"

"You said that Fiona didn't want him, and yet she was his wife."

"He didn't like her after a while. She wasn't pleased with how he treated her. She was difficult."

"All I know for certain is that Fiona wasn't a very good housekeeper. Just look, Aunt Arleth, everything is falling to bits and much of it has to do with a dusting cloth, or a mop and bucket—not my groats. Now I suggest that you calm yourself and have a cup of tea. I intend to set things aright here. You may either help me or I will simply go through you."

"I won't have it!"

"I'm speaking truthfully, ma'am. Will you cooperate with me or will I simply pretend you're not here?"

Goodness, she sounded firm and wonderfully in charge. Sinjun wanted to throw up she was so scared in that moment. Her first ultimatum. She'd pictured her mother as she'd spoken, and that had given her a goodly dose of confidence. No one ever gainsaid her mother.

Aunt Arleth shook her head and left the hall, her shoulders squared. Sinjun was rather relieved she couldn't see the good lady's face. She'd won; at least she could believe that she had.

Why, Sinjun wondered, staring at a thick, deep cobweb that was draped over the immense chandelier overhead, hadn't Mrs. Seton done any housekeeping? She seemed competent; she seemed eager. She got the answer to her question an hour later, once the Great List was done and each of them was sipping a cup of tea.

"Why, my lady, Miss MacGregor didn't allow it."

"Who is Miss MacGregor? Oh, Aunt Arleth."

"Aye. She said that if she saw anyone doing anything to make this pile of filthy rubble look cleaner, she would personally take a whip to them."

"But she just told me how much she hated how everything was going to rot and how the crofters' children were crying with hunger."

"What wickedness! Our crofters' children are never hungry! Och, if the laird had heard her say that, he'd have lost his wig right 'n tight!"

"How very odd. She's trying to sow dissension. Now, why would she want to do that? Surely it couldn't be just for my benefit." And Sinjun wondered about the other things she'd said. Were they lies, too? Very probably.

"After her sister, Lady Judith, died some five years ago—that was his lordship's mother—Miss MacGregor believed that the old laird would wed her, but he didn't. I believe he bedded her, but it wasn't marriage in the kirk he had in mind. Men, och! All alike they are, save for Mr. Seton, who has no interest at all in the desires of the flesh."

"I'm very sorry, Mrs. Seton."

"Aye, my lady, I am, too. In any case, Miss MacGregor was very angry, and as time passed she became more and more bitter. Petty, I guess ye'd say, with all of us. Ah, but she loved and pet Malcolm—the Kinross laird for such a short time, he was—and she treated him like a little prince. Malcolm even preferred her to his own mother, he did, because she spoiled him into rottenness and his mother swatted his hands but good when he was naughty. He'd run to Miss MacGregor and whine. Och, it wasn't good for his character, needless to say. A wastrel he became, beggin' yer pardon, my lady, but a wastrel he was, truly, just like his pa. Then he died all unexpected like, and Master Colin became the Kinross laird. We've yet to see what he will do. At least he isn't a wastrel, and he's fair. Perhaps there is more, but I don't know of it. As to the state of the castle, why, gentlemen rarely notice the state of things, until the cobwebs fall into their soup an' wind about their spoon. O' course, my lady, Fiona didn't care. When finally I did mention it to the new laird, he said we had no money for anything."

"Well, now we have money, and we have the will to do something, and you and I will see to it. By the time his lordship returns, Vere Castle will look like it did in his mother's time."

"Och, 'tis a fine day indeed when his lordship found ye to buy him."

"I would prefer that you said that a bit more diplomatically, Mrs. Seton."

"Aye, my lady."

Sinjun left the housekeeper's room whistling, tickled with herself that she'd had the foresight to remove her still nearly two hundred pounds from Colin's keeping. She wondered what he'd think when he missed the money.

Sinjun lay in the huge laird's bed, aware that even though the sheets were clean and the covers well aired, there was still a clinging musty smell of a room left closed up too long.

Her first three days at Vere Castle had passed quickly. Goodness, there was so much to be done. Mrs. Seton had already hired a good dozen women and another six men to come and clean the castle. Sinjun herself planned to scour this room. If she'd waited as her husband had demanded, her list for him would have stretched to the North Sea. Naturally, she'd never had any intention of waiting. Mrs. Seton was a fount of local knowledge, and on the morrow Sinjun would ride to Kinross, a fishing town that boasted both a seamstress and a man who worked with wood, and every sort of shop one could wish for. She had visited Colin's room in the north tower and had been charmed and dismayed. The stairs reaching the room were dangerous, the wood rotted in many places. Treacherous. The room itself was moldy, and all his books were in danger of rotting if she didn't act soon. She intended it to be in perfect condition before her husband ever again ventured up to his tower room.

Mrs. Seton, Murdock the Stunted, who came only to Sinjun's armpit and was one of Colin's most trusted servants, who did a bit of everything, and Mr. Seton the Kinross steward—the abstinent steward—all had accompanied her. If the men believed she would let them deal with the carpenters alone, they soon learned their mistake.

Kinross-shire was a small, quite pretty country town, mainly a base for the fishermen for nearby Loch Leven. A narrow road clung to the northern edge of Loch Leven, and the horses they rode knew the path very well indeed. The water was startling in its blueness and the hills that rose from it were alternately lush and green or barren and rugged and looked impassable. Nearly every foot of land was tilled, and now, in early summer, the land was covered with barley, wheat, corn, and rye.

Mr. Seton had quickly pointed out the kirk when they entered Kinross, extolling the local minister's virtues and condemnation of all those who were ripe for the nether regions. He pointed to the old town cross that was still attached to the iron collars for wrongdoers. As for Murdock the Stunted—all of four feet three inches in height, with a great head of red hair—Sinjun saw that he avoided going anywhere near the kirk or that town cross with its iron collar.

She'd discovered quickly enough that she might be the countess of Ashburnham, but all the locals were leery of her ability to pay the bills, and she knew she had to hoard the two hundred pounds. After all, as old Toothless Gorm pointed out, the old laird had sold the Kinross Mill House, hadn't he? And now a demned ironmonger was living there and lording it over all the locals. It took Mrs. Seton at her most undiplomatic—aye, my lady's an heiress, just dripping groats, and the laird got her married to him right and tight!—to bring old Toothless Gorm and the others back to smiles and enthusiasm. They'd purchased materials for new clothes for the children, for the servants, and for Sinjun, new plates for the servants' hall, new linens, and the list went on and on—Colin's list that he would never see, and many items were now duly crossed off. What a day it had been, full and satisfying.

Sinjun now turned onto her side in the huge bed. She was tired but that didn't help her to sleep. She thought of Kinross Mill House. She'd asked Murdock the Stunted to take her there. It was a lovely house with superb gardens planted in the seventeenth century and an old mill with its wheel still poised above the water of a rushing stream. She'd stood there, looking at the lovely fish ponds, the graceful statuary, the topiary, and the immensely beautiful rose gardens, and vowed that somehow she and Colin would bring Kinross Mill House back into the family. Their children and grandchildren deserved to have their heritage restored.

She missed Colin dreadfully. He, on the other hand, didn't appear to be in any hurry at all to return to her. She had come to realize that men had to have women, it was that simple. Not just kissing, but their sex had to come into a woman and they had to release their seed. She would have to suffer this to make him content with her. And it had doubtless been the three times that had hurt her so much, that followed by the hard riding the following day. If she could convince him that just once would be sufficient for his needs, she could bear that easily. Once a night? Once a week? These were things she didn't know. As for her brothers Douglas and Ryder, she wondered how often they made love to their wives. Why the devil hadn't she spoken to Alex and asked her some pointed questions? Ah, she knew why. She'd believed she'd known everything there was to know. She'd read all of Douglas's Greek plays, after all, and they weren't at all reticent about matters of the flesh.

Blessed hell. She pictured Alex and Douglas, always touching, those two, kissing ardently when they believed no one was looking. And Ryder and Sophie were much the same. Ryder laughing as he fondled Sophie, teasing her even as he was nibbling on her ear. She would like Colin to do those things as well. It was just the other. Why hadn't she asked Alex? And Alex was such a small woman, much slighter than Sinjun, and Douglas was as large as Colin. It didn't make sense that Alex could possibly tolerate it. Blessed hell.

She sighed and rolled onto her back. It was then she heard the noise. She cracked an eye open and stared off into the darkness in the direction of the noise. It was just a very low scratching sort of noise. She must have imagined it. It was a very old house. All old structures had strange, unexplained shudders and sounds. She closed her eyes and snuggled down.

The noise came again, a bit louder this time. Scratching, as if something were trapped in the wainscoting. A rat? She didn't like that thought.

It stopped yet again but Sinjun was tense, waiting for it to resume.

It did, louder now. There was another sound with the scratching. Behind it, sort of. It sounded like something dragging along the floor. Something like a chain, heavy and slow, dragging across a wooden floor but oddly muffled.

Sinjun bolted up in bed. This was absurd!

Then there was a moan, distinct, sharp, a human moan that made gooseflesh rise on her arms. Her heart pounded. She strained to see in the darkness.

She had to light the candle. She reached out toward the night table to grab the lucifer matches, but she knocked them to the floor instead.

The moans stopped suddenly, as did the scratching. But the chain, dragging slowly, was louder now, and it was coming closer, still muffled, but it was coming, closer. It was in the bedchamber now.

Sinjun knew such terror she very nearly screamed. But the scream stuck in her throat. There was now a flicker of a light coming from the far corner of the bedchamber. Just a flicker of very white light, almost like smoke, because it was thin and vague, too. She stared at that light and knew such fear she nearly swallowed her own tongue.

The moans came again, and suddenly the chain slapped hard against something or someone. There was a cry, as if it were indeed a person the chain had struck.

Oh Jesus, she thought. She couldn't just sit here trembling like a twit. She didn't want to, but she forced herself to slither off the bed. She fumbled to find the matches. They'd slid somewhere and she couldn't find them. She was on her hands and knees when the moan came again, sharp and loud and filled with pain.

She paused. Then, still on her hands and knees, she crawled toward the end of the dais. She kept close to the floor. When she reached the end of the dais, she peered about the edge. There in the far corner the light burned more brightly. And the look of it was so very strange, so floaty and vague, yet so white.

Suddenly there was a horrible scream. Sinjun nearly leaped to her feet to run from the bedchamber. The hair lifted off her neck. She was shaking with cold terror.

Just as suddenly, the light was gone. The corner of the room was perfectly black again. There were no more moans.

She waited, so cold now she was shaking from that and not fear. She waited and waited, nerves stretched to the limit.

Nothing. No more scratching, nothing more.

Slowly, Sinjun reached up and pulled the covers down to the floor. She wrapped herself in them and curled against the dais. Finally she fell asleep.

It was Mrs. Seton who found her the next morning. Sinjun cocked open an eye to see the lady standing over her, saying over and over, "Oh, och! Ye're hurt, my lady! Oh, och!"

Sinjun was sore and all stiff from her hours on the hard floor, but she wasn't hurt. "Mrs. Seton, ah, please help me up. Yes, thank you. I had this dream, you see, a hideous nightmare actually, and it frightened me so I curled up down here."

Mrs. Seton merely arched one of those tremendously thick black brows at her and assisted her to her feet.

"I'll be fine now. If Emma could fetch some water for a bath, I'll be downstairs soon."

Mrs. Seton nodded and walked toward the door of the bedchamber, only to draw up short and stare at the floor. "Och, what is this, pray?"

It was the far corner of the bedchamber.

"What is what?" Sinjun's voice sounded creaky and harsh.

"This," Mrs. Seton said, pointing to the floor. "It looks like some sort of ooze from the Cowal Swamp, all black and smelly and thick. "Och, there are even wee lumps of—" Her voice broke off and she stepped back. "My mither always said it takes a lang spoon tae sup wi' the devil."

Mrs. Seton, who normally spoke the loveliest English, had fallen into a very thick Scottish brogue.

She got hold of herself in short order, however, and said thoughtfully, "However did it get here? Goodness, the swamp isn't all that close to Vere Castle." She gave Sinjun an odd look, then shrugged. "No matter. I'll send someone to clean up the mess."

Sinjun didn't want to see the mess up close, but she did. It was disgusting, as if something or someone had ladled out some of the filth onto the floor—that . . . or dragged it in, perhaps with a chain.

It was really quite well done of them, she thought as she stepped into her bath. Really quite well done.

11

SINJUN MADE HER WAY around four local men yelling at one another in a language that wasn't at all English. They'd lowered the huge chandelier, replaced the dangerously rusted chain, and were now cleaning off the years of filth before the women began to wash all the crystal.

She spoke to them, smiled, and continued on her way to the smaller dining room, which was called the Laird's Inbetween Room. She drew to a halt to see Aunt Arleth berating a serving woman who was on her hands and knees in the massive Tudor entrance hall, scrubbing the marble squares.

"I won't have it, Annie! Get up and get out of here!"

"What is the problem?" Sinjun asked calmly.

Aunt Arleth whirled on her. "I don't approve of this, any of it, my girl. Now look what she's doing! Those squares have been as they were for years upon years."

"Yes, and so filthy, poor Annie must have pads on her knees she's been scrubbing so long."

"I told you that you didn't belong, young lady, and I meant it. And now you have the gall to spend the laird's money for this sort of nonsense."

"Oh no," Sinjun said, smiling. "It's all my money, I promise you."

"I think it looks nice, Aunt."

Serena, looking even more like a princess who'd lost her bearings than the last time Sinjun had seen her, floated down the wide staircase and into the entrance hall wearing a soft pale blue silk gown.

"What would you know? You, who do nothing but take and take. Just look at you! You're daft!"

"Look at what, Aunt? I look beautiful. Mirrors don't lie. You're old, so I understand that you would be jealous. Now, dear Joan, how may I be of service?"

"Well, that is very kind of you, Serena. Why don't you come into the Laird's Inbetween Room now and we'll discuss it over breakfast."

"Oh, I don't wish breakfast now. I believe I will pick some purple thistle, it's the emblem of Scotland, you know."

"No, I didn't know."

"Oh yes. It seems that some Vikings came ashore to rape and plunder, but one of them stepped on a bed of thistles and cried out in pain. It alerted all the native Gaels, and they were able to escape the enemy."

"Silly nonsense," said Aunt Arleth. She added under her breath, "Why don't you go sit under a rowan tree?"

"That is unkind, Aunt. Even if I did, nothing would happen. I become stronger by the day. I'm a witch, you know, Joan, but a good witch. I will speak to you later, Joan."

She floated through the massive front doors, humming softly to herself.

"What's a rowan tree?" Sinjun asked.

She heard Annie suck in her breath.

"Just never you mind."

"Very well. You will kindly leave Annie alone, Aunt Arleth. Should you like to have breakfast with me?"

"I will rid this place of you," Aunt Arleth said in the meanest voice Sinjun had ever heard. Then she turned on her heel and walked quickly from the entrance hall, not outside, as Serena had done, but upstairs. Now what was upstairs for her to ruin? Nothing, Sinjun thought, relieved.

"When you're tired, Annie, please stretch your legs and go to the kitchen. Cook has made big urns of coffee and tea for everyone, and I do believe there's also a grand tray of broonies." Sinjun rolled her tongue as she said the name of those tasty little oatmeal gingerbread biscuits.

"Thankee, m'lady."

Sinjun smiled, hearing the carpenters working on the stairs. After all the main stairs were repaired, the railings sound again, they would continue to repair the stairs that surrounded the minstrel's gallery. Then it was onward to the stairs in the north tower. All was proceeding apace. Sinjun felt quite pleased with herself.

She went into the Laird's Inbetween Room and was delighted to see Dulcie seated between Philip and Dahling.

"Good morning, Dulcie, children."

Dulcie said, "Good morning to ye, m'lady. Philip, dinna frown like that, it'll put creases in yer forehead fer all yer lifetime, ye ken? Dahling, stop smearing yer eggs on th' tablecloth!"

Another normal breakfast, Sinjun thought, remembering the breakfasts with all of Ryder's children. Bedlam, sheer and utter bedlam.

She served herself from the sideboard and sat down in Colin's chair, since it was closest to the children.

"That's Papa's chair."

"Yes, and it's a very nicely carved chair. It's even big enough for him."

"You don't belong there."

"You don't belong *here,*" Dahling added.

"But I'm your father's wife. Where do I belong if not here, at Vere Castle?"

That stumped Dahling, but not Philip.

"Now that Papa has your money, you could go to a convent."

"Master Philip!"

"But I'm not Catholic, Philip. What would I do there? I don't know anything about crucifixes or matins or confessions."

"What's matins?"

"Prayers said at midnight or at dawn, Dahling."

"Oh. Go to France and be the queen."

"That's quite good, Dahling, but unfortunately there isn't a queen of France at the moment, there's just Empress Josephine, Napoléon's wife."

Both children were at an impasse. "This is delicious porridge. The fresh oatmeal makes all the difference. I love it with brown sugar."

"It's better with a knob of butter," Philip said.

"Oh, really? Then I will try it with a knob of butter tomorrow." She took the last spoonful, sighed with pleasure, took a sip of her coffee, and announced, "I have worked very hard for the past three days. This morning I have decided to reward myself, and you will be the rewards.

You will go riding with me and show me around."

"My tummy hurts," Dahling said, grabbed her middle, and began to groan.

"Then 'tis buckbean ye be needing, Dahling."

"I'll ride with you," Philip said. Sinjun caught the evil wink he gave to his sister.

It took Philip less than two hours to get her lost in the Lomond Hills. It took Sinjun another three hours to find her way back to the castle. However, the morning wasn't a waste by any means. She'd met five crofters' families and drunk five different ciders. She found one man who could write—Freskin was his name—and thus he had a quill and some foolscap. She began to list all their names and what needed to be done in repairs. They had little grain, and nothing could keep the fear from Freskin's wife's face when he said it. They needed a cow and a couple of sheep; ah, but it was grain that was most important.

If any of the men, women, or children believed it a pitiful state of affairs for her that she was here only because of her healthy stock of groats, they were polite enough not to say so. Sinjun began to understand more and more of the local dialect. It was either that or drown in lilting sounds. A sweetie wife, she learned, meant a gossip. Freskin's wife was certainly a sweetie.

Since the day was beautiful, she let her mare canter over the soft rolling hills and through the forests of larch, pine, birch, and fir. She drank from her cupped hands from Loch Leven. The water was so cold it made her lips tingle. She let her horse wander through a clump of fir trees and nearly stumbled into a peat bog. She held her mare to a walk over the harsh barren moors of the eastern hills. All in all, when she returned to Vere Castle she was tired and had quite enjoyed herself.

She paused atop the rise she and Colin had halted at such a short time before. Vere Castle still looked magical, perhaps even more so now that she felt a part of it. She reminded herself to purchase some material to make pennants to fly from those four castle towers. Perhaps she could even find a lovely young girl with golden hair to sit in one of the tower windows and plait and unplait her hair.

She was singing when she espied Philip surely on the lookout for her, near the massive Tudor front doors.

"Why, Master Philip, what a fine chase you led me! Goodness, you did best me, didn't you? You just wait until I take you with me to visit my home in southern England. I'll get you lost in the maple woods. But I will leave a trail of bread crumbs for you to follow home."

"I knew you'd come back."

"Yes, naturally. I live here."

Philip kicked a pebble with a very worn shoe. "I'll do better next time."

She didn't pretend to misunderstand him. She grinned and ruffled his beautiful thick black hair—his father's hair. "I have no doubt you will try to do better, but listen, Philip. I am here to stay, you know. Best accustom yourself, don't you think?"

"Dahling's right. You are ugly."

Sinjun was lying in her bed, wide awake, staring up at the black ceiling. It had been well over a week now, and still no word from Colin. She was worried; no, she was angry. The Tudor rooms were all immaculate and nearly all her two hundred pounds were gone. She was tempted to go to Edinburgh, not just to track down her husband but to get more funds. The people who were working for her surely deserved money for their efforts, not promises.

The carpenters were ready to move on to Colin's north tower. Perhaps she should wait; perhaps she should allow him to oversee the work. No, damn him. He didn't deserve the fun. She turned on her side, then flopped again onto her back and sighed.

She'd had her first visitors today, a local viscount and his wife, and they had come to see the heiress who'd saved the laird's hide.

She chanced to hear Aunt Arleth say, "'Tis a mighty burden for all of us, Louisa. She might be an heiress, but she's most ill-bred and has no respect for her betters. She pays me no heed at all, ordering everyone about, she does."

Sir Hector MacBean had been looking about him with growing appreciation and no little astonishment. "I fancy her orders have accomplished a great deal, Arleth. The place smells positively clean. Louisa, just look up at the chandelier. I vow I used to fear walking beneath that monstrosity. Now it sparkles and it looks to have a new chain holding it up."

And that, Sinjun thought, arranging the skirts of the only gown left to her, was her cue to enter, which she did, all smiles.

The visit had gone off nicely. Philpot, attired in his new uniform of stark black and white, served Cook's clootie dumplings, surely the most delicious dish in all the world. He was as regal as King George III on one of his better days, and just as frigidly polite.

Aunt Arleth looked ready to spit. Sinjun had offered her a clootie dumpling, saying, "The custard sauce Cook makes defies description. Isn't it delicious, Aunt?"

Aunt Arleth was stuck. She could but nod.

The MacBeans were pleasant and appeared sincerely fond of Colin. When they were on the point of leaving, Lady Louisa smiled at Sinjun, patted her arm, and said in a low voice, "You seem a very competent girl. There is much here at Vere Castle that is odd, and all those damnable rumors, of course, but I fancy that you will bring things aright and ignore the talk, for it is nonsense naturally."

Whatever that meant, Sinjun thought, thanking the woman.

She remained on the front steps to wave them away. Aunt Arleth said, "You think you're so much better than the rest of us. Well, I daresay that Louisa saw through you. She will tell everyone that you are a mushroom, a no-account upstart that—"

"Aunt Arleth, I'm the daughter of an earl. If that makes me a mushroom, then you have need of further education. You will cease your diatribes. I have much to do." She turned, not giving Arleth a chance to say more. "Dahling! Come here, sweeting, we have a gown to fit on you."

The night before there had been a snake in Sinjun's bed: long and black and slithering frantically about, trying to hide. She'd blinked, then smiled. Wrapping it gently around her arm, she had carried the poor snake downstairs and let it escape into the overgrown gardens.

She wondered what they would do this night. She hadn't long to wait. It turned out to be a repeat of the first hoary ghost performance. They were quite talented actually, and Sinjun, smiling into the darkness, said aloud in a quavery voice, "Oh dear, not you again. Leave me, O Spirit, please leave me."

The spirit departed shortly thereafter, and Sinjun would have sworn she heard a soft giggle.

Colin called out her name even as he strode up the well-indented stone steps of the castle.

"Joan!"

It was Philip and Dahling who greeted him, Dahling flinging her arms about his leg, crying that Sinjun was mean and nasty and ugly and utterly cruel.

As for Philip, he kept still. Colin hugged both his children and asked them where Joan was.

"Joan?" Philip said blankly. "Oh, her. She's everywhere at once. She does everything. She won't let anyone rest. It's provoking, Papa."

Then Aunt Arleth was there, hissing as close to his ear as she could get that the *girl* he'd had to marry was giving *everyone* orders and ruining *everything*, and what was he going to do about it? It lacked but Serena, and she made her entrance in the next minute.

She smiled at him sweetly, went up on her tiptoes, and kissed him on the mouth. He was startled and drew back. Her smile didn't falter.

"I am glad you're back," she said in her soft voice, and his eyebrow arched upward a good inch.

"All of you—Dahling, let go of my leg now; Philip, take your sister away from here. Where? Anywhere, I don't care. Arleth, a moment, please. Where's Joan?"

"I'm here, Colin."

He looked up to see her coming down the wide staircase. She was wearing a new gown, a very simple muslin of soft pale yellow, not at all stylish, a gown such as a country maid would wear, but, somehow, on Joan it looked smart as could be. He'd missed her. He'd thought of her more than he'd liked and had come home before he'd accomplished all he'd needed to in order to see her. Yes, he thought, she looked very nice indeed, and he couldn't wait to strip off that gown and kiss her and plunge into her. Then he sniffed, and his pleasant fantasy vanished. Beeswax and lemon. Images of his mother rose to his mind and he stiffened, for that was surely impossible.

Then he looked around and what he saw made him blink.

Everything was spotless, not that he'd ever noticed that it had been particularly dirty before. But now he remembered, oh yes, he remembered.

The chandelier looked to be new, the marble floor was so clean he could see his reflection. He didn't say anything. He was stunned. He walked into the drawing room, then into the Laird's Inbetween Room. There were new draperies that appeared nearly the same as the old but weren't, and there were what couldn't be new carpets, yet their blues and reds shone vivid in the afternoon sunlight.

"It's nice to see you, too, Colin."

He looked at his wife, saw that her lips were pursed, and he said low, "I see you have been busy, Joan."

"Oh yes, we all have. You will notice the draperies, Colin. They are new but I copied the same fabric. Can you believe the warehouse in Dundee still carried the same fabric? It's a pattern from nearly fifty years ago! Is it not wonderful?"

"I liked the draperies as they were."

"Oh? You mean you liked dust and years upon years of grime dripping onto the floor?"

"Those carpets look odd."

"Assuredly so. They are clean. They no longer send up clouds of dust when you walk across them."

He opened his mouth but she forestalled him, raising her hand. "Let me guess—you preferred them as they were."

"Yes. As I said, you have been busy, have done things I did not approve."

"Should I perchance have lazed about on a chaise, reading novels that you don't have in that moth-eaten chamber you call a library, eating broonies?"

He realized they were standing three feet apart, but he made no move to close the distance. He was in the right and he had to make her understand, make her apologize. "You should have waited for me. I specifically asked you to make your lists for my review and then we—"

"Papa, she is cruel and nasty to Philip and me! She even made me stay in my room one morning and it was a lovely day."

"Even my children, Joan?" Colin looked down at his daughter. "Go to Dulcie. I wish to speak to your stepmother."

"We don't want her here! You will tell her not to beat us anymore?"

Sinjun stared at the little girl, then gave a shout of laughter. "That is really quite good, Dahling. A front shot of the cannon. Quite good."

"Go, Dahling. I will see to Joan. Ah, Aunt Arleth, you are here, too? Please leave now and close the door. I'm speaking to my wife."

"You will tell her to stop ruining everything, will you not, Colin? After all, 'tis you who are the laird, the husband, and the lord, not this girl here. It isn't she who is in charge at Vere Castle, it is you. You will see that she—"

"Send her to a convent!" Dahling yelled, then disappeared from the doorway.

Arleth merely nodded and took her leave. She closed the door behind her very softly. They were alone in the middle of the beautifully clean and scrubbed Kinross drawing room. Even the battered old furniture had a fine patina to it, but Sinjun wasn't paying any attention to all her accomplishments at the moment. All her attention was on her husband. Surely he wouldn't believe Dahling's dramatic performance, surely . . .

"Did you strike my children?"

She stared at him, and he was beautiful and her pulse speeded up just at the mere sight of him, but now he seemed a stranger, a beautiful stranger, and she wanted to hit him.

"Did you, Joan?"

It was absurd, ridiculous. She had to stop it and stop it now. She quickly walked to him, laced her fingers behind his neck, and rose to her tiptoes. "I missed you dreadfully," she said, and kissed him. His lips were firm and warm. He didn't open his mouth.

He grasped her arms in his hands and drew them down. "I have been gone for nearly three weeks. I came back only to see you, to assure myself that you were safe, that the damned MacPhersons hadn't tried anything. I couldn't find that damned Robbie MacPherson in Edinburgh. He's avoiding me, curse his coward's hide. Of course, I would have been told if something had happened, but I wanted to come myself and see for myself. You are quite the queen of the castle, aren't you? You have made yourself quickly in charge and done whatever it was you wished to do. You had no care for my opinions. You ignored my wishes. You ignored me."

She felt his words wash over her. She wasn't used to words that hurt so very much. She looked at him now and said simply, "I have done what I believed best."

"You are too young, then, to be trusted to know."

"It's absurd and you know it, Colin. Ah, here is Serena, doubtless here to kiss you again. Do you wish to continue your sermon with Serena present? I can call the children and Aunt Arleth again if you like. Perhaps they can harmonize in a chorus, singing of my sins to you. No? Very well then, if you wish, you may come to your tower room. You might as well relieve yourself of all your bile now."

She turned on her heel and strode away, just like a young man, he thought, his jaw tightening, almost no female sway to those hips of hers, yet he knew the feel of her, and his hands fisted at his sides. He followed her, saying, "It would have been nice had you made an effort to befriend my children. I see they still think you're an interloper. I see that you dislike them as much as they dislike you."

She didn't turn about to face him, merely said over her shoulder,

"Louder, Colin. Children tend to behave in the ways of their parents, you know."

He shut his mouth. He kept on her heels all the way to the north tower. He could smell the beeswax and the lemon here and knew that she'd had the gall to do as she pleased to his room—the only room that was truly his and only his—as well as to the rest of the castle. He speeded up. When he saw the repaired tower stairs, he said, "I didn't wish to have them repaired in this way. What the devil have you done?"

She was three steps above him when she turned. "Oh, what would you have authorized, Colin? Perhaps you wished to have the stairs placed diagonally? Or perhaps skipping every other stair, with a dungeon below for those who were not careful walkers?"

"You had no right to interfere with what is mine. I told you not to."

He said nothing more, pressing past her on the narrow stairs. He opened the brass-studded door of his tower room, and the fresh smells that assailed him were more than he could bear. He stopped in the middle of the circular room, staring at the vase of summer roses set on his desk. Roses, for God's sake, his mother's favorite flower, and the smell mingled with the tart scent of lemon.

He closed his eyes a moment. "You have overstepped yourself, madam."

"Oh? You prefer filth, then? You prefer that your books continue to rot? They were quite close to it, you know. Naturally, the shelves upon which they sat had worm rot and beetles and God knows what else. It was a close thing."

He turned then to face her, furious and feeling utterly impotent. She was right, damn her, he was being a dog in the manger, but he'd wanted to oversee things, it was his home, his rags and his tatters, his responsibility. But no, she'd set herself up as the arbitrator of everything, and done just as she'd wished to do and without any direction or permission from him. He could not forgive it. He'd exiled himself to protect her, and she'd done him in, taken over, all without a by-your-leave. He continued to wax eloquent in his mind, then blurted out, a new outrage coming to the fore, "I despise lemon and beeswax! The smell of roses makes me want to puke."

"But Mrs. Seton said your mother—"

"Don't you dare speak about my mother!"

"Very well, I won't."

"You came into my room, the only private room in this entire pile of rubble that has belonged to me since I was bloody well born. You came in here and you changed it to suit you."

"I changed nothing, if you would but cease being an unreasonable boor and look about you. The roses, yes, but nothing else, and they're not a change, just a mere temporary addition. You think you would prefer that the tapestries your great-great-grandmother wove lose all their magnificent colors in years upon years of filth and fray until they turn to dust? And the stones, Colin, you could have easily broken your leg had they not been replaced and reset. I did nothing differently. You will even notice that the damned stones match. And the carpet, dear God, that beautiful Aubusson carpet, at least now you can see the vibrant colors in it."

"It was up to me to have it done."

He was dogged, she'd give him that. Once the bone was in his mouth, he wasn't about to let go of it. She drew on her depleted control. "Well, it cost little to replace the stones. Why didn't you do it, then?"

"What I did or didn't do is my affair. I don't have to explain any of my actions to you. This is my house, my castle. What you have done is wrong."

"I am your wife. Vere Castle is also my home. It's my responsibility."

"You are only what I allow you to be."

"By all that's fair, you're being an idiot! I've waited and waited for you to return home. Nearly three weeks and not a single bloody word from you. Well, my lord, you seem to forget that you also have responsibilities—such as your children."

"My children! They appear to dislike you as much as they did when you first met them, and there's probably an excellent reason for it. You did raise your hand to them, didn't you? You probably saw yourself as taking my place—what with you having all the damned money—and you decided that a man would stride about and give everyone orders and buffet children who didn't immediately conform to what it was you wanted."

Sinjun was careful not to touch the first-edition Shakespeare. She chose instead a thick tome written by some obscure sixteenth-century churchman and hurled it at him.

It struck him solidly in the chest. He grunted, stepping back. He stared at her, not believing that she would hurl a book at him. Had she had a sword available to her, she probably would have tried to run him through.

He'd looked forward to coming home, be it just for a day or two, had looked forward to seeing his bride, and she'd thrown a book at him. He'd seen himself seated at the grand dining table, she as his bride in her place, his children, well scrubbed—doubtless by her own soft hands—smiling and laughing, happy as little clams with their new stepmother. He rubbed his palm over his chest, staring at her still. His pleasant fantasy vanished. Damn her, but he was in the right of it. Because she was the heiress, she'd thrust herself into his role and made herself the master of his home. He wouldn't tolerate it.

"I believe I'll lock you in the laird's bedchamber. You can cause no more discord there."

She stared at him. The day was warm and his beautiful black hair was windblown. His face was tanned, his eyes such a deep blue, a treacherous blue, she thought, hard now with his anger and his dislike for her. She said slowly, "Just because I've tried to become a Kinross you would punish me?"

"A true Kinross wife wouldn't force everyone to obey her commands. She would be sensitive to others' feelings. She would obey her husband. Just because you're the heiress, you cannot behave as if you are also the laird. I won't have it."

She walked away from him quickly, saying nothing more. He started forward, only to stop. She went through the narrow open door and he heard her light step going quickly down the circular stairs, the newly repaired circular stairs.

"Well, damn," he said.

Sinjun walked straight to the stables. She wished desperately that Fanny were here, but nothing had yet arrived from Northcliffe Hall, not her trunks or her mare. Murdock the Stunted was there. When he saw her face, pale and set, her eyes wide with something he didn't understand, he quickly saddled the mare she'd been riding, a rawboned bay whose name was Carrot.

Sinjun wasn't wearing a riding habit. She didn't care. She saw that Murdock hadn't put a sidesaddle on the mare. She didn't care about that, either. She grabbed a shock of the horse's mane and swung herself up. Her skirts were at her knees, showing her white silk stockings and her black slippers.

She was out of sight of the castle quickly.

"Good. She's gone."

Colin stared at Aunt Arleth. "What do you mean?"

"I mean she rode away from here and the hussy wasn't even wearing a riding habit. Her gown was hiked up showing her stockings. I watched her from the dining room windows."

"Will you be able to keep her money, Colin?"

This was from Serena, who was flitting about the entrance hall, looking at herself in every shiny surface she passed.

He had no time to answer, for at that moment Murdock the Stunted appeared in the doorway, his frayed red cap in his gnarled hands.

"I be a mite worried, milor'" was all he said.

Colin cursed, long and fluently. Murdock looked upon him with grave disapproval. Aunt Arleth opened her mouth to round on Murdock, but she didn't have time. Colin was out the front doors.

He cursed all the way to the stables. His own stallion, Gulliver, was blown. He took Old Cumber, a gentle ancient fellow who'd known more feud fights than most men who lived here.

"Which way did she ride?"

"Toward the western end of the loch."

He didn't find her, not a trace, not a single damned track. He spent two hours searching, alternately cursing her, then so worried that one of the MacPhersons had stolen her that he shook. He found himself doubting that Latham MacPherson, the old laird, had truly managed to forbid any further raids on Kinross land. Hell, it was quite possible Robbie MacPherson had left his father's side—that is, if he'd ever gone to it in the first place. He sweated. Finally, as the sun was beginning to set, he returned to the castle. Her mare, Carrot, was munching on hay.

Murdock the Stunted merely shrugged, but he didn't meet the laird's eyes. "She came in a good hour ago, milor'. Quiet she were, but all right an' tight."

"I see," Colin said, and flicked his riding crop angrily against his thigh.

He wasn't overly surprised to find the laird's bedchamber not only empty but as sparkling clean as the rest of the castle. It was still as dark as before, but not nearly so dreary now. He hated to admit it. When he went downstairs for dinner, bathed and dressed in formal evening attire, he decided he would hold his tongue. He didn't want another scene in front of the entire family.

He saw her standing beside the empty fireplace, wearing the same gown, holding a glass of sherry. Aunt Arleth was holding forth about something doubtless unpleasant, Serena was seated on a settee looking dreamily off into space, and the children were there, sitting side by side on a love seat, Dulcie standing like a big-bosomed pixie guard behind them.

Sinjun looked up to see him striding into the room. Damn, but he was splendid. She didn't want to take his place, the stupid lout. How could he be so blind? She wanted her own place, not his, she wanted to be beside him, laughing with him, working with him, kissing him and feeling his body with her hands.

"Good evening," Colin said to all assembled.

"Papa, she said we couldn't have any dinner, but since you're here she had to give in."

Dulcie gasped and grabbed Dahling's arm. "Ye're a wicked wee mite, ye are, Dahling Kinross!"

"A veritable witch, I see," Colin said.

"You overdid that one a bit, Dahling," Sinjun said, smiling toward her stepdaughter, "but it was a worthy try. I will give you dramatic lessons. You mustn't ever overdo a role, you know, that's the cardinal rule of the theater."

"I should like to tread the boards," Serena said. "That is the correct way the English say it, isn't it, Joan?"

"That's exactly the way. You already walk so gracefully it's as if you float. The rest would be easy for you."

"All of this is nonsense," Aunt Arleth said, standing. "What are your intentions, Colin?"

"To dine, Aunt Arleth. Joan, here's Philpot to announce our dinner. Give me your arm."

She didn't want to, particularly, but everyone was watching and she had no choice. She tensed as he patted her hand, preparing for battle. "Oh, my dear, not here. When I tell you what I expect from you it will be from behind a locked door in my bedchamber—the laird's bedchamber—the laird's very clean bedchamber."

12

Colin was good to his word. He gently shoved Sinjun into the laird's bedchamber, then closed and locked the door. He watched her even as he slipped the key into his vest pocket. He watched her walk to the center of the vast room and stop, rubbing her arms with her hands.

"Should you like me to light a fire?"

She shook her head.

"Perhaps it would be a good idea. You will shortly be naked, after all, and I won't wish to have you shivering from cold. I want you shivering just from me."

So this was a man's punishment, she thought, looking back at him now. He was completely in control, his size alone gave him that, and he looked mean and determined and oddly angry. She'd said nothing to draw forth that anger, at least not at the dining table. He was probably smelling the dreaded beeswax and lemon again.

But Sinjun had been blessed with two singularly unmanageable, obstinate, very intelligent brothers, who had taught her a lot about men and their strange outlooks and unaccountable behaviors.

Here was Colin acting like the sultan, and she was here to be his slave girl. The image pleased her. It would have pleased her more were he laughing and teasing her. Ah yes, veils, dozens of veils in all colors, and she would dance for him and . . .

"What the devil are you smiling about?"

"Veils."

"Joan, have you lost your wits?"

"Oh no, I was just seeing you as the head sultan and me your slave girl for the night, and I was wearing veils and dancing for you."

He paused, at a loss. She was unexpected; what she thought and said were unanticipated. Even when she said something that he could possibly expect, at the edge of his brain it still shook him that she could speak so clearly and candidly and without guile. He didn't like it.

"I think that a charming and apt idea. However, tonight you will simply dance for me naked. I will clap my hands for you if you need accompaniment. I will fetch you some veils when I return to Edinburgh. Then we can try it again, conforming more to your vision."

"Ah, so it is your intention to leave in the morning, then? Before dawn, I daresay. Whilst I'm still asleep, naturally. I understand, Colin. The last thing you want is to face a pathetic wife who just might beg you not to leave her here again, not to leave her stuck in your home, on your lands, in your damned foreign country. Do you think perhaps I could change your mind about leaving? No, I didn't think so. Oh yes, I mustn't forget the pleasant relatives you have immured me with. Aunt Arleth is a treat. She hates you, she hates me; as far as I can tell the only ones she loved were your brother and your father, who played her false, at least in her mind. As for Serena, I have no idea if she is of this world or of the fairies. She's daft, but pleasantly so. The children—why, I will simply continue to beat them whenever it suits my fancy."

"I don't wish to argue with you any more this night. Just know, Joan, that you will do absolutely nothing more whilst I'm gone. Nothing. You will try to present a pleasant face to all my people and to my children. That is what I expect of you, my wife."

"Go to the devil, Colin."

He watched her chin go up and felt his blood quicken, felt his damned blood rush from his brain to his groin. This girl, who'd worshiped him so ardently in London, who'd begged for his man's body all the way to Scotland, ah, why she'd become a termagant. There was no ardent devotion in her Sherbrooke-blue eyes at the moment. There was a good deal of fire, and oddly it looked cold as the moon. It also excited him.

He took a step toward her. She stood her ground. She wasn't about to let him chase her around the laird's bedchamber, although she'd heard

Alex shrieking once when Douglas was chasing her. And then the shrieks had stopped and Sinjun had known that what they were doing was wonderful. But this wouldn't be wonderful.

"I will let you kiss me, Colin. I much enjoy that. I already told you."

"Oh yes, I will kiss you."

"If you wish I will also kiss you."

"Yes, I expect you to kiss me back."

"No, I mean I will kiss your sex and caress you, if you wish. It was enjoyable that first time to hear you moan and see your body tighten and jerk and all because of what I was doing to you."

He stopped dead in his tracks at that. He swallowed. He also hardened considerably. He easily pictured her above him, touching him with her mouth and her hands. He could still feel her hair spread over his belly.

"No," he said, "I don't want you to do that," and felt his body nearly revolt.

"Why not? You liked it. I don't know why you made me stop so quickly that first time. I was just learning how to do it. I could continue on and on tonight. I don't wish to have you do the other thing to me. We have already decided that you will not. You are too large."

"I told you that you didn't know anything. For a girl who's so intelligent, so very well educated, your ignorance in this matter is laughable. I will make love to you, Joan, and I will come inside you the way I am supposed to, the way men and women have come together since the moment God set them in Eden."

"Very well, I see you are quite set on this. I was just testing the waters. I'm willing to compromise with you, Colin. I will be able to endure one time, I think. It shouldn't be so bad. But more than one time I cannot allow. It would be cruel of you to insist."

He laughed, he couldn't help himself. God, he'd missed her, and he hadn't wanted to, damn her Sassenach hide. No, he'd wanted to take other women, but he hadn't, though several ladies had issued invitations that only a blind man would have missed. No, he hadn't touched another woman, and he'd thought about her, those long white legs of hers, but most of all her absolute honesty. He cursed. He didn't believe for a minute that she would ever lay a finger in anger on a child, any child, even Dahling at her most irritating.

"No, we'll do it right. I have endured abstinence. I'm not meant for celibacy. At least no more of it. I will take you as many times as it pleases me to do so, and you will enjoy it, Joan. You will trust me."

She didn't move an inch, didn't twitch. "You force me to bare my soul, so to speak, to mortify myself, which I don't like to do." She drew a deep breath and stared him right in the eye. "I'm not pregnant, Colin."

"It is just as well that you aren't. You and I need more time together before you bear my children. We need more understanding between us. You must needs learn your role in my house and what I expect from you."

"No, I mean I'm not pregnant right now."

He felt an earthquake of frustration. He felt all the blood in his groin whoosh back to his brain. If there had been a full moon, he'd have howled and run like a crazy man over the Lomond moors.

He looked at her with a thread of hope. "You mean you didn't discover you weren't pregnant last week, say?"

"No, right now. Right this very minute as we speak."

"Perhaps you are nearing the end of it?"

"No."

Did he expect her to tell him the truth? As a matter of fact, he did.

"Well, blessed hell," he said.

"That's my brothers' favorite curse," she said, "all except for Tysen, who's the clergyman."

"I must have heard your dear brothers say it enough. It always preceded their attacking me."

"They love me," she said simply. She waited. He didn't say a word, didn't even look as though he wanted to, but simply lacked the proper words or the ability. "Yes," she said, "blessed hell."

"Come here and I will kiss you."

It wouldn't solve anything, but it would be pleasant, of that she had no doubt. She walked to him with no hesitation. "I would like that. Thank you, Colin."

For a Colin kiss, it wasn't his best, she thought, wishing he would kiss her as he had on their wedding night. He gently set her away from him but kept his hands on her upper arms. He breathed in the sweet scent of her. He felt the softness of her flesh beneath his fingers.

She said, her eyes never leaving his mouth, "Edinburgh is but a half day from here."

"Yes, I know."

"You could come home every few days, Colin."

"Yes, but I won't, not until everything is handled to my satisfaction."

"Where is Robert MacPherson? Have you spoken to the old laird?"

"I have no idea where Robert MacPherson is right now. Perhaps he followed me back here. I don't know. But it seems most likely that he will remain in Edinburgh, to try to get to me there. He hasn't tried anything so far. I have met with old Latham, his father, and he doesn't understand why Robbie is acting like such a cowardly sod. He's put out the word for his son to see him, but to date he hasn't shown himself. He says that Robbie told him I had no proof of anything and he himself would admit nothing to his father. We will see. He will have to come to me sooner or later."

"Why don't you just kill him?"

Colin blinked down at her. "You're a woman," he said slowly. "Women are supposed to be gentle, to despise violence and war. You want me to kill him?"

She looked thoughtful, then nodded. "Yes, I suppose you must. He sounds unbalanced, a bit like Aunt Arleth. I don't wish to live in fear of his hurting or killing you. Yes, I think you should kill him, but cleverly, of course."

He could find no words.

"I could write my brothers and ask them how best to proceed."

"No," he said quickly, "oh no, don't do that. Listen, it's possible he hasn't had anything to do with the trouble. I don't believe that myself, but it's possible. After all, you were the one hurt in Edinburgh. Robbie is a good shot. It's difficult to believe he missed."

"You're forgetting London. And I should say that trouble is a passionless word for trying to kill someone, Colin."

"I can't be certain. It is likely, but not certain."

"So you will remain in Edinburgh until he either kills you or you manage to kill him in the act of trying to kill you?"

He gave her a lopsided grin. "I expect that's about it."

"Sometimes I think gentlemen are too soft."

"I shouldn't wish to hang."

"Oh, you're much too smart to have anyone think you'd done it. Aren't you?"

"I don't know. I've never before killed anyone with any kind of premeditation."

He released her and watched her walk to one of the huge overstuffed leather chairs. She stood behind it. "Nor have I. I wish you would consider it, though. Now, Colin, I wish you would apologize to me for your distressing behavior today."

He stiffened up like the fireplace poker. "You and I had a bargain. You didn't keep to your end of it. You disobeyed me."

"And if I weren't indisposed at the moment, you would punish me for it."

"Lovemaking isn't punishment, damn you!"

"Ha! I'm your wife and I'm in a very certain position to know that it is! It's painful, humiliating, and isn't at all pleasant except for the man, who could doubtless rut a goat and still enjoy himself!"

He cursed, nothing original from what Sinjun could hear, but it showed a frayed state of mind. Not being an unkind person, she said, "It's all right, Colin, I will forgive you even though you can't find it in yourself to apologize. I will continue to improve upon matters here, but I will tell you that I have spent all the two hundred pounds."

"Good, then you will be done with your damned meddling."

"Oh no, if you don't provide me with more funds, I shall simply smile and let Mrs. Seton continue reminding all the tradesmen how you, the fortune-hunting laird, managed to snag an heiress."

"Continue?"

"Oh yes, she much enjoys getting back her former consequence. She's even fond of me, since I'm the bottomless pit of groats. It was quite easy to win her over."

It was as if he were sinking in the treacherous Kelly peat bog with no hope of rescue. "I will speak to her and tell her to keep her tongue behind her teeth." It was a pitiful attempt to regain a semblance of control and he knew it. However, she didn't have to grin at him.

Colin sighed. "I came home to see you, truth be told. And my children, of course. I wish you would make a push to gain their affections."

"Children do things in their own good time. Philip and Dahling are no different. I'm quite pleased with our progress, actually."

"You are but nineteen, not ninety-nine! You don't know everything about children!"

"Of course I do. I have found them to be unpredictable and perverse and immensely creative. But bad feelings don't suit them, not really. We will see. It would help if you were to remain and assist them to see their new stepmother as a very charming person."

"I'm going to Clackmannanshire to oversee the purchase of sheep. The cattle are coming from Berwick. I will return home when that is taken care of and Robert MacPherson is either dead or I judge him innocent."

Sinjun gave him a long look. "There are several lists for you in the estate room, from the crofters I have visited. I trust you wish to see to them?"

He cursed again, but she said nothing more, simply went behind the musty Oriental screen and put on her nightgown.

He was gone the following morning before she awoke.

Sinjun smiled as she heard the huge clock downstairs strike twelve times. Ah, the stroke of midnight. It shouldn't be long now.

It wasn't. Not ten minutes later she heard the soft scraping sounds, like light-footed scurrying rats in the wainscoting. There were the familiar moans, the slapping of the chains.

Very slowly, she sat up in bed and counted to five. Finally she cried out, sounding so terrified she scared herself. "Oh, please stop, halt, I say! Oh, dear heavens, save me, save me!" Then she moaned herself. "I cannot bear it, I shall have to leave this haunted place. Ah, Pearlin' Jane, no, no."

Finally the sounds ceased.

She was grinning like a half-wit when she slipped out of bed an hour later.

Philip was twitching in his sleep. He was dreaming about a large fighting trout he'd caught in Loch Leven the previous week, when he'd gone with Murdock the Stunted. The trout grew as his dream lengthened. It got bigger and bigger and its mouth seemed now the size of an open door. Then Murdock the Stunted was touching him, telling him what a fine fisherman he was, his voice soft and softer still . . .

But it wasn't Murdock the Stunted's fingers or his voice. Suddenly the trout was gone and he was back in his own bed, but he wasn't alone. He felt it again, like soft fingers on the back of his neck, and he heard the soft voice saying, "You're a bright lad, Philip, so bright and so kind. Och, aye, a good lad." He lurched upright and there, beside his bed, hand still outstretched, was a dead lady.

She had long, nearly white hair and wore a flowing white gown. She was young and beautiful, but she looked ghastly. Her hand was but inches from him and that hand and all its dead fingers were whiter than her gown.

Philip swallowed, then yelled at the top of his lungs. He grabbed his covers and yanked them over his head. It was a nightmare, his brain had made the trout into a ghost, that was all, but he burrowed farther down into the feather mattress, clutching the covers over him like a lifeline.

There was the soft voice again. "Philip, I'm the Virgin Bride. Your new stepmother told you about me. I protect her, Philip. Your Pearlin'

Jane is afraid of me. She doesn't like the way you and Dahling are trying to scare off Sinjun."

Just as suddenly the voice stopped. Philip didn't move. Since he couldn't breathe, he made a small tunnel beneath the bedclothes to the edge of the bed. He waited, his breath coming in huge gasps.

It wasn't until dawn that he eased his head out from under the covers. Dull morning light was seeping into his bedchamber. There was no sign of anything or anyone. Not a sign of the Virgin Bride.

Sinjun went about her usual duties, outwardly serene, smiling, wishing Aunt Arleth would drop into a deep well. Colin had been gone four days now, and she was so angry with him that she occasionally shook with it.

She was very tempted to go to Edinburgh. Or would he now be in Clackmannanshire or Berwick? Damned man.

Her trunks and Fanny her mare arrived late that morning, delivered by James, one of the head Northcliffe Hall stable lads, and three of his companions, stable lads all. She danced about like a child, so excited that she even kissed James and hugged the other stable lads. All was well at Northcliffe Hall, including her mother, the dowager countess, who was, nevertheless, according to James, a bit downpin because there was no one else about for her to improve upon. James delivered letters to Sinjun, saw Dulcie smiling at him as if he were a prince, and was more than delighted to spend the night at Vere Castle.

After she saw James and the stable lads off the next morning, their satchels filled with food for them and letters for her family, she went to the stables and saddled Fanny herself.

"She be a foine mare," said Murdock the Stunted. Young Ostle, all of twenty-two years old, agreed fervently. George II, a mongrel of indeterminate lineage, barked wildly at the scent of the new animal, and Crocker yelled at him in language so colorful Sinjun vowed to make him her teacher.

The day was warm, the sun bright overhead. Sinjun click-clicked Fanny onto the gravel drive, now widened and newly regraveled—with the assurance, naturally, that the laird would pay for it upon his return. She was smiling. She'd ordered other things done as well the same day that Colin had left again. Three of the crofters' huts were getting new roofs. She'd purchased seven goats and distributed them to all the crofters with children and babies. She'd sent Mr. Seton—never loath to impress his neighbors and the tradesmen with his importance—to

Kinross to purchase more grain and sorely needed farming implements. A score of barrels and several dozen chickens had been duly distributed to the crofters. Ah, yes, she'd been busy, she'd meddled to her heart's content, and if Colin didn't return home soon, she fancied she would begin another wing to Vere Castle. She'd also set the local seamstress to work on pennants for the four Vere Castle towers. The Kinross tartan pattern was of red, dark forest green, and black. She wished she could see Colin garbed in a Highland kilt, but they'd been outlawed after Culloden in 1746. It was a pity, but the pennants would proudly fly the Kinross tartan.

Sinjun set Fanny into a gallop all the way to the very edge of Loch Leven and loosed the reins so her mare could drink the cold water. She looked toward the eastern moors that stretched up the sides of the Lomond Hills themselves. Barren and empty and immensely savage. Even at this distance she could see patches of purple heather, sprouting up between rocks and out of deep crevices in the land. And to the west, the land was verdant, rich and lush, and every acre of it tilled and flowering with growing wheat and barley and rye. A land of contradictions, a land of beauty so profound she felt it touch the deepest part of her. It was now her land, and there was no going back.

She patted Fanny's sleek neck. "I'm being a romantic and you're fat," she said, sniffing in the clear sweet air, the scent of honeysuckle and heather light and teasing. "Douglas has been letting you eat your head off in the stables, hasn't he? A good gallop is just what you need, my girl."

"I occasionally say that to my women."

Sinjun turned slowly in her saddle. A man was seated on a magnificent bay barb not six feet from her. Why hadn't Fanny whinnied?

"I wonder why my mare didn't alert me to your presence," she said aloud, straightening now and looking at him.

He frowned. A bit of fear would have pleased him. At least a show of surprise at his unexpected appearance. Perhaps her wits were slow and she hadn't understood his small jest.

"Your mare didn't alert you because she's drinking from the loch. The loch water is magical, 'tis said, and a mare will drink until her stomach bloats."

"Then I should stop her." Sinjun gently tugged the reins back, forcing Fanny's muzzle from the water. "Who are you, sir? A neighbor, perhaps?"

"I suppose I'm a neighbor. You are the new countess of Ashburnham."

She nodded.

"You're quite lovely. I expected a rabbit-toothed hag, truth be told, since you're such a full-blooded heiress. Colin must believe he's the luckiest bastard alive."

"I'm pleased I'm not a hag, for Colin never would have wed me, regardless of the number and weight of my groats. As for his feelings of luck, I cannot attest to that."

He frowned at her. "Colin is a fool. He's not worthy of any woman's regard."

She looked at him more closely now as he spoke. He was tall, perhaps taller than Colin, though it was difficult to be certain, since he was sitting atop his stallion, his posture indolent, his expression amused, his clothing of the best quality and fitting him perfectly. And he was very slender, to the point of delicateness, but surely that was an absurd thought to apply to a man. He had a full head of very soft blond hair and his forehead was high and wide. If anything, his features were too refined, too soft, almost feminine. His complexion was fair, his eyes a pale blue, his jawline and his chin as soft and delicate as a woman's. This quite pretty man was vicious?

"Who are you?" she asked.

"I am Robert MacPherson."

"I suspected as much."

"Did you now? Well, that does make it easier, doesn't it? What has the bastard said about me?"

Sinjun shook her head. "Did you try to kill Colin in London?"

She saw that he hadn't; the surprise was too sharp in his eyes, his hands tightened too quickly and roughly on his stallion's reins. So it had evidently been a coincidence after all. He laughed as he flicked a fly from his stallion's neck. "Perhaps. I try to take advantage of opportunities when they present themselves."

"Why would you wish to kill Colin?"

"He's a murdering sod. He killed my sister. Broke her neck and threw her off a cliff. Isn't that an excellent reason?"

"Do you have proof of your accusation?"

He drew his stallion closer to the mare. The mare flung back her head, nervous, her eyes rolling at the stallion's scent.

"No closer, if you please." Sinjun calmed Fanny, crooning to her, ignoring Robert MacPherson.

"I don't understand why you aren't frightened of me. I now have you in my power. I can do as I please with you. Perhaps I will ravish you until your womb takes my seed. Perhaps you will bear a child and it will be mine."

She cocked her head to one side, studying him. "You sound like a very bad actor in an inferior play in Drury Lane. It is curious, I think."

Robert MacPherson was nonplussed. "What is curious, damn you?"

Sinjun's look was remote. "I had pictured you otherwise. Don't you find that is so often the case? You thought I would be a hag, but I'm not. I had thought you would look something like Colin, or perhaps MacDuff—you must know MacDuff, don't you?—but you don't. You are . . ." She stopped. *Pretty* wasn't a particularly politic thing for her to say. Nor was *graceful* or *elegant* or *quite lovely, really.*

"I am what?"

"You seem quite nice—a gentleman, despite your vicious words."

"I'm not at all nice."

"Did your sister resemble you?"

"Fiona? No, she was dark as a gypsy, but beautiful, aye, she was more beautiful than a sinner's dream, blue eyes the color of the loch in winter, and hair so black it was like the devil's own midnight. Why? You are jealous of a ghost?"

"I don't think so. But I am curious. You see, Aunt Arleth—that's Miss MacGregor—she says that Fiona fell in love with Malcolm and betrayed Colin, and that's why Colin killed her. I find that odd, since Colin is the most perfect man in the world. What woman could conceivably want another man, if he were her husband? Do you think it's possible?"

"Perfect man! He's a bastard, a murdering bastard! Damn you, Fiona loved only her bloody husband. She wanted only him from the time she was fifteen years old, no other, certainly not Malcolm, although he did want her. Our father pushed for Malcolm, since he would be the laird after his father's death, but she wouldn't hear of it. She nearly starved herself until our father gave in. She got Colin, but she wasn't happy for very long. All I remember now was that she was always accusing Colin of infidelity, she was so jealous of him. He couldn't look at another woman without Fiona shrieking at him, trying to claw his eyes out. He grew bored with her and her insane jealousy, even I understand that, but he had no right to rid himself of her. He had no right to hurl her over that damned cliff. And to claim that he had no memory of it. Absurd."

"This is all quite confusing, Mr. MacPherson. No one tells the same story. Also, I don't understand how Fiona could have possibly believed Colin to be unfaithful. He would never break his vows."

"What nonsense! Of course he broke his vows. He slept with women far and wide. Fiona was once filled with laughter and charm. Men couldn't keep their wits about them when she was near, and it pleased Colin's pride to have it so, but only at first. Her jealousy extended even to the servants at Vere Castle. That's when he bedded other women, to punish Fiona. But that doesn't mean he didn't also sleep with her. She would tell me how he'd take her in a frenzy, his need was so great for her. She was a witch, Fiona was, a jealous witch. Even while he despised her, he was filled with lust and desire for her. And she for him, more's the pity. But she's dead now, dead because he was tired of her and he found it expedient to kill her.

"I have had to wait for retribution because my father believed Colin innocent of the crime. But now he's an old man with an old man's failing wits. He still refuses to take action. His man tells me he sits and drools and dreams aloud of long-ago nights with his men, raiding the lowlands or fighting the Kinrosses. Ah, but it doesn't matter now, at least to me. I do as I please. Soon I will be laird.

"I've been watching Vere Castle for several days now. I know Colin is waiting for me in Edinburgh, waiting to confront me, perhaps even to try to kill me as he killed my sister. But I decided on another course. I came back here. At last you have come out alone. You will now come with me."

"Why?"

"You will be my prisoner, and thus Colin will be at my mercy. I will at last see justice done."

"I cannot tell you how difficult it is to take you seriously when you quote such atrocious lines."

He snarled with fury and raised his fist.

"I don't think so," Sinjun said, and quick as a streak of lightning, she slashed his face with her riding crop.

He yowled. His stallion, startled, reared back, unseating his rider. He fell off, landing on his side, but he was up in an instant.

Sinjun didn't wait to see what he would do. She forced Fanny to run straight at his stallion and, at the last moment, to swerve away. She grabbed the stallion's reins and pulled them over his head. She felt her arm nearly pulled from its socket as the stallion balked at being led, but finally he broke into a run, coming neck to neck with Fanny.

She heard Robert MacPherson yelling curses behind her. Unlike Douglas's stallion, Garth, this animal didn't respond at all to his master's voice. Thank God.

He was a very odd man, she thought.

13

SINJUN SAID NOTHING about her encounter with Robert MacPherson to anyone. Who was there to tell, anyway? She could just imagine what Aunt Arleth would say. Blessed hell, she would probably clap her hands and cheer Robert MacPherson on. She would probably drug her and have her delivered to MacPherson in a gunnysack.

She'd released his stallion close to the border of MacPherson land and slapped its rump. She hoped that MacPherson had a very long walk ahead of him.

Colin must be fetched immediately from Edinburgh. On the heels of that thought, she shook her head. What she needed to do was think, then act, quickly.

But, she thought, as she changed from her riding habit to a soft muslin gown of dark green, if Colin were here, what would he do? Hunt MacPherson down? Challenge him to a duel? MacPherson was a weasel, a very pretty weasel. He'd shown his true colors in Edinburgh, when he'd tried to shoot Colin and gotten Sinjun instead. She touched her cheek, remembering the shard of rock slicing into her. It had healed now with no scar, not that it mattered much. No, she couldn't take chances with Colin's life. She knew he would behave with honor; he was that kind of man. She doubted MacPherson had much of that attribute in any significant quantity. She would simply have to do away with MacPherson herself. Yes, gentlemen were too nice in their notions; they were bound by concepts of behavior that had no practical use when it came to the sticking point. She had to do something, and she would do something. She wanted Colin safe and home with her and the children. It wasn't likely that he could learn to care for her if he never came home.

She walked quickly up the stairs of the north tower to Colin's chamber. She wanted a gun and he had an adequate collection kept there. She would not ride out again from Vere Castle without one. The door stood partially open. Puzzled, she quietly pushed the door open more widely.

Philip stood in front of his father's gun collection, his hand lifted to pull free an old dueling pistol that Sinjun doubted could still be fired with safety.

"Philip," she said very quietly.

He jumped and whirled about, his face deathly white.

"Oh, it's just you," he said, and his shoulders slumped in relief. "What are you doing here in my papa's room?"

"I might ask you the same thing. Why do you want that dueling pistol, Philip?"

"It's none of your affair! Besides, you're a stupid girl and you wouldn't understand!"

She arched an eyebrow at him and said, "You think so, do you? Well, if you wish to test your beliefs, why don't the two of us go to the gardens and have a bit of a competition?"

"You can shoot a gun?"

"Naturally. I was raised by my brothers, you know. I am also a champion with a longbow. Are you?"

"I don't believe you."

"There is no reason for you not to. Once I shot a very bad man in his arm and quite saved the day."

He turned away from her then and she saw that he was wringing his hands.

It hit her hard when she realized what was wrong. The Virgin Bride had scared him, truly scared him, and it was her fault. She'd never before played the ghost with a child. She hadn't thought, hadn't imagined that it would so terrify him. She drew a deep breath, feeling so guilty she bit her lip.

"What's wrong, Philip?"

"Nothing."

"Did I tell you that Pearlin' Jane has visited me several times since I've been here?"

He started, his face flooding with color. "Silly ghost, she doesn't exist. You made it up because you're a girl and you get scared of anything."

"Boys aren't scared of ghosts?"

He looked on the verge of a faint. But his chin—his father's chin—went up and he gave her an excellent sneer. "Certainly not!"

"Do you remember me talking about the Virgin Bride—she is the ghost that lives at Northcliffe Hall?"

"Yes, but I didn't believe you."

"Well, you should. She is there, truly. However—" Sinjun drew a very deep breath. "However, she isn't here at Vere Castle. As far as I know she's never traveled, though I imagine she'd find Scotland charming."

Philip made a grab for the dueling pistol, but Sinjun jerked his arm away. "No, Philip, she isn't here. Come with me, I have something to show you."

He followed her, wariness stiffening every line of his body.

"This is my papa's bedchamber."

"I know. Come in."

Sinjun dismissed Emma, who was dusting the heavy armoire. She waited until Emma had left the room, then she opened the armoire doors and burrowed in one of the corners and opened a small bandbox.

"Here, Philip."

She brought out the long wig and the white gown.

She thought he was going to collapse, but he just turned paler and backed away.

"No, it's just a costume. I made the wig out of raw wool and goat hair. You and Dahling tried to frighten me with your Pearlin' Jane performance, which, I must tell you, was quite excellent. You scared me half to death that first time. I decided to have a bit of revenge. I visited you during the night, after your last ghostly visit to me."

He stared at her. "You were the ghost who patted me on the neck and told me to leave Sinjun alone?"

"Yes." She wanted to tell him she was very sorry for having frightened him so desperately, but she could just imagine how a proud boy would take that.

"Why does Papa call you Joan?"

That made her blink, then chuckle. "He thinks Sinjun sounds too much like a man's nickname, which it is, but it is also my name and I quite like it and am quite used to it. Would you like to call me Sinjun?"

"Yes, it doesn't sound like a silly girl or an—"

"An evil stepmother?"

He nodded, his eyes still riveted on the wig and white gown.

"How did you know that it was Dahling and me and not Pearlin' Jane?"

"The swamp ooze. By itself, it would have been quite terrifying, but with the chains and the moaning and the scurrying behind the wainscoting, it was overdone, if you know what I mean. Also, that next morning, just to be sure, I asked Dulcie and she told me that you'd gone out with Crocker and your direction was the Cowal Swamp."

"Oh."

"You don't need that dueling pistol, Philip."

"If I did, I could use it, and I could beat you at any competition."

Little boys, she thought, marveling at him, were indeed splendid. Little boys became men who didn't seem to change at all in this regard. "Do you fence?"

That took him aback. "No, Papa hasn't yet taught me."

"Well, there is something both of us could learn together, then. MacDuff said that he would be coming back soon for a visit. If your papa isn't yet returned, perhaps he could give us a lesson."

"You can really shoot a crossbow?"

"Yes."

"There's an old armory up in the south tower. There are all sorts of weapons there, including crossbows and swords. Crocker keeps them up. It's his hobby."

"Would you like to learn to shoot a crossbow?"

He nodded slowly, his eyes going to that white wig and floaty gown. "I think Sinjun is all right. Joan sounds like a cocker spaniel."

"My sentiments exactly."

MacDuff arrived the following afternoon to find Sinjun and Philip in the apple orchard with crossbows two hundred years old and in perfect condition. Crocker was sitting on a fence whittling new arrows, his mongrel George II at his feet.

At the sight of the huge MacDuff, George II bounded up and barked maniacally.

"George, old boy, down!"

For a dog named after a king, he was singularly obedient. He sank back down at his master's feet and rested his head on his paws, his tail wagging as frantically as a flag in a strong wind.

Sinjun heard the dog bark but she didn't turn around. "Now, Philip, that's excellent form. That's right, right under your nose and keep your left arm perfectly straight and still. Yes, that's it."

The target was a straw-stuffed scarecrow that Sinjun had borrowed from the wheat field. It was only twenty paces distant.

"Now, very easy . . . that's it, easy."

He released the arrow and it sped toward the scarecrow, striking it squarely in the groin.

MacDuff yowled in feigned pain.

"Good shot," Sinjun said, and turned to face her cousin-in-law. "MacDuff! Goodness, it's about time you came back to visit. Your timing is quite perfect. Do you shoot?"

"Oh no, Sinjun, not me. I've never had to. I'm far too big and too ugly for any man or any three men to try to take me on." He held up a meaty fist and shook it at her. "This is all the protection I need, at least bullies think so."

"You're right," Sinjun said. "Did you see Philip's shot?"

"I certainly did. Where did you learn, Philip?"

"Sinjun," the boy said. "She's quite good. Show him, Sinjun."

She did, deftly targeting the scarecrow and releasing the arrow quickly, with no fuss. It struck the scarecrow right through the neck, the arrow coming out six inches through the back.

"My God," MacDuff said. "That was excellent. Your brothers taught you?"

"Oh yes, but they have no idea that I can now outshoot them. Perhaps they do but it would never occur to them to admit it."

"You're wise not to tell them," MacDuff advised. "They would be crushed, their male pride stomped underground."

"Men," Sinjun said. "What does it matter?"

"I don't know, but it does."

"Philip, why don't you tell Aunt Arleth that MacDuff is here. You will stay some time with us?"

"A couple of days only. I'm on my way to Edinburgh and just wanted to see if there was anything you needed."

Yes, I need my husband, she wanted to say, but said instead, "You were staying here in the neighborhood?"

"I have friends, the Ashcrofts, who live near Kinross."

"Well, I'm glad you're here, for even so short a time."

MacDuff merely nodded, watching Philip race back to the castle. He said, wearing a small smile, "I see you have quite won over Philip. How goes Dahling?"

"Ah, she's a tough little nut, but I believe I've found her weakness."

"She's only four and a half years old, Sinjun, and she already has a weakness?"

"Oh yes, she's quite horse mad. I took her out to see my mare, Fanny, and I thought she would burst the seams of her gown. It was love at first sight. I haven't yet let her ride Fanny. But when I do, that should quite drop her into my net."

"You're dangerous, Sinjun. So all goes well, then."

"I suppose all goes. How well or not is a matter of the time of day and the mood of the inmates here."

They walked together to the castle, Sinjun stopping every so often and frowning.

"What is the matter?"

"Oh, I'm just making a mental list of things that still need to be done. It's endless, really. The chickens need a new roof on their house, and the fencing there needs mending. I imagine we've lost many hens due to that. Ah, there's so much. Let me show you the new garden. Cook is all atwitter about it and the scullery maid, Jillie, is sheer magic with plants. She is now only a scullery maid half of the time and a gardener the other half. Cook is happy, Jillie is radiant, and our meals are better by the day. All that remains is talking Cook into trying her hand at some English dishes."

"Good luck to you," MacDuff said, and laughed. He admired the garden, still stubby green sprouts just showing above rich dark earth. "Colin isn't happy," he said suddenly, coming to a halt near the cistern. He leaned his elbows on the worn stones and looked down.

"It's very deep," Sinjun said. "The water is sweet."

"Yes, I remember that it is. I see that you've put a new chain and that's a new bucket."

"Yes. Why isn't Colin happy?"

MacDuff lowered the bucket, letting it down slowly, listening closely until it finally hit the water. He raised it and took the wooden mug hanging from a hook and dipped it into the bucket. He drank.

"As good as I remember," he said, and wiped his mouth with the back of his hand.

"Why isn't Colin happy?"

"I believe he feels guilty."

"He should. I'm here and he's not and there is another thing—Robert MacPherson . . ." She broke off, wanting to kick herself. Colin would come riding home *ventre à terre* to protect her. MacPherson wouldn't care how he got to Colin and with Colin here, there were too many possibilities, including the safety of the children. No, she would have to deal with MacPherson. There was no other way as far as she could see, and she'd thought about it very hard, listing out pros and cons as Douglas had taught her to do when faced with any problem.

"What do you mean about MacPherson?"

She shrugged, looking guileless as a nun. "I just wondered what Colin was doing about the man."

"Nothing. He's gone to ground. Colin visits the old laird, and he's learned that Robert's been going behind his back with his people, trying to get the power. Distressing, but true. Colin's in a bit of a bind because, truth be told, he likes the old laird, despite Robert and Fiona."

"He will figure it out," she said shortly, looking out over the barley rows to the east. "It hasn't rained in three days. We need it."

"It will rain, it always does. This is paradise for growing. Colin is truly blessed with all the arable land. Here on the Fife Peninsula there are usually mild temperatures and ample rain. Much of Scotland is barren crags and empty moors and savage hills. Yes, Colin is very lucky to have Vere Castle. His ancestors, naturally, were lucky to be here and not in the Highlands or the borderlands."

"I doubt the first Kinrosses had their pick of where they wished to be in Scotland. Who are these Ashcrofts, MacDuff?"

He smiled. "Friends of my parents. It was a long-overdue visit."

"We're long overdue as well. I'm glad you're here."

"I wish to see all that you've done. Incidentally, what does Colin think of all your improvements?"

"Not much."

"I hope he hasn't hurt your feelings."

"He has. I fancy you know that."

"Perhaps. Try to understand, Sinjun. Since he was a little boy, Colin usually lost those things that were his. He learned secrecy. He learned to guard what was his. But even then he wasn't always successful. He was the second son, you see, and as such, anything that was his that his brother Malcolm wanted, why, it was taken away from him. I remember he had this small stash of items, nothing valuable, you understand, just things that were his and were important to him, things he didn't want taken away from him, and Malcolm would have, I never doubted it. Anything that was Colin's he wanted. Colin hid them in this small carved box in the trunk of an oak tree. He would go to the oak tree only when he knew Malcolm was somewhere else.

"Perhaps that explains why he still wishes to keep the doing of things here at Vere Castle to himself. You see, everything is now his and what is his, he protects. He guards jealously."

"I see," Sinjun said, but she didn't, not really. It made no sense. He was no longer a boy, he was a man.

"It has sorely chafed him that there was no money to bring the castle back into its former splendor. You have made a very big difference, Sinjun."

"Why does Aunt Arleth hate him so?"

"She's a strange old witch. The workings of her mind have eluded any meaningful analysis. Malcolm was her favorite, I don't know why. Perhaps because he'd be the future laird and she wanted him to look at her with lasting respect and affection. She treated Colin like he was a gypsy's get, of no importance at all. I remember she told Malcolm about Colin's love of poetry—he got that from his mother—and Malcolm told his father that he also loved poetry and he wanted Colin's book. He got it."

"But that wasn't fair!"

"Perhaps not, but the laird saw the Kinross future as being in Malcolm's hands, thus Malcolm wasn't thwarted in anything he wanted. It ruined his character. Naturally Aunt Arleth hated her sister for the simple reason that she wanted the earl for herself. The word is that she got him after her sister died, but only in her bed, not at the altar. Odd how life goes, isn't it?"

Sinjun shivered, not because wispy gray clouds had moved to block the afternoon sun, but because she'd never seen such behavior in her family. Her mother had always been a trial, but it hadn't mattered. It was even amusing now that she could think about it from a goodly distance and not have to live with it.

"But now Colin is the laird. He's a good man and I daresay he's found himself an excellent wife."

"That's true," she said, voice tart. "It's just a pity that he isn't here to enjoy his good fortune."

What to do?

Sinjun chewed over all alternatives she could think of during the next two days, always changing and honing down her list of pros and cons. There was no word from Colin. MacDuff was helpful and kind. He consented to give both her and Philip fencing lessons and both of them proved adept with foils. He complimented her continually on the state of the house, and her reply was only that soap and water were not expensive.

"Aye," he said, "but it takes fortitude to hold out against Aunt Arleth and all her plaints."

She herself studied Colin's gun collection, finally selecting a small pocket pistol with a silver butt cap and a double barrel, not more than fifteen years old, that would hide itself in the skirt pocket of her riding habit.

Now she had to rid herself of MacDuff and be available for Robert MacPherson to come upon. She'd decided on making herself bait. It was the cleanest, most straightforward way of getting him. She didn't doubt for a moment that he or one of his minions was watching Vere Castle. For that reason, she kept both Philip and Dahling close. They were never alone, and if they wondered at her firm stricture, they didn't voice it.

It was at breakfast the morning of MacDuff's departure that Dahling swallowed her porridge and said, "I've decided that you aren't ugly, Sinjun."

MacDuff stared at the little girl but Sinjun only laughed and said, "My thanks, Dahling. I have nearly broken my mirror in my anxiety."

"May I ride Fanny?"

"Ah, I understand now. The child is attempting a stratagem," MacDuff said.

"Would I be ugly again if I said no?"

Dahling looked undecided, but finally shook her small head. "No, you just wouldn't be a Great Beauty, like I will be."

"Well, in that case, why don't we compromise? I'll set you in front of me and we'll both ride Fanny."

The little girl beamed at that, and Sinjun, knowing quite well that the child had gotten exactly what she wanted, didn't mind a bit.

"So both children call you Sinjun now."

"Yes."

"I daresay that Colin will have to come around. Is there any message you wish me to deliver to him?"

Now she realized that she didn't want him around, not until she'd dealt with MacPherson, and only the good Lord knew how long that would take. She said only, "Tell him that the children and I miss him and that all goes well here. Oh yes, MacDuff. Tell him that I would never steal that box of his in the oak tree trunk."

MacDuff leaned down from his great height and lightly kissed her cheek. "I don't believe Colin has read any poetry since Malcolm took his book."

"I will think about that."

"Good-bye, Sinjun."

Sinjun marveled that MacDuff's horse, a hard-jawed hacker a good eighteen hands high, didn't groan when he swung onto his back. Indeed, the stallion even managed to rear on his hind legs. She remained on the deeply indented front stone steps until he was gone from her sight.

Now, she thought, now it was time to act.

But it was Philip who prevented her. He begged and begged to show her the Cowal Swamp. He even promised her, in a voice that offered a great treat, to let her bring some of the swamp ooze back for her own uses. And that, she thought, wondering how Aunt Arleth would react, convinced her.

Crocker accompanied them, and Sinjun noted that he was well armed, despite the fact there'd been no further violence. She wondered if Colin had told him to arm himself. Very likely. Crocker had said the MacPherson name but once, and he'd spat after he'd said it.

It was a good hour through some of the most beautifully savage moors Sinjun could have imagined. Then, quite suddenly, there was a peat bog that deepened and thickened into a sluggishly repellent swamp, with rotting vegetation hanging into the mucky shallow waters.

Crocker gave her a history that included any moving lumps that one could see rippling beneath the surface of the water. Sinjun wouldn't have placed a single toe into that swamp had her life depended on it. The odor was nasty, like sulfur and outhouses that hadn't been limed, both mixed together. It was hotter here, which seemed curious, but it was so. Hot and wet and smelly. Insects buzzed about, dining off the newcomers, until finally Sinjun called a halt. She swatted at a huge mosquito and said, "Enough, Crocker! Let's fill our buckets and leave this odious place."

It rained all the way back to Vere Castle, thick, sheeting rain that turned the afternoon to night very quickly. The temperature dropped dramatically. Sinjun took off her riding jacket and wrapped it around a shivering Philip. As for Crocker, his single cotton shirt was plastered to his stocky body.

Sinjun fretted about both of them, seeing to it that Crocker bathed in front of the fire in the kitchen and Philip in his bedchamber. He appeared to be fine at bedtime.

The following morning Dahling climbed onto Sinjun's bed, ready to ride Fanny.

"It's late, Sinjun. Come along, I'm all dressed."

Sinjun opened an eye and stared with blurry vision at the small girl sitting beside her.

"It's very late," Dahling said again.

"How late?" Her voice came out a croak, hoarse and raw. Sinjun blinked to clear her vision. A shaft of pain over her eyes nearly knocked her senseless. "Oh," she moaned and fell back against her pillow. "Oh no, Dahling, I'm ill. Don't come any closer."

But Dahling was leaning forward, her small palm on Sinjun's cheek. "You're hot, Sinjun, very hot."

A fever. It was all she needed to go with the pain in her head. She had to get up and get dressed. She had to see Philip and make her plans to get MacPherson, she had to . . . .

She tried but couldn't make it. She was too weak. Every muscle, every fiber of bone and sinew and muscle ached horribly. Dahling, worried now, climbed off the bed. "I'll go get Dulcie. She'll know what to do."

But it wasn't Dulcie who came into the laird's bedchamber some ten minutes later; it was Aunt Arleth.

"Well, felled at last."

Sinjun managed to open her eyes. "Yes, it appears so."

"You sound like a frog. Crocker and Philip are quite well. I suppose one would expect an English miss to be the one to become ill."

"Yes. I should like some water, please."

"Thirsty, are you? Well, I'm not your servant. I'll have Emma fetched."

She left without a backward look or another word. Sinjun waited, her throat so sore that it hurt to breathe. Finally she fell into an uneasy sleep.

When she awoke Serena was standing beside her bed.

"Water, please."

"Certainly." Serena turned and left and Sinjun wanted to cry. Oh God, what was she going to do?

Unlike Aunt Arleth, Serena returned with a carafe of water and several glasses. She filled a glass and put it to Sinjun's lips.

"Drink slowly, now," she said, her voice soft and crooning. "Goodness but you don't look at all well. Your face is quite pale and your hair a ragged mess. Your nightgown looks sweaty. No, you don't look well at all. It came on you so quickly, too."

Sinjun didn't care if she looked like a goat. She drank and drank and drank. When she didn't want any more, she lay back, panting with the effort it had cost her.

"I can't get up, Serena."

"No, I can see that you are quite ill."

"Is there a physician nearby?"

"Oh yes, but he's old and infirm. He doesn't visit just anyone."

"Have him come here at once, Serena."

"I will speak to Aunt Arleth about it, Joan." And she left, floating out of the bedchamber in a rich silk gown of deep crimson that was so long it trailed the floor behind her like a train. Sinjun tried to call after her, but her voice came out a whisper.

"We haven't the money to pay any doctor."

It was Aunt Arleth. Sinjun felt light-headed now. It was difficult for her to focus on the woman. It was late afternoon, according to the clock that stood near the bed. She was thirsty again, terribly hungry, and she had to relieve herself.

"Fetch Emma or Dulcie for me."

"Oh no, Dulcie is quite occupied with the children. Goodness, it's so very warm in here, isn't it? You must needs have some fresh air."

Aunt Arleth shoved open the windows and tied back the pale gold brocade draperies. "There, that should cool your fever. Do get better, my dear girl. I will look in on you later."

She was gone again. Sinjun was alone. The room was getting colder by the minute.

She managed to relieve herself through sheer effort of will, and stumbled back into bed. She burrowed under the covers, her teeth chattering.

The following morning, Philip slipped into the room. He ran to the bed and looked at Sinjun. She was asleep, but she was also shivering. He put his palm on her forehead and jerked it back. She was burning with fever.

He realized then that it was very cold in the room. The windows were open. Aunt Arleth, he thought. He'd known she'd come to see Sinjun, for she'd told the rest of them that she had, and that Sinjun was very nearly well. She was still lying abed because she was English and thus slothful, enjoying ordering everyone about. She'd meant mischief, that was clear. His mind balked at pursuing that thought.

Philip closed the windows and untied the draperies. He fetched more blankets from his own bedchamber and piled them on top of his stepmother.

"Thirsty," Sinjun whispered.

He held her head in the crook of his elbow and put the edge of the glass to her lips. She was so weak her head lolled against his arm. He felt a shaft of fear.

"You're not better," he said, and Sinjun dimly heard the fear in his voice.

"No. I'm glad you're here, Philip. You're here . . . I've missed you. Help me, Philip." Her voice trailed off and he knew that she was more unconscious than asleep this time.

Aunt Arleth had told them all to stay away from the laird's bedchamber. She didn't want any of them catching their stepmother's slight cold. She'd assured them that all was well, that their stepmother didn't want them to come see her.

It was more than a cold. Aunt Arleth had lied. Sinjun was very ill.

He stood there, staring down at her, wondering what to do.

"You disobedient little boy! Come out of here now! Do you hear me, Philip? Come here!"

Philip turned to face Aunt Arleth, who stood ramrod straight in the open doorway.

"Sinjun is very ill. You were wrong about her condition. She must have help."

"I've been giving her help. Has she said anything? If so, she's only trying to gain your sympathy, to turn you against me. You see? I'm here yet again to help her, you silly child. I don't want you to be near her, you might sicken as well."

"You said she was just lying about because she was lazy. How could I get sick from laziness?"

"She still has just a touch of fever, nothing much, but it is my responsibility in your father's absence to see that you're well taken care of. That means seeing to it that you don't become ill."

"Sinjun was taking care of both Dahling and me very well."

"She's a shallow chit, thoughtless and clearly negligent, or she never would have gone to that wretched swamp with you. Surely you see that she was just playing at being responsible. She cares naught for either you or Dahling. She cares naught for any of us. She merely enjoys telling us all what to do and flinging her wealth in our faces. Oh yes, she sees all of us as mere poor relations she must tolerate. Why do you think that your dear father isn't here in his own home? It's because of her; he can't bear her company because she rubs his nose in his own poverty and lords it over him. She doesn't belong here, she's a Sassenach. Come away now, Philip. I shan't tell you again."

"The windows were open, Aunt."

"Oh, for heaven's sake! She ordered me to open them. I told her it wasn't wise, but she just kept fretting and whining until finally I simply obliged her."

She was lying, he knew it, and he was suddenly very frightened. He didn't know what to do. He looked back at Sinjun and knew deep down that if something wasn't done she would die.

"Come away from her, Philip."

Slowly, he walked toward Aunt Arleth. He even nodded as he came up to her. He knew exactly what he was going to do.

He turned to watch Aunt Arleth place her hand on Sinjun's forehead and nod. "Ah yes, I knew it. Hardly any fever at all now. No need for a doctor."

Philip left the bedchamber.

14

Northcliffe Hall
Near New Romney, England

ALEXANDRA SHERBROOKE, the countess of Northcliffe, was napping in the middle of a warm Wednesday afternoon. She was permitted this indulgence, her mother-in-law had assured her, even going so far as to pat her cheek with what could be termed affection, because she was carrying another child for Douglas—as if she were some sort of vessel for her husband's use, Alex had thought, but nonetheless had slipped off her gown and fallen quite easily to sleep.

She dreamed of Melissande, her incredibly beautiful sister, who had just borne a little girl who greatly resembled Alex, even endowed with Titian hair and gray eyes. It was justice, Douglas had told her, since their own twin boys were the very image of the glorious Melissande, a happenstance that still made Tony Parrish, Melissande's husband, grin like a smug bastard at Douglas. But in her dream something was wrong with Melissande. She was lying motionless on her back, her beautiful black hair spread like a silk fan against the white of the pillows. Her face was pale, faint blue shadows showing beneath her skin, and her breath was hoarse and low.

Suddenly, her hair wasn't black, it was chestnut, and drawn into a long thick braid. It wasn't Melissande's face now, either. No, it was Sinjun's.

Alex blinked, dragging herself from sleep. What a strange dream, she thought, as she closed her eyes again. She'd just written to her sister-in-law, so that was perhaps why she'd taken Melissande's place in her dream.

Alex quieted. Gently and easily, she dozed, but this time there wasn't a dream awaiting her, there was a soft voice, a woman's low voice, and it was near her ear, saying over and over, "Sinjun is ill . . . Sinjun is ill. She is in trouble. Help her, you must help her."

Alex frowned, then moaned. She awoke with a jerk. There beside her bed stood the Virgin Bride, calm and still, her white gown gently shimmering in the silent bedchamber, and she spoke again, but the words were in Alex's mind, not coming from the ghost's mouth, soft and quiet, but insistent. "Sinjun is ill . . . in trouble. Help her, help her."

"What's wrong? Please, tell me, what's wrong with Sinjun?"

"Help her," the soft voice said, pleading now. The beautiful young woman was clasping her hands in front of her. Odd how her fingers were long and so very slender, yet they seemed to be clear, the bones showing through as dark shadows. Her exquisite long hair was so blond that it shone nearly white in the afternoon sunlight. "Help her. There is much trouble for her."

"Yes, I will," Alex said, and rolled off the side of the bed to her feet. She saw the ghost nod, then gently retreat toward the corner of the countess's bedchamber. Alex watched her simply fade into a pale reflection of herself, lighter and lighter, until there was nothing there. Nothing at all.

Alex drew a deep breath. The ghost hadn't come to her in months and months, and the last time the ghost had smiled and told her that Farmer Elias's cow had survived the colic and could now give milk to the ailing baby in the house. And she'd been here when Alex had needed her, when she'd been screaming in labor with the twins, so torn with the agony that she didn't believe she would live through it. The Virgin Bride had come to her then and told her that she would be all right and she wasn't to doubt it for a moment. Alex would have sworn that a soft hand had touched her forehead, then her belly, and the pain had lessened. Of course, Douglas informed her that she'd simply been delirious. She never should have told him. He was so stubborn about it, and she knew why. Men couldn't bear to accept something they couldn't understand, something they couldn't grasp by the throat and look at and speak to and throttle if they didn't like it. The Virgin Bride couldn't be explained, thus she couldn't exist.

And now she'd come again to tell her that Sinjun was in trouble and ill.

Alex felt a slight spasm of dizziness but it passed quickly. Her heart was pounding hard and she stopped, drawing deep breaths.

Douglas wasn't here. He'd had to return to London to meet with Lord Avery at the Foreign Office several days before.

Well, he would be of no use in any case. If she told him what the Virgin Bride had said, he'd sneer and laugh and be an ass about it. No, it was a good thing that he wasn't here because she knew that he wouldn't allow her to take any action—he'd gone so far as to swear her to near complete inaction during his absence—and she knew she had to.

Alex informed her household that she was going for a visit to her brother and sister-in-law in the Cotswolds. Hollis, their butler, stared at her as if she'd lost her wits instead of her breakfast, but her mother-in-law seemed overly pleased to see the back of her for a while.

Sophie had received her own visits from the Virgin Bride over the past five years. Together they would figure out what to do.

Vere Castle

Philip crept out of the castle at ten o'clock that night. He wasn't scared, not so much that he couldn't think, anyway. Any fear he did feel was overcome by his worry for Sinjun.

He made the stables without a single bark from George II, whom he saw just in time to scratch behind his mangy ears before the dog could howl the house down.

Philip didn't pause in the stables. The lads were asleep in their chambers off the tack room. He saddled his pony, Bracken, and quickly led him well down the drive before mounting.

He had a long ride ahead of him, but he was determined. He just prayed that he would be in time.

He'd wanted to tell Dulcie what he was going to do, but he knew deep down that she wouldn't be able to keep her mouth shut. He told her instead, as he was yawning deeply, all ready for his bed, to please look in on his stepmother, and give her water to drink and keep her covered with as many blankets as she could find.

Dulcie had promised. He prayed as he sent his pony into a gallop that Aunt Arleth wouldn't come upon Dulcie and dismiss her, or worse, hurt her.

There was a half-moon overhead and the dark rain clouds of the past three days had disappeared, replaced by soft white ones that did little to obscure the moon or stars. He could see quite well enough.

When he heard hoofbeats behind him, Philip thought his heart would burst through his chest. He quickly guided Bracken into the thick brush beside the road and clamped his fingers over the pony's nostrils to keep him from whinnying.

There were three men riding toward him. When they neared he heard them speaking clearly.

"Aye, 'tis a wee-witted lassie she be, but I'll hae her non' the less."

"Nay, she be fer me, ye louthead, her father promised me an' th' laird is fer th' banns."

A third man laughed aloud, a smug, triumphant laugh. He spat and said, "Well, yer both off the mark, ye are. Dinna ye ken, I already bedded wi' her, she's all mine. I'll tell th' laird, an' 'tis done. I'll tell ye something else, lads, her tits bain't be wee."

There were howls and yells and curses, and the horses were whinnying and plowing into each other. Philip stayed still as a stone, waiting, praying that the strongest of the men would get the wee lassie and the other two would go to the devil.

The fight lasted another ten minutes. Finally, Philip heard a loud curse and then the loud report of a gun. Oh God, he thought, swallowing so hard he nearly choked himself.

There was a yell, followed by a profound silence.

"Ye kilt Dingle, ye fool."

"Aye, he bedded wi' her, he deserved t' croak it."

The other man groaned, then shouted, "An' wot if she's got his seed 'n her belly? Yer a stupid sod, Alfie, MacPherson'll have our guts fer his breakfast."

"We'll nae say a word. 'Tis a bloody Kinross wot kilt him. Away, then! Away!"

They left the third man there. Philip stood irresolute. Then he left Bracken tied to a yew bush and quietly made his way back to the road. The man was sprawled on his back, his arms and legs spread wide. There was a huge red stain covering his chest. His eyes were wide with surprise, his teeth still bared in a snarl. He was quite dead.

Philip threw up. Then he ran back to Bracken and sent him back onto the road.

He'd recognized the man. It was a bully whose name was Dingle, and he was one of the MacPhersons' meanest fighters.

His father had pointed him out once to Philip on a visit to Culross Palace, telling him that the fellow was a cretin and an excellent example of the caliber of MacPherson's men.

Philip rode until Bracken was winded and blowing hard. He fell asleep astride his mare. It was Bracken who nudged him awake. Philip, not knowing how much time had passed, panicked. But his pony couldn't sustain a steady gallop and he was forced to slow. He saw more men and several peasant women. What they were doing up and about in the middle of the night would remain a mystery. He avoided them, though he heard one of the men shouting after him.

He was on the ferry to Edinburgh at four o'clock in the morning, paying the ferryman every shilling he had taken from his father's strongbox save one. He nestled down between two bags of grain for warmth. He reached his father's house in Abbotsford Crescent just past six o'clock in the morning. It had taken him a good hour to find the house, and he'd nearly been in tears when, finally, he'd spotted it.

Angus opened the door, yawning deeply as he did so, and stared down at the boy, mouth still agape.

"Oh och, 'tis ye, th' young master! By gawd, bain't this be a treat fer th' laird. Who be wi' ye, laddie?"

"Quickly, my father, Angus. I must see my father." While Angus was gaping at him, trying to gather his wits together, Philip ducked around him and raced up the stairs. He didn't stop running until he reached the laird's bedchamber and flung open the doors, banging them loudly against the walls.

Colin came awake in an instant and bolted upright in bed. "Good God, Philip! What the devil are you doing here?"

"Papa, quickly, you must come home. It's Sinjun; she's very sick."

"Sinjun," Colin said blankly.

"Your wife, Papa, your *wife*. Quickly, come now." Philip was pulling back the covers, so frightened and relieved that he'd found his father that he was shaking with it.

"Joan is ill?"

"Not Joan, Papa, Sinjun. Please hurry. Aunt Arleth will let her die, I know it."

"Blessed hell, I don't believe this! Who came with you? What the devil happened?" But even as he spoke, Colin flung off the covers and jumped off the bed, naked and cold in the gray light of dawn.

"Speak to me, Philip!"

Philip watched his father pull on clothes, watched him splash water on his face, watched him wave Angus away when the old man appeared in the doorway.

He told him about the Cowal Swamp and the rain on the ride back to the castle and how Sinjun had taken off her riding coat and made him wear it. He told him about the cold room and the open windows and the lies Aunt Arleth had told them. He stopped then, stared with frightened eyes at his father, and started to cry, low deep sobs that brought Colin to his son instantly. He enfolded him in his arms and hugged him close. "It will be all right, Philip, you'll see. You've done very well indeed. We'll be home soon and Joan will be all right."

"Her name is Sinjun."

Colin forced his exhausted son to eat some hastily prepared porridge. Within a half hour, they were on horseback and off. He'd suggested that his son remain here because he was so weary, but Philip wouldn't hear of it. "I must see that she's all right," he said, and in that moment Colin saw the future man in the boy, and he was pleased.

Sinjun felt strangely peaceful. She was also incredibly tired, so very weary that she just wanted to sleep and sleep, perhaps forever. There was no more pain, just this sweet desire to release her mind from herself, to give in to the gentle lassitude that tugged persistently at her. She moaned softly, the sound of her voice odd in her ears, far away really, as if that sound came from someone else. Tired, she was so very tired. How could she be so tired and not sleep? Then she heard a man's voice, echoing in her head as if it came from a great distance, and wondered if it was her own voice she was hearing and if it was, why she was speaking. Surely there was no need to speak, not now, not forever. No, his voice was strong, deep, impatient, and commanding, surely a man's voice, a man who wasn't pleased about something. She'd heard that tone of voice enough times in her life from her brothers. But it wasn't Douglas or Ryder. It couldn't be. Now the man was speaking more closely to her, next to her ear, but she couldn't understand his words. They weren't important, surely not. She heard another man speaking as well, but his voice was old, softer, blurring at the edges of her mind, not intruding, bumping gently against her consciousness, then rolling away, harmless and indistinct.

The hard man's voice was retreating, at last. Soon she would be free of it. It was gone now and her head lolled to the side, her mind eased. She felt her breath slow and slow yet more.

"Damn you, wake up! I won't tell you again, Sinjun, wake up! You shan't give up like this. Wake up, you damned twit!"

The shouting brought her back with a lurch of pain. Douglas shouted like that but she knew it wasn't Douglas. No, he was far away. She felt as if she were teetering on the edge of something that was very close to her but still unseen; she was drawn to it, yet still wary of it. It was strangely seductive.

The man's voice came again, a loud, horribly grating voice that made her brain pound. She hated it, she wanted to scream at him to be quiet. She stepped back from the edge, so angry at the interference that she even opened her eyes, wanting to protest, to yell at the man. She opened her mouth but didn't make a sound. She was looking up at the most beautiful man she'd ever seen in her life. Her mind absorbed his image, his black hair and incredible dark blue eyes, and that cleft in his chin, and she managed to say in a raw whisper, "You are so beautiful," then she closed her eyes again, for she knew he must be an angel and she was here in heaven, and she wasn't alone, and for that she was grateful.

"Damn you, open your eyes! I'm not beautiful, you little twit. Good God, I haven't even shaved!"

"An angel doesn't curse," she said clearly, and once again forced her eyes open.

"I'm not an angel, I'm your bloody husband! Wake up, Sinjun, and do it now! I won't have any more of your lazing about! No more dramatics, do you hear me? Wake up, damn your Sherbrooke eyes. Come back to me and do it now, else I'll beat you."

"Bloody husband," she repeated slowly. "No, you're right, I must come back. I can't let Colin die. I don't want him to die, not ever. He has to be saved, and I'm the only one to do it. He's too honorable to save himself. He isn't ruthless and only I can save him."

"Then don't leave me! You can't save me if you die, you understand me?"

"Yes," she said, "I understand."

"Good. Now, I'm going to pick you up and I want you to drink. All right?"

She managed a nod. She felt a strong arm beneath her back and felt the cold glass touch her lips. She drank and drank and the water was ambrosia. It ran down her chin, soaking into her nightgown, but she was so very thirsty nothing mattered but the sweet water trickling down her throat.

"There, enough for now. Listen to me. I'm going to bathe you and get that fever down. Do you understand me? Your fever's too high and I've got to get it down. But you won't sleep again, do you understand me? Tell me you understand!"

She did, but then it escaped her. Her brain tripped off in another direction when she heard a woman's shrill voice say, "She worsened suddenly. I was just on the point of fetching that old fool Childress when you came, Colin. It isn't my fault she got sicker. She was nearly well before."

Sinjun moaned because she was afraid. She tried to pull away from that woman, tried to curl up in a ball and hide from her. The beautiful man who wasn't an angel said in a very calm voice, "Leave, Arleth. I don't want you inside this room again. Go now."

"She'll lie to you, the little bitch! I've known you all your life. You can't take her side against me!"

She heard his voice come again, but he was pulling away from her.

Then there was blessed silence. She suddenly felt a cool wet cloth on her face and she tried to lean upward to bury her face in it, but there was his voice again, this time soothing and so gentle, telling her to lie still, that he would see to it that she felt better. "Trust me," he said, "trust me." And she did. He would keep the woman away from her.

She heard the other man, the one with the old voice, the soft voice, saying, "Keep that up, my lord. Wipe her down until the fever lessens. Every several hours, make her drink as much as she'll take."

She felt the cool air touch her skin. She vaguely realized that someone was taking off the sweaty nightgown, and she was thankful for it, for quite suddenly she felt the itchiness of her skin. She felt the wet cloth wipe over her breasts and ribs. But it didn't go deep enough. She was still so very hot, deeper inside, and the wonderful cold of the cloth didn't reach it. She tried to arch her back to bring the cloth closer.

She felt a man's hands on her arms, pushing her back down, and he was saying quietly now, that beautiful man, "Hush, I know it burns. I had a very bad fever once, as you well know, and I felt as if I were in flames on the inside, where nothing could reach, and I was burning from the inside out."

"Yes," she said.

"I'll keep doing this until that burning is gone, I promise you."

"Colin," she said, and she opened her eyes and smiled at him. "You're not an angel. You're my bloody husband. I'm so glad you're here."

"Yes," he said, and felt something powerful move inside him. "I won't leave you again, no matter what."

It seemed then she must make him understand. She tried to lift her hand to touch his face, to gain his attention, and her voice was hurtling from her throat, the words raw and ugly. "You must leave, it's safer for you. I didn't want you to come back until I'd taken care of him. He's a weasel and he would hurt you. I must protect you."

That made Colin frown. What the devil was she talking about? Who, for God's sake? She closed her eyes again and he continued to wipe her down, from her face to her toes. When he turned her onto her stomach, she moaned softly, then sprawled boneless on the sheets.

He continued rubbing her with the damp cloth until she was cool to the touch. He closed his eyes for a moment, praying for her and praying for himself, that God would find him ample enough in grace to listen to him. Finally the fever was down. "Please, God, please let her be all right," he said aloud in the silent bedchamber, a litany now.

He covered her when he heard the bedchamber door open.

"My lord?"

It was the physician. Colin turned, saying, "The fever is down."

"Excellent. It will rise again, doubtless, but you will handle it. Your son is sleeping on the floor outside the door. Your daughter is sitting beside him, sucking on her thumb and looking very worried."

"As soon as I've put my wife in a nightgown, I will see to my children. Thank you, Childress. Will you remain here at the castle?"

"Yes, my lord. If she will survive, we'll know by tomorrow."

"She will survive. She's tough. You will see. Besides, she has a powerful incentive—she's got to protect me."

And he laughed.

Sinjun heard the woman's voice and she knew deep sudden fear. She was afraid to move, afraid to open her eyes. The voice was vicious and mean.

It was Aunt Arleth.

"So you're not dead yet, you little slut. Well, we'll just have to see about that, won't we? No, no use you struggling, you're weak as a gnat. Your precious husband, the young fool, left you. Aye, left you to my tender mercies, and you'll get them, my girl, oh aye, you'll get them."

"Aunt Arleth," Sinjun said as she opened her eyes. "Why do you want me dead?"

Aunt Arleth continued speaking, her voice softer now, running on and on, the words melting together. "I must move quickly, quickly. He'll be back, doubt it not, the young fool. He doesn't want you, how could he? You're a Sassenach, not one of us. Aye, perhaps I must needs place this lovely soft pillow over your face. Yes, that will do it. That will send you away from here. No, you don't belong here, you're an outsider, a no-account. Yes, the pillow. No, that's too obvious. I must be more cunning. But I must act, else you might live to spite me. Aye, you'd make my life even more a misery, wouldn't you? I know your sort—vicious and mean and not to be trusted. Aye, and pushy, treating us all like worthless savages and taking over. I must do something or we're all lost. Even now you're planning to send me away."

"Aunt Arleth, why are you in here?"

She whirled about to see Philip standing in the open doorway, his hands fisted on his hips. "Papa told you to stay away from here. Get away from her, Aunt."

"Ah, you wretched little giblet. You ruined everything. You're a disgrace to me, Philip. I'm taking care of her. Why else would I be here? Go away, boy, just go away. You can go fetch your papa. Yes, go get the bloody laird."

"No, I will stay here. 'Tis you who will leave, Aunt. My papa isn't a bloody laird, he's *the* laird and he's the very best."

"Ha! Little you know what *he* is! Little you know how his mother—aye, my own sister and your grandmother—played her husband false and fell in with a kelpie, aye, a kelpie she called up from the devil himself to dwell in Loch Leven. He became a man in the form of her husband, but he wasn't her husband because it was me he loved, and he didn't look at her anymore. No, the man she fornicated with wasn't her husband, for the real laird was mine in all ways. Hers was this kelpie and he was one of Satan's minions, a false image, evil through and through, and the son she bore this false husband was Colin and he is as evil and bone-deep blighted as was his kelpie father."

Philip didn't begin to understand her. He prayed his father would come, and quickly, or Mrs. Seton or Crocker, anyone, anyone. Please God, bring someone. Aunt Arleth was agay wi' her wits, as Old Alger the barrel maker was wont to say.

Philip was afraid; he didn't see any of his fervent prayers being answered. Aunt Arleth was moving toward Sinjun. He dashed forward, hurling himself up onto the bed next to his stepmother, covering her body with his, trying to shield her from Aunt Arleth.

"Sinjun!" he shouted, grabbing her arms and shaking her. He shouted her name again, and this time she opened her eyes and stared up at him.

"Philip? Is that you? Is she gone yet?"

"No, she isn't, Sinjun. You must stay awake now. You must."

"Get out of here, boy!"

"Oh God," Sinjun whispered.

"And did you know, you silly boy, that her real husband—your grandfather—put a rowan cross over the door to keep her from entering? He knew she was fornicating with a kelpie. Ah, but Satan had sent a charm that protected her even from the rowan cross."

"Please go away, Aunt."

She drew herself up and slowly stared from the boy to the woman who lay on the bed, those damned covers to her chin. Her eyes were open and filled with fear. It pleased Arleth to see that fear.

"You fetched your pa. You filled his ears with lies, aye, you brought him back with lies, you made him feel guilt. He didn't want to come back, you know. He wants her to leave. He has her money, so why bother with the likes of her?"

"Please go away, Aunt."

"I heard you speaking of a rowan cross and kelpies. Hello, Aunt, Philip. How is Joan?"

Philip jumped at the sound of Serena's voice. She'd glided up silent as a ghost to stand beside him at the edge of the bed. "Her name is Sinjun. Take Aunt Arleth away from here, Serena."

"Why ever for, my dear boy? Now, about the rowan cross. They are nasty things, you know, Aunt. I detest them. Why would you speak of them? I'm a witch, true, but the rowan cross has no effect on me."

Philip wondered if he wasn't losing his wits. He wasn't afraid now. No matter what else Serena was, she wouldn't allow Aunt Arleth to hurt Sinjun.

"Go away, Serena, else I'll crown you with a rowan cross!"

"Oh no you won't, Aunt. You can't hurt me and well you know it. I'll always be too strong for you, and too good."

Aunt Arleth looked pale and furious, colder than the loch in January.

Then, to Philip's utter relief, his father strode into the room. He stopped short and frowned at his son, who was hovering on the bed next to Joan as if he were protecting her, for God's sake. Serena was looking vague and beautiful, like a fairy princess who had mistakenly stepped into Bedlam and didn't know what to do.

As for Aunt Arleth, there was no expression at all on her thin face. She was looking down at her pale hands, at the age spots that dotted the backs.

"Colin?"

He smiled now and walked to the bed. Sinjun was awake and had her wits about her, finally. "Hello, Joan. You're back again. I'm pleased with you."

"What's a kelpie?"

"An evil being that lives in lochs and inland lakes. He can assume different forms. He gets his power from the devil. It's an interesting question. Why do you wish to know?"

"I don't know. The word just kept coming into my mind. Thank you. May I have some water?"

It was Philip who helped her to drink. "Hello to you," she said to him. "What's wrong, Philip? Do I look that horrid?"

The boy lightly touched his fingertips to her cheek. "Oh no, Sinjun, you look fine. You're better, aren't you?"

"Yes. You know something? I'm hungry." She looked at Aunt Arleth and said, "You dislike me and you wish me ill. I don't understand you. I've done nothing to harm you."

"This is my house, missy! I will—"

Colin said mildly, "No, Aunt Arleth. You will stay away. No more from you." He watched her leave the room, slowly, unwillingly, and he was afraid that her mind, tenuous at best, was losing its meager hold. He turned back to hear his wife say to Philip, "Get me the pocket pistol, Philip. It's in the pocket of my riding habit. Put it under my pillow."

Colin said nothing. He wanted to tell her not to be such a fool, but in truth he couldn't be at all certain that Arleth, from some misguided notion of loyalty, hadn't tried to hurt her.

He said now, seeing that his son was fairly itching to get the pistol for her, "I will speak to Mrs. Seton about some invalidish dishes for you, Joan."

"I remember you called me Sinjun."

"You wouldn't respond to your real name. I had no choice."

Sinjun closed her eyes. She felt beyond tired, her bones so weak she knew she couldn't lift the small pistol even to save herself. The fever was rising and she was shivering. She wanted some more water badly.

"Papa, you stay with Sinjun. I'll talk to Mrs. Seton. Here's the pistol, Sinjun. See, it's right under your pillow."

Colin gave her water to drink, then sat down beside her and watched her. She felt the flat of his hand on her forehead, then heard him curse quietly.

The heat became cold from one instant to the next and she knew that if she moved, her body would crack, just as ice would crack. She felt brittle; she knew that if she blew her breath out, she would see it, for the air was frigid in her lungs.

"I know," Colin said. He stripped off his clothes and climbed into bed beside her. He drew her against the length of him, pressing her even closer, trying to give her all his warmth. He felt the tremors, the convulsive shaking, and it hurt him, this pain of hers. He wanted to know many things, but now wasn't the time.

He held her close even when he began to sweat. When she finally slept, he still held her, his hands stroking up and down her back.

"I'm sorry I wasn't here," he whispered against her hair. "I'm so sorry." He was very aware of her breasts pressing against his chest, her thighs against his, and her belly . . . no, he wouldn't think of that. Oddly enough, even though he was hard, he felt more protectiveness toward her than lust. It was odd, but it was so. He wanted her well again. He wanted her yelling at him when he again took her to bed, only this time she wouldn't mind at all when he came into her. He would see to it that she welcomed him. He wouldn't be a clod.

The fever broke the following day.

Colin, more exhausted than he'd been in his life, smiled at the doctor. "I told you she'd survive. She's tough."

"Most odd," said Childress. "She's English."

"What she is, sir, is my wife. She's now a Scot."

That night one of the crofters came to the castle. MacPherson had stolen two cows and killed MacBain and his two sons. Colin felt such rage he shook with it.

"MacBain's wife said the brutes told her to tell ye that it was t' pay fer Dingle's life ye took."

"Dingle! Why, I haven't seen that miserable lout in longer than . . ." Colin cursed soundly. "I don't know when I last saw him. What is it, Philip? What's wrong? Is it Joan?"

"No, Papa, but I know all about Dingle."

When Colin heard the story he felt his guts knot at how close his son had come to disaster on his journey to Edinburgh. However, he managed to pat his son's shoulder, and retreat to his tower chamber.

He could see no hope for it. He wanted the feuding to stop. He would have to speak to MacPherson. But tell him what? That he truly couldn't remember a thing about Fiona's death or how he came to be unconscious by the cliff edge?

Sinjun was sleeping fitfully. There was a strange light at the edge of her mind, a soft, very white light that was soothing and clear, yet somehow shadowy and deep, filled with meanings buried in mysteries that she wanted very much to understand. She tried to speak but knew it wouldn't help her. She lay still, her mind and body calm, waiting. A flicker of darkness appeared in the white light, then faded only to glitter again, like candlelight flickering in a breeze. Then it seemed to grow stronger and shimmer in its own pale way. And then there was a female figure, a very ordinary young female figure, her expression good-natured, and she was all gowned in pearl-covered white material. So many pearls—never had Sinjun seen so many pearls. Surely the gown must be very heavy with all those pearls.

Pearlin' Jane, Sinjun thought, and smiled. She'd left the Virgin Bride to come to another ghost and now this one must needs make her acquaintance. She felt no fear at all. She'd not harmed this ghost nor had Colin. She waited.

The pearls glittered in a light that strengthened, growing stronger and brighter until Sinjun's eyes hurt from the intensity of the light. The pearls flashed and sparkled. The ghost did nothing at all, merely looked at her, her expression studious now, as if she didn't know what kind of person Sinjun was and wanted to.

"He tried to buy me off," she said at last, and it seemed to Sinjun that her lips moved. "He did indeed, the betraying fool, with naught but a single cheap pearl, but I knew what he was about. He'd kilt me, hadn't he? Not a brow he raised when he ran me down in his carriage, his lady love beside him, her nose in the air, like I was nothing more than a bit of trash beside the road. So I demanded enough pearls to cover my gown and then I would leave him alone."

That answered that question, Sinjun thought, and she thought again, *But you were already dead, weren't you?*

"Aye, dead as a mousie rotting in the wainscoting, but I took care of that demned blighter, aye, I did. Made his life a misery, I did, and his little wifey, aye, I tormented that bitch until she couldn't bear the sight of him. I see my portrait's gone again. Fetch it back; it goes between the two of theirs, always in the middle, between them, separating them in death as it did in life, that's where my portrait must hang. See that you do it. I don't know why it was taken down. Put it back up. I will trust you to see that it stays in its rightful place."

"All right. Please come again whenever you wish."

"I knew you wouldn't be afraid of me. 'Tis good you're here."

Sinjun slept deeply now, a healing sleep, and when she awoke late the following morning, she sat up in bed and stretched. She felt wonderful.

15

PHILPOT OPENED THE DOORS and gaped. Two stylish ladies stood on the front steps, a traveling carriage with a high-nob crest on the side on the graveled drive behind them. The two magnificent bays in harness were blowing and stamping.

There were two outriders, who had pulled their horses to stand protectively on either side of each lady. The man driving the carriage was whistling, his whip upright on his leg, looking at Philpot with ill-concealed suspicion. Damned Sassenachs, Philpot thought, insular buggers, all of them.

The ladies themselves were in traveling gowns of the highest quality—Philpot might be the son of a Dundee baker but he knew excellence when he saw it. They were also dusty, a bit on the wrinkled side, and one lady, in a gray gown with military gold braiding on the shoulders, had red hair, not really absolutely red hair but dark red hair that wasn't all that dark. . . . He shook his head. She also had a spot of dirt on her nose. The other one was just as pretty and just as travel-worn. She was gowned in a deep forest-green traveling gown and her chestnut hair was thick and braided atop her head with a nonsensical little bonnet perched on top. Part of the thick braid had come loose and was hanging over her shoulder. They had traveled quickly. Philpot wondered how far they'd come in how short a time.

The lady with the red hair that wasn't really all that red, just sort of red, stepped up, a wide smile on her face. "This is Vere Castle, home of the earl of Ashburnham?"

"Aye, my lady. Might I inquire as to who you—"

There was a shriek from behind him and Philpot paled hearing the countess. Oh Gawd, had she fainted? He whirled about as quickly as his age and dignity permitted. She was leaning against a decorative suit of Elizabethan armor just behind him, pale as could be, staring at the two ladies.

"Alex? Sophie? Is that really you?"

The lady in green rushed forward. "Are you all right, Sinjun? Oh, please, my dear, tell me you're all right? We were so dreadfully worried about you."

"I think I am now, Sophie. But why are you here? Are Douglas and Ryder outside? Why—"

"You have been ill! I knew it. No matter now, Sinjun, Sophie and I are here to see that everything will be all right. You're not to worry about anything anymore."

The two ladies had swept past Philpot as they spoke, and quickly converged on the sickly countess and took turns hugging her and patting her pale cheeks and telling her how much they'd missed her.

Finally, after all the affections had been duly dispensed, Sinjun introduced them to Philpot, then said, "Do you know where the laird is?"

"Ye shouldn't be out of yer bed, m'lady," he said, sounding as disapproving as a bishop.

"Don't scold me, Philpot. I was sinking like a dead stone into the feather tick. Had I remained abed any longer I would have smothered myself. But you're right, I'm feeling a bit shaky. I'll sit down in just a moment. Please send for the laird. Tell him we have guests, my sisters-in-law, to be exact. We'll all be in the drawing room. Alex, Sophie, come with me."

Her ladyship tried to lead the way, but she faltered. Philpot jumped forward, but the two ladies were quicker. They all but carried her into the drawing room.

Sinjun was settled on the sofa, her feet put up, a cushion beneath them, another pillow behind her head.

"Are you warm enough, love?"

"Oh yes, Alex, I'm just fine, though I am much enjoying seeing the both of you hovering. Ah, you're really here, it's wonderful. I can't believe it. How?"

Alex looked at Sophie, then said simply, "The Virgin Bride sent us. She said you were ill."

"Douglas and Ryder?"

Sophie gave an elaborate shrug and didn't look one whit guilty. "Douglas was easy. He's in London, so Alex just left Northcliffe Hall to come visit me, bringing the twins with her. Ryder, however, presented more of a strategic difficulty. We had to wait until he went to the Ascot races with Tony, a three-day outing, thank heaven. I pleaded an indisposition, as did Alex. Then we left, simple as that." She paused a moment, then said, "I believe Ryder thinks I'm pregnant. He was giving me all these male possessive looks and tender pats on my stomach. It was difficult not to laugh. I wanted to ask him if he thought being with child was catching—since Alex is pregnant, you see."

Sinjun groaned. "They'll come," she said. "They'll come and try to kill Colin again."

"Again?" This from both Alex and Sophie together.

Sinjun groaned again, leaned her head back against the cushion, and said, "Yes, again. Alex knows about the first time. She herself coshed Douglas with a walking stick to help me break up their scuffle. There were two other times as well, both here in Scotland. Did you bring the boys?"

"No," Alex said. "Directress Jane of Brandon House is free to enjoy all three of them whilst we're gone. That is the title she selected, you know. She insists upon it whenever I introduce her to someone. The twins feel like they've arrived in heaven when they get there, what with Grayson and all the Beloved Ones. That's a total of fourteen children right now. But who knows—Ryder just might bring home another child from Ascot."

"Lucky Jane!"

"Oh yes," Sophie said serenely. "She is indeed. Grayson would kill any number of dragons for Jane. As for Alex's twins, Melissande will doubtless visit them nearly every day, since they look like her. She calls them her little mirrors. It very nearly renders Douglas incoherent with nausea. He will look at the boys, shake his head, gaze heavenward, and wonder aloud what he did to deserve the two most handsome male children in the world, which will undoubtedly ruin their characters and make them insufferable."

"Sit down, both of you. Now, my head is awhirl. The Virgin Bride came to you, Alex? She told you I was ill?"

Before she could answer, the door opened and Mrs. Seton, bearing a large silver tray, her dark eyes nearly crossed in her excitement, came into the drawing room. To a stranger she would have looked stiff and proper as a duchess, only Sinjun wasn't fooled for a minute.

"Thank you, Mrs. Seton," she said formally, maintaining Mrs. Seton's pose. "These two ladies are here to visit us awhile. They are my sisters-in-law, the countess of Northcliffe and Mrs. Ryder Sherbrooke."

"Charmed, my ladies," Mrs. Seton said, and gave them a curtsy that would have done justice to the Queen's drawing room. She lacked but a feather in her hair.

"I shall prepare Queen Mary's room and the Autumn Room," she added with more ceremony than Sinjun's mother would have deemed appropriate, and proffered another quite impressive curtsy. "The footmen are seeing to your valises. Emma will unpack for you."

"You are very kind, Mrs. Seton. Thank you."

"This is the laird's castle, my lady. Everything is done properly here."

"Yes, certainly," Sinjun said, and watched Mrs. Seton take herself out of the room. "Phew! I never knew Mrs. Seton had quite so much . . ."

"I don't know the word, either, but it was impressive," Alex said.

"Also we only have one footman, Rory, and he does everything in addition to any footing. However, Emma is an excellent girl and it is she who will take care of you. Now, back to the Virgin Bride."

Before Alex could say anything, the drawing room door opened again and Colin strode into the room like the master of his castle, looking at once belligerent and wary. He saw only two young ladies seated beside his wife, cups of tea in their elegant, albeit somewhat wrinkled, gloved hands. The one he recognized as Douglas's wife. Oh Lord, the bounder had to be here somewhere. He craned to see the rest of the room.

"Where are they? Are they armed this time? Pistols or foils? Are they hiding behind the sofa, Joan?"

Sinjun laughed, a weak laugh, but it made him smile.

"Good lord," Sophie said, and stared at her sister-in-law's husband. "You look like a bandit!"

Indeed, if a bandit were wearing naught but a white flowing shirt, unlaced at the top to show some of his hairy chest, and tight black knit breeches and black boots, his black hair windblown, his face tanned from the summer sun, then Colin was a bandit. Sophie happened to look at Sinjun. Her sister-in-law was staring at her husband with such wistful besottedness that it made Sophie lower her gaze.

Colin looked at his wife then, saw her pallor, and frowned. He strode to her, leaned down, and lightly pressed his palm to her forehead. "No fever, thank God. How are you? Why are you downstairs? Philpot was more concerned about telling me that you'd been tottering about than he was about our visitors. Welcome, ladies. Now, Joan, what the devil are you doing downstairs?"

"I was growing mold in bed," she said, and raised her hand to touch his jaw, the cleft in his chin. "I couldn't bear it any longer. Please, I'm fine, Colin. These are my sisters-in-law. You know Alex already. This is Sophie, Ryder's wife."

Colin was charming but cautious. "Ladies, a pleasure. Where are your husbands?" he asked as soon as could be, still standing, still wary.

"They'll be coming," Sinjun said. "But it will take a while, I hope, because Alex and Sophie are smart."

"Smarter than you were, I trust," he said. He turned to the ladies. "We arrived in my house in Edinburgh to find Douglas and Ryder already in residence, waiting to kill me. It was my manservant's blunderbuss that saved us."

"And put a big black hole in the drawing room ceiling."

"That was a sight," Colin said. "Actually, it still is. I haven't yet had it repaired."

Alex looked very interested. "Odd that Douglas didn't mention that. He did mention your house in Edinburgh, Colin, but no talk of violence. What was the other time they attacked you? He said nothing about another time, either."

Colin flushed, Alex was sure of it. Her curiosity rose to unprecedented heights. She happened to look at Sinjun and saw that she was utterly crimson, all the way to her hairline.

Sinjun said quickly, "Colin, they got together and came to me because of the Virgin Bride."

"Isn't that the ghost at Northcliffe Hall you were telling the children about?"

"Children?" Alex said blankly.

Colin flushed again as he was lifting a cup of tea. He moved about in his seat. "Yes," he said, "children."

"I have two wonderful children," Sinjun said smoothly. "Philip and Dahling. They are four and six, and delightful little heathens, just like all our others. I told Colin all about Ryder's Beloved Ones."

"You didn't mention the children in your letters, Sinjun," Sophie said, her voice reproachful.

"Well, no. You see—" She stalled. "Colin, the Virgin Bride came to Alex and told her I was ill. So she and Sophie came as quickly as they could get away, because they were worried about me."

"It was more than that," Alex said, allowing herself to be sidestepped. Another mystery. It was fascinating. "She also said you were in trouble."

"Oh dear," Sinjun said, and looked at her husband, who appeared sincerely puzzled. Douglas would have been sneering and carping on about idiot nonsense. Ryder would have been laughing his head off.

"There is no trouble," Colin said. "Well, maybe a bit, but nothing I can't handle. What the devil is going on here? I want the truth now, all of it."

"We have come for a visit," Alex said, giving him a fat smile. "A simple visit, that's all. We will oversee things until Sinjun is well enough to take over again. Isn't that right, Sophie?"

"Exactly," Sophie agreed, nodding as complacently as a maiden aunt as she ate her second scone. "We both have different household talents, you see, Colin, thus the both of us are necessary so that all may continue to run smoothly. Delicious tea, Sinjun."

Colin looked at her, one dark brow arched up a good inch. "Indeed," he said. "Joan is blessed in her relatives."

"Joan?" Sophie said, frowning. "Wherever did you get that, Colin?"

"I prefer it to her man's nickname."

"Oh. But—"

"It doesn't matter, Sophie," Sinjun said, adding quickly, "Thank you both for coming. I'm so glad you did." She added, without thinking, "It's been rather harrowing."

"What do you mean?" Sophie asked, licking a dollop of sweet raspberry jam from her finger.

Sinjun darted a look at her husband, saying quickly, "Later, Sophie, we will speak of it later."

Colin was frowning ferociously. "You will go back to bed, Joan. You look pale as my shirt and you're sweating like a Caerlaverock goat. I don't like it. Come along. I'll carry you up. I want you to stay in bed this time. I'll tell you when you can get up again." He didn't wait for her to reply, merely picked her up in his arms and carried her to the door. He said over his shoulder, "You may follow us, if you like, ladies. It will help you get the lay of the land."

And so Sophie and Alex, relieved that Sinjun was all right and confused to their eyebrows at the notion of children and harrowing things, silently followed their brother-in-law up the impossibly wide staircase.

"Think of it as an adventure," Alex said to Sophie behind her hand. "Would you look at the gentleman in that portrait! Goodness, he's naked!"

Colin smiled but didn't turn, merely said over his shoulder, "That's my great-great-grandfather, Granthan Kinross. The stories have it that he lost a wager with a neighbor, the result being that he had to have his portrait painted without his plaid. There is a judiciously placed yew bush in front of him, though."

"What was the wager?" Alex asked.

"The story goes that Granthan was a wild young man and much in demand with all the local ladies. He took it on as his mission in life to see that they were all happy. One neighbor said Granthan would never seduce his wife no matter what his blandishments, because of her unflagging virtue, and a bet was made. The wife, it turns out, was really a young man in disguise and Granthan did indeed lose the bet and his clothes for the painting."

Sophie laughed. "You're right, Alex. It's going to be a grand adventure."

That evening after dinner Sophie and Alex came to Sinjun's bedchamber and settled themselves by her bed. Colin let them be, adjourning himself to the children's nursery.

"No, don't ask about my health again. I'm fine, just bloody weak. I got sick from a good dousing in the rain, nothing more, nothing less, except that Aunt Arleth tried to kill me."

Sophie and Alex gaped at her.

"The devil you say," Alex said at last.

Sophie said, "She's a sour old thing—not at all happy to see us, I can tell you that!—but to try to kill you? Why?"

"She doesn't want me here, just my groats. Maybe not even my groats, I'm not certain. When I was ill, Colin was in Edinburgh. She opened windows, left me alone; all in all, she sent me to the edge of oblivion. Philip rode by himself throughout the night to fetch his father. He's a wonderful little boy. Later she tried again. I don't know if she was really serious, perhaps she's just unhinged. She speaks of many things but makes little sense. Now, what do you think of my children?"

"They were only allowed for a few minutes in the drawing room. They're the image of their father, which is to say that they're quite handsome. Dahling hid behind her father's leg, her thumb in her mouth, but Philip came to me and said he was glad we were here. He lowered his voice and told us to be careful for you. He didn't want you hurt again. You have quite a champion there, Sinjun. He will also break ladies' hearts one of these years."

"Just as his father, hopefully, won't break mine."

"Why should he?" Alex demanded. "You're everything a man could wish for in a wife."

"My heroine," Sinjun said fondly, patting her sister-in-law's hand.

"There are problems," Alex said. "You might as well tell us everything, Sinjun. I have this dreadful presentiment that the husbands will arrive here yelling and demanding our heads by dawn tomorrow morning."

"No," Sinjun said firmly. "We'll have more than two days of respite before the husbands descend. We must. You two did very well. It will take them time to get together and make their plans. Didn't you say Ryder was with Tony at Ascot?"

"Yes, but that won't matter," Sophie said. "I agree with Alex. Somehow they'll know and they'll get together. Tomorrow at dawn. And you know how they'll behave—Douglas will be enraged because Alex is pregnant and traveling without his godship's permission, and Ryder will want to skin my hide for keeping secrets from him."

Alex just laughed but didn't disagree. "No, don't worry about me, I feel grand. No more retching in indecorous places, thank God! At least I haven't retched in a day and a half. Talk, Sinjun."

"Sophie's right. We must move quickly. Lying here whilst you were all downstairs gave me the perfect plan. I just need a bit of time to get it into motion."

"Plan for what?" Sophie asked.

Sinjun began with the MacPhersons and moved to Pearlin' Jane, a ghost that both Sophie and Alex readily accepted.

"Do you think," Alex said thoughtfully when Sinjun paused in her recital, "that ghosts can somehow communicate with each other? How did the Virgin Bride know you were ill and in trouble? Did this Pearlin' Jane tell her?"

It was a question to which there was no answer. But Sinjun said, "Oh dear, I forgot to place Pearlin' Jane's portrait and the other two back in their places. She won't like it and I did promise."

"What is all that about, do you know?"

"Evidently Pearlin' Jane wanted all the pearls she could get from the benighted earl, a long-ago Kinross who'd seduced her and left her and then killed her, and she wanted her portrait painted—from her lover's memory, of course—and placed between his portrait and his wife's. Every time it was moved, something unpleasant happened to either the master or the mistress of Vere Castle. Oh, not being struck down by a bolt of errant lightning, but just something unpleasant, like becoming ill eating something bad. I don't want that to happen to me. I think Aunt Arleth moved all the portraits, hoping some affliction would strike me. I'm guessing, but it surely sounds like her."

"A thoroughly dreadful woman," Alex said. "We're here now so she doesn't dare try anything."

"I find Serena the odd duck," Sophie said as she dropped to her knees on the stone hearth and began to build up the fire. "So ethereal, in both her manner and her mode of dress. That gown she was wearing tonight was really quite lovely, not to mention very expensive. Now, that's a good question. If Colin didn't have any money, where did she get the gold for the gown? She was pleasant to us, don't misunderstand me, but vague, cryptic, you could say."

"I'd say she's daft," Alex said.

"Perhaps," Sophie said thoughtfully. "But you know, Sinjun, it's almost as if it's all an act. I don't think she's so out of touch with things as she wants you to believe."

"She did tell me that Colin doesn't love me, that he loves *Another.* She also likes to kiss him on the mouth when he doesn't expect it. But on the other hand, she seems to accept me. She is certainly strange." Sinjun shrugged and yawned. "As to the cost of her gowns, that's an excellent question. Why don't I ask her tomorrow?"

"Only if your husband allows you out of bed," Sophie said, and grinned at her.

"Oh dear, you do look tired, Sinjun."

"All I need is another good night's sleep," Sinjun said firmly. "Tomorrow I must set my plan into motion. Day after tomorrow—no later—we must act. Don't forget the husbands. They will come, no doubt about that."

"All right," Sophie said. "We'll pray you're right about them not being here until Friday. We'll breakfast with you tomorrow and you can tell us this plan of yours. All right?"

"What plan?" Colin asked from the doorway.

"He walks as quietly as Douglas does," Alex said. "It's provoking."

"Our plans for the day, naturally," Sophie said smoothly, rising from her position in front of the hearth and dusting off her skirt. "Dividing up the housekeeping chores, all that sort of thing. Things that would never interest a gentleman; you know, Colin, discussing Alex's pregnancy and how she feels, knitting blankets and tiny baby slippers—that sort of thing."

Colin appreciated her tactics. He said, a wolfish gleam in his dark blue eyes, "You think I have no interest in women's matters? Why, they're my matters, too. Goodness, as soon as I can manage it, Joan's belly will be swelling up with my child."

"Colin!"

"Yes, perhaps I'll even take up knitting and the two of us can sit in front of the fire, our needles clicking away, selecting names for our progeny."

Sophie said, ignoring him, "There, the fire is set now for several hours. Thank you for letting us visit you, Colin. Come along, Alex. Good night, Sinjun."

When the door was closed, Colin walked to the bed and sat down. He gave his wife a brooding stare. "They are as dangerous as their husbands. It is only their stratagems that differ. I don't trust them an inch. Nor you, for that matter. Now, you will tell me what's going on, Joan."

She yawned again, this one manufactured specifically for the occasion. "Nothing at all. Goodness, I feel I could sleep a week."

"Joan, you are to stay out of my affairs," he said quietly, too quietly.

"Certainly," she said, starting to pretend to another yawn and then changing her mind.

He raised a brow at that. "You said a lot of things when I came back from Edinburgh. There were no brakes on your tongue when you were so ill. You went on and on about protecting me, not that that's anything out of the ordinary or new, merely there is MacPherson. I'm ordering you, my dear wife, to keep to the castle. You will leave me to deal with that bastard."

"He is very pretty," she said without thinking, then realized what she'd done and gasped, her expression now perfectly horrified.

"So," Colin said, leaning closer to her now, his hands on the headboard of the huge bed, on each side of her face, "you have met Robbie, have you? When? Where?"

She tried to shrug but it was difficult, for his fingers were now lightly stroking her throat. She wondered if he would strangle her. "I was riding and met him at Loch Leven. He was a bit nasty and I left him, nothing more, Colin."

"You're lying," he said, and sighed, rising to stand beside the bed.

"Well, I did, ah, take his horse. Nothing more, I promise." She paused, then opened her mouth, but he forestalled her.

"You took his horse. Damnation, I never knew a woman could positively thrive on being so bloody meddlesome. No, don't add to your deceit, just promise me that you will stay safe in the castle."

"No," she said finally, "I can't promise you that."

"Then I will have to lock you in our bedchamber. I won't have you disobeying me, Joan. Robert MacPherson is a dangerous man. You had the cut on your cheek to prove it."

Sinjun felt only mildly concerned; after all, both Sophie and Alex were here. Amongst the three of them, they'd save Colin from any possible danger.

"I agree," she said. "He is dangerous. It's odd since he is so pretty."

"Perhaps that has something to do with his viciousness, but I'm just guessing. As he grew into manhood, his face didn't grow into hard lines, his features softened. He became more difficult, more severe and violent, inside and out. Now, wife, will you obey me?"

"In most things, Colin, you know that I do willingly. But in some things you must grant me leave to behave as I deem proper and right."

"Ah, yes, and one of the *some things* is our having sex together."

"That's right."

"You speak with such confidence. Is it because you know I am not enough of a bastard to take you whilst you're still weak from your illness?"

He had a point there and Sinjun was forced to nod.

He sighed, plowing his fingers through his hair. "Joan, I wasn't very kind to you when I came home before."

"You were a mean-spirited sod."

"I wouldn't go that far," he said, giving her a harassed look, "but I realize that at least now my children care a great deal for you. My small six-year-old son risked his life to come to me in Edinburgh."

"I know. It makes my blood run cold to think of it. He is a very brave boy."

"He is my son."

She smiled at that.

"Also Dahling—when she can be convinced to take her thumb out of her mouth—now sings your praises. Well, your mare's praises more than yours, actually." He sounded a bit baffled and, strangely to Sinjun, a bit put out.

"Will you also allow that it is my right and responsibility to be in charge of the household?"

"I suppose so. MacDuff said he had a message from you. It was something about you not stealing my box. What does that mean?"

"It means that I don't want to take anything away from you, like the box you hid in the oak tree to keep it safe from your brother's greed. I simply want to share what is ours. I'm not Malcolm nor am I your father."

He turned away from her. "MacDuff's mouth overworked itself, I see."

"He just wanted me to understand you. When is your birthday?"

"The last day of August. Why?"

She just shook her head and smiled. She wondered what poets he liked best. Then she yawned, a true yawn, and he said, "You will rest now. I doubt not that your two brothers will be on their wives' heels. You have my permission to protect me from those two. The wives, I see, didn't know about their husbands' bursting into our bedchamber."

"No, thank God."

"Perhaps I should tell them."

"Colin! Oh, you're jesting."

"Yes, I am. Another thing, do Douglas and Ryder know their wives are here?"

"Why, certainly they know."

"How could they let them come alone? No, I don't want to know the tale, it would likely grizzle my hair."

Colin stepped toward the fire and began to strip off his clothes. He was very aware that his wife was looking at him, he could *feel* her looking at him.

He said, "I think Alex is imprudent to have come here. It is a great many miles and it's early days yet. I wouldn't ever want you to risk losing a child with such foolishness. When you are pregnant you will do as I tell you."

Sinjun just smiled at his back, knowing she would do just as she pleased, and willed him to turn around and face her. She wanted to see him, all of him. He was naked now and she stared at the long line of his back, his buttocks, his legs. He was perfect, no doubt about that. She couldn't imagine another man in the world looking as he did.

"Colin?" Her voice sounded hoarse to herself.

"Yes?" he said slowly, turning to face her now, knowing, she thought, just knowing what she was thinking and wanting.

She swallowed. She stared and she wished he would remain there for another hour or so. Perhaps she could take up painting and he could agree to pose for her. She wondered if he would agree to such a ruse.

"Yes, Joan?"

"Will you sleep with me tonight? Hold me?"

"Oh yes. I know you enjoy that. It doesn't threaten you, does it? I will even kiss you and you do like that very very much."

He walked to the bed, knowing she wanted to look at him and allowing it. Her fascination amused him and, truthfully, pleased him inordinately. It was splendid for a wife to admire her husband, yes indeed. He heard her suck in her breath and frowned. He looked at himself. Under her gaze, his sex had aroused itself with predictable enthusiasm, and now she was afraid. Well, what did she expect—that he would shrivel?

Damnation. He wanted her to be well again, quickly. This nonsense of hers was irritating to his nerves.

"You will stay home now, Colin?"

"Yes, as I told you, since MacPherson is here now, causing more trouble, I must deal with him here. And I will, Joan—without any help from you. Also it appears I must protect you from Aunt Arleth."

"I appreciate that, Colin."

He climbed into bed with her and she willingly came into his arms. They lay on their sides, facing each other, their noses nearly touching.

"You still have your bloody nightgown on."

"Perhaps it best stay on."

"You're probably right, damn you." He kissed her mouth, then grinned. "Open up, Joan. You've forgotten what I taught you. No, not like a fish or an opera singer. That's right. Ah, yes. Give me your tongue."

He wanted her very much and if he wasn't mistaken she wasn't at all averse to his continuing with his mouth and with his hands, but he knew she was still weak, not at all up to snuff, and he didn't want her to become ill again. He kissed the tip of her nose and gently pressed her cheek down to his shoulder as he turned onto his back. It was damned difficult but he did it. He felt at the height of his nobility. She gave a small gasp of disappointment and tried to kiss him again.

"No, Joan, I don't wish to tire you. Hush, that's right. Just relax now.

I'll hold you, that's all. Was Philip right? Did Aunt Arleth really try to kill you?"

Sinjun was nearly stuttering with lust. She was trembling against him, trying to control herself, but it wasn't easy. She had very little experience in turning off the spigot, so to speak. She wanted to kiss him until she couldn't breathe. She wanted her hands all over his body. She wanted to kiss his belly, his sex, take him into her mouth again. Ah, but it was difficult to simply stop, to simply forget that he was against her, his body hot and hard and fitted against hers so perfectly. She strained against him, unable to help herself. Her hand fisted over his belly. Slowly, very slowly, she flattened her hand over his stomach and felt the heat and hardness of him, and the crispy hair lower on his groin.

Colin closed his eyes and bit his lip. "No, Joan. Hold still, you must really, sweetheart. Move your hand before you make me very uncomfortable. Please, answer my question."

She realized then, vaguely, that he was also trying to control himself, and she supposed she appreciated his concern with her illness, but she would rather take her chances with another fever. Her fingers moved lower, just touching him now. He jerked away from her. He was bent on nobility. She sighed, then said, "She didn't come right out and force poison down my throat, but she wanted me to die, no doubt about that. She even opened the windows to assist me to my eternal reward. After you came, she found me alone once and spoke to me about how she would use a pillow to smother me. She then decided it wasn't the way to do it, it was too obvious. She said that I had ruined everything, that I would make her life even more miserable. There were so many things she said on that day, Colin, so many things she's said at other times, and things I've found out about during your absence." She told him about the kelpie ramblings, how she'd forced Mrs. Seton to keep the castle filthy, how Colin's father wasn't really his father, rather it was the kelpie demon, and the laird had loved her, Arleth, not her sister, who was a fool and evil. Colin asked many questions, but it was confusing. Finally, though, when she was too exhausted to speak another word, he said, kissing her left temple, "I will see to it that she is removed from Vere Castle. She is a danger to herself and to us. Lord knows what she could do to the children were her mind to snap in another direction. Odd that I've never before noticed her strangeness, just her dislike of me—obvious enough, of course—and I paid no heed to that.

"Sleep now. Please, move your hand upward. Yes, that's right. My chest is not such a dangerous place."

She smiled against his shoulder. Nothing could happen to her with him here. As to something happening to him, she would do what she had to do. He could rant and be as lordly and autocratic as he pleased, but it would make no difference. He had no chance against the three sisters-in-law.

No chance at all.

16

DOUGLAS AND RYDER didn't appear at Vere Castle at the crack of dawn, much to the wives' combined relief and chagrin. At eight o'clock that morning, in the laird's bedchamber, Sophie finally voiced her worry. "But where are they? Do you think they've been hurt, Alex?"

"Oh, no, I don't believe so," Alex said, her brow lowering. "I'm beginning to think they're angry and not coming. It's a lesson. Douglas is tired of trying to have his way and only succeeding half the time, and thus he's punishing me with his absence."

Sinjun looked from one to the other and started to laugh. There were two identical expressions of outrage but she couldn't stop laughing. "I can't believe the two of you—you sound as if you want them to come this very instant."

"Oh no!"

"How absurd!"

Sinjun looked from one glum face to the other. "Did either of you brilliant sweetings bother to leave a note as to where you were bound?"

Alex looked at Sinjun as if she were a half-wit and gave her a disdainful shrug that would have done Douglas proud. "Why, naturally I told him where I was going! What kind of a person do you think I am? I would never want to worry Douglas."

"And what did you write to Douglas?"

"Ah . . . that I was off to see Sophie. Oh damn."

Sinjun turned a twinkling eye to Sophie, who was now frowning ferociously down at her pale green slippers. "And you? Did you tell Ryder where you and Alex were bound?"

Very slowly, eyes still firmly on her feet, Sophie shook her head. "I just wrote to him that we were going to do a bit of sightseeing in the Cotswolds and that I would write him to tell him when we would return."

"Oh, Sophie, you didn't!" Alex threw a pillow at her. "I can't believe you didn't tell him the truth. What were you thinking, for God's sake?"

"Well, Alex, you did no better!" Sophie rounded on her and threw the pillow back, striking her magnificent bosom. "You only told part of the truth because you were the first leg of the deception, so to speak. You didn't have to lie like I did."

"You should have realized that there was no need for a lie! You should have thought, but you didn't think, you—"

"Don't you dare call me stupid!"

"I didn't call you stupid, but if the glove fits—"

"That's enough from both of you," Sinjun said, trying desperately not to laugh. Alex's splendid bosom was heaving; Sophie was red in the face, her hands fisted at her sides.

It was Alex who said finally, her voice reeking of catastrophe, "What are we going to do?"

Sinjun didn't crack that smile; the laughter was no longer bubbling up in her throat. She said very firmly, "Ryder and Douglas will figure it out quickly enough. I know they will. If it makes you feel better, then both of you write letters to them right this instant and I will have one of our stable lads go to Edinburgh with them. I don't believe it's necessary, though."

"That will take forever!"

"It isn't necessary," Sinjun repeated. "Now, trust me. I promise that both husbands will be here before too much longer. Indeed, I still hold to Friday, no later. Would the two of you like to shake hands now and we'll get on with the business at hand?"

Sinjun realized she felt quite good as she watched her sisters-in-law continue to grumble at each other even as they hugged. Yes, she felt stronger than she had the day before. Not up to full snuff yet, but she was clear-headed and her brain was functioning quite well. She didn't feel wilted any longer.

They discussed their plan until Sinjun, at least, was pleased, and all the consequences she could think of were covered. Sophie and Alex didn't like the plan but Sinjun convinced them it was the only way. "Would you prefer that I just shoot him and toss his body in the loch?" she'd said, and that had shut down most of their objections. She'd written her letter the afternoon before and had Ostle brought to her. Him, she had sworn to secrecy. Pray God he would keep mum about what he'd done.

Sinjun looked from one sister-in-law to the other. "Now, we will act this morning. We can't take the chance that we'll have another day. You may not have faith in Douglas and Ryder, but I do."

Both Alex and Sophie had brought pocket pistols. Both knew how to shoot, not as well as Sinjun, but well enough. The sight of the pistols brought their feet firmly to the ground.

"The Virgin Bride said trouble, Sinjun," Alex said. "We're not stupid, no matter we didn't think of *everything*. Or *write* everything. Now, where's your pistol?"

Sinjun drew the small pistol from beneath her pillow. "I'm strong enough for us to do it this morning. I will ensure that Colin is off doing something else and not paying any attention to either of you or to me. I'll manage it somehow. Now come here and listen carefully."

Getting rid of Colin wasn't as easy as Sinjun had hoped it would be. Finally, at her wits' end, she played the invalid and began to cough pitiably, bending over and clutching at her ribs as she coughed and coughed. She had the headache, too, of course, a pounding pain over her left eye. Ah, and she could barely catch her breath. She did it well, her eyes even tearing as the raw scraping coughs came from her throat. She even managed some convincing shudders.

"Damn, I thought you were so much better," Colin said, his big hands rubbing up and down her back as he cradled her against him. It was he who insisted on riding himself for the physician Childress, but not before he gained both Alex's and Sophie's promises not to leave her. An easy promise to make and to keep. Talk about guilt, Sinjun was about ready to sink with it at his show of concern, but she knew she had to hold a steady course, they all did.

If men weren't so bloody intractable, she thought, but it was an absurd wish.

"I feel just excellent," Sinjun said in reply to Alex as she dressed quickly in one of her riding habits, a blue serge that was shiny with age and wear. "I'll probably be as weak as a sick goat later, but for now everything's fine. Don't worry, you two. We must take care of this before the husbands arrive. No, don't glare at each other. They will come, and soon."

"Where are you going?"

It was Philip. He strode into the bedchamber, paying no heed to either Sophie or Alex, and walked straight to Sinjun, stopping and staring at her, his hands on his hips, a stance just like his father's. "Where are you going?" he asked again. "You're wearing a riding habit, not a nightgown. Papa won't be pleased, Sinjun. Nor am I."

Sinjun wanted to ruffle his hair but restrained herself. She contented herself with giving him a small smile. "I'm just taking your two new aunts about the grounds. I feel quite good, Philip, and I will be careful. As soon as I tire I'll come back to bed."

"Where is Father?"

"He's doubtless with Mr. Seton going over accounts or perhaps visiting the crofters. He was gone for three weeks and there is much that requires his lordly attention. You didn't ask him?"

"I wasn't downstairs when he left. Dahling was throwing a tantrum and trying to bite Dulcie's leg. I had to protect Dulcie."

"Well, whilst I'm being an excellent hostess, why don't you keep watch on Aunt Arleth for me."

His eyes lit up. "Yes," he said. "I'll do that, but Sinjun, don't tire yourself, all right?"

"I promise." She watched Philip leave the bedchamber and felt the knife of guilt turning in her innards. "I hated doing that, but he's just as protective as his papa."

"You're a wonderful actress, Sinjun," Alex said as they slipped down the back servants' stairs. "I've never been that good."

"I hate it, but it had to be done," Sinjun said on a sigh. "Ah, the guilt. But I must keep Colin safe. He will know how important it is to me. He will understand, if, that is, he ever discovers what we did."

"Your optimism is built on sand, my dear," Sophie said. "He's a man. I shouldn't hold my breath were I you. Understanding isn't a virtue men necessarily cultivate, particularly if it relates to a wife."

"Sophie's right," Alex said. "If Colin does find out, and in my experience husbands usually discover *everything* you don't want them to know about, he will feel enraged and worried to his toes because you might have been hurt; and being a man, he would naturally blame you for worrying him. It all makes sense to them. Strange, but it does."

"A man can't accept that there is anything he can't do," Sophie continued. "If his wife succeeds where he can't, why, he'll be so furious he'll spit nails. And he'll blame her for succeeding."

"I know," Sinjun said on a deep sigh. "I'm married now and I realize well enough that Colin is no different from Douglas and Ryder. He shouts and yells and carries on until I want to cosh him. But surely he will understand that he's left me no choice but to do what I must."

"Ha," said Alex.

"Ha, ha," said Sophie.

"That is if he ever finds out."

"You're dreaming," said Alex.

"More a drunken fantasy," said Sophie.

The three ladies were lost in gloomy thoughts until they reached the stables. Sinjun spotted Ostle and ordered Fanny and two horses for the other ladies.

"I dinna like this, m'lady," he said once, and then again and once more. "It bain't be right."

"You will hold your tongue, Ostle," Sinjun said with such force that her sisters-in-law stared at her. "Now, you will ride to Edinburgh today as soon as we're gone and make the other inquiries. It's critical that you don't let anyone know what you're about. It's critical that you return as quickly as possible. And you must contrive to see me alone. Do you understand me, Ostle?"

He was miserably unhappy, but he nodded, the sweet guineas piled thick in his pocket, tipping the scales against telling the laird what was up.

Unfortunately, due to the depletion of the Kinross stables, there was only one other mare suitable for a lady to ride.

"Very well," Sinjun said after a moment. "I'll ride Argyll, Sophie will take Fanny, and Alex, I'm sorry, but you will have to ride Carrot."

Carrot, a very docile swaybacked mare of ten years, looked at Alex, blew loudly, and nodded her long head.

"We'll do," Alex said. A horsewoman of some renown, she was delighted.

"Er, m'lady, Argyll bain't be in a sporting mood t'day, nay, he bain't. His lordship was going t' ride him, saw that he was nastiness hisself, and rode Gulliver instead. Nay mere than ten minutes ago his lordship left."

Gulliver was the bay Colin kept in Edinburgh. Gulliver was the bay he rode back with Philip because he'd been so worried about her. She gulped and said, "Well, nasty or not, it's Argyll for me. Ten minutes, hmmm. Do hurry, Ostle, and don't worry, all will be well."

She'd never before ridden Colin's stallion—lord, she thought as she swung up on his broad back, he could outrace the rain in a storm. She prayed Colin wouldn't notice he was missing. But if he did, it wouldn't matter. He wouldn't know which direction they'd taken. Ostle wouldn't be here to question. She drew a deep breath and dug her heels into Argyll's muscled sides.

Short minutes later they were galloping smoothly down the long tree-lined drive of Kinross Castle, the summer air warm and soft on their faces, slivers of bright sunlight slicing through the dense canopy of green leaves overhead.

"It is so beautiful here," Sophie said, craning back to see the castle on its rise at the end of the long drive.

"Yes," said Sinjun, and gulped. "Colin said one of his ancestors—the one who is painted naked—planted all the trees. They're very lovely. Of course, there aren't any gardens like yours at Northcliffe, Alex."

"Perhaps not, but these trees. I shall do it at Northcliffe Hall," Alex said. "What do you think—pines and birches and oaks?"

Sinjun knew both of them were scared to death of her plan and scared for her. Alex was babbling about trees; Sophie was looking grim as a defeated general, staring straight between her Fanny's ears. Sinjun said nothing. She was set on her course. She directed them immediately off the narrow road. No tracks for Colin to follow if he happened to be in this exact spot and so inclined.

They rode steadily, not speaking now, staying close to Sinjun's stallion, Argyll, who seemed pleased as could be to have her on his back. Not a bit of trouble did he cause her, which was fortunate, because Sinjun didn't want to deplete her store of strength on a damned recalcitrant horse.

Sinjun called for them to halt in another mile. They were near the barren Craignure Moor. "The MacPherson castle—St. Monance—is but seven miles, over this desolate stretch, then into the Aviemore Hills. I know a short way around—I asked Ostle. We'll be there in an hour. Are both of you ready for this? Are you certain?"

"I don't like it at all, Sinjun," Sophie said, "and neither does Alex. There must be another way. It was easier to talk about and agree to than it is now, actually doing it. It's dangerous. Anything could happen."

Sinjun shook her head. "I've thought and thought. The last thing I want is to have him come across me or Colin by accident, or by design, for that matter. He's already tried to kill Colin once, and possibly twice; the second time I was hurt by mistake." Their breaths sucked, for she hadn't told them about the attempt in Edinburgh, and she continued inexorably, "No, I must be the one in control, the one with a plan. We will take him by surprise. I know there are problems with this, unknowns, if you will, but I couldn't think of anything else. It will work. You must trust me on this. Ostle will find out what we need to know in Edinburgh. It won't take many more days, probably two at the most. Even if the husbands do arrive, why, then I will simply sneak away and finish things off. Then let Colin yell and pound the furniture with his fists if he discovers what I've done. It won't matter. Indeed, I shall enjoy hearing him carry on because I know he'll now be safe. Now, my dears, let's go."

"Your husband will yell and pound the furniture and then he'll kill all of us."

"I will lie to him and he will know it, but how will he ever guess the truth?"

"What lie have you planned to tell him to explain your absence and ours?" Alex asked. She held up her hand. "You see, Sinjun, there's today and then yet another day to deal with, and perhaps even another and another after that. The scheduling of this is difficult, even without the husbands' interference. Now, what will you tell Colin?"

"Truth be told, I haven't the faintest idea now, but with Colin yelling at me, I doubt not that something wonderful will spring to mind. It always does. First things first. Let's go." Argyll galloped forward, spewing pebbles in his wake.

They rode hard and saw very few people. The deeper they rode into the hills, the more difficult the going became. Purple heather sprang up thick from between sharp-edged rocks, giving the landscape a savage beauty.

"You're certain this is a shorter route?" Alex asked.

Sinjun nodded. "Nearly there."

Actually, St. Monance Castle, home of the MacPherson clan, was set at the very end of the Pilchy Loch, a narrow body of water that had grown thinner during the past century. There were trees aplenty surrounding the loch, sufficient arable land that Sinjun could see. Unlike Vere Castle, St. Monance looked its age. Because it was summer, there were brilliant flowers about, softening the ravages of time, but there were more weeds than blossoms, and everything looked untended and uncared for. Everything looked weathered and poor. It was what Crocker had told her. The weathered gray stone had crumbled or caved in at many places on the castle walls. Once there had been a moat, but now there were only tall weeds and a swampy area that stank nearly as badly as the Cowal Swamp in the warm morning air.

"This place desperately needs another heiress, Sinjun."

"From what I've learned, nearly every Scottish clan needs a huge ration of money, particularly the Highland clans. We're lucky here in Fife. There is arable land aplenty, so there is no question about sheep being brought up and the people shoved off their land, which is what is happening in the Highlands. Why the MacPhersons are poor, I don't know. Goodness, I'm starting to babble like you, Alex." Sinjun drew a deep breath. "I do hope that Robert MacPherson is here. Now, as you know, I told him in my letter that I would be alone, and that I would be here this morning. If he isn't here, well, then I've failed. Keep your fingers crossed. Stay here and keep hidden. With any luck I'll have him with me very soon. Now, I need the two of you to assure me that a man would just look at me and become cross-eyed with lust."

"At least cross-eyed," Sophie said, and she meant it.

This was the part of the plan that both Sophie and Alex had serious qualms about, but Sinjun seemed so very sure of herself. "Ostle swore he delivered the letter," she said. They looked at each other but could think of no more to say. They pulled to a halt in the midst of birch and fir trees and prepared to wait. "If you aren't back with him within a half hour, we're coming in to fetch you," Alex told her.

Sinjun rode directly to the front of the castle. Chickens and goats and dogs scattered before Argyll. There were perhaps a dozen men and women about outside, and they stopped their tasks to watch the lady ride up.

She saw two men look at her, then disappear through the great iron-studded front doors. She pulled Argyll to a stop at the bottom stone step and smiled at the people around her.

To her wondrous relief, Robert MacPherson appeared in the open doorway. He stood there and simply stared at her. Slowly, saying nothing, he strode down the deeply pitted stone steps, stopping when he was on eye level with her.

"So," he said, his arms crossed over his chest. "You came. My question, my lady, is why you would come to my lair all alone, and no fear in those beautiful eyes of yours?"

He was so pretty, she thought, each of his features so finely drawn, from the perfect arch of his fair eyebrows to the thin aristocratic nose. His eyes were just as beautiful as her Sherbrooke blue eyes, surely. She contented herself with simply staring at him for a few moments longer.

"Come ride with me," she said.

Robert MacPherson threw his head back and laughed. "You think me that witless? Doubtless your husband is over there, yon, in the birch trees, waiting with a dozen men to shoot me down."

"You weave that notion from cobwebs. You truly believe Colin Kinross so lacking in honor that he would send his own wife to fetch his enemy to him?"

"No," MacPherson said slowly, "Colin has too much pride to do that. It's not a question of honor. It's an arrogant man you married, my dear, overly proud and vicious. He would come himself, ride up to my door as you have done, and challenge me."

"So you are also saying he is fearless?"

"No, his unbridled vanity leads him into stupidity. He would probably die without understanding how it could happen. Have you come to challenge me?"

"You have misunderstood my letter, then? My trip here was for naught?"

"Oh no, I understood your every word, dear lady. I will say that your servant nearly relieved himself in his breeches he was so afraid. But not you. That interests me. But, truth be told, it doesn't seem plausible to me that you would want to see me. Our last encounter didn't leave me with the impression that you wished my company again. Indeed, our last encounter made me rather angry with you. It was a long walk."

"It was your own fault. You underestimated me because I am a woman. You were, frankly, a boor. You should not have tried to force yourself on me or threaten me. I don't take kindly to such things. I'm now offering you a chance to improve your manners and gain a new friend, perhaps."

"Ah, that is what fascinates me. Why?"

Sinjun leaned down in her saddle toward him. She said softly, her breath warm on his face, her eyes as blue as the cloudless sky, "You're too pretty for a man. It has teased me, this prettiness of yours. I want to see if you are a real man beneath those britches of yours, or a pretty boy prancing about in a man's body."

His eyes narrowed in fury. He grabbed her, but she gently raised her hand, the pistol not six inches from his face.

"I told you I didn't appreciate boors, sir. Now, will you prove yourself to me? What is it to be—a pretty boy or a man with a man's desires?"

Now she saw lust spring to life in his eyes, raw and deep. She'd practiced this so many times during the past day and she'd won, but it was terrifying.

"How do I know you won't take me into the woods and shoot me with that pretty little pistol?"

She smiled at him. "You don't."

He studied her face a moment longer. "You're a bit pale now. Perhaps you are a bit frightened?"

"A bit. After all, you could have your men hidden about to shoot me. But it would sorely hurt your reputation were you to kill a woman. On the other hand, who knows? And I have always thought life should be experienced to the fullest and if there are no risks, then why bother? Do you have men hidden about?"

"No. As you said, you're only a woman. You're also an Englishwoman, an earl's daughter. I've never met another woman like you. You fascinate me. Why did you marry Colin if you didn't want him? You've been married two months, isn't that right?"

"Perhaps you've also heard that of that time, we've spent very few days—and nights—together. He remains in Edinburgh and I am stuck here in that moldering castle of his. I'm bored, sir, and you appear to be something out of the ordinary. I knew you were different from Colin the moment I saw you. You are quite pretty, you know."

He gave her a brooding look, saying finally, "Come to the stable. I will get my horse and then, my dear, I will take you to this special place and show you that a man can have a pretty face and be endowed with splendid attributes as well."

"As splendid as Colin?"

He stiffened taut as a poker.

"I could say many things about my husband, but the fact is that he is every inch a man. It's just that he doesn't care about me, just my money."

"He is nothing," MacPherson said at last. "I will prove it to you shortly."

Sinjun sincerely doubted that could be true, but she held her tongue. She wanted him to come with her, not howl with fury and try to knock her from her horse. The last thing she wanted to do was to have to shoot him here on his own lands. It didn't seem the politic thing to do.

Ten minutes later Robert MacPherson was surrounded by three ladies on horseback, each of them pointing a pistol at him. He turned to Sinjun. "So, I see I was right."

"Not at all. Colin knows nothing about this. You see, Colin has much too much honor just to hunt you down like the wretch you are and do away with you. Thus, sir, we three have decided to remove the burden from his shoulders. I cannot allow you to try to harm him again. You really shouldn't have tried to kill him in London or in Edinburgh. You really shouldn't have burned our crofters' huts and killed our people.

"You will pay for your crimes and it will give me vast relief to have you long gone from here. Incidentally, my husband didn't kill your sister. If he wouldn't kill a vermin like you, why then, how can you possibly believe that he would ever harm a woman who was his wife?"

"She bored him. He was tired of her."

"Perhaps you have a point. After all, after only two meetings, you bore me quite beyond reason. However, even though I am tempted to toss you off a cliff, I won't, even though in addition to being a boor, you're a bully and a sneak and a man who knows no honor. I understand from Colin that your father is a good man and I wouldn't want to distress him overly. Enough of this. Alex, Sophie, I've said my piece. Shall we tie him to his horse?"

Colin was at first utterly confused, then so furious he wanted to spit and curse at the same time, something that wasn't easily accomplished.

He stood in front of his son and said in a voice so angry it sounded calm, far too calm, "You are telling me that your stepmother and your two aunts are out wandering about the estate?"

"That's what Sinjun told me, Papa. She said she felt wonderful and wanted to show them around. I asked her where you were and . . . she didn't tell me the truth, I guess."

"You bloody well mean she lied! Damn her eyes, I'll beat her, I'll lock her in my bedchamber, I'll—"

"My lord," Dr. Childress said, touching his age-spotted hand to Colin's sleeve. "What is amiss here? The countess isn't ill after all?"

"My wife," Colin said between his teeth, "pretended to be very ill, all to get me out of the way. Damnation! What is she up to?"

He was silent for several moments, then slapped his palm to his forehead. "How could I be so stupid?"

He turned on his heel and raced for Gulliver, who was chomping contentedly on some of Aunt Arleth's white roses beside the front steps.

Philip said to the doctor, "I fear my mother has enraged my father. I'd best go after him and protect her. Forgive us, sir." And Philip raced after his father.

Dr. Childress stood alone, bemused, listening to the boy's footsteps echo off the entrance hall stones. He'd known Colin since the moment he'd slipped from his mother's womb. He'd watched him grow straight and tall and proud. He'd watched his father and his older brother try to kill the spirit in him, and fail, thank the good Lord. He said aloud, his voice pensive, "I fear the young lady has unleashed a tiger."

The tiger pulled to a stop in the cover of some fir trees and stared toward St. Monance Castle. Gulliver was blowing hard, and as he watched the castle he gently patted his stallion's neck. "You're a good old fellow, aren't you, Gull? Well, you're in a damn sight better position than my wife, who isn't going to like the way her day proceeds after I get my hands on her. Another thing," he continued to his horse, "Ostle is gone, supposedly ill and back in his bed. I don't think that sounds at all believable. Another thing, that fool wife of mine had the gall to take Argyll." He shuddered even as he said those words to his horse. Gulliver paid no heed, just shook his head to get the flies off.

Colin couldn't make out anything unusual at St. Monance Castle. MacPherson folk were going about their tasks. There didn't seem to be anything out of the ordinary, no massing of men, no shouting, nothing at all unusual.

What had Joan and the wives planned to do? That stymied him. What was she plotting? Had she indeed come here?

He realized after another ten minutes of quite boring observations that he was wasting his time. Unless he intended to ride up to the big iron-studded doors of St. Monance and demand to know where his wife was, then sitting here like a blind fool would gain him naught. His fear and fury at his wife had made him act without thinking.

Where the devil was Joan? Where were the wives?

He drew a deep breath, turned Gulliver, and stared at his son, who was sitting there astride his pony, quiet as could be. Colin said nothing. He hadn't even heard Philip ride up. He was in bad shape. He shook his head. Together, father and son rode thoughtfully back to Vere Castle.

He supposed he wasn't overly surprised to see all three horses returned to the stables, in their stalls, eating their heads off. It was obvious to the meanest eye that they'd been ridden hard. Damn her eyes. Argyll looked up at him and stared, as if to say, "She really did it this time, my good man."

Colin grinned, but it wasn't an amused grin. He was ready to kill. What the devil had she done? And she'd ridden that damned horse, curse her eyes.

He strode to the house, his riding crop slashing against his thigh in rhythm to his walk.

He didn't say anything to anyone. He shook his head at Philip when he would say something, and took the stairs two and three at a time.

"Remember, Papa," Philip shouted after him. "Remember she's been ill!"

"She'll pray for a fever before I'm through with her," Colin shouted back over his shoulder.

He saw Aunt Arleth. She, in turn, saw his rage and smiled. It was obvious to Colin that she was devoutly praying that he would murder his wife. It was a thought, but he preferred torture and slow strangulation. Emma was coming out of one of the wives' bedchambers. She saw the earl and quickly dashed back inside.

"Smart of you," he said under his breath. He wanted to crash into the laird's bedchamber and start yelling. At the last minute he forced himself to calm. These ladies had to be handled carefully. They were used to men who yelled; yelling wouldn't yield the desired effect of making them fall in a faint and stutter and plead and stammer out the truth.

Very gently, his fingers nearly cramping with the effort to contain his ire, Colin opened the bedchamber door. Odd, but he wasn't at all surprised to see the two wives gowned as gloriously as society ladies all set for tea. They looked elegant, fresh, and beautiful; his wife was lying in bed, her hair soft and curling around her face, wearing a lovely lace-covered peignoir. She looked very young and elegant and innocent as a lamb. She was holding a book in her hand. All looked tranquil. It could have been an English drawing room in Putnam Square. There wasn't a hair out of place on any of their heads. There wasn't a wrinkle in any of their gowns. They were giving him inquiring looks, as if to say, "Goodness, a gentleman is here. How very strange. He came without an invitation. What should we do with him?"

Sinjun called out, her voice as sweet and innocent as her damned face, "Oh, Colin. I'm delighted you're back. Do forgive me for sending you on that quite useless errand to Dr. Childress, but I felt much better nearly the exact moment after you'd left. Strange, isn't it? I tried to call you back but you left too quickly. I'm just fine now, as you can see. Aren't you pleased?"

"What I see," Colin said mildly as he walked into the room, "is a quite perfect stage setting. My God, it would do any Drury Lane theater proud. The three of you are really quite good. I've always known that Joan could move quickly—indeed, accomplish incredible tasks in very little time, just witness our elopement—and now I see that you two aren't to be left in the dust. Even the color of your gowns and her peignoir complement each other. Remarkable. I applaud you."

Sinjun said nothing. The wives were silent, blank smiles firmly affixed to their faces, their hands steady in their laps.

He walked to Sinjun and sat beside her on the bed. He very lightly traced his fingertips over her cheek. She looked suddenly flushed as a very ripe apple. He was so furious he wanted to strangle her. He looked at her white neck wistfully. Her hair was soft and lovely, so very thick and curly. He ran his fingers through several strands. He remained silent, just looking at her, touching her face and hair.

Sinjun had believed he would storm into their bedchamber and yell and rant. But he hadn't and now she wasn't so sure. She waited, keeping quiet. There wasn't a word in her head in any case.

"How very lovely you look," he said after another few moments of silence. "Lovely and clean and there's not even a hint of horse smell on you."

"We only rode for a very little while. I did tire quickly."

"Yes, I imagine you did. Poor darling, are you certain you're better? I don't have to fear another relapse?"

"Oh no, Colin, I feel just grand. It's kind of you to be concerned for me."

"Yes, isn't it? Actually, what I want from you, Joan, what I want this very instant, is the truth. If you lie to me, I will know it and I will punish you."

"Punish me? Really, sir, such a threat isn't at all civilized."

"At this moment I'm not feeling at all civilized. I'm feeling quite savage. Speak to me, Joan. Now." His voice was so low and calm and quiet, yet his words . . . Oh dear, he couldn't be any more dangerous than Douglas or Ryder at their best, could he?

She darted a look toward Sophie and Alex, who both looked nailed to their chairs. Then Sophie, bless her, jumped to her feet. "Goodness, Colin, all we did was ride out a bit, nothing more. Then Sinjun felt a bit weak and we came back to the castle and put her to bed. Surely you aren't angry about that."

Colin said pleasantly, "You're lying, Sophie. Unfortunately, I'm not your husband so I can't beat you. But this simpleton here is my wife. She belongs to me. She is supposed to obey me; however, I've yet to experience that blessed phenomenon. She will have to learn that—"

Alex grabbed her stomach, groaned loudly, and jumped to her feet.

"Oh dear! The baby—my stomach. Sophie, I'm going to be ill. Oh dear!"

It was a tableau worthy of Emma Hamilton, and Colin wasn't untouched by the talent to produce it. He began clapping. "Bravo," he said. "Ah, yes, bravo."

Alex fell to her knees and vomited on the newly cleaned Aubusson carpet.

17

"SHE WAS ALWAYS THROWING UP when she was pregnant with the twins," Sinjun said, struggling to get out of bed. "The first three months kept everyone on their toes trying to keep basins near her. Poor Alex."

"No, stay put," Colin said to his wife. He strode over to Alex, who was clutching her sides now, nothing more in her belly, trying to catch her breath. He grasped his sister-in-law under her arms and pulled her upright. He took a look at her pale face and the sweaty strands of hair plastered to her forehead, and swung her into his arms. He said gently, "You're feeling miserable, aren't you? I'm sorry, but it will get better soon." Sighing, Alex lay her face against his shoulder.

"Get some water and dampen a towel, Sophie," Colin said, and laid Alex next to Sinjun on the bed.

"At least she didn't eat much breakfast," Sinjun said. "Poor Alex, are you all right?"

"No," Alex said, and groaned. "Stop calling me 'poor Alex.' It makes me feel like a gouty maiden aunt."

Sophie alerted the servants to the disaster and for the next few minutes pandemonium reigned. Emma stared wide-eyed at the mess, two other serving maids stacked behind her, gawking. Sophie brought a wet towel,

Rory the footman behind her, craning to see into the bedchamber. Mrs. Seton trailed her with a basin of cool water.

"Here, drink this," Colin said, and lifted Alex slightly. She sipped at the water he'd poured into a glass from the carafe on the bedside table, promptly grabbed her stomach, and groaned again.

"I remember drinking water sometimes made her stomach cramp," Sinjun said. "Mrs. Seton, what we need is some hot tea."

"Poor little mite," said Mrs. Seton, and efficiently wiped Alex's face. "Aye, birthing isn't always an unafflicted joy."

Alex groaned again, and Sophie announced, "I wasn't sick for a minute."

"Shut up, Sophie," Alex said, teeth gritted. "First you don't have the good sense to tell Douglas where we are and now you're bragging about how wonderful you felt carrying Grayson when I want to die."

"Shush," Colin said, taking the cloth from Mrs. Seton and wiping Alex's clammy face. "You'll feel just the thing very soon, I promise."

There were suddenly loud footsteps in the corridor, coming closer and faster, as if a battalion of crusaders had just arrived to free the Holy Land. It needed but this, Colin thought, staring at Douglas Sherbrooke as he burst into the bedchamber, flinging the door so hard that it slammed against the wall. Ryder nearly rammed into Douglas's back, and there was Philpot, consternation writ plainly on his face, jumping up and down behind Ryder.

"My lord," Philpot yelled above the jumble of voices. "They truckled right ov'r me!"

"It's all right," Colin said on a sigh. He continued to wipe Alex's face. "Hello, Douglas, Ryder. Do come in. Philpot, they won't attempt violence in front of their wives. Ah, Emma, stop staring at the mess. Please clean it up. The rest of you—out!"

"I knew you'd come," Sinjun said, beaming at both of them. "But this is faster than I expected, even for you two."

Sophie was staring down at her slippers.

Alex just groaned and closed her eyes.

Douglas said dispassionately, as he strode to the bed and stood there, staring down at his wife, "So you were sick, were you? And on the beautiful carpet, I see. Well, Sinjun, it's your own fault. You know how Alex is. Blessed hell, she threw up on every carpet of value at Northcliffe Hall. Didn't you have the foresight to put a basin in every room? She even threw up on my favorite burgundy dressing gown."

"You deserved it," Alex said without opening her eyes.

Ryder wasn't at all dispassionate. He strode to his wife, grasped her arms, and shouted two inches from her face, "Damn you, look at me, Sophie!"

"I'm looking!"

"You left me! You vex me, woman; your gall has gone too far this time."

"My gall has never gone anywhere before! And you're here, Ryder, here with Douglas, just as we knew you'd be, although Alex was beginning to think that Douglas wouldn't come just to punish her with his absence."

"Yes, I'm here. I would never use absence as a punishment and neither would Douglas. Blessed hell, I was worried about you, nearly fretted myself out of my mind until I realized it was all a lie. You're not pregnant."

"I never said I was. You were strutting around all arrogant and pleased with yourself. I simply didn't gainsay you."

"I will beat you. Where is your bedchamber?"

"I shan't take you to my chamber. Alex is sick. Sinjun was sick but she's better now. Colin appears philosophical but I don't trust it. You and Douglas are as you always are. Sinjun knew you'd be here. But I don't know how you could be here since I didn't tell you where we were going."

"Yes," Alex said, "how did you know, Douglas?"

Douglas was looking at poor Emma, who was cleaning up the carpet. He turned to his wife and said, "You twit. You think I couldn't very quickly determine where you'd gone?"

"I told you I was going to see Sophie," Alex said, refusing to open her eyes.

"Och, here's a cup o' tea for her ladyship," Mrs. Seton said, and marched to the bed. She gave Douglas a severe look and he obligingly moved. She sat down and gently put the rim to Alex's lips. "Oh, that's good," Alex said, her head falling back on the pillow after three healthy sips.

"The two of you look quite remarkable in that bed, side by side," Ryder said.

"I want you to feel better," Douglas said to his wife. "I have quite a bit to say to you, madam."

"Oh, stow it, Douglas," Sinjun said, and immediately regretted opening her mouth, because her brother, frustrated because his wife was ill and thus immune from his displeasure for the moment, bent the full force of his anger on her. "So, little sister, you've been up to all sorts of nonsense again, haven't you? I can see you're well enough again for any sort of just deserts. I would personally enjoy taking your skirts up over your bottom, but you've a husband now and I must deny myself that pleasure. However, I must hope that he will do it. She is well enough now, isn't she, Colin?"

Colin smiled. "Yes, she certainly is well enough now."

"Good," Douglas said, rubbing his hands together. "I hope he won't suffer your pranks as I've had to over an interminable number of years."

"I daresay I won't suffer pranks at all."

Sophie interrupted. "Listen, Douglas, I want to know how you and Ryder knew to come here. Sinjun said you'd be here Friday, but that's just because she thinks you're both gods."

Alex moaned softly. Mrs. Seton reached in one of her large pockets and drew out a fat scone, wrapped in a napkin and bulging with raisins. "Try this, my lady, 'tis soft an' easy for the belly. 'Twill make ye settle, ye'll see."

Sinjun was staring at Douglas. He looked uncomfortable; he was actually flushing. He rose and strode across the bedchamber and back again. He was clearly agitated.

But it was Alex who was eyeing him with dawning comprehension as she chewed on her scone. "It was the Virgin Bride! She came to you and told you where we were. What else did she tell you?"

"That's utter nonsense!" Douglas shouted. "Nothing of the sort. That bloody damned ghost. She doesn't exist—"

"Naturally not," Sinjun said. "She's been dead for centuries. It's her ghost that hovers about."

"Shut your mouth, Sinjun. I merely applied a few mental processes—very few were necessary, given you two—and quickly realized that you would go haring off to Scotland."

Ryder was frowning at his brother. "You fetched me from Ascot. You told me we had to go get our wives, that they'd heard from Sinjun, and that she was ill and that there was trouble. I didn't think to question you then. I thought Alex had left you a letter, but obviously she hadn't. How did you know Sophie was involved? What's going on here, Douglas?"

Douglas plowed his fingers through his hair, standing it on end. He looked clearly harassed, defensive, and wary. "I just got this feeling, that's all. A simple feeling. We all have simple feelings from time to time, even you, Ryder. This bloody feeling came when I was sleeping in Alex's bed because Mother had insisted on having my mattress restuffed and pounded, God knows why. I like flat goose feathers. I just felt them then, during the night, these simple feelings when I was thinking about Alex, that's all. Simple feelings and simple deductions."

Colin had moved to stand by the fireplace, leaning negligently against the mantel, his arms crossed over his chest. He looked utterly unmoved by all the carping and ghost talk. He even appeared mildly amused to Sinjun's fond eye, at least she hoped he was amused. He'd be easier to deal with if he was amused. He said at last when there was a moment's break, "The carpet wasn't all that expensive. Don't worry about it, Alex. I think Emma's done an excellent job."

Alex cocked an eye open. "Thank you, Colin. You're very kind to a sick lady, unlike—"

"Don't even think about saying it," Douglas said. Mrs. Seton had left, albeit with a lagging step, and he had resumed his seat on the bed by his wife. "No, not a damned word. I am your husband and it is I who am kind to you, no other man, do you understand?"

Her eyes twinkled at him for the first time. "I understand. But Douglas, you must have seen the ghost and she told you where we'd gone."

"No, dammit!"

"What I don't understand," Sophie interrupted, "is why the Virgin Bride would tell Douglas. Doesn't she think we're capable of dealing with the situation by ourselves?"

"Oh God," Sinjun said. "Sophie!"

Sophie clapped her hand over her mouth, darting an agonized look at Colin.

"So," Colin said, "there is a situation, not that I ever doubted it. It must involve MacPherson. I assume you took care of him once you'd gotten rid of me this morning. My dear wife, what have you done with him? Is he dead? Did the three of you draw lots to see who would kill him?"

"Never," Alex said.

"I would have liked to kill him," Sinjun said wistfully, "but I didn't think you'd approve. You're fond of his father. No, the bounder isn't dead. You do understand, don't you, Colin? I had to do something. I had to protect you. You're my husband. He would have snuck up on you, stuck a knife in your back; he's that sort of man. Or he would have sent some of his bullies, like he did in London when you got stabbed in the leg. He has no honor, no—"

Colin didn't move a muscle, but Sinjun saw the tic by his right eye.

He said with superb calm, "This is all quite interesting, don't you agree, Douglas, Ryder? My wife, who is also your little sister, thinks I'm helpless as a motherless foal. She enjoys unmanning me. She believes me feeble, a fool, unable to see to the truth of things, unable to protect myself when appropriate. What do you think I should do to her?"

He didn't sound very amused now, Sinjun thought.

"You're her husband," Douglas said. "You will do whatever is necessary to keep her safe."

"I should like to know," Ryder said thoughtfully, disregarding Colin and Douglas and still clutching his wife's upper arms, "how you three all got together."

"The Virgin Bride visited Alex, naturally," Sophie said. "She normally only appears in the countess's bedchamber, as Douglas very well knows, except for that time when I first came to Northcliffe Hall. Then she welcomed me in your bedchamber, Ryder."

"Bosh," said Ryder. "You were anxious for me to make love to you, and when I didn't come to you quickly enough, your female brain decided upon something dramatic to relieve your anxiety. That or Sinjun played the Virgin Bride again. Alex's brain has done the same thing."

"But she does usually visit only the countess's bedchamber," Alex said. "As Douglas very well knows."

"That's not entirely true. Once—" Douglas stopped and cursed. "Listen, all of you. Enough is enough. For whatever combination of reasons, all of us are here. There is a situation. I should like to get it resolved. Now, Sinjun, what have you done with this MacPherson fellow whom we don't yet know?"

"We manacled him and locked him in a deserted croft."

The three men stared at Sinjun, speechless for the first time in fifteen minutes. The chamber reeked with the blessed silence.

"We weren't overly cruel," Sinjun continued. "He has some length on the chain so he can walk about a bit and do private things as well. But the manacle was necessary. We couldn't risk his escaping."

"I see," Colin said slowly. "And is Robbie to starve to death?"

"Oh no," Alex said, eyes firmly on Colin, not on Douglas. "We're taking turns going to the croft to feed him. We didn't want you to suspect anything." She sighed. "I suppose it's all blasted to hell now."

Douglas's dark eyes twinkled, he couldn't help it. "No," he said, patting his wife's pale cheek, "no, it's not at all blasted anywhere." He rose. "Ryder, Colin, shall we handle this situation to our satisfaction now?"

Sinjun gasped. "No, we won't let you! Why don't all of you just go back home—"

"I am home," Colin said.

"You know what I mean. We don't need your interference. Everything is going splendidly. There is no more situation. I have everything in hand. All plans will . . . Oh damn, just go away, all of you."

"Where is the croft, Joan?"

"I shan't tell you. You'll just let him go and then he'll kill you and I'll be a widow even before I'm scarcely a wife, and it isn't fair."

"I fully intend that you become a full and complete and happy wife," Colin said, and was pleased when she closed her mouth. "Where is the croft?"

Sinjun just shook her head.

Douglas said, "All right, Alex, where is it?"

Alex batted her eyelashes and looked utterly helpless. She heaved a deep sigh, which sent her husband's eyes immediately to her glorious bosom. She fluttered her hands. "I don't remember, Douglas; you know how horrid I am with directions. It was all this way and then that way and only Sinjun knows. Sophie and I were hopelessly lost, weren't we, Sophie?"

"Hopelessly."

"I'm going to beat you now," Ryder said, and hauled his wife tightly against him. He leaned down to say something, but kissed her instead, full on her mouth. He raised his head and grinned. "Don't worry, Douglas, Colin. I can get anything at all out of her with enough time. She melts like a candle. It's really quite charming and—"

Sophie sent her fist into his belly.

He sucked in his breath but continued to grin. "Now, love, don't deny it, you know that you adore me, that you worship me and the very shadow of my footsteps. You're like a lovely rose that opens to the sun each morning."

"Gawd," Sinjun said, "you're a horrible poet, Ryder. Just be quiet and let Sophie lone."

Colin, frowning, said, "I would like to know what you three intended to do with MacPherson. Surely you don't want to have to feed him three times a day for the next thirty years?"

"No," Sinjun said. "We have a plan. If you would simply go away and drink brandy or something, all will be taken care of."

"What is the plan, Sinjun?" Douglas asked. He rose now to walk around to her side of the bed. She shook her head and stared at the middle button on his buff riding jacket.

"Sinjun," he said, leaning down over her, "I held you in my arms when you were born. You burped up milk on my shirt. I taught you how to ride. Ryder taught you how to tell jokes. We both taught you how to shoot and enjoy books. Without us, you would have grown up to be scarce anything at all. Now, tell us what your plan is."

She shook her head again.

"I can still whip you, brat."

"No, unfortunately you can't, Douglas," Colin said. "But I can and I firmly intend to. She swore to obey me when we were wedded but she hasn't yet gotten beyond the abstract to the concrete."

"How the devil could I obey you when you were in Edinburgh? Ignoring me, I might add. You were happy as a lark in that damned house with the black hole in the drawing room ceiling, weren't you?"

"Ah, a bit of anger, Joan? Perhaps you would like to tell everyone here why I have remained in Edinburgh?"

"Your reasons were absurd. I reject them. I spit upon them."

Colin sighed. "It's difficult. I wish to deal with you properly but I can't, not with your damned brothers hovering about. Douglas, Ryder, why don't you remove your wives from this bedchamber? Then I can question Joan suitably."

"No, I want Alex and Sophie to stay here! I'm hungry. It's time for lunch."

"Ah," Colin said. "And which of the wives is to take MacPherson his lunch?"

"Go to the devil, Colin."

Ryder laughed. "Well, we'll have our answer soon enough. Unless they wish MacPherson to starve, they will have to take him food sometime. Then we will know."

"Why did you remain in Edinburgh, Colin?" Douglas asked.

"To protect my wife," Colin said simply. "And my children. That morning when she had the cut on her cheek, it was from a bullet ricocheting off a rock and striking her. I couldn't allow her to remain in Edinburgh with me. I thought she would be safe here, and she was until MacPherson decided to leave Edinburgh and go to ground back here."

"What children?" Ryder asked, looking at his brother-in-law blankly.

"Not again," Sinjun said. "I have two stepchildren, Philip and Dahling. You will meet them shortly. They will adore you, Ryder, as all children do. They might not even run screaming from you, Douglas, if you would stop your scowling."

Douglas was giving Colin a brooding look. Finally he sighed. "There is much here to consider. I think I shall take my wife to bed—so she can rest, naturally—then I would like to meet my new niece and nephew."

"Come along, Sophie, you may accompany Alex. If I get you alone, I just might behave in a manner ill-suited to our blissful married state."

When Colin and Sinjun were alone, Colin shoved off the mantel and strode over to her. His expression was bland but his eyes, those beautiful dark blue eyes of his, were hot with anger. He sat on the bed beside her. He said nothing, merely leaned down over her, his face inches from hers. He looked into her eyes. Finally he said very quietly, "You have gone too far this time. I will tolerate no more insults from you, no more interference in my affairs. Where is MacPherson?"

"If I tell you he might be able to hurt you. Please, Colin, can't I continue with my plan?"

He leaned back a bit and crossed his arms over his chest. "Tell me this plan of yours."

"I am delivering Robert MacPherson up to the Royal Navy. I understand they aren't terribly discriminating about who is delivered up to them, whether or not the man wishes to be there or not, you understand."

"Oh yes, I understand." He looked away from her now. "It isn't a bad plan," he said mildly. "Which ship of the Royal Navy do you have in mind?"

"I sent Ostle to Leith to see which ships were available to us. There's bound to be at least one, don't you think?"

"Yes, if not right this minute, then not long from now. However, there is something you couldn't have known that makes it impractical."

"And what is that, pray?"

He grinned at the rancor in her voice. "The word clan comes from the Gaelic *clann* and means simply 'children.' So you see, the Clan MacPherson are really the children of MacPherson. If you eliminate one of the clan, or children, the others are bound to seek revenge and retribution. If you make the son of the laird disappear, the Kinross clan will be the prime suspects, and there will be violence. It will escalate with scarce any provocation at all. It's a vicious cycle. Do you understand?"

Sinjun nodded slowly. "I didn't realize. Oh dear, what shall I do now, Colin?"

"First, you will promise me that you will never again take matters into your own white hands. You will never again keep secrets from me. You will never again seek to protect me from any enemies."

"That's a lot to promise, Colin."

"You did it before and you lied to me. I will give you another chance, mainly because you're too weak for me to beat you with any sort of efficacy."

"I will promise if you will promise the same thing."

"I'll beat you despite your weakness."

"Do you want to?"

"Not really, perhaps fifteen minutes ago I would have thoroughly enjoyed it, but not now. Actually, it was strangulation I was thinking of. I would prefer now to strip that nightgown off you and kiss every inch of you."

"Oh."

"Oh," he repeated, mimicking her.

"I think I should like that, at least the kissing part."

"I will kiss you once you have told me where MacPherson is so I can deal with this."

Sinjun didn't know what to do. She was frightened for her husband and unfortunately it showed on her face. He said, "Don't even think it, Joan. Tell me the truth now and tell me all of it. Then you may give me your promise to keep yourself out of my affairs."

"He's in the croft that lies just on the western edge of Craignure Moor."

"An excellent hidey-hole. No one goes there. He should be quite enraged by now."

"He hasn't been there all that long, no more than three hours now."

"I will see you later," he said, and rose to stand beside the bed. "I wish you to rest and regain your strength. I've realized that keeping away from you wasn't a good idea. You're my wife. I will sleep with you tonight and every night for the rest of our lives."

"That would be nice," she said, then began twisting the covers in her long fingers. "I want to go with you, Colin. I want to see this through."

He looked at her for a very long time. "Remember I told you the message MacDuff brought to me in Edinburgh? That you had no intention of stealing my box? I looked at him as blankly as a cutpurse caught in the act, and he explained that he'd told you about my father and my brother. I wish he hadn't, but now it's done. I also realize, a bit perhaps, that you want to be important to Vere Castle and to me and to the children. Very well, Joan, you and I will go see Robert MacPherson."

"Thank you, Colin."

"Let's wait for another couple of hours. I should like him to be raw-brained with rage."

Sinjun grinned at him. To her deep pleasure, he smiled back at her. "I will come back to awaken you. Sleep now."

It was a very good start, she thought, watching him leave the bedchamber. An excellent start. She hadn't the heart to tell him she was quite hungry, not at all sleepy.

It was close to ten o'clock at night. Sinjun was sitting in her husband's lap in a deep wing chair that sat facing the fireplace. She was wearing a nightgown and a pale blue dressing gown. Colin was still in his buckskins and white batiste shirt. The evening was cool. Colin had lit a fire and the warmth of it was soothing. Sinjun laid her face against her husband's shoulder, turning slightly every few moments to kiss his neck.

"The brothers and wives seem to be speaking to each other again," Colin said. "I would further say that if Sophie isn't with child right now, she soon will be. Ryder was looking at her all through dinner like a man starving."

"He always looks at her like that, even when he's furious with her."

"She's a lucky woman."

Sinjun looked up at his shadowed jaw. "Perhaps you could look at me like that sometimes."

"Perhaps," he said, and tightened his hold on her. "How do you feel?"

"Our adventure with Robert MacPherson didn't tire me out at all."

"Ah, so that's why you slept for two hours upon our return home?"

"Maybe a little bit," she conceded. "Do you think he'll draw off the attack now? Do you think you can believe him?"

Colin thought back to the hour he and Joan had spent in the dismal little croft with Robert MacPherson. They'd arrived in the middle of the afternoon and he'd allowed her to enter the croft first. She walked like a general leading her troops. He smiled at the back of her head. He was glad he'd brought her with him. Two months before he couldn't have imagined doing such a thing, but Joan was different; she'd made him see things differently.

Robert MacPherson was so furious he couldn't at first speak. He saw her coming through the door of the croft and he wanted to leap upon her and cuff her senseless. Then Colin came in behind her and he froze, frightened for the first time, but he refused to let the bastard see his fear.

"So," he said, spitting in the dirt floor in front of him, "it was a lie. You did know about this. You sent your damned wife to get me. You rotter, you damned slimy coward!"

"Oh no," Sinjun said quickly. "Colin has come to rescue you from me. I would have given you over to the Royal Navy and let you swab decks until you reformed or got kicked overboard and drowned, but Colin wouldn't allow it."

"You don't look very comfortable, Robbie," Colin said, stroking his jaw. MacPherson lunged forward, but only three feet. He was pulled to an ignominious halt by the chains.

"Get these things off me," he said, panting with rage.

"In good time," Colin said. "First I'd like to talk to you. A pity there are no chairs, Joan. You're looking just a bit white around your jawline. Sit on the packed dirt and lean back against the wall. That's right. Now, Robbie, you and I will discuss things."

"You bloody murderer! There's nothing to discuss! Go ahead and kill me. Aye, you do that, you murdering sod. My men will destroy Vere Castle and all your lands. Go ahead!"

"Why?"

"What the hell do you mean, why? You killed my sister. You killed poor Dingle."

"Oh no, Dingle was killed by another of your own men. As it happens, my son, Philip, witnessed the whole thing. It was a fight about a woman, naturally. Alfie killed him."

Robert MacPherson shook his head and said in disgust, "That damned chit! I told them—" He broke off and jerked forward once more against the chains. They held firm. "All right, I will give you that one. Still, you murdered my sister."

Sinjun opened her mouth, then closed it. This was up to Colin, and she realized that it was important that she keep still. MacPherson must know now that she loved her husband to distraction, must believe she'd lie for him without hesitation, all true naturally. It was difficult, but she kept quiet, and watched.

"Your sister died nearly eight months ago. Why didn't you act immediately against me?"

"I didn't believe you'd killed her then. My father was certain you were innocent and I believed him. But then I found out the truth."

"Ah," said Colin. "The truth. Could you tell me the source of this truth?"

MacPherson looked suddenly crafty. "Why should I? I have no reason to doubt the source. My father wouldn't either if he had an unconfused thought left in his pathetic brain."

"Your father was quite clear in his thinking the last time I visited him," Colin said. "Go back to Edinburgh and tell him. See if he agrees with you. My guess it that he will laugh at you. I think you're afraid to tell him, Robbie, afraid of his scorn at your damned credulity. Well? Answer me. No? I will tell you something else. I believe you prefer skulking about in the shadows, hiring your bully boys. I believe you prefer claiming your father is brain-soft and that is only because he won't agree with you about me. Thus, you want to toss him out with the rubbish. Tell him, Robbie. He's the MacPherson laird. He's your father. Trust him, for God's sake. Now, who told you I killed your sister?"

"I won't tell you."

"Then how can I allow you to leave here? I don't wish to die, nor do I wish to have to worry all the time about Joan's safety and my children's safety."

MacPherson looked at the chafed flesh on his wrists. Chained to the bloody wall like a damned criminal, and all by that ridiculous little chit who sat on the floor, watching him with her wide blue eyes. She'd tricked him; she'd made a fool. He pulled his eyes away from her. He stared at Colin Kinross, a man he'd known all his life, a man who was tall and lean and trustworthy, with a man's strong features, not pretty as he was, a man women adored and sought out. The man Fiona had loved despite her insane jealousy. No one doubted Colin's virility; oh yes, he'd heard the silly girls giggling about him, his endowments, his skills as a lover. No one questioned that he was less than a man. He felt the jealousy grind into him and looked away. He said, his voice low, "If I promise I won't attempt to harm either this girl here or your children, will you release me? Good God, man, Philip and Dahling are my nephew and niece, for God's sake! They're Fiona's children; I wouldn't hurt them."

"No, I believe that would be beyond even you, Robbie. However, that leaves Joan. She is my wife. She also has this unfortunate habit of trying to save me all the time. It's appealing when it isn't enraging."

"She should be beaten. She's only a bloody woman."

"I daresay you wouldn't feel that way were she always on the lookout to keep you safe. Who told you I killed Fiona?"

"I won't harm her, damn you!"

"But you will keep trying to hurt Colin, won't you?" Sinjun was on her feet now. She felt no charitable leanings toward MacPherson. Were it up to her, she'd leave him chained here until he rotted.

He saw her feelings on her face and grinned at her. Colin said, "Sit down, Joan. Keep out of this."

She subsided, but her brain was working furiously. Who had accused Colin of murder? Aunt Arleth? That seemed a distinct possibility. With him dead, she could do as she pleased. But it made no sense, not really. Aunt Arleth much appreciated the money Sinjun's dowry had brought to the laird. If I were dead, she would rejoice, Sinjun thought, but Colin? What if Aunt Arleth did hate him enough to want him dead, because she somehow believed he was responsible for his brother's death? Sinjun felt a headache begin to pound at her over her right temple. It was too much, all of it.

Colin jumped as a log rolled off, scattering embers out onto the hearth. He was pulled abruptly back from his memories of the afternoon with MacPherson. He hugged his wife closer as she said, nestling closer as she kissed her husband's throat yet again, "Do you believe him, Colin?" She kissed him again. He tasted warm and salty and utterly wonderful. She could kiss him until she cocked up her toes.

"I don't wish to speak of him anymore tonight."

"But you let him go! I'm frightened!"

"You'll be safe. He swore on his father's name."

"Ha! He is a little weasel, pretty but deadly."

"Hush, Joan. I want to kiss you now." He gently shifted her in his arms and brought his mouth to hers. He tasted of the sweet, darkly mysterious port he'd drunk with Ryder and Douglas after dinner. His mouth was firm and when his tongue came gently between her lips she felt a desire to lock her arms around his neck and never let him go. "That feels wonderful," she said into his mouth. His tongue touched hers and she squirmed a bit.

He raised his head and looked at her. "I've missed you. Tonight, Joan, you'll learn pleasure. Will you trust me and cease your babble about my being too large for you?"

"But you're still as large as you were, Colin. That can't change. I still don't see how it can be at all wonderful for me when you have to come inside me."

He just grinned down at her. "Trust me."

"I suppose I must, since I want to see your beautiful face every day until I die. You're very important to me, Colin. You must take good care of yourself. All right?"

"Yes, and I'll also take good care of you."

He kissed her again and yet again. He continued kissing her, lightly then more deeply, nipping at her lower lip, kissing her until she was gasping and pressing herself against him, her fingers wild in his hair and on his shoulders. He made no move to caress her breasts or touch her anywhere but her back and her arms. Kissing seemed to be the only thing on his mind. Sinjun was very happy about it, for about five minutes.

She wanted more. It was disconcerting, but she didn't mind at all. She felt that tugging sensation low in her belly, a sort of burning that was intense yet still vague and indistinct, but she knew there had to be more and she wanted it. She vaguely remembered those feelings now, oh yes, she'd had them before, but they'd vanished when he'd hurt her. She grabbed his hand and pulled it to her stomach. She pressed his palm against her belly. "I feel very strange," she said into his mouth, her breath warm, her voice hoarse. She began to kiss him wildly, without restraint, her hands in his hair, stroking his face and shoulders.

"Yes, I can feel that you do," he said. His fingers didn't move for the longest time, merely rested lightly on her stomach. But he continued to kiss her until she moaned into his mouth. Then his fingers slipped slowly downward. Sinjun sucked in her breath, waiting. She felt frantic, and very very warm. She felt as if there was something wonderful waiting for her, and it was close now, very close.

"Colin," she said, and moaned into his mouth.

"What would you like now, Joan?"

18

COLIN HAD A STRATEGY and he had no intention of allowing himself to forget it or modify it. No, he had no intention of losing his control. No, tonight he was going to make his wife want him desperately, then he would see.

She was getting close and he was both delighted and immensely relieved.

He continued to kiss her. She was warm and soft and urgent and he wanted very much to cover her with his fingers, to ease inside of her, to feel her around him, to feel the softness and warmth of her. But he held off. No, let it build within her, this passion he would continue to inflame, until she was moaning with it, then yelling. He closed his eyes, trying to picture her face when her pleasure took her.

"I want—" she began, then touched her tongue to his and gasped.

"Yes, I'll give you that," he said, and deepened his kiss. His fingertips were lightly cupped over her, but not moving, not caressing her, just lying there.

Sinjun wondered what was happening. She remembered that he'd been a wild man before and he'd hurt her. She realized dimly that he was being very careful with her, very restrained. Did he believe her still weak from her illness?

No, he didn't want to scare her off again. She smiled against his wonderful mouth. She said quite without thought or hesitation, "I love you, Colin. I loved you from the first moment I saw you. I think you're the most remarkable man in Scotland."

He jerked at her words. He felt something move deep inside him, something he'd never felt before in his life, something hot and frantic, yet strangely gentle and tender. It scared the hell out of him. At first. Then he eased, allowing the feelings into himself, and her words. Yes, her words. He would think about it later. He kissed her again, tasting the sweetness of her mouth, and kissed her three more times before saying, "Only Scotland?"

"All right, perhaps in all of Britain."

"Kiss me, Joan."

Her mouth was red and swollen with his kisses, and yet again she leaned up against him without an instant's hesitation, and he saw the need in her beautiful eyes, felt the slight trembling of her mouth as his tongue slid between her lips.

When her tongue was warm in his mouth, his fingers suddenly dipped lower. His middle fingers pressed inward, hot as the devil against the light lawn of her nightgown. She thought she'd leap from his lap.

"Let's get you out of this damned thing," he said, feeling the soft material dampen beneath his fingers. He brought his fingers to her lips and gently pressed against them. "That's the taste of you, Joan. It's very nice, don't you think?"

She could but stare at him. Slowly, she nodded. He straightened her and pulled the gown over her head. He sat her there on his thighs, the firelight glowing behind her, her breasts in profile to him and her narrow waist and her flat belly. He'd never in his life seen a more beautifully made woman. And she was all his. His hands trembled and he flattened them to his thighs. No, he would hold control. He wouldn't frighten her, ever again. He would hold to his plan, but it was difficult, damned difficult.

He leaned his head against the chair back. The old leather creaked comfortably under the pressure. "What would you like me to do, Joan?"

"I want you to kiss me some more."

"Where?"

He heard her breath suck in sharply. "My breasts," she said, lightly stroking her fingers over his chin. "You're still clothed, Colin. That isn't fair."

"Forget fairness for the moment," he said, gently clasping her arms and pulling her against him. He wasn't about to let her see him naked. It would probably make her forget her passion. It would probably scare her out of her mind.

"I think your breasts can wait a bit," he said, and, still careful not to touch her anywhere that would make her tremble and shudder, he kissed her mouth, and again and then once more, his hands cupping her face, his fingers sliding through her hair, holding her head still for him. When she was squirming against his thighs, very lightly he cupped her left breast in his warm palm.

"Oh!"

"You're quite nice." His knuckles were rubbing lightly over her nipple. "Lie back against my arm."

She did, staring up at him. She watched him lean down even as his arm brought her upward, and when his mouth closed over her, she nearly yelled with the power of it. He smiled, tasting her sweet flesh, quivering himself, but experienced enough to keep it from her. His sex was hard as a stone and he wanted her very much, so much that he considered briefly just carrying her to the bed, spreading her thighs for him, and coming into her. Surely she was ready for him now. But no, he was a fool even to consider it for a moment.

He stopped himself and kissed her breast, fondling her with his fingers and his tongue until he knew she was very ready for him. His hand flattened on her belly and he felt the muscles tighten. "Now, I want you to close your eyes, sweetheart, and just picture in that lively mind of yours what my fingers are doing."

He didn't hold back now. His fingers found her quickly and he began a rhythm that was at once deep and gentle, light and urgent. She had no chance to object, no chance to feel embarrassed. All she could do was feel how her body was jerking, her legs clenching, then opening to him, and he saw those feelings clearly on her expressive face. She stared up at him, her eyes vague and bewildered. "Colin," she whispered and ran her tongue over her lower lip.

"Come along now, Joan. I want you to think about what my fingers are doing to you. I'm going to kiss you and I want you to let yourself go and cry out in my mouth."

At that moment, he eased his middle finger into her and nearly cried out himself at the wondrous feeling of her. He kissed her as if he would die without her and he wondered vaguely in those moments if it wasn't true. His fingers were on her swelled flesh again, stroking her, caressing her until she stiffened and pulled back. He looked at her face and smiled at her, painfully. "Yes, sweetheart. Come to me now."

She did, from one moment to the next, she was gasping, her legs stiff, such sensations pulsing through her that she couldn't begin to understand what was happening to her. Whatever it was, she prayed it would never stop. It was so strong and so deep and he was there, staring down at her, that smile in his eyes, and he was saying again and again, "Come to me, come to me . . ."

The feelings crested, flinging her into a world that was fresh and magical, a world that held her now and would never release her. She quieted. His fingers quieted, soothing her now, no longer inflaming her.

"Oh goodness," she whispered. "Oh goodness, Colin. That was wonderful."

"Yes," he said and there was both pain and immense pleasure in his voice and he never stopped looking at her, and now he leaned down and kissed her, softly, lightly. Ah, the bewilderment in her Sherbrooke blue eyes, and the vagueness and the excitement. It pleased him, pleased him to his soul.

Sinjun drew a deep breath. His pleasure, she thought. He hadn't received any pleasure from her. Would he hurt her now? Oh no, he wouldn't ever hurt her again. But his pleasure . . . Her heart slowed. Her eyes fluttered closed. To Colin's chagrin and amusement, she was asleep in the next moment.

He held her for a very long time in front of the warm fire, looking down at her, then into the dying flames, and wondering what this woman had done to him.

When Sinjun awoke the following morning, she was smiling. A silly smile, one that was absurdly content, one that held only one thought, and that thought was of her husband. Of Colin. God, she loved him. Suddenly she stilled and the smile slid off her face. She'd told him she loved him, loved him from the first moment she ever saw him, and he hadn't replied. But he'd given her such pleasure that she'd wondered even as she prayed it would never end if she would die from it.

She'd told him she loved him and he'd said naught.

Well, she'd been a fool, but she didn't care. It seemed ridiculous to her now that she would hold back anything from him. He cared for her, she knew that. Now he knew that she loved him. If it gave him power over her, then so be it. If he used the power to hurt her, so be that as well.

She was herself. She couldn't change. She was a wife, Colin's wife. God had given him to her; she would never hold back from him. He was, quite simply, the most important person in her life.

Still, when she entered the Laird's Inbetween Room some forty-five minutes later for her breakfast, she felt flushed and nervous and embarrassed. Colin was there, seated at his ease at the head of the table, a cup of coffee in his hand, a bowl of porridge in front of him, a curl of heat rising from it. The bowl sat on a beautiful white linen tablecloth she'd bought in Kinross.

Her brothers weren't there. Neither of the wives was there. The children weren't there. Neither Aunt Arleth nor Serena was there. There was a bloody castle full of people and they were alone.

"Everyone finished thirty minutes ago. I've been waiting for you to come down. I didn't think you would appreciate a full table."

Was that ever the truth, she thought, pinned a smile to her mouth, and walked in, head up.

He grinned at her like a wicked potentate. "I thought perhaps you'd want to speak to me about how I made you feel last night. In private, naturally. I thought perhaps you'd be disappointed because I only brought you to pleasure one time. I'm very sorry you fell asleep, Joan, but I was too much the gentleman to wake you and force you to climax yet again. You've been ill, after all, and I didn't want you to have to feel too much like a wife all at once."

"You're very kind, Colin," she said. She met his eyes and she flushed. He spoke as boldly as did her damned brothers. She never colored up like a silly chit when they were outrageous. She willed her tongue into action; her chin went up. "I'm not disappointed, husband, but I did worry about you. You were too kind. I told you, I would be your wife, but you didn't allow me to give you any respite."

"'Respite,'" he repeated. "What a gloomy word to use for screaming, thumping sexual pleasure. 'Respite.' I must mention that to my friends and see what they think."

"I would that you not do that. It is a rather private matter. Very well, I will take back 'respite' and be more like my brothers. I'm sorry you didn't have any sexual screaming, Colin."

"That's better. What makes you think there was no pleasure for me? I watched you climax, Joan. I watched your eyes get bluer, if that's possible, then grow dim and vague and it was quite charming. Indeed, I felt your pleasure, for you were trembling beneath my fingers and moaning and when you made those cries in my mouth I assure you I wanted to howl with masculine pleasure. Along with you."

"But you didn't," she said, slipping into her chair.

He gave her a look that was completely unreadable to her and said as matter-of-factly as a fifty-year husband, "Should you like some porridge?"

"Just toast, I think."

He nodded and rose to serve her. "No, remain seated. I want you strong again."

He poured her coffee and set her toast in front of her. Then, without warning, he grasped her chin in his hand and lifted her face. He kissed her, long and hard, then very gently. When he released her, her eyes were vague and dazzled and she was leaning against him, her arms loose at her sides.

"Philip told me he would forgive you for lying to him if you asked him nicely," he said, and walked back to the end of the table. "It appears he understands you very well. He said that you would walk through fire to save me, thus a lie was nothing if it served your cause in serving me."

She stared at him. Philip was a smart boy. She continued to stare at Colin, at his mouth. A word of affection would have been nice, she thought. Perhaps an endearment. Perhaps an acknowledgment that he was touched that she loved him. She tasted him on her own mouth. She just looked at him helplessly, all that she felt on her face.

He gave her a pained smile that vanished as quickly as it had appeared. "Eat, Joan." His expression remained unreadable, the sod.

She chewed on her toast, wondering why God, in his infinite wisdom, had created men to be so very different from women.

"I also wished to tell you that I intend to question Aunt Arleth this morning. If she was the source Robert MacPherson claims told him I killed Fiona, then I will get the truth out of her."

"Somehow I can't believe it was her. But she does cherish an amazing dislike for you. But then again, she heartily disliked Fiona. It was only your father and your brother she loved, if I understand what worked its way out of her mouth. Actually, Aunt Arleth makes little sense at the best of times. Remember all her talk about a kelpie being your father? She's very strange."

"It doesn't matter. Once I've either confirmed or rejected her part in this, she's leaving Vere Castle, her strangeness with her."

"She has no money, Colin."

"As I told you, she has family and I've already sent her brother a message. He and his family live near Pitlochry, in the central Highlands. They have no choice but to provide her a home. I'm sorry she behaved as she did toward you."

Nearly killed me dead, truth be told, Sinjun started to say, then stopped. It didn't matter now. She would soon be gone. She said, "If she wasn't Robert MacPherson's source, then who was?"

"I don't know, but I will find out. In the meantime, as you know, Robbie has promised to keep his men in control as well as himself. He's promised to speak to his father and to listen to him, really listen. Don't mistake me, Joan, if he attempts more violence against any of us or against any of our people, I will kill him. He knows it. Perhaps he will seek to be reasonable now."

"Serena is his sister. It makes more sense that she would have accused you to him."

He looked amused and vain as a very young man with his first compliment from a lady. "Oh no. Serena loves me. At least she's told me so countless times, and all those times since I married you. I'm also seeing that she returns to her father."

"Goodness, the castle will be bare! Please, Colin, it isn't necessary. Serena is an odd duck, perhaps daft, but harmless. If she tries to kiss you again, though, perhaps I will have to speak to her."

Colin laughed. "She doesn't realize how ferocious you are, how possessive of me you are. I should tell her that she isn't safe around you if she touches me again. She should request that I send her back to her father. Now that you're here for the children, there's no need for either of those ladies. Do you agree?"

"I quite agree," Sinjun said.

"Everything is happening now," he continued after a moment. "The sheep will be arriving within the next two days—not sheep to force our people off their lands, just enough to provide enough raw wool and milk. And the cattle, naturally, enough for all our people. I have also called a meeting of all my crofters and tenants. My proposition is that they will go from one croft to the next. I will furnish all the supplies and equipment we need. We will make all necessary repairs, from roofs to fences to bed frames. There will be no more want or uncertainty for the Kinross clan. Thank you, Joan."

"You're welcome," she said, and swallowed. He'd spoken to her like his partner. "Why are you telling me all this?"

He was silent for a moment. He took a spoonful of porridge and chewed thoughtfully. "It's your money that allows all this. It's only proper you know its disposition."

She felt a streak of disappointment, for his voice was cool and dismissive, but she managed to say calmly enough, "Tell me what to do. The household is shaping up quite nicely, but there is still much repair to be done. I also need gardeners."

"Yes, Alex has already filled my ears with what needs to be done outside. I shouldn't be surprised to find her out there weeding around the rosebushes. She was very impassioned about it. You will speak to Mr. Seton. He will bring men to you to interview. It will all take time, but time is something we now have. The creditors are no longer breathing down my neck. We are afloat; indeed, we are rowing smartly forward. We will make up that infamous list together quite soon. Now, Douglas and Ryder wish me to take them around and show them what we're doing. They wish to meet some of our people. Should you like to accompany us?"

She looked at her husband. He was including her. Did he finally understand she wouldn't steal his box and this was the proof of it? No, probably not. It was her money, as he'd said. He didn't want her to feel excluded. He was being kind. Blessed hell, but she hated kindness from him; kindness was a bloodless emotion.

"No, not this time," she said, tossing her napkin on her plate and rising. "I wish to visit with the children, particularly Philip. I owe him an apology, and since he is very much your son, I imagine he will make me grovel before absolving me."

Colin gave a shout of laughter.

"Also, the wives will want to know what's happened with MacPherson."

"I already told them everything at breakfast. Alex was arguing toe to toe with me when she turned green, grabbed her stomach, and sprinted from the room. Douglas sighed and hefted up the basin Mrs. Seton had given him and went after her. Ryder and Sophie were alternately laughing and yelling at each other. They were trying to look interested in all my projects, but failed woefully. Your brothers are charming, Joan, when they're not trying to kill me."

She grinned, picturing the scene without difficulty. "How did Aunt Arleth and Serena react? Guilty? Angry?"

"Aunt Arleth said not a word. Serena looked vague. It was Dahling who had all the questions. She wanted to know why you didn't take her to confront MacPherson since it was a ladies' battle. She then asked Serena why her brother was such a bad man. Serena said he hated his angel's face and thus he cultivated his devil's soul."

"It appears I must apologize to her as well. Are you certain Aunt Arleth didn't look guilty?"

"No, afraid not. Still, I will speak to her privately."

"I'm still afraid, Colin."

He rose and strode to the end of the table where she was standing. He stood there beside her, looking down at her. Then he opened his arms. "No one will ever hurt you again," he said, and pulled her up against his chest. "Dear God, you scared the very devil out of me."

She nuzzled her face into his throat. "Good," she said, as she kissed his chin. "You had a great deal of wickedness. A little less won't serve you ill."

He laughed, hugged her more tightly, and stood there, holding her. "Do you feel well today?"

"Much better. Just a bit on the weak side."

"That was from last night. You'll feel that way nearly every morning from now on."

She raised her face to kiss him.

"Papa, surely Sinjun doesn't like to have you pet her at the breakfast table."

Colin sighed, kissed her lightly on her chin, and released her. He looked down at his son, who stood in the doorway, hands on his hips, a stance just like his father's.

"What do you want, Philip? Joan was shortly to be on her way to find you. She is quite prepared to give you an abject apology. She is prepared to grovel, to cook you sugared almonds until your teeth rot out. She is quite ready for you to abuse her endlessly, since you are my son."

For a brief moment Philip managed to look severe, but then he said, "It's all right, Sinjun. I know you. I doubt you'll ever change." Then he turned immediately to his father. "Uncle Ryder asked me if I wanted to visit him and Aunt Sophie and all their children. He says there are more than a dozen now and I would quite enjoy myself. Brandon House is where they all live and it's right next to his house. Did you know that he saves children, Papa, from all sorts of terrible situations? He becomes their guardian and takes care of them and he loves them. He didn't say that but I could tell that he does and Uncle Douglas told me that he does. I think it embarrasses him when people think he's good. Uncle Ryder told me about his brother-in-law Jeremy, who's at Eton and lame and quite the best fighter he's seen in a long time. He said Jeremy can also ride like the wind. He said he'd teach me how to fight dirty if it was all right with you. He said I'm nearly the age Jeremy was when he taught him. Please, Papa, can I?"

"Uncle Ryder and Uncle Douglas," Colin mused aloud. "I'll tell you what, Philip. I'll fight dirty with your uncle Ryder and whoever wins will teach you, all right?"

Philip, no fool, said, "Perhaps it would be best if both you and Uncle Ryder taught me how to fight."

"He should be in the diplomatic service," Colin said to his wife, hugged his son to him, and continued. "The two uncles and I will discuss all this. You rest, Joan. I will see you later."

"Oh, Papa, Sinjun is teaching me how to shoot a bow and arrow. But there's still fencing. MacDuff gave us some beginning lessons, but then he had to leave. You can do that, can't you?"

"Joan was learning with you?"

"Yes, and I must continue. I can't let Philip get ahead of me."

"I didn't know you were so accomplished."

He sounded a bit miffed. She cocked her head to one side and grinned. "You sound just like Ryder and Douglas when I happen to outdo them at something. They taught me to shoot, to be an excellent archer, to ride like a veritable Diana, to swim like an—well, never mind. My point is they taught me all the manly sorts of things, but when I prove proficient, they act scandalized."

"They're unreasonable, naturally. A man enjoys having his wife don his britches and ride off to do battle with his enemies, leaving him to flounder about with nothing to say, nothing to do."

"I've decided it's not just a matter of wives. I think it's just that men must always feel that they are the ones in control."

"For all your daring, Joan, for all your bravery, for all your passion for my welfare, and your terrifyingly creative mind, you are still weaker than I. Any man, be he brilliant or a half-wit, could hurt you. That's why you have men. We really are useful creatures. It's our responsibility to protect our wives and our children."

"Ha! You know that's nonsense, Colin. This is no longer medieval times, when robbers roamed the land."

"Why are you arguing?" Philip asked, looking from her to his father. "Both of you are right. Boys, too, can prove worthwhile in a fight. Didn't I ride to fetch you, Papa, from Edinburgh? Without me, Joan would have been really ill."

They looked at each other over Philip's head. Sinjun grinned. Colin said, "You believe every family member should contribute his bit, eh? Everyone should have the chance to be a hero once in a while?"

"That would mean even Dahling would get her chance," Philip said, frowning. "What do you think, Sinjun?"

"I think your father has finally grasped the right straw."

"Now, Philip, if you will accept Joan's apology—"

"Her name is Sinjun, Papa. I accept, Sinjun. You'd do anything for Papa, so I suppose I shouldn't hold it against you."

"Thank you," she said humbly. She watched Colin's left eyebrow go up a good inch; she watched father and son leave the Laird's Inbetween Room, Colin leaning down to hear what Philip was saying.

She loved him so much it hurt.

Who the devil had told Robert MacPherson that Colin had murdered his wife?

The late afternoon was cool. The sky was clear—Sherbrooke blue, Sophie had remarked to her husband, then kissed him.

Colin had wanted to be alone, for just a little while. He frowned now at the water stain on the book he held in his hand. He could tell that the book had been carefully cleaned, its binding oiled, but the stain had been there a long time and would remain there. She'd cleaned it, of course. And all the other books as well. He'd known that she had, only he hadn't realized until now that she'd treated each book as a treasure in itself, carefully and with respect. He laid the book down and walked back to his desk. He sat back in his chair, his arms behind his head, and closed his eyes.

He was in his north tower room. He could smell the fresh heather and roses. And the lemon and beeswax. It smelled of his mother, and now he didn't feel anger at his wife, he felt profound gratitude. He fancied that before long when he smelled lemon and beeswax, it would be his wife he thought of, not his mother.

I love you.

Colin supposed he'd always known she loved him, though the notion of that sort of emotion upon meeting another person he couldn't easily credit. On the other hand, she'd taken his side from the very beginning. She'd never wavered in her belief in him. Even when they'd argued, he'd known that she'd die for him if it came to it.

It was humbling.

He was so damned lucky he couldn't believe it. He'd gotten his heiress. He'd also gotten a lady who was a wonderful mother to his children, a lady who was an excellent wife. Albeit stubborn; albeit much too impulsive.

Just when everything seemed at last to be coming out from behind that awful black cloud, there was an enemy still hidden. He wondered if he should have simply beat the name out of MacPherson. Probably. Joan wouldn't have held him back at the croft. She probably would have argued with him to hit MacPherson herself.

That made him grin. She was bloodthirsty when it came to his safety. He thought of Aunt Arleth, a woman who'd lost her grip on things, only he hadn't recognized it in time. Because of his blindness, Joan could have died. He clenched his teeth at the thought. It was quite true, Aunt Arleth had even admitted that the little slut would be better off dead. Then things would return to normal; then she would be in charge again.

But she hadn't told MacPherson anything. Colin sighed and opened his eyes when he heard footsteps coming up the tower stairs. He recognized the light step and leaned forward in his chair, his eyes fixed on the iron-studded door.

It was Joan, pink with exertion, her forehead damp with perspiration.

He rose immediately and went to her. "You're still not back to your Amazon self. Come and sit down for a moment and regain your breath."

She did as she was bid. "It's lowering to be puffing about over some simple stairs. Hello, Colin. I haven't seen you. Are you all right? I wanted to get away from everyone for a while. Did you, as well?"

"Yes, but I'm glad you're here."

She drew a deep breath. "I came for a reason."

"You want to know about Aunt Arleth."

"Perhaps, but not really. That is, there's something else, but I don't think it was Aunt Arleth or you would have hunted me out immediately. No, it's about something else entirely, but it can wait. I see you're holding a book."

He cocked one of those black eyebrows of his, then handed the book to her. "Thank you for trying to mend this book. It was my grandfather's. He used to read to me from it. It's Chesterfield's *Letters to His Son.* I was thinking it was time for me to read the letters on mythology and history to Philip, and I was right."

"Chesterfield's son was named Philip also. Isn't that curious? Douglas didn't introduce me to Chesterfield, but I found him very quickly.

He was miserable with his wife and thus has a very low opinion of women, but Douglas said he'd never met me so he'd been deprived, thus I wasn't to pay him any attention. Ah, this is one of my favorites: 'Wear your learning, like your watch, in a private pocket. . . . Above all things, avoid speaking of yourself, if it be possible.'"

He could but stare at her. He wondered if she would continue to surprise him for the rest of their lives.

"My books from home are still in crates. There's been no time to unpack them." She looked at him then, and her expression was tentative. "Also I don't know where you would like me to put them."

Colin felt like a self-centered ass. If she hadn't been the kind of person she was, he would have completely terrorized her, ground her under. Even now she wasn't at all certain of his reception. About her damned books, for God's sake.

"You know," he said slowly, smiling at her, "there are dozens of rooms in the castle. You can use any of them you wish to. However, if you would like, I should be delighted to share this chamber with you."

She gave him a dazzling smile and jumped to her feet. "Oh, Colin, I love you so much." She leaped into his arms.

He held her, laughing and kissing her ear and her nose and smoothing her eyebrows with his fingertips. He whirled her about. "All this just for the offer of this benighted room and a few bookshelves?"

It was part of himself he was offering, something he'd held dear and very close so it wouldn't be taken from him, but she didn't point that out. He was offering it to her because he trusted her; he knew she would never take from him. "I came to see you for a specific reason," she said, her eyes brilliant. She kissed his chin.

"Yes, but you didn't tell me what it was."

"I came to make love to you, Colin."

"You mean you want me to make you scream with more pleasure?"

"No, I want to do it to you."

He was nonplussed. He was the man, dammit, he was the husband. It had been his plan to seduce her slowly, so when he finally came into her she wouldn't realize what had happened. Now here she was . . . No, he couldn't be certain what she meant.

"I think it's foolish to continue as we have. I have forced you to it and you have been very kind, very giving, too giving. I have been selfish. But now, I want to do everything with you."

"As in everything?"

"Oh yes."

19

"BUT THIS ISN'T THE WAY it's supposed to be done," Colin said slowly, staring down at his wife, all visions of his future very gentle and tender seductions taking flight toward the window.

She just stroked his face with her fingertips, hugged him close, kissed his mouth a dozen times, his chin, his nose, tugged on his earlobe with her teeth. She said between kisses and bites, "I've been selfish and quite childish. I've been a coward. You're a man. You expected a woman when you married me. That's what you will have, right now. I don't care about any pain. It's not important. I want to give you what it is you must have. I will give myself to you as often as you wish, with no moaning or plaints."

"Ah, Joan, but the pain. I know you remember the pain. I have no wish to torture you. I don't wish to make you weep."

"I won't weep. I'll be strong. I was raised to be stoic by Douglas and Ryder. Ryder used to box my ears when he thought I was acting like a girl. I won't disappoint you, Colin, ever again." She drew a deep breath. "I swear it."

He gripped her forearms in his hands, slowly pulling her arms from about his neck. "I can't allow this sacrifice. It's too much to ask of you. Perhaps once a year you will allow me to come inside you—to create a child, nothing more." He sighed deeply and assumed the expression of a martyr. "I don't mind, truly. To give you pleasure night after night will suffice me. It must. I'm no monster to make you scream with pain."

"Oh, Colin, you're so noble, so very kind, but I have made up my mind. I've decided that I will do it right now. That way I should be fully recovered by dinner. Also, if I happen to cry out from the pain, there's no one near here to hear me. Now, I wish to undress you."

He could only stare at her, utterly amused, trying to keep the laughter well under hatches. "To believe you love me so much to offer yourself to me like this," he said, his voice thick with emotion. "Despite what you know will happen, you are still willing to open yourself to me. It moves me, Joan. It makes me realize how very strong and giving you are. It humbles me."

She was fumbling with the string on his shirt, tugging at the buttons on his britches. He laughed, slapping her hands away. "We'll do it together, all right?"

She nodded, not looking at him now, and proceeded to strip off her clothes.

She wanted to seduce him on the carpet? She wanted to ravish him right here? Upon brief reflection, he thought it was a grand idea.

Colin was tugging off his left boot when she was naked, standing in front of him, her hands at her sides. She was trying to give him a siren's smile, but failing woefully at it. She looked scared but determined. She looked like her namesake Joan of Arc on her way to martyrdom, elated that she was guarding her dignity even whilst she contemplated the flames. The foolish little twit.

When he was naked, he knew her eyes were on his belly and nowhere else. He wasn't fully aroused, so she shouldn't yet scream with fright.

He started to resume his role of the tender seducer, to end this damnable charade, when she jumped at him. His quick reflexes saved both of them. She was holding him in a strangle lock about his throat and kissing him until he was laughing.

Let her do it, he thought. He stroked his hands over her buttocks and hefted her legs around his waist.

"Oh," she said and kissed him until she had to stop for a breath.

"What do you want me to do now, Joan?"

"I want you flat on your back so I can kiss you. I don't want you to move, Colin."

He obliged her, easing both of them onto the Aubusson carpet. Late afternoon sunlight sent silver beams through the narrow windows into the chamber. The air was soft and warm. She was lying on top of him, her legs between his, his sex hard against her belly.

He saw the fear in her eyes when he moved inadvertently against her, but then she smiled at him and leaned back. "You're very beautiful, Colin. I'm the luckiest of wives."

"Er, thank you," he said, aware that his sex was responding to her more quickly than he'd thought possible. He was big and hard as a stone against her now. Still, she didn't hesitate. He heard her draw a deep breath.

"I don't want you to move, Colin. I want you to lie very still. I'm going to kiss you just like you kissed me. Is that all right?"

He choked, nearly swallowing his tongue. This was madness. He managed to nod.

She kissed his throat, his shoulders, his chest, her fingers soft and busy in the mouth's wake. She covered him with kisses. He thought he'd burst. He twitched. He raised his arms to pull her down.

"No, don't move, you promised."

He hadn't promised anything, he thought wildly. But he forced himself to stillness. He fisted his hands at his sides. This was what she wanted. She would learn, oh yes, she would soon learn.

When her warm mouth touched his belly, he heaved and shuddered.

"Joan," he said. This was pain, he thought, this was truly very real pain.

She looked up at him and grinned. "Do you feel like you made me feel? Urgent? As if there's a fire building up inside you, but you'd kill to make it even hotter?"

"Close enough."

She touched his sex with her hand. She stroked him. She was looking intently at him, then at her hand holding him. He was oddly embarrassed. He felt strange. Then she frowned slightly. "No," she said more to herself than to him. "I want more and I want to see how you taste." She took him in her mouth and he jerked and moaned and his chest heaved. He thought, quite simply, that he was going to die.

"Ah," she said, feeling his wonderful response to her, and set out to make him scream with pleasure.

He nearly did, so close did he come to his release. "Joan, no, sweetheart, you've got to stop. I'm different from you. I'll spill my seed if you continue. Then your sacrifice will have been in vain."

"Oh," she said, and drew back. "You must spill your seed inside me. That's the way of things. You're a man and that's what you want, I know.

This you enjoy as well, but the other . . . that's what it must be. Very well."

Before he knew what she intended, she came up over him and straddled his hips.

"Oh no," he said as she tried to bring him into her. If he weren't hurting so much for her, he would have laughed. She wasn't near to ready to take him into her and yet, here she was, trying to impale herself.

She looked at him as he spoke, and he saw she was paler than a moment before; she was afraid of the coming pain.

He smiled, stroking his hands up and down her arms. "Not yet, Joan. Don't try to force me inside of you just yet. I'm not ready for you. Not even close. No, no, it's true. I must have more so that I will enjoy myself. I can't reach my full potential unless—" He stopped at her gasp.

She looked at his sex and then back at his face. She looked at him as if he were mad. "You mean to say there'll be even more of you? But you were moaning, Colin, and twitching. You're sweating. Surely there can't be that much more."

"But there is," he said, desperate now. "I'm a man and I've got to have more. Believe me. You must trust me in this. I'm the one with the experience. I must have more, else my pleasure won't be anything beyond the ordinary. It won't be worth the passage of moments it will take to bring me to it. You do want me to have more pleasure rather than less, don't you?"

"Of course. I promised you that I wouldn't be selfish about it. If you wish to increase in your size even more, if that's what makes you scream with pleasure, then so be it." She drew a deep breath. "What do you wish me to do now?"

He smiled painfully. "Roll over onto your back. No, no, I'm not taking charge, nothing like that. I just must show you what's necessary for you to do to make me scream with pleasure like I made you do last night."

She nodded, looking dubious, but did what he'd asked. She lay on her back, and she was looking at him coming over her and he saw that damned fear in her eyes again, but he couldn't blame her, his sex was hard as a stone, fully aroused. And she thought he'd get bigger?

He calmed himself. He wasn't about to let this wonderful surprise turn into another fiasco.

He lay between her legs as she had between his. He settled himself over her, balancing his weight on his elbows. "Now," he said. "Look at me, Joan. Yes, that's right. Now, I must have you kiss me some more. It's important, else I'll just have to pretend I'm enjoying myself. Surely you don't want me to feign enjoyment with you."

"Oh no," Sinjun said, finding no fault with his program. When she was kissing him, she could momentarily forget about that part of him pressing against her belly, huge and hot and it would hurt, impossible for it not to, but she was resolute, she wouldn't let him down this time. She wouldn't ever again let him down. He wanted her and she would have him in any way he wished.

Colin took his time. He kissed her, parting her lips, and slipped his tongue into her mouth. He kissed her until finally, blessed be to the kind heavens above, she moaned and squirmed beneath him. He smiled a bit painfully, then eased down her body to caress her breasts. She tasted wonderful and the feel of her sent him shuddering with need.

"You want me enough now, Colin?"

He ducked his head down at the sound of that strained little voice. "No, no, not just yet. I need more, Joan. It takes me time to grow into my need."

"Very well."

"Are you enjoying what I'm doing to you? That is, sweetheart, it's not necessary, but you might as well as long as I am."

"Oh yes, it feels quite nice."

Just you wait, sweetheart, he thought, as he moved down until his tongue was lightly caressing her white belly. He felt the deep clenching of her muscles, felt her quiver then, and he knew that she didn't know what he would do, but she was very interested, she was excited, she was nearly ready to have him topple her over the edge.

He gave her his mouth in the very next instant, and she yelled, her hands fisting in his hair.

He kissed her and caressed her with his mouth. His fingers eased into her and he thought he'd burst with the joy of it. She was ready for him. Very ready. He brought her to the edge, then quickly reared up over her, lifting her hips in his hands.

"Look at me, Joan."

She opened her eyes as he eased inside her. He saw her Sherbrooke blue eyes widen and he knew she was tensing, waiting for pain, but she would wait in vain. Yes, indeed. There would be no pain.

He kept easing into her, lifting her hips to take more of him. He felt her flesh stretching to accommodate him, but there was no pain, of that he was certain. Her warmth made him grit his teeth to keep his control.

"Colin?"

"What's the matter, doesn't that feel nice?"

"Oh blessed hell, yes. I don't understand. Why aren't I feeling that awful hurt again? I'm stretching to take you, I feel filled with you, but it doesn't hurt. It feels quite nice, actually."

He drove forward, seating himself to his hilt inside her. Then he came back down over her and began to kiss her. "Move against me, Joan, it will enhance my pleasure. It's what you want for me, isn't it?"

"Oh yes," she said, and moved in rhythm to him, jerkily at first, but then her body responded without her mind's interference. He kissed her and fondled her and moved in a fierce rhythm in and out of her. Finally, when he knew he couldn't keep his brain in charge any longer, he eased his hand between their bodies and found her.

He watched her face as his fingers caressed her.

She looked, quite simply, absolutely astounded.

"Colin," she said on a high thin wail.

"Yes, sweetheart. Let's meet this together, shall we?"

"I don't understand what's happening here—" she began, then threw her head back, her back arching, and cried out, her body convulsing around him, and he let himself go.

She was utterly still beneath him.

Colin finally slowed his breathing. He pressed his palm to her breast. Her heart was still galloping. He grinned. He wanted to dance.

"Easy now," he said, and feathered her lips with his.

Her breathing slowed. Her hand fluttered up, then dropped to her side. He rather wished she would hug him but decided he'd exhausted her. It was rather nice to do that to one's wife, particularly when she had fully expected to be impaled and ravaged.

"You were very brave, Joan," he said, serious as a man in the confessional. "I think you're wonderful to hide your pain from me, to make me believe you were enjoying yourself. I'm the luckiest of men to have such a giving and noble wife."

The next instant he was groaning and rubbing his arm. "Giving and noble and mean," he said. "Why did you hit me?"

"You lied to me, you damned man. No, damn you, don't raise one of your supercilious eyebrows at me. You lied to me. You agreed with me that the pain was horrible. You were laughing at me, knowing, and I hate you!"

He laughed aloud now, and felt himself coming out of her. He shut his mouth. He didn't want to leave her. Just thinking of himself in her, just feeling the softness of her, the heat of her, he swelled and eased more deeply.

"No, that was your nonsensical idea. Don't rewrite the past, Joan. I know our first time—"

"First time! You ravaged me three times!"

"Very well. It wasn't well done of me and I did apologize to you if you'll recall. Also, if your memory wasn't completely burned out in your recent pleasure storm, I told you that it wouldn't ever hurt again, but you refused to believe me. Now you know that I was telling you the truth. I told you this morning that men are useful creatures. We're good for protection—if you allow us to protect you—and we're useful at giving you pleasure. Now that you know all about pleasure, why then, should you like to do it again?"

She looked up at him. She looked ready to spit in his face. Her blue eyes were narrowed to slits. She said, "All right."

He loved her slowly and it lasted longer than three minutes this time, which pleased him. When she twisted and moaned, he closed his eyes against the soul-deep pleasure of it and let his own release take him.

"Admit it, Colin, you have been laughing at me, haven't you?" she said later as she shifted herself to her side.

"A bit, perhaps. Up my sleeve, for the most part. You were so sincere, so convinced that my body couldn't possibly fit with yours. Yes, it was amusing, when it wasn't painful. You see, I wanted you very much. Ah, perhaps I want you again. What do you think? No, wait, it will be the infamous three times again. Think carefully before you answer, Joan."

"All right," she said immediately, and arched up to kiss him.

They were late to dinner. They were more than late. Philpot and Rory were serving blueberry-and-currant tarts when they arrived. Philip and Dahling had already eaten and been duly removed by Dulcie back to the nursery.

Serena, the brothers, and the wives were there. Aunt Arleth was in her room and would remain there until her brother sent a carriage to fetch her home.

Douglas raised an eyebrow but kept his mouth shut. Sinjun wondered at his discretion until she saw his mouth was full with tart.

Ryder's mouth was full only of wickedness. He sat back in his chair, his hands clasped over his lean belly. His blue eyes gleamed with devilment. "Sinjun, I think you have a look on your pretty face that makes me want to kill Colin. You're my baby sister. You have no right to look that way, no right to do what you've quite obviously done with great abandon."

"Be quiet," Sophie said, and stuck the tines of her fork into the back of his hand.

"It's true," Douglas said, once he'd swallowed the tart, and prepared to launch his own salvo.

"Don't you get into it," Alex said. "She's a married lady. She's no longer ten years old."

"That's a fact," Colin said, grinning at his new relatives, kissed his wife's nose, and seated her in the countess's chair. "Actually that's two facts."

He strode to the head of the table, eased himself down, raised his wineglass, and said, "A toast. To my wife, a beautiful, quite challenging lady who's been mired in female confusion and wrong thinking to the point that—"

"Colin! You will be quiet!" Sinjun heaved her soup spoon at him. It fell short since the table was twelve feet long, clattering against a vase of daffodils.

Philpot cleared his throat loudly but no one paid him any heed.

Serena sighed, looked from Colin to Sinjun, and said, "Colin never looked at Fiona or at me like that. It's not just a man's lust he's taken care of, no, it's something beyond that. He looks like a cat who's eaten more cream than he deserves. I think he's very selfish. I hope he vomits up all that cream. I think you've quite ruined him, Joan. Philpot, would you please give me some tarts?"

Philpot, poker-faced, gently placed the plate of tarts in front of her.

"I'm relieved he's beyond lust now," Ryder said in great good humor to his sister. "You have a witches' brew, little sister? Perhaps you've been sharing that recipe with Sophie here? She is so greedy, so without pity for me, that it requires all my nobility to remain bravely standing in the face of her demands. Regard a man who's striving with all his might to provide her with another child. She won't leave me alone. She's after me constantly. I am safe from her only at the dinner table."

"Surely she will stab you again if you don't close your mouth," Alex said. "I just hope, Sophie, that when you're with child again, you will turn green and lose your breakfast just once."

"Oh no," Sophie said. "Not that, never that. Besides, I'm much too nice a person to have that happen. I think it's your husband, Alex. It's he who makes you sick."

All three wives were laughing.

Douglas was frowning at his sister-in-law.

Ryder puffed out his chest. "No, Sophie will never know a day's illness. I will simply forbid her to."

Alex just shook her head back and forth and said to Sophie, "Sometimes I forget what they're like. When I'm reminded, why, I realize that life is more than sweet, it's delicious. It's even better than those blueberry-and-currant tarts Douglas is gobbling down."

"Now that you've spoken the pure truth," Douglas said, "I beg you not to run out of here toward the basin Philpot set in the entrance hall."

"I would that we shift the subject a bit," Sinjun said.

"Yes," Ryder said, "now that Douglas and I see that you're pleased with this man, Sinjun, we will move on to other matters. Douglas and I have given this situation a good deal of thought, Colin. It seems to us that the person who told Robert MacPherson that you'd killed his sister is quite likely the same person who killed her himself."

"Or *her*self," Alex said.

"True. But why would anyone want Fiona dead?" Sinjun asked. "And to have Colin there, unconscious by the edge of the cliff, all ready to blame because he couldn't remember anything. It was a carefully thought-out plan. Serena, do you know of anyone who hated your sister that much? Someone who knew enough about potions and such to erase Colin's memory?"

Serena looked up from her tart, smiled vaguely at Sinjun, and said in her soft voice, "Fiona was a faithless bitch. I quite hated her myself. I also know enough about the effects of opium and henbane and the maella plant. I could have done it quite easily."

"Oh."

"Let's go another step," Douglas said. "Serena, who hated Colin?"

"His father. His brother. Aunt Arleth. Toward the end, Fiona hated him because she was so jealous of him and he didn't love her. She was even jealous of me, but I never touched you then, Colin. I was very careful."

Colin went very still. He slowly lowered his fork back onto his plate. He said mildly, belying the pain Sinjun knew he must feel at Serena's words, "My father didn't hate me, Serena. He merely had no use for me. My brother was the future laird. I wasn't important. I understood that as much as I realized it wasn't right or fair, as much as it hurt me. It would be like Joan and me having a son and disregarding him because Philip is the firstborn.

"As for my brother, why, Malcolm had no reason to hate me, either. He had everything. If there was any hate to be festered, why, I should be the one brimming with it. As for Aunt Arleth, she loved my father and hated her sister, my mother. She wanted my father to marry her after my mother died, but he didn't. It's true she dislikes me amazingly and believed my brother was a prince among men, but I doubt even she understands why. It was as if she feared me, perhaps, because I was also a son, a possible future earl."

"I don't hate you, Colin."

"Thank you, Serena. I truly don't know how Fiona felt about me before she died. I pray she didn't hate me. I never wished her ill."

"I would never hate you, Colin, never. I only wish I had been the heiress. Then you wouldn't have had to go to London and marry her."

"Ah, but I did and there's an end to it. And you, my dear, will go to Edinburgh to live with your father. You will go to parties and balls. You will meet many nice men. It is for the best, Serena."

"All adults say that when they wish to justify what they're doing to someone else."

"You're an adult," Sinjun said. "Surely you don't wish to remain here at Vere Castle."

"No, you're right. Since Colin won't make love to me now, I might as well leave." With those words, she rose from her chair, not waiting for Rory to assist her, and, oblivious of the stunned silence, wafted her way from the room.

"You have very odd relatives, Colin," Douglas said.

"What about your mother, Douglas, and how she treats me?"

"All right, Alex. Most families have strange members," Douglas said, grinning at his wife. "Serena . . . I don't know, Colin. She seems fey, if you know what I mean. Not daft, not really, just fey."

"Yes, as if both her feet weren't quite planted firmly on the grass. She's always fancied the notion that she was a witch, and she's dabbled with her plants for many years now."

"But you don't believe she would kill her own sister. And drug you so you would take the blame?"

"No, I don't, Joan. But as Douglas says, Serena is odd. She always has been. Fiona adored her though, insisted that she live here with us, though I wasn't overly pleased about it."

"Did she try to kiss you in front of her sister?"

"No, Alex, she didn't. That began after her sister died. When I brought you back, she tried to waylay me behind every door."

"It would be nice to have some clarity here," Douglas said.

"Perhaps," Sinjun said, "we should call Dahling. She has opinions on everything and everyone."

"Joan," Colin said suddenly, frowning down the table at her, "you haven't eaten and it doesn't please me. I must insist that you regain your strength. Philpot, please serve her ladyship a noble plate."

At that, both brothers and both wives looked at each other, then burst into merry laughter. Colin blinked; then, to Sinjun's surprised delight, he flushed, again.

Colin, a celibate for too many weeks, had no difficulty in pleasing his wife yet another time before they slept. And Sinjun, laboring under misapprehensions for too many weeks and delighted with her newfound knowledge, was nothing loath.

They both slept deeply until suddenly, without warning, Sinjun was instantly awake, her eyes wide open to the darkness of their bedchamber.

There, shimmering in a soft light with her brocade gown weighted down with dozens and dozens of glistening pale cream pearls, was Pearlin' Jane, and she was upset, Sinjun knew it, deep down.

"Quickly, Aunt Arleth's room!"

The words were loud in Sinjun's mind, so loud she couldn't believe that Colin hadn't come roaring awake.

Then Pearlin' Jane was gone, vanished from one instant to the next. Not like the Virgin Bride, who gently eased out of view, slowly moving away until the shadows and she became one. No, Pearlin' Jane was there and then she wasn't.

Sinjun shook Colin even as she threw back the covers.

"Colin!" she shrieked at him as she pulled her discarded nightgown over her head.

He was awake and confused, but her urgency shook him. "What, Joan? What's the matter?"

"Hurry, it's Aunt Arleth!"

Sinjun ran from the bedchamber, not bothering with a candle. There was no time.

She shouted as she passed by each brother's door but she didn't slow.

When she reached Aunt Arleth's room, she flung open the door. She stopped on the spot, frozen with horror. There was Aunt Arleth hanging from a rope fastened to the chandelier in the ceiling, her feet dangling at least a foot from the floor.

"No!"

"Oh God."

It was Colin, and he shoved her aside as he ran into the bedchamber. Quickly, he grasped Aunt Arleth's legs to push her up, relieving the pressure of the rope around her neck.

Within moments, Douglas, Ryder, Sophie, and Alex were crowding into the room.

Colin held her firmly against him, yelling over his shoulder, "Quickly, Douglas, Ryder, cut that damned rope. Perhaps we're not too late."

There was no knife to be found, so Douglas stood on a chair so he could reach the knot at the base of the chandelier. It took him several moments, moments that stretched longer than eternity, to untie the knot. Slowly, Colin eased Aunt Arleth down into his arms and carried her to her bed. He gently untied the knot about her throat and pulled it away.

He laid his fingers to the pulse in her throat. He slapped her face several times. He rubbed her arms, her legs, slapped her again, shook her. But there was nothing.

"She's dead," he said finally, straightening. "Dear God, she's dead."

Serena said from the doorway, "I knew she'd be dead. Your mother's kelpie lover came for Arleth because she told Joan about your origins. Oh yes, the kelpie was your father, Colin, and now Arleth is dead, as she deserves to be."

She turned and left the bedchamber, her pale nightgown floating around her as she walked. She paused and said over her shoulder, "I don't believe in that kelpie nonsense. I don't really know why I said it. But I'm not sorry she's dead. She was dangerous to you, Colin."

"Oh God," Alex said, and to her own astonishment, she crumpled where she stood.

20

"SHE DIDN'T KILL HERSELF," Colin said.

"But the stool beside her," Sinjun said, "it was kicked over, as if she—" her voice simply stopped. She swallowed, her head lowered. Colin hugged her tightly to him.

"I know," he said quietly. "I know. If only we'd been just a few moments sooner, perhaps—"

Douglas rose and strode to the fireplace. He stood there, leaning against it, a cup of hastily prepared coffee in his hand. "No, she didn't kill herself. I'm positive of that. You see, I untied the knot that was at the base of the chandelier. She simply wouldn't have had the strength or the ability to fashion such a knot."

"Shouldn't we have Ostle fetch the magistrate?" Sinjun asked her husband.

"I am the magistrate. I agree with Douglas. I have only one question for you, Joan. How did you know to wake up and go to her room?"

"Pearlin' Jane woke me. She told me to hurry to Aunt Arleth's room. We went immediately, Colin, there was no hesitation. I wonder why she waited so long. Perhaps she didn't realize Aunt Arleth wouldn't survive, or perhaps she didn't want her to live; she wanted her punished for what she did to Fiona and to you, Colin, and to me. How can we possibly understand a ghost's motives?"

Douglas shoved away from the fireplace, his face red. "Dammit, Sinjun, enough of this bloody damned ghost talk! I won't have it, not here. At home I have to bear it because it's a damned tradition, but not here!"

On and on it went. Sinjun was so tired, so shocked into her tiredness that she simply sat there, listening but not really hearing everyone as they voiced their opinions. And being Sherbrookes and wives of Sherbrookes, they all had opinions and all their opinions were contrary to one another's.

At one point Sophie shuddered and stepped quickly back, bumping into a chair. Ryder, frowning, immediately went to her and brought her into the circle of his arms. He leaned down, pressing his forehead against his wife's. "It's all right, Sophie. Tell me what's wrong, love."

"The violence, Ryder, the horrible violence, the pain. It just brought it all back to me, all of Jamaica. I hate the memories, dear God how I hate them."

"I know, sweetheart. I'm sorry about this, but you're with me and you will remain with me and no one will ever hurt you again, ever. Forget your damned uncle, forget Jamaica." He rubbed her back, rocked her gently against him.

Douglas said, "Why don't you take Sophie to bed, Ryder. She's had quite enough. She looks as fatigued as the rest of us doubtless feel."

Ryder gave his brother a nod.

Some five minutes later, at four o'clock in the morning, Colin said, "Douglas is right. Everyone is exhausted. Enough for tonight. We will speak of this again tomorrow."

He held Sinjun close, his arms locked around her back, his face pressed against her temple.

"Who killed her, Colin?"

He felt her warm breath against his throat. "I don't know," he said, "blessed hell, I don't know. Maybe she was an accomplice in Fiona's death, just maybe . . . I don't know. Jesus, what a night. Let's get some rest."

The next morning there was surprisingly little conversation at the breakfast table. Colin had told Dulcie to keep Philip and Dahling with her, he wanted no horrific tales spun in front of their young faces.

Still, there wasn't much more to say.

Serena said nothing at all. She ate her porridge, chewed slowly, even nodded occasionally whilst she chewed, as if she were carrying on a private conversation with herself, which, Sinjun thought, she probably was. She would never understand Serena; she wondered if Serena understood herself.

As if at long last, Serena became aware that Sinjun was looking at her. She said, her voice as calm and serene as a warm starlit night, "A pity it wasn't you, Joan. Then Colin would have all your money and me. Yes, a pity. I like you, naturally, it's difficult not to. But it's still a pity." With those words that made Sinjun's blood freeze in her veins, Serena merely smiled at everyone and left the Laird's Inbetween Room.

"She's frightening," Sophie said, and shuddered.

"I think she's all talk," Alex said. "And I think she speaks that way for effect. She loves to shock. Sinjun, pull yourself together. It was just words, nothing more."

Colin said, "I will see that Serena returns to Edinburgh as soon as may be. In fact, it might be best if I sent Ostle with a message to Robert MacPherson. He could come for her himself. There's no reason to wait."

Robert MacPherson did come to Vere Castle, and with him were half a dozen of his men, all armed to the teeth.

"You'll notice Alfie isn't among my men. I hanged him for killing Dingle."

He dismounted, waved his men to do the same, and entered the castle, careful that the great doors remained open. "There is much improvement," he said, then nodded to Sinjun. "You're quite the housekeeper, aren't you?"

"Oh yes," she said, wondering why she hadn't shot him when she'd had the chance. She didn't trust him an inch, this pretty man with his evil heart.

"I will take Serena to Edinburgh now. I did promise you that I'd speak to my father, though I warn you, Colin, he's not as he should be in his mental parts."

"He was all that he should be when I last saw him," Colin said. "If you simply told me who it was who claimed I killed your sister, we would both save ourselves a lot of time."

"Oh no," Robert MacPherson said, casually flicking a speck of dust from his coat sleeve. "To tell you would lead to nothing. You would try to kill the person in a rage, and I would still be left with doubts. No, I will speak to my father. I will tell him about this person who accused you. I will listen to what he has to say. Ask no more, Colin."

"I wouldn't kill your damnable informant!"

"If you didn't, then your bloodthirsty wife would."

"I surely would," Sinjun said. "He's right about that, Colin."

Colin suddenly realized they were all standing in the entrance hall. He didn't want MacPherson in his home but he had come for Serena. He had to be somewhat civil, but that didn't mean taking him into the drawing room and giving him a cup of tea. They would remain in the entrance hall. Colin said, to break the uncomfortable silence, "You know the wives, do you not?"

"Oh yes, bloody savages those two. Ladies," Robert MacPherson added, and gave them each a deep bow. "And their husbands, I presume. I'm relieved that you both are here. These two charming females should be kept under lock and key."

He turned back to Colin. "Now, your letter said you wanted me to remove Serena. May I ask why, at this particular moment in time?"

"Aunt Arleth died last night. Hung in her room."

"Ah, I see. You lured me here to accuse me of murdering the old witch. Fortunate that I brought my men with me, isn't it?"

"Don't be a fool, Robbie. It was made to look like a suicide, but Douglas rightfully pointed out that Arleth wouldn't have had the strength to tie the rope knot so tightly to the chandelier. No, someone killed her, perhaps this informant of yours was her accomplice. Perhaps he feared she'd talk and did away with her."

But Robert MacPherson just looked at him. He did move a bit closer to the open front doors, closer to his men on the steps outside, all of them at the ready.

"Dammit, Robbie, that means someone got into the castle and murdered her!"

"Perhaps she was strong enough with the bloody knot," he said. "Arleth was more robust than she appeared."

Colin gave it up. He fetched Serena. She looked at him as he walked beside her down the wide staircase as if he were her lover. She looked at him as if he were Romeo to her Juliet.

"I'm very relieved that she's leaving," Sophie whispered to Sinjun. "She frightens me, be it all an act or not, it doesn't matter."

"Me too," Sinjun said.

"Sister," Robert MacPherson said, nodded briefly at her, and motioned for his men to fetch the two valises from Colin.

"Hello, Robbie," Serena said. She stood on her tiptoes to kiss her brother on his mouth, "you're more beautiful today than you were even six months ago. I pity your wife. She will have to compete with you for beauty. When we go to Edinburgh, you must promise not to escort me anywhere."

He sucked in his breath, and for one horrible moment Sinjun was afraid that he would strike his sister. Then he smiled and said easily, "I will grow a beard."

"I'm pleased you are able to," Serena said. She turned to Colin, stroked her fingers over his cheeks, then rose onto her tiptoes and kissed him full on the mouth, just as she'd done her brother. "Good-bye, my love. A pity you prefer this one. A pity she is kind, but I am pleased that you married her because she was an heiress."

Without another word, Serena walked past her brother out the front doors.

Colin simply nodded to Robert MacPherson. He walked beside him outside. The day was overcast and chilly. He watched Serena mount a mare her brother had brought for her. He watched one of Robbie's men fasten her valises to the back of his saddle. He watched them all mount, watched them ride down the long tree-lined drive of Vere Castle.

"You will come to me once you've spoken to your father," Colin called after him.

"I will certainly do something," Robert MacPherson yelled back over his shoulder.

"Actually," Colin said to his wife as he turned back into the entrance hall, "I'm glad I married an heiress as well, particularly this heiress."

Sinjun grinned up at him, though it was difficult. He was trying to lighten everyone's mood, but it was tough going.

Sophie rubbed her hands together. "Now," she said, "we have a mystery to solve. Sinjun, I want to hear more about Pearlin' Jane. Why do you think she came to you and told you about Aunt Arleth?"

Douglas turned on his heel and left the castle. He said over his shoulder to Alex, who was standing there staring at him, "I'm going riding. I'll return when you're done chewing over this damnable ghost nonsense."

"Poor Douglas," Ryder said. "He's a man who must maintain his stand once he's taken it."

"I know," Alex said. "I can talk him around to just about anything, but not the Virgin Bride. Sophie's right. It's time to discuss this fully."

Colin said, "It would be simple if the castle were to be locked up tightly every night, but it isn't. Anyone who's remotely familiar with the castle could get in and go anywhere he pleased."

"That," Sinjun said, "is a great pity. I did fancy Serena, blast her eyes."

They talked and debated and argued until finally the children interrupted them, their faces pale because they'd heard of Aunt Arleth's death from the servants.

"Come here," Colin said. He gathered both children to him and hugged them. "It will be all right. We'll figure out what happened. I'm smart. Your uncles and aunts are smart. Your stepmother even occasionally comes to proper conclusions, once she's been nudged onto the suitable path. Everything will be all right."

He held them for a very long time. Then Dahling looked up at him and said, "Papa, let me go now. Sinjun needs me."

Dahling fell asleep in Sinjun's lap. Philip took up a stand at her side, her protector, she thought, and smiled at him with all the love she felt.

Aunt Arleth's body was removed by her brother, Ian MacGregor, the following afternoon. If he was surprised or upset by the news that she'd been murdered in her own bedchamber, he hid it well. It became clear very quickly that he simply wanted to leave Vere Castle as soon as possible. He didn't wish to involve himself. It was that simple. He had a wife and seven children, after all, he told them all in a pious manner that made Sinjun want to slap him. He had no time to spend here. He had to return home. He would bury Arleth, yes he would, but he would let Colin—as was only proper since she was dispatched in his home—solve the mystery of her death. She'd always been odd, she had. Always wanted what her sister had. Aye, a pity it was, but life was many times a pity.

He said to Sinjun as he prepared to leave, "I trust you won't get yourself killed like poor Fiona did, although I suppose it's not all that important now that Colin has married you and has your money in his pockets."

They watched him ride beside an open wagon that held Aunt Arleth in a casket covered with a black blanket.

"He's my uncle," Colin said more to himself than to anyone else. "He's my bloody uncle and I haven't seen him since I was five years old. He's married to his fourth wife. He has many more than seven children. It's seven children from this, his fourth wife. One wife dies from too many births in too short a time, and he immediately weds another and does the same thing. He's a paltry fellow."

There was no disagreement to this pronouncement.

"You have something of the look of him, Colin," Douglas said. "Odd that he is so very handsome and such a rotten man."

Sinjun turned to burrow against Colin's chest. "What are we going to do?"

"What truly disturbs me is that someone came into the castle and murdered Aunt Arleth. It couldn't have been Serena. At least I pray it wasn't."

"But I tell you Serena couldn't have managed it," Douglas said. "I even looked at her upper arms last night. Skinny arms, no muscle at all. Sinjun could have managed it, but not Serena."

Colin didn't find that observation to his liking. He gave Douglas a look, but the earl of Northcliffe only shrugged.

"It's true, Colin," Sinjun said. "I'm very strong."

"I know," Colin said, kissed Sinjun's forehead, and sighed.

Sinjun was sitting in a pile of straw, playing with some kittens whose mother, a stable cat called Tom, had delivered in the third stall, thankfully empty, some four weeks before. She heard Ostle speaking to Crocker. She heard Fanny snort in her stall two doors down, doubtless wanting some hay.

She was tired but also blessedly numb, although the fear was still waiting deep inside her to come out again. She'd left Colin speaking with Mr. Seton. Her brothers were with the crofters doing hard physical labor. "It calms my mental works," Ryder said when Sophie asked him why he was doing it.

"Douglas wanted to sweat as well," Alex had said. "It's frustration. It's been two days since Aunt Arleth's death."

Sinjun had left the two wives arguing even as they went about the castle checking every door for possible clues. She wanted some private peace of her own. The kittens soothed her. Even now, two small toms were climbing up her skirt to settle into her lap, purring while kneading her legs through her many petticoats.

She patted them absently. Ostle's voice was far away now, growing dimmer. Had he said something to her? No, surely not. And Crocker was hard to hear now as well. Fanny snorted again, but Sinjun only dimly heard her. She felt very relaxed. Soon she slept.

When she awoke, not much time had passed at all. The kittens were asleep in her lap. The sun was very high in the sky, shining fully through the big window in the stable.

MacDuff was on his haunches beside her.

She shook her head, smiling up at him. "Hello, what a wonderful surprise. Let me get up and greet you properly, MacDuff."

"Oh no, Sinjun, you needn't move right now. Have some consideration for the kittens. Cute little buggers, aren't they? No, just stay there, I'll join you."

"All right," she said, and yawned. "So much has happened, so very much. I just wanted to get away from everyone for a little while. Have you seen Colin? Do you know about Aunt Arleth? Are you here to help us?"

"Oh yes," he said. He leaned down very close to her. He gently lifted the sleeping kittens from her lap and placed them on an old blanket.

"Now," he said, and drew back his fist and slammed it into her jaw.

Colin looked around the drawing room. It was late afternoon and everyone was assembled for tea.

"Where's Joan?" he asked.

"I haven't seen her since just after lunch," Sophie said. "Nor has Alex, for we were together all afternoon."

"We were looking for clues, specifically which door the murderer entered to come into the castle. But we couldn't find any clues or a plausible entry."

Sophie threw a scone at her. "You are so stubborn, Alex! We did find the door. It's the small one off the kitchen, Colin. I know it had been forced, but Alex here claims that it was just normal use because it is so old."

"I will look at it," Colin said. "Thank you both for trying."

"Where the devil is Sinjun?" Ryder asked the drawing room at large.

It was a small son of one of Colin's crofters who delivered the letter.

"Don't move," Colin told the boy as he ripped open the envelope. He read it once and then again. He paled. Then he cursed.

He questioned the boy, but he could tell him nothing. It was a gentleman, the boy said, his hat pulled down over his eyes, and he wore a scarf that muffled him to his ears. He did look something familiar, but he didn't know, not really. He was on a horse and he never got down from the big brute.

Colin walked into the drawing room and handed the letter to Douglas.

"Good God, I don't believe this!"

There was pandemonium until finally, it was Ryder who read aloud:

Lord Ashburnham,

I have your heiress wife. I will kill her if you don't bring me fifty thousand pounds. I give you two days to fetch the money from Edinburgh. I suggest you leave immediately. I will be watching. When you return to Vere Castle with the money I will contact you again.

"Blessed hell," Alex said.

A few moments later Philpot came into the drawing room to announce that one of the lads had just found both Crocker and Ostle bound and gagged in the tack room. Neither man knew who had done it to them. Just talkin' they were, an' knocked all over their heads.

Colin turned to stride from the room.

"Where are you going?" Douglas asked, catching his arm.

"To Edinburgh, to get the damned money."

"Wait a moment, Colin," Ryder said slowly, stroking his long fingers over his jaw. "We must do a bit of thinking now. I do believe I have a plan. Come along."

Sophie flew to her feet. "Oh no you don't! We came here to help Sinjun and you shan't exclude us now!"

"No indeed!" Alex shouted, then clutched her belly and ran to the corner of the room, where Philpot had placed a basin.

MacDuff watched Colin ride from Vere Castle early the following morning, riding that huge brute stallion of his, Gulliver. Fast as the wind, that one was. He'd supposed that Colin would have left immediately, but then again, this marriage hadn't really been to Colin's liking. He'd married Joan Sherbrooke only to get his hands on her money. Why should he hurry? Why should he care overly if she was killed?

Of course, his honor would demand that he ransom her.

Colin rode alone. MacDuff rubbed his hands together. With luck, Colin would return to Vere Castle sometime tonight, money in hand. He'd decided to let them all gnaw on their fear for her, and not deliver the other letter until the following morning. But something urged him to bring it all to a close. There was no reason to draw it out.

He rather liked the notion that both her brothers and their wives were here at Vere Castle. He hoped they would try to interfere, that they would somehow try to fool him with some stupid plot, and come with

Colin into the trap MacDuff had set for him. He would enjoy showing them up as inept English bastards. He was rather pleased they were here; he couldn't have planned it more to his liking.

The English losing soundly. That had a delicious irony to it and MacDuff was pleased. It dulled the ever-present pain in his chest.

He waited a while longer to see if either of Sinjun's brothers would leave the castle, but no one came through the great front doors. He waited another hour. Finally satisfied that nothing was afoot now, MacDuff mounted his horse and rode back to the small croft.

It was Jamie, the youngest of the crofter lads, who slipped into the side door off the kitchen, the infamous doorway Sophie swore was the one used by the murderer to get into the castle. He was only one of a dozen small boys who'd been stationed around the castle in a wide perimeter, well hidden, waiting and watching.

Colin was waiting there, seated at the kitchen table, a mug of thick black coffee in his hand.

"'Tis a man, milor'. 'Tis yer cousin, th' giant wi' all th' red hair. MacDuff ye calls him."

Colin paled. Ryder's hand came down on his shoulder.

"Who is this MacDuff, Colin?"

"My cousin. Douglas met him in London. Dear God, Ryder, why? I don't understand any of it."

Ryder gave Jamie a guinea. Jamie, mouth agape, gasped and said, "Thank ye, milor', thank ye! Me ma'll bless yer soul, aye, she will."

Colin rose. "Now, Jamie, take us to the place you saw him."

Douglas slipped through that side door off the kitchen an hour later. His eyes glittered with ill-suppressed excitement. He looked up to see the same look in his wife's eyes. "We're two of a kind, aren't we?"

"Oh yes. And soon we'll have MacDuff. Remember him, Douglas? He was the very nice giant of a man who came to see Colin in London. Colin was knocked off kilter. He doesn't understand why MacDuff would do this."

"Dear God."

"I know. It's a shock. Colin and Ryder went with the lad who saw him to the place he is hiding."

"Soon we'll have Arleth's murderer as well as Fiona's. I do wonder what his motive was."

Alex just shook her head. "I don't know, Douglas. Neither does

Colin. Of course, Sophie is claiming she would have suspected him instantly if only she'd been in London with us to meet him."

Douglas laughed.

When Douglas rode back to Vere Castle at seven o'clock that night, he knew MacDuff was watching him and from what vantage point. He was careful to keep his face averted from that dense copse of fir trees. He was careful to ensure that MacDuff got a good look at the bulging packet fastened to his saddle. He hoped MacDuff wouldn't notice that Gulliver wasn't sweating from his hard ride. Indeed, Gulliver had been running only about ten minutes. He was a terror, Douglas thought, wondering if Colin would sell him the horse.

Thirty minutes later, Philpot retrieved the letter that had been left on the front steps. He opened it and read it. He smiled.

MacDuff was whistling as he pulled his horse to a stop in front of the deserted croft that huddled beneath some low-lying fir branches just short of the eastern edge of the Cowal Swamp. It was a damp, utterly dreadful place, redolent with rotted vegetation and stagnant water. The croft itself was on the verge of collapse. Supposedly an old hermit had lived there for years upon years. It was said that he'd just walked into the swamp one night during a mighty storm, singing to heaven that he was on his way. There was one window, long since stolen and now boarded up, but even the boards were sagging and loose, one constantly swinging by its rusty nail. He pulled off his gloves and strode into the one room. There was a packed dirt floor, one narrow rope bed, one table, and two chairs. Sinjun was tied securely to one of them. He'd brought the table and chairs. He didn't fancy sitting on the dirt floor to eat his meals. There were rats to eat the remains. He imagined that they'd kept Sinjun excellent company whilst he'd been gone.

Sinjun eyed the huge man when he walked through the door. His head barely missed the frame. He looked very pleased with himself, damn him. She closed her eyes a moment, picturing Colin and her brothers. They would find her. She didn't doubt it for a moment. On the other hand, it would never have occurred to her not to try to escape. She was nearly ready.

"Not long now," MacDuff said as he sat down on one of the chairs and rubbed his large hands together. The chair creaked ominously under his weight. He cracked his knuckles, a ripping sound in the silence. He opened a brown bag and pulled out a loaf of bread. He tore off a huge chunk and began to eat. "No," he said, his mouth full, "not long. I saw Colin riding back from Edinburgh just a while ago. I left the letter on the front steps. No sense waiting until morning. Perhaps he wants you back alive, my dear. Who can say?"

"He is very honorable," Sinjun said, her voice carefully neutral. She wasn't stupid. She was afraid of MacDuff.

MacDuff grunted and swallowed the bread. He ate steadily until the entire loaf was gone. Sinjun felt her stomach knotting with hunger. The bastard didn't care if she starved.

In that moment she found herself wondering if he truly intended to let her go as he'd promised.

"I'm hungry," she said, eyeing the other brown bag.

"A pity. I'm a big man and there just isn't enough for you. Maybe a bit for the rats, but not for you. Yes, a pity."

She watched him eat until both bags were empty. He wadded them up and threw them into the far corner. The air was redolent with the smells of sausage and bread. "If the rats want the crumbs, they'll have to eat through the bags." He laughed at that.

Nearly free, she thought. Nearly there. He rose then and stretched. With his arms over his head, they touched the sagging roof of the croft.

"Perhaps you'd tell me now why you're doing this?"

He looked at the bruise on her jaw where he'd struck her the previous afternoon. "I was tempted to strike you again when you asked me that last night." He made a fist and rubbed it against his open hand. "You don't look like such a lady now, my dear Countess of Ashburnham. You have more the look of a frowsy slut from Soho."

"Are you afraid to tell me? Do you think I can somehow free myself and kill you? You're afraid of me, aren't you?"

He threw back his head and laughed.

Sinjun waited. She prayed he wouldn't hit her again. Her jaw hurt dreadfully. She prayed he wouldn't go ahead and kill her now.

"So, you want to taunt me into talking, huh? Well, why not? You're not stupid, Sinjun. You must know that, if I please, I can easily kill both you and Colin. You are so very different from Fiona. Colin must believe he's already died and gone to mighty rewards. You have an independent spirit and you have money, an irresistible combination. I will think about it. But, you know, telling you makes no difference to the outcome and we must pass the time. So why not tell you?"

He stretched again, then took a turn around the small room. "What a filthy place," he said more to himself than to her.

She waited, working her hands that were tied behind her.

"Colin is a bastard," he said abruptly, grinning hugely at her. "Ah, yes, a real bastard, as in his mother was a whore and slept with another man. Arleth knew but since she nurtured hopes of marrying the earl herself after Colin's mother died, she feared he'd turn on her if she told him the truth, so she just made up that story about Colin's mother and her kelpie lover. Ah, some kelpie! A flesh-and-blood man with a flesh-and-blood rod.

"The old earl never married Arleth. He bedded her, but nothing more. Then he died and Malcolm became the earl. Arleth loved Malcolm, none of us could figure out why. Malcolm was a rotter; he was petty and mean-spirited. He was occasionally quite cruel. Ah, but then he, too, passed on to his just rewards in Hades and Colin became the earl of Ashburnham.

"But you see, he was a bastard. It is I who should have become the next earl, I who should have inherited Vere Castle. Arleth was distraught when Malcolm died. She hated Colin, oh aye, she certainly did. She promised to give me proof of his illegitimacy, the old hag. She promised me the proof so Colin would be set aside and I would be the earl of Ashburnham."

Sinjun held perfectly still. She didn't even blink. He was furious, nearly out of control. She was more afraid than she'd ever been in her life.

He seemed to calm. He was sweating profusely. When he spoke again, his voice sounded a bit singsong, as if he were reciting words that had been in his mind for a very long time, playing themselves over and over. A justification, perhaps, for any guilt.

"Arleth tried to kill you through neglect. It was revenge against Colin because he was alive and Malcolm was dead. You survived, more's the pity. Then the old witch had an attack of conscience. After all these bloody years, an attack of conscience! I killed her because she refused to give me the proof. I wanted to snap her scrawny neck, but I thought perhaps you would all believe her guilty of killing Fiona if you believed she'd hung herself."

"You tied the knots much too tight at the base of the chandelier. She wouldn't have had the strength to do that."

He shrugged. "It doesn't really matter now. I will have fifty thousand pounds. I will go to America, I believe. I will be a wealthy man there. I've decided not to kill you or Colin, unless you force me to it. Then again, perhaps I shall. There's no reason to really, though. I've never hated you or him. But killing—it exhilarates me, makes me happy in those precious moments."

"Did you kill Fiona?"

He nodded, his expression suddenly dreamy. "Perhaps I should kill Colin. He always had what I wanted, even though he never realized it. Fiona was besotted with him, but he didn't give a good tinker's damn about her. She drove him mad with her ceaseless jealousy. She shrieked at him if he even looked in the direction of another woman. She didn't care about Vere Castle or any of its people. It was just Colin, only Colin. She wanted him to be her lapdog. He should have just beaten her, it would have helped, but he didn't. He just withdrew from her. But I wanted her, loved her, but she rejected me. Yes, Arleth gave me a potion to pour into Colin's ale. Since the old earl and Malcolm were both dead, she didn't care if the whole bloody castle died; she was quite ready to assist all of them to the grave. Colin drank it and passed out. I broke Fiona's pretty neck and tossed her over the cliff. She pleaded and promised she would love only me, but I didn't believe her. Perhaps I wanted to for a moment or two, but then there was that odd exhilaration again. I couldn't stop once I'd begun. I was quite the artist, Sinjun. I arranged Colin's unconscious body right there, nearly over the edge but not quite. Had I been lucky, he would have fallen; had I been lucky, he would have been hung for her murder. But I wasn't lucky at all."

He stopped then, as if the spigot had turned off.

But Sinjun had to know. "Did you hire a man to kill him in London?"

"Yes, but the fool failed. I came to visit my dear cousin all happy as a clam in the home of the damned earl of Northcliffe. Safe from me, he was, but I was busy. I thought, were he to die in London, far away from Scotland, things would be easier for me, and they would have, damn him. Your brother behaved as I suspected he would when I sent the letter accusing Colin of killing Fiona. But you, Sinjun, you were completely unexpected. Whisked your lover away from London, away from your family's interference, away from me.

"Colin blamed Robert MacPherson for everything, though all Robbie did was steal a few sheep and butcher a couple of Kinross crofters. He did try to shoot Colin in Edinburgh and even botched that up. He hit you, the blundering sod. He believes himself so cruel and wicked, does Robbie. He does it because he's so pretty. The meaner he is, the less pretty people will see him to be. I told him that Colin had killed Fiona and he believed me because I also told him a very real truth—that I loved his sister and that I couldn't bear that Colin get away with her murder. I convinced him that it was his responsibility to avenge his sister's death."

He turned then and yawned. "I don't wish to speak any more. Indeed, I've told you more than another living soul. If you have more questions, my dear, perhaps you can ask God when you reach heaven—if I decide to send you there, of course. Ah, a decision to sleep on." He laughed.

"I think I'll take a short nap. Perhaps a long one. You just relax, my dear, listen to the rats and their gnawing. I'll try not to snore."

He unfolded several blankets, spread them on the floor, and careful not to touch his clothes to the dirt, he lay down. His back was to her.

She gave him twenty minutes. She'd needed but ten minutes to work her hands free, finally. Her wrists were raw and bleeding. It didn't matter. Soon now, very soon.

21

HE DIDN'T SNORE, damn him. If only he would, she could be certain that he was really sleeping.

She couldn't afford to wait longer. If he was pretending in order to catch her, then so be it. She had to try. Slowly, Sinjun leaned down and began to untie the knots at her ankles. It took longer to untie the knots than it took the rats to eat through the paper to get to the crumbs.

At last she was free. She rose. Quietly, very quietly. She immediately collapsed back onto the chair. Her legs wouldn't hold her. She rubbed her ankles, rubbed her legs, one eye on her hands, the other on MacDuff. He shifted suddenly. Her breath stuck in her throat. He turned onto his back now.

Oh God, don't let him awaken.

She tried to rise again. This time she succeeded. Slowly, she walked toward the croft door.

A rat shrieked. Sinjun froze in her tracks.

MacDuff stirred, then groaned in his sleep.

She had her fingers clutching the handle. She pressed it down. Nothing happened. She pressed again and shook it.

There was a loud squeaking noise. MacDuff jerked and sat up. "You little bitch," he screamed at her, and jumped to his feet.

Sinjun had sheer terror in her favor. She jerked open the croft door and plunged into the darkness outside. Thank God for the fetid damp night, deep and fathomless. The ground beneath her feet was suddenly spongy, then wet, the wetness slapping against her slippers, sucking and loud. Her feet suddenly sank into quagmire, the dank muck pulling at her skirts, weighing her down. Smells were all around her, awful smells and strange sounds from creatures she would rather not see.

He was right behind her, yelling, "You damned bitch! You'll die in the swamp! I told you it was unlikely I would kill you! Come back here, all I want is the money and you'll be free! Surely even you don't think I could get away with murdering both you and Colin and perhaps your brothers, as well! Don't be stupid, get back here!"

Oh no, she thought, oh no. He sounded close, knocking against branches behind her. She turned, panicked, and ran into a tree. She nearly knocked herself out. She stood there, trying to get her bearings again, hugging that damned tree. It was bent forward toward the still, thick water and its trunk felt slimy. She felt herself being drawn deeper into the thick mud. She clutched the trunk, trying to pull herself free. It didn't work. She was sinking, the filthy slime nearly to her knees now. Her great plan, all for naught. Either she would sink here in this swamp or MacDuff would kill her. Why didn't he sink like a stone? He weighed three times what she did, why the devil didn't he sink?

"Jesus, you stupid bitch, I should leave you here to be sucked under."

MacDuff hauled her free of the muck and without hesitation threw her over his shoulder. "Any more trouble from you and I'll strike you again."

She was breathing hard, her face hitting his shoulder. She wanted to be sick but she had no intention of succumbing. She swallowed hard. She had to do something. She'd wanted only to run away from him. Damnation, all for naught.

Then, quite suddenly, she was flying off MacDuff's back, striking the ground and rolling onto her stomach. She heard Colin's voice and it was cold and furious. "All right, you damned bastard, it's all over."

Sinjun turned over quickly. She saw Colin holding a pistol on MacDuff. Thank God he hadn't tried to fight him. MacDuff would have broken him in half. Then there were her two brothers and Sophie and Alex, all of them there in a half circle, watching, silent as stones. All of them holding pistols.

Colin dropped to his knees and gathered her up. "Sinjun, are you all right?"

She stared up at her husband. "What did you call me?"

"I asked you if you were all right, damn you. You're filthier than a Loch Ard goat."

"Yes, certainly. Colin, you called me Sinjun."

"It was a slip of the tongue, done in my excitement. Now, MacDuff, we will all go to that dismal little croft and I want some answers from you."

"Go to the devil, you filthy devil's spawn! How did you manage this? Damn you, I saw you riding Gulliver to Edinburgh and coming back to Vere Castle. I saw you! It isn't possible that you knew I was there!"

Douglas spoke for the first time. "It was me you saw. As for discovering your hidey-hole, we had a dozen or so lads stationed all about the perimeter on the lookout. Jamie spotted you. It was quite easy after that."

MacDuff just stared at Douglas. Then he turned back to Colin. "I wouldn't have killed either you or Sinjun. I just wanted to leave. My father left me little money, Colin. You could afford fifty thousand pounds since you married her. I just wanted a little bit of her fortune. It was all Aunt Arleth's fault."

"You killed her," Colin said, his voice shaking with fury, with betrayal. "God, I trusted you. All my life I trusted you, believed you were my friend."

"Yes, was. Only, things change. We became men." He looked down at his feet, then, with a fierce cry, he rushed at Colin, grabbed his gun arm, jerking it upward, and crushed his cousin to him, his massive arms tightening around his back, cracking his ribs.

Sinjun was on her feet in an instant. She froze in midstride. The gun went off.

Sinjun screamed.

Slowly, so very slowly, Colin pushed free of MacDuff. He crumpled to the ground. He didn't move.

There was utter silence. The night sounds became louder. Sinjun fancied she heard one of the rats shriek.

"He knew he couldn't get away from all of us," Douglas said slowly, looking at the pistol he held in his own hand. "He saw that Ryder and I were armed."

"We were, as well," Alex said.

Colin stared down at his cousin, the man he'd loved as a boy and respected as a man. He was dead. He looked over at his wife. A look of intense pain crossed his face. "So many people lost to me, so many. Did he tell you why, Sinjun?"

She felt his pain, his wrenching betrayal. No more, she thought, no more. She looked at him straight in his beautiful eyes. "He told me that he murdered Fiona because she rejected him. He killed Aunt Arleth because she had proof that he'd killed Fiona. He was in financial difficulties, as he told you. He wanted to leave Scotland and he had to have money. We were the likely source. That's all there was to it, Colin. Nothing more."

Colin's head was bowed. "Nothing more?" he asked, not looking at her.

"No, nothing more. He didn't want to kill either of us, Colin. I think he was sorry for all the tragedy he'd caused. Thank you for saving me."

"Ah," said Douglas, "then you're not going to claim that it was the damned Virgin Bride or the absurd Pearlin' Jane who sent us here to save your white hide?"

"Not this time, brother dear." She smiled up at her husband. He looked at her closely. He lightly ran his fingertips over the bruise on her jaw. "You're a mess," he said. "A beautiful mess. Does your jaw pain you much?"

"Not much now. I'm all right. Just dirty and awfully tired of these foul swamp smells and sounds."

"Then let's go home."

"Yes," Sinjun said, "let's go home."

Two days later, Sinjun went to Aunt Arleth's bedchamber. No one had been in the room since they'd found her body. Thank God the rope had been taken away. There was no sign that a tragedy had occurred here, yet the maids wouldn't even come as far as three feet from the door.

Sinjun closed the door quietly behind her and stood there for a moment, just looking around. She saw signs quickly enough that MacDuff had searched in here to find his proof that Colin was illegitimate. But he hadn't found that proof. It was still here, unless Aunt Arleth had lied to MacDuff about it, and Sinjun didn't believe she'd lied about that.

She searched methodically, but at the end of twenty minutes she hadn't found a thing out of the ordinary. She had no idea what she was looking for, but she knew she would know when she found it.

Another twenty minutes of searching and she was nearly ready to concede that Aunt Arleth had spun the fantasy from her own tortured brain.

She sat in the chair that faced the small fireplace, leaned her head back, and closed her eyes.

What would the proof be?

Suddenly, she felt a warmth steal over her, a prodding sort of warmth that made her rise instantly from the chair. She stood perfectly still, wondering what the devil was going on, and then, just as suddenly as the warmth had come to her, she understood it. It was Pearlin' Jane and she was here to help her.

She walked directly to the long brocade draperies that hung from ceiling to floor on the far east side of the bedchamber. She knelt down and lifted the hem of the drapery. There was something very solid sewn into the wide hem.

The thread wasn't all that secure. She gently pulled it open. Out fell a small packet of letters tied with a faded green satin ribbon.

They were letters from a Lord Donnally and they were yellowed with age, the paper crinkly. They covered a three-year period, the first one dated nearly thirty years before.

Well before Colin's birth.

All the letters were from Lord Donnally's estate in Huntington, Sussex. She read a few lines, then hastily folded the paper and slipped it back into the ribbon. She withdrew the very last letter in the packet. It was dated after Colin's birth.

She read the faded black ink written in a spidery hand:

My dearest love,

If only I could see my son, hold him, just press him against my body once. But I know it can't be. Just as I've always known you could never be mine. But you have our son. I will abide by your wishes. I will not seek to see you again. If ever you need me, I am here for you. I will pray that your husband will cease his cruelty, that he won't hurt you . . .

The handwriting was blurred here and she couldn't make it out. But it didn't matter. She'd read quite enough.

Sinjun dropped the letter into her lap. She felt the wet of her tears slowly drop on the back of her hands.

The warmth seemed to swirl around her. She knew of course what she had to do.

Sinjun left Aunt Arleth's bedchamber ten minutes later. The room was warm from the fire that had burned briefly.

She went into the drawing room and walked directly to the fireplace. She stood there, looking up at Pearlin' Jane's portrait. It was between the earl's and his wife's, just as Pearlin' Jane demanded that it should be.

"Thank you," she said softly.

"Who are you talking to, Sinjun?"

Her name on his lips was wonderful. She turned around to smile at Colin, her husband, her lover, the man she would willingly give her life for. Now he was safe and so was she and they had life ahead of them.

"Oh, I was just talking to myself, really. I think that Pearlin' Jane's portrait needs a good cleaning. Is there someone qualified at minor restoration?"

"There must be. If not in Kinross, why then, in Edinburgh."

"I think Pearlin' Jane deserves the best. Let's take the portrait to Edinburgh. Also, it just occurred to me that I would have been sorely in the wrong had I sent Robert MacPherson to Australia."

"It would doubtless have improved his character, but it wouldn't have been justice. I'm rather relieved that you failed in that particular endeavor. Incidentally, I saw him this morning, told him all about MacDuff."

"Don't tell me he apologized to you."

"Oh no, but he did offer me a mug of ale. In his house. And none of his men or servants held guns or daggers toward me. Also, it appears he's trying to grow a beard."

"Did you see Serena?"

"No. He sent her posthaste to Edinburgh to take charge of their father's household. He fancies he's washed his hands of her, but somehow, knowing Serena, I doubt it."

Sinjun grinned at him. She walked into his arms and hugged him close. "Did I tell you yet today that I adore you? That I worship you? That I would peel grapes for you if any were available and pop them into your beautiful mouth?"

"That would be nice," he said, and kissed her mouth and the tip of her nose, and smoothed his fingertip over her eyebrows.

"I love you, husband."

"And I you, my lady wife."

"Ah, that sounds wonderful, Colin."

"Before I attempt to have my way with you here in the drawing room, where are the wives?"

"The last time I saw the wives, Sophie was arguing with Alex about where the rose plants would be best situated."

"Douglas and Ryder are out working with the crofters. Indeed, I had planned to come in and simply say hello to you and perhaps just give you one kiss. I told them that they were old married men and thus didn't deserve the same benefits that I was entitled to. Kiss me, Sinjun."

She did, with gratifying enthusiasm.

He kissed her until she was breathless, then he squeezed her tightly against him. "Jesus, if anything had happened to you I couldn't have borne it."

She felt his big body shake. She hugged him more tightly, kissing his neck. Then she felt the soft warmth again, swirling around her, about both her and Colin, but he didn't appear to feel it. Then it began to recede, but there wasn't any coldness in its place. No, in its wake was perfect stillness and a sort of softness in the air itself. Then, suddenly, Sinjun heard a faint lilting sound that could have been a laugh, perhaps.

Colin said as he nibbled on her earlobe, "I like your laugh, Sinjun. It's soft and warm and as sweet as a moonless night."